Sufferborn

Book I

J.C. HARTCARVER

Dorwik Publishing

Sufferborn
Copyright 2019 Jesslyn Carver

This is a work of fiction. Names, characters, businesses, places, events, locales, and incidents are either the products of the author's imagination or used in a fictitious manner. Any resemblance to actual persons, living or dead, or actual events is purely coincidental.

Cover art "Sufferborn Trio" oil on linen, back cover art "Conspiracy" oil on canvas, and all interior illustrations by Jesslyn Carver.

Fan mail can be sent to J.C. Hartcarver via the "contact" page on her website: www.jchartcarver.com.

ISBN: 978-0-9982104-4-5 (paperback)
978-0-9982104-5-2 (hardback)
978-0-9982104-6-9 (ebook)

Dorwik Publishing
Greenbrier, TN

Table of Contents

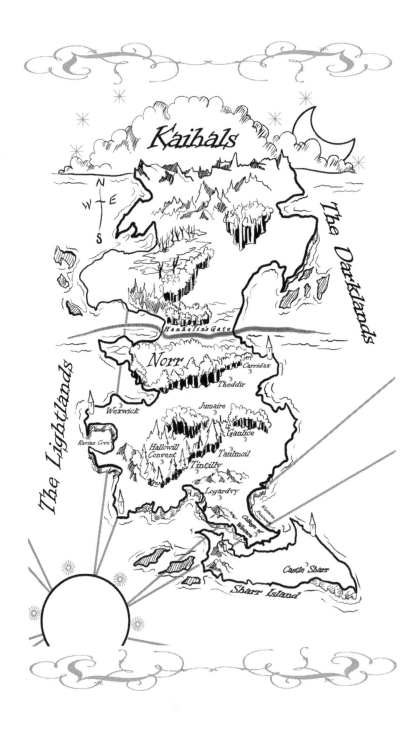

For Timmy.
Thanks for putting up with Dorhen.

Sufferborn

Prologue

A spasm shot through Daghahen's body. Dropping to the floor, he writhed and fought back a scream. Seconds later he relaxed, the ceiling blurring in his glazing vision.

"No," he groaned. "Please." His eyelids closed, suddenly heavy. With a deep breath, he grasped the side of his bed and pulled himself up.

The cloaking spell had failed, but at least the warning spell he'd cast over the area worked. Daghahen rushed out of the bedroom, whipping aside the canvas tarp acting as a door. He dashed to the hearth, stopped, and flitted to the basin, pausing to align his thoughts.

The sound of a horse's breath huffed outside. Long-forgotten nightmares he'd pushed deep into the darkest pits of his mind were crawling into the light again. A suffocating old sensation of being stuck in binding situations and being enslaved to shameful duties pressed on his heavy head once again, as if after fifteen years nothing had changed. The sweetness of freedom vanished. His brother had found him.

Go outside and turn him away, Ibex instructed. The voice in his head usually offered good advice, though sometimes difficult or complicated. Come to think of it, he hadn't heard from Ibex in years.

Daghahen approached the door and peeked through a thin, carved slot. He had built his little two-room cabin with security in mind; it possessed peepholes on each wall rather than windows. Not much could be seen from the current angle. He wiped his eyes, widened his stance, and opened the door.

Outside, a cloaked figure swung his leg over the rump of a huge black horse and stepped onto the muddy ground. A fierce wind ripped through the dense, ice-covered trees. Removing his hood, the visitor turned toward Daghahen. A bright flare of yellow-blonde hair spilled out, as Daghahen remembered it.

"Lambelhen." The name crawled up Daghahen's throat with a rush of bile. Lambelhen's face displayed a new smoothness, like porcelain, with yellow eyes glassier than ever before.

Lambelhen paused, his brow narrowed, and he pointed to Daghahen's clothes. "What have you been doing?"

Daghahen finally noticed the blood all over his woolen tabard. He brushed at the fabric with his hand, but the stains were set and dried.

"Oh, um. Sorry. I forgot. I'm so…tired. What brought you all the way out here?"

Lambelhen gave one of his signature fake smiles. "I'm passing through Norr. Thought I'd try and find you while I'm here. It's been so long. How is my dear brother getting on?"

Daghahen eyed him up and down again. "Must've been hard findin' me."

Lambelhen's smile slacked into a smirk. "Indeed. I could have missed it in this wilderness. How is it my only flesh and blood would leave so fast and go so far? And without a word of goodbye?"

Daghahen's heart hammered hard against his sore ribs. He shook his head. "I was called—called away."

"Did you build this house?" Lambelhen stepped forward.

Daghahen took a tiny step back, staring at him. Gauging. Predicting. He let his eyes rest on a tree behind Lambelhen.

"Yes. I wanted to see Norr, the place we were born… We spent so little time here. I wanted to see it, and I liked it here. I think I…lost track. Started to settle in." Swallowing again, he managed a long blink, reluctant to open his eyes again. "I was comin' back, but got delayed. I swear."

"I see," Lambelhen said. "If I know my dear brother, he has no plan, no organization."

"I have a wife." Daghahen narrowed his eyes at him. "As well as a child."

Lambelhen showed teeth. "How unexpected. How old is your child?"

"Just a…a few hours actually."

"Male or female?"

"A *saeghar*."

"Ah, always good luck to have a son born first. I must say, I always thought you would produce the rare *farhah* as a first child." A smile spread wide on Lambelhen's face. "That's why you're such a mess. I imagine delivering one's own child would be an overwhelming job."

"First month, seventh day," Daghahen said, frowning. "My child's birth. It happened today."

Lambelhen cocked his head for a moment and drew his cloak tight around his shoulders. "It's cold out today, isn't it? Do I smell mint tea in there?"

Daghahen pulled a long stream of air in, trying not to let it show.

A different voice rang musically from inside the house behind him. "Daghahen, do we have a visitor?"

"Yes," he called back.

"Well, aren't you going to bring him in? The draft is coming in."

Daghahen's eyes grazed over his brother while he went over spell chants in his head to see if he remembered them. A gleaming sword in an exquisite scabbard hung off the newcomer's hip.

That's it! Take it away from him. Take it!

Daghahen responded to Ibex in his head, *Now I know you're nothing but a mad figment of my imagination, you crazy goat.*

Grinding his teeth, Daghahen stepped upon the threshold and widened the door.

"How long have you been married?" Lambelhen entered the house, his eyes scanning the inside.

"Almost a year." Daghahen took his cloak and hung it on the wall.

The sound of the beautiful feminine voice filled the air again. "Daghahen." Whenever it called his name, he resisted wrenching his clothes and weeping. "Who is it?"

"It's my brother, here to call on us, my dear."

"Wonderful. Bring him in. Tell him not to be shy."

"Come this way," Daghahen said. "They're in the bedroom. Orinleah hasn't even put him down yet." Daghahen's weak lips barely smiled.

The tall, wooden heels of Lambelhen's boots clomped on the hollow floor with that familiar impression of egocentricity, transporting Daghahen back to darker days when they had lived in confiscated wooden inns or the oppressive stone tower of Ilbith.

Daghahen drew aside the tarp leading to the bedroom. Orinleah, his wife, sat against a pile of pillows, packed under all the blankets and skins they owned, cradling her sleeping infant. When the two brothers entered, her radiant, smiling presence offered an oasis of color and warmth in this bitter winter. Perfect little teeth glowed between her warm, pink lips. A silky lock of dark brown hair fell over one of her eyes, and she brushed it aside with a delicate hand.

"Daghahen didn't tell me he had a brother. Your name is—" Orinleah would've guessed it correctly. She seemed to have Desteer talents but ignored them. Thanks be to Daghahen's lucky stars, she'd chosen to marry him.

"Lambelhen," he finished for her as he sat on the stool by the bed.

"*Lambelhen*, like one who is headstrong?" she asked.

"And you must be Orinleah."

She giggled, covering her mouth. "You two look alike."

"We're twins, which means we're practically the same flesh."

"How unusual. I'm honored to meet you, Lambelhen." She held out her hand to him.

Lambelhen hesitated before carrying out the elven custom of grasping her hand briefly in both of his. Daghahen watched his face, noting a slight twitch of his eyebrow.

Orinleah flashed him a warm smile. "I'm happy to finally meet someone from Daghahen's clan."

Her eyes flitted to Daghahen, and she shared her luminous smile with him as well. The lass beamed in the presence of their visitor after a long year being cooped up in this drafty cabin, all because of Daghahen and his selfishness. She'd chosen him and all the faults he harbored.

"I'm happy I decided to come," Lambelhen said.

Cradling his head, she held out her swaddled child. "Meet your nephew now."

He leaned in. The baby's dark hair matched his mother's.

She said, "His ears are perfectly shaped, like his father's…and yours." Orinleah paused and blushed at what she'd said.

The infant let out a whine.

"I'm in love with his eyes. He's awakening, so look while you can."

The baby's blue-green eyes flashed in the candlelight. Lambelhen turned away and cleared his throat. Daghahen sat on the edge of the bed beside her.

"What's the child's name?" Lambelhen asked.

Another blush touched her face. "Dorhen."

Lambelhen's eyes narrowed to slits. "Are you mad?"

"I've dreamt about this over and over, and no other name fits the way this one does."

"So…you've decided to jinx your house right at the start of it?"

"No, not at all—"

Lambelhen pointed a finger at her. "You should know even better than him." His pointing finger changed to Daghahen.

"I trust Orinleah's decision," Daghahen said.

Lambelhen smirked and shook his head. "The forbidden name, that's what you've given your first son."

Frowning and breathing harder, Orinleah said, "But the name is so—"

"Insane?" Lambelhen finished for her. "It means 'stranger.' Every *saehgahn* with that name so far has been one."

"But Dorhen won't be!"

Daghahen stood and put a hand between his wife and his brother. "Stop this! You're upsetting her."

Lambelhen didn't offer any more protests.

Orinleah cleared her throat. "I am *faerhain*," she said, reminding them both. "I know what I've done might seem frightful, but I've never been so sure about anything in my whole life. It's like he told me his name. It's my duty to say it aloud. My mother and grandmother were apt at determining names too. They named all of their children perfectly; none grew up incomplete. As I feel complete in my name, I know it will be the same for him."

The two *saehgahn*, the male elves, blinked at her, and Daghahen turned to Lambelhen's contorted face.

"I know you don't walk the path of tradition, but Orinleah and I do. If she says his name is Dorhen, I guess it must be. There. My saying it aloud completes the ceremony." Daghahen reached over and stroked the baby's dark brown hair. "Dorhen," he said again, mostly for himself.

Lambelhen scoffed. "Tradition? Your wife is barely old enough for her *faerhain* naming ceremony, and you insist on tradition?" He licked his lips, shifting in his seat, and jerked his head toward Daghahen. "Tell me, how did you convince the Desteer to let you have her? Did she send you the little wooden token? Better yet, tell me the story of how you met. Full of whimsies and romance, I'll bet. Her family didn't even know about it, did they? I'll bet the Desteer didn't know either."

Lambelhen turned his bright eyes back to Orinleah. "Tell me how you fell in love with him, darling. Was it the sweet words on Daghahen's tongue? My brother has a special talent. Do you know of it?"

Daghahen bristled. He'd grown so tired of Lambelhen's mouth in the past, but the bastard never cared about anything past his own selfish desires.

Orinleah looked at Daghahen, her innocent eyes sparkling. "Daghahen and I are married because I chose him. He's my *daghen-saehgahn*, my husband and my guardian, as his name suggests. He carries his name, and so Dorhen will carry his too." She glanced at the baby. "My son is strong."

She spoke truth. The books said to expect long labors for *faerhain*, and it had taken at least three days for Orinleah to give birth to their son. Praise to both the One Creator and the Bright One, no complications occurred. Orinleah had done well; she appeared bright again already. Dorhen himself was impressively heavy and loud.

Lambelhen flared his hands. "Dorhen, then. The stranger. The one who brings bad luck to his clan."

Remember. Remember, Ibex's voice rumbled.

Daghahen perked up, dismissing Lambelhen's cutting words. "Right. You said you wanted tea." He rose and went straight to the hearth in the other room. He hadn't slept in three days. He'd stayed on his feet, working hard to keep the house warm. His *saehgahn* protection instincts were peaking today.

As Daghahen made his way back with a cup of tea, Lambelhen swept the tarp aside to emerge from the bedroom. His yellow eyes caught the dim firelight and glowed. They always did. Sometimes they flared bright enough to seem disembodied, like a wild animal on the prowl. Daghahen's eyes were blue; their mother used to differentiate them by their eye colors when they were two little blonde *saeghar* playing in the mucky alley behind the old inn where they had grown up.

He extended the steaming clay mug with both hands. "You came so far out of your way and managed to find my house. Sit and relax. Spin tales with me a bit before ya go."

Lambelhen waved the offering away. "Thanks, but I can't stay long."

"Please. You must. You should." He stepped to the side, blocked Lambelhen's path, and pushed the mug closer.

Lambelhen smirked, his eyes moving from the mug to Daghahen's eyes. "No, Dag."

"Why not?"

"I've been corresponding with the bishop of Carridax. You know, at the cathedral near the coast. He's…shall I say…interested in what I do and what I offer."

Daghahen smiled. "You still work for Ilbith?"

"Of course. It's my home. My practice keeps my ailments in check, as always." He fiddled with a huge ruby ring on his index finger as his eyes darted to the bedroom and back. "So as I was saying, the bishop and I have exchanged many letters, favors, and items. We're friends, but now he's ill and might die. He's leaving me a fortune. Such is why I'm in the Lightlands again. I can't stay long."

Lambelhen's journey all the way down here from the Darklands for a bishop's money sounded true enough. He'd donned plain clothing without his usual red cloak, which announced his Ilbith affiliation. Even if it was all true, how long had Lambelhen really been looking for him? Daghahen's cabin was too far out of the way for a convenient and spontaneous visit.

"Thanks for sharing the warmth of your home. But I sadly must leave—I was only passing through, after all. Lucky I found you at all."

"All right." Daghahen set the mug on the hearth and used the old iron poker to stir the logs in the fire. "I understand. You were always busy. Ambition is the name of *my* dear brother. You know what ya want. I admire you. Well…"

Daghahen savored the weight of the iron rod. His sweaty palm itched against the dingy old rag wrapped around its handle. How he'd love to put this poker into Lambelhen's eye. He adjusted his fingers around the handle and squeezed.

Lambelhen stared back at the bedroom tarp, behind which Daghahen's innocent wife and child sat defenseless. Behind Lambelhen's back, Daghahen hung the poker on his own belt like a sword and dropped his long, hanging tabard over it. He fetched his brother's cloak off the peg.

"Here," he said, regaining Lambelhen's attention.

Lambelhen reached for his cloak, and Daghahen dodged his hand gracefully, waving the cloak as if in a dance. "Oh no, allow me. You're my guest." His body movements were always graceful, along with his words. He had relied on them in his youth. However, Lambelhen knew all about that. He most likely suspected Daghahen was planning something, but he had to try anyway. He retained the cloak as long as possible to buy time to complete the incantation; waving it a bit made for a good distraction too.

Melah doena haxil, melah doena haxil. He couldn't merely think the words, the spell required saying them. The words slid out in low murmurs, bending his lips as little as possible. Turning his head as naturally as he could and using his unkempt hair to mask his face, he finished his chant and gave the cloak a flourishing twirl. It landed on Lambelhen's shoulders. If Lambelhen noticed his lips moving, he'd know. And if he knew, Daghahen and his family would be in trouble.

Their eyes locked. With the cloak now resting on Lambelhen's shoulders, he squinted at Daghahen.

He knows!

Daghahen smiled, proceeded to tie the string for him, and carried on as if he'd done nothing out of place.

"Short journey, smooth road," he said, and opened the door for his brother.

Lambelhen approached the threshold. He spun around. "Daghahen."

"Yes?" Daghahen's pounding heart buried the sound of his own voice.

Lambelhen's grin widened. "You're a lucky *saehgahn.*" He strode out, mounted his horse, and cantered off through the tangle of trees.

Daghahen closed the door and leaned against it. A clammy sweat formed on his upper lip and temples. Lambelhen hadn't seen it. His hands shook uncontrollably as they reached under his bloodstained tabard and retrieved the exquisite sword he'd managed to steal with the simple switching spell. Now it hung on his belt by its hilt. If luck was on his side, Lambelhen wouldn't notice the fireplace poker in his scabbard for at least the rest of the day considering he didn't actually use it. The sword acted more as a good luck charm for Lambelhen than a weapon.

Daghahen bent over to catch his balance as the room suddenly spun around him. It had been so long since he'd used magic. He wanted to quit, he really did. The cloaking spell he'd cast over this house had lasted ten years. It must've weakened for Lambelhen to have dispelled it so easily. Of course, Lambelhen wouldn't have ceased his sorcery practice. He'd always been the better spell caster. Daghahen relied on his natural ability to charm and read the stars. He'd gone soft. His blissful abandonment of magic would be his demise so long as Lambelhen still lived. He had to resume his practice.

He straightened, the dizziness fading. A sculpted nude figure was molded on the cross section of the sword's hilt, its arms crossed over its midsection like a dead body, just as Daghahen remembered. The deeply-etched word, "HATHROHJILH," ran along the opposite side of the blade. It remained as shiny and mar-free as it was years ago when the twins obtained it.

What have I done?

Ibex rumbled in his head, *Gained the edge, that's what. You'll kill him.*

"Daghahen, are you all right?" Orinleah called from behind the tarp.

"Yes, my dear. I'm just exhausted."

"You can sleep in here next to me. I'm sure we'll be fine while you rest."

"Orinleah," he said, leaning against the door again.

"Yes?"

"Did I ever tell you I love you?"

Her voice shook now. "No. Please come here. I dearly want to see you!"

His eyes never left his warped reflection in the blade. This must be it. It had never occurred to him to steal the sword before. He knew little about it, but he'd find out whatever he needed to know to prepare for Lambelhen's certain return.

He put the sword down and scrambled to a certain corner, clawing at the floorboards with his long fingers. He lifted up the loose ones and found a tattered book lying amongst wispy cobwebs in its hollow under the floor.

He brushed the dust off the cover, labeled with the burnt symbol of a hideous swine's face made up of tiny runes, long ago covered by fabric. Someone in the past had tried to hide the book's identity. The fabric had faded to grey and hung in threads off the book's edges. Though the book was not terribly thick, its weight dragged on his muscles.

He shuddered. His old sorcery grimoire. He closed his eyes, not quite ready to see it again. Could this be his best defense?

"See there? The posts?" Daghahen asked, pointing to the three skinny logs he'd hewn from felled trees. They stood in the ground, decorated with feathers, bones, and green cloth tied to them.

It took her a moment; the posts were somewhat camouflaged by their ornamentation. "Yes," Orinleah answered when her eyes settled. Their one-year-old son lay against her, sucking his thumb with his head laid under her chin.

"Many posts like it are erected all around our house... By *saehgahn* law, you're never to go beyond them."

"What?"

"They're for our safety. I've planned it out; they're set wide enough for us to reach each area most important to us."

"But—but what if we need to go to a clan to ask for food or help or..."

He put his hand on her shoulder and squeezed. "Please trust me. If you need anything, I'll go and get it for you. You'll still have the berry patch. Wild onions grow all around. We'll have mushrooms, and we have our stream for water and fishing. If you want other kinds of fish, I'll go to other places to get them. I'll also gather firewood from outside the barriers."

She exhaled and leaned against him, putting her forehead on his chest. "I trust you, *saehgahn*... It's not as if I can go home to visit my family anyway. Even if I needed to speak to the Desteer, I can't. I made my decision."

He wrapped his arm around her, bringing her and Dorhen in close. "You don't need them anymore. We're establishing our own clan."

"You're a good *saehgahn*, Dag. I'm lucky you came to me. We *will* make our own clan. A strong one."

He kissed the top of her head. Making themselves stronger was their sole option. They couldn't run away from Lambelhen's impending return. Refuge found in the human lands in comparison to what Norr provided was like comparing a nut to a boulder. They'd be hard-pressed to find any other corner of Norr where they could slip under the nose of the ruling clan or the telepathic reach of the Desteer. It had taken him long enough to find this spot years ago. This place, this homestead, offered their best hope.

Later that night, Orinleah made silent steps through the tarp door to join Daghahen by the hearth. He'd surrendered to the comfort of the white ox pelt spread across the floor. Customarily, all married couples kept a white ox pelt in their home, and Daghahen had found one for her recently, making up for a custom he couldn't fulfill when they were first married.

When he had presented it to her, she hugged it to her chest and said, "Now we're complete." It made her smile so brightly he hadn't the heart to confess how he'd bought it from a roadside peddler during his last trip into the human lands for supplies.

She knelt beside him and, in an excited haste, her hands went straight to his hair. She slid one sleek leg over his lap and her lips went to his throat.

"What about the lad?" he asked.

"He's asleep already."

She wrapped her legs around his middle. That usual sense of hesitation came over him, put in place by various events in his repulsive past, but he slowed his breath and concentrated in an attempt to relax, as he usually had to do. They hadn't made love much at all in the year since Dorhen was born. Refusing her offer would seem odd. Daghahen couldn't put his mind to anything but Lambelhen's unexpected visit.

"Are you sure, lass?"

She cut him off, shushing him. "Of course I am. You said we would start our own clan. We can't start a clan with only one child."

She unclasped his poncho and threw it aside. Sliding her hands around to rub his shoulders and the back of his neck, she plunged her tongue into his mouth. Her moves worked.

Pulling her mouth away, she traced her lips to his ear and whispered, "I dreamed about you again."

"What?"

"Mmm-hmm. You might be interested to know I've experienced a few of them since we met."

He kept silent and resisted at first when she pushed him to lie flat. She pulled his shirt off and insisted he lie down. The furry surface of their marriage pelt comforted his bare back with its thick, tickling locks of wool.

"Although," she continued, tracing her fingers across his stomach to the laces on his leggings, "in the dreams, you're always more wild. And you like it when I'm on top. I wonder if you prefer that in real life. You've never made any requests."

"Um." He swallowed and closed his eyes while she did her work. He abandoned whatever response he might have offered. None of that sounded like him, though. He'd never been a wild lover, and harbored no particular favor for any position. He decided not to worry about it. If her dreams excited her so much, he owed it to her to make them real. She deserved all the love he could lavish upon her, along with the clan she desired to establish.

Daghahen left the house each day and made it home later each night. At first, he told Orinleah he had been fishing, and when he couldn't find time to bring home evidence, he said he had visited Theddir to earn some dendrea. All of it was putrid lies.

His answers to her questions became less elaborate and more brief, and she asked so many questions: Were the fish not biting today? What is Theddir like? Where's the money you made today? Do you think the thief who robbed you will get caught? With dwindling answers and sharp diversions, he carefully trained her to stop asking.

But he was still their guardian and provider. Some days, he managed to bring home fish and silver dendrea with funny Lightlandic letters and fat-nosed faces embossed on them. He balanced covering his lies with his sorcery practice. Sorcery always demanded more time, more energy. He gave it what it wanted, and its demands increased.

The years passed, and Dorhen grew into an adorable and mischievous little *saeghar*. But Daghahen could hardly delight in this fleeting novelty. Each night he returned home, Dorhen greeted him with loving and inspired praises and whatever sort of trinket he had made from clay with his mother's help earlier in the afternoon. Daghahen always stepped past him and rushed to the dark bedroom to collapse on the bed. Orinleah's voice shushing and turning Dorhen away from the room reverberated in his ears as he drifted to sleep.

"Daghahen, wake up, my love."

"Hmm?" Daghahen opened his heavy eyelids. His wife, lying beside him, nudged his shoulder. He had fallen asleep wearing his clothes from yesterday.

"I have to talk to you. I'm frightened."

He raised his head a bit more. In the deep hour of the night, Dorhen slept soundly on his cot. "Who frightened my Orinleah?"

"I saw a spirit in the forest. It wasn't the first sighting."

"You were dreaming," Daghahen said, and patted her head, hoping she would lay it down and go to sleep. Her voice sounded so high and energetic, she must have been awake all this time. He shushed her so she wouldn't wake Dorhen.

"It appears on rainy days. It looks like a *saehgahn*, but it has blue hair.

Have you seen it?"

Daghahen had seen many spirits but wasn't about to tell her about them. "No. Go to sleep, my love."

"It has wings too, which it wears like ornaments of pride. Oh, and sharp eyes! It wants something from us."

"Orinleah, you're—"

"There's more. A horrible episode... Dorhen played in the creek the other day, and he caught a frog. I said, 'Put that poor thing down,' and when I got a closer view, I saw no frog. A tiny person with legs *like* a frog sat in his hands, trying to kick its way out. When I screamed, it wriggled free and escaped. I grabbed him and ran away so fast his shoes are still on the bank. The fairies are after our son, I think. What do we do?"

Stretching his arm around her, he snuggled her in close and spread his lips into a smile. Though he couldn't see her in the dark, she might sense it somehow. The lass often demonstrated strong intuition. He'd have to work hard to keep his secrets from her.

"Don't worry about them, lass. They're pests. Put some dirt on his face. They won't steal a dirty *saeghar*."

She didn't speak again, so he took the chance to fall back to sleep.

Standing in the damp forest, Daghahen threw off his tan tabard and unwound the dirty grey strips of cloth from his arms. He'd wrapped them to hide the numerous cuts he had made during his sorcery practice. Orinleah hadn't asked about them, so she might not have noticed them yet. He slapped the old grimoire onto a rock and flopped it open, snapping pages over in search of spells he could use to counter Lambelhen's magic. The barrier posts wouldn't be enough.

Sorcery was for the literate. It worked by contacting demons or pixies and satisfying their demands in return for their aid. Anything from information to a temporary power or new learned spell could be acquired.

Daghahen and Lambelhen had discovered it when they'd traveled the Darklands together after their mother died. Daghahen had wanted nothing to do with it at first, but Lambelhen found it to be profitable. Its soothing effects also tended to suppress his lusts.

Early in their practice, the two had fallen in with a small, cave-dwelling cult of practitioners who tried their hardest to contact a spirit called Naerezek. Lambelhen sneered and referred to the other members as simpletons behind their backs.

One day, he managed to steal their leader's grimoire. Never sure how he worked differently, Daghahen watched his brother summon the disturbing jackal-headed beast over a huge bonfire they built in the forest. It happened, and right as Daghahen began to doubt the spirit's existence. Pleased with Lambelhen's offerings, Naerezek proposed to be his pettygod, and to transform Lambelhen's debilitating lust into a strength. Afterward, sexual intercourse restored his energy so he could sleep less and practice more.

When the twins returned to the cult's cave, Lambelhen used a new spell, courtesy of Naerezek, to shapeshift into a large beast with fur and fangs and rampage through the cave's chambers. When the echoing screams stopped, Daghahen entered the cave, shaking all over. Bypassing the heaping carnage littering the tunnels, he found his brother in the dead leader's chamber, laughing in delight, naked save for all the blood of his victims, rummaging through the leader's store of riches and magical objects.

Now, Daghahen remembered his thought in that moment so long ago: escaping his brother would be difficult. He had been right.

Sorcerers worked in factions, and kept a dark spirit, or pettygod, as their deity. Ilbith worshipped five pixies with enormous magic power loaned to the sorcerers, who studied diligently to keep their favor. Naerezek was one, which helped the twins' entry to the faction because Lambelhen already flaunted its favor. The others were Hael, Ingnet, Wik, and Thaxyl, although Thaxyl was now out of commission.

Thaxyl had once been great centuries ago, almost like a real god. It appeared for Daghahen over a murky concoction of ingredients in a large bowl merely as a grey wisp struggling to stay aglow. Fairies set out in this form as wisps drifting about, collecting energy from various sources. This one had evolved all the way to pixie form.

A corpse-like face flickered within the wisp. A voice raked Daghahen's mind. "Feed my children and we'll talk."

Daghahen cocked his head. "Children?"

"A fool as old as you should've seen them. Do not let them die. If you will feed them, I can collect their energy."

Daghahen's days of sating another person's desires were over. "I contacted you to get information, and I see you've degraded. Ilbith has four deities left now, I suppose." Back during his time there, Ilbith boasted about having Thaxyl's favor regardless. With some investigation into the remaining four, he might find out how to break through the spell barriers protecting Lambelhen's life. "At least tell me what happened to you."

"Creating the Thaccilians spent all my energy, and now observe their status. If they don't feed, they'll die out."

"Ah yes, the heart-eaters. I've seen 'em. Didn't know you ceased to be a pixie because of them. So they supply you with a fast channel of energy to feed your reserves—that is, if they were faring any better. If they go extinct, it'll take you a millennia to evolve into a pixie again. Do your sorcerer-followers know about your debacle?"

"Yes. They've tried to free my children and failed."

"Do you know Lambelhen McShivvey in Ilbith?" Daghahen asked.

"Maybe."

"You choose not to answer?" The glowing wisp blinked out but managed to return. "I want to know what sort of enchantments he wears or what blessings have been placed on him to keep him alive. I tried to kill him once and failed. He has many tricks in play."

The little grey hovering flame blinked out again. "Please!" Daghahen tossed another fistful of bone dust into the bowl. The wisp flickered back in. A hiss scraped his skull, and Daghahen groaned and covered his ears.

"Ask Hael…" The wisp faded again, and the glow died for good.

Hael. Another of Ilbith's pettygods. The texts said it dwelled among and drew energy from the dying. It might be beyond Daghahen's ability to contact. In fact, it required a series of small contacts before a real audience could be arranged, and Hael might not be the only pixie involved. However many Lambelhen used, Daghahen would have to please each pixie, outdoing whatever sacrifices Lambelhen had first offered them.

In his diligent practicing, Daghahen's skin took on a long-lasting clamminess, and the corners of his mouth drooped. Sorcery, a dark and demanding mistress, drained one's energy and happiness. It sucked the light bonded to one's soul—drove a wedge straight between a person and the Creator. His light had been restored in his new life, but again it withered.

He awoke early each morning and collected the necessary animals and plants he needed to weave his spells. His nights were filled with baleful chanting, slaughtering followed by sticky organ arrangements, bleeding, and blazing bonfires. When at home, he had no energy to answer questions, feign interest in his family's chatter, or eat.

"Poor Dag," Orinleah cooed one night in her flirty way as she reached a hand toward his hair in the dark. He swatted it away and went to sleep with her sobs lingering in his head.

The next night, he walked in through the door to the sound of Dorhen whimpering in his sleep in the bedroom.

"I ran out of the salted fish you usually bring, so I used radishes for the stew. It's on the table." Orinleah pointed to the bowl.

He curled his hands into fists and hid them in his draping tabard by his sides. "You've no idea how difficult the human towns can be. They demand money. They're not as kind and helpful as your old clan was!"

"I…"

"I, what? Radishes are fine! Go find more. And how can I sleep with Dorhen in there crying?"

"He's not crying. He's sleeping, and he's been having bad dreams lately."

"Then wake him!"

Orinleah stepped back, clutching the lapel of her aging elven *hanbohik*. "I can't. He has to face the dreams on his own." She dropped her eyes and scrambled out of his way.

The next morning, he found her gathering up the radish stew he hadn't touched last night. He watched her for a moment. She didn't say a word or even look at him, keeping a distance between them, her head stayed low. A bigger problem faced them than their silence, and coddling her back into his confidence wouldn't help. His twin *would* return.

He set it all up. A dead raven lay split open and spread in the perfect layout on the sacrificial rock. The herbs and spices poured in lines wove the correct pattern. He'd arranged leaves along the sigil and tied a rag in the center of the raven's open chest. An uncorked bottle of wine stood to the side. As he clicked the striker to light the rag, he focused, going over the words in his head. If he could make this work, he would be granted an audience with Hael, the death pixie, to ask about the state of Lambelhen's protected mortality.

A spark from the striker ignited the oiled rag. Watching the moon, Daghahen commenced the chant. The flame grew and ate its way down the rag. He gazed into the flame, searching for some indication of a presence. Where would it show this time?

He drew near to the end of the chant, speeding up to race the flame, his hand on the bottle's neck. As Daghahen tipped the bottle over the fire, the wind picked up and blew it out too early.

"Damn!" He smashed the bottle of wine across the setup and stabbed the broken neck of the bottle into the dead raven.

His hand slipped down the slick glass and smashed onto the other shards, cutting him. He roared and swiped his arm across the rock, knocking everything to the ground. Daghahen collapsed on the rock, pressing his face into the bloody entrails until his tantrum passed.

Orinleah no longer waited for Daghahen's return. With the warmth washed out of his face, he'd become frightening. He moved around like a ghost, disregarding her and their son.

When she worked up the nerve to ask him why he'd skipped so many meals, he yelled, "Because I'm ill!" He ran his fingers through his hair. "Sorry, I…I'm not well these days. I'll be fine. It's just…I dunno." He drifted out the door and disappeared into the rows of white trees.

Falling to her knees, Orinleah stared at the forest through the open door. Dorhen wrapped his little arms around her neck and laid his head on her shoulder. Her heart slowed. She placed her hand on his head. At least she had her *saeghar*; she would always have him.

One day, in Daghahen's absence, she packed some clothes and led Dorhen past Daghahen's post barrier, many miles through Norr's forest terrain to her old village. Leading her young child by the hand, she squared her shoulders and walked into the little village from the dense trees.

Little round houses were built along a large circular path with a big round Desteer hall standing in the center. The male answer to clan authority, the elder's house, stood over on the north side. The practice yards were arranged on the west side where the *saeghar*, young males, were practicing. Soon Dorhen would be among them. In the distance, childish voices growled and huffed as they exercised. The wooden fighting sticks clacked in a musical rhythm. At intervals, a gruff adult voice barked a new command, and the rhythm changed.

Not so long ago, Orinleah and her friends had gone to the practice yards to watch the ranks of adult *saehgahn* in their sparring. Every young *farhah* dreamed of growing up and running her own household. Each *farhah* tasked herself with studying the *saehgahn* closely and, after becoming full *faerhain*, chose the best one out of the group to marry. Experience was critical: the young *saeghar* worked hard to graduate to the *saehgahn* order to be considered eligible. By strict commandment, only true-blooded Norrians could be eligible for marriage. If the Desteer decided one was tainted with foreign lineage, and the possibility of the Overseas Taint, he was branded "*sarakren*" and banished to the wilds—if not executed.

Six short years had passed since she was a *farhah*. The unexpected sight of Daghahen lurking about the forest had happened so fast. She would never forget the first day she had met him in the wild strawberry patch.

"Excuse me."

Orinleah dropped her basket, her eyes darting upward. An odd *saehgahn* stood between two trees bowing toward each other like a doorway. When he removed his hood, yellow hair spilled out and shone in the dappled sunlight. All the *saehgahn* in her clan had dark hair.

"Yes?"

"I see you've got water. Can I trouble you for a sip of it? I've walked a long way today."

"Of course, *saehgahn*." She untied the water gourd from her belt. His hand brushed the back of hers when he took it, an improper contact, but she forgave him for it. He smiled, and his vibrant blue eyes reflected like a butterfly's wings.

He plopped down on the dirt before her, his layers of robes pooling around him, and she did the same. Her training helped her judge the best *saehgahn* for marriage, and by the look of his form, he showed promise. All his features were exotic like his hair color. He wiped his mouth on his sleeve and handed the gourd back.

"You've done me a great kindness. Thank you, lass... You *are* purely a lass, aren't you?"

"Not exactly—I'm nineteen. I'm practically *faerhain!* Won't be long now and I'll be married."

"Sorry. You strike me as young, is all."

Young? What nerve! Orinleah straightened her back and pushed a lock of hair behind her ear. "What clan are you from?"

"McShivvey. That's my family name. I'm Daghahen."

"Where is your clan located?"

"I didn't grow up there, wherever it is. I've been in the human lands most o' my life. Especially Theddir, which is in the south." He pointed out to the side. "Not far out of Norr. I've been all over, up north as well."

"Really? Have you seen Hanhelin's Gate?"

"Seen it? I've been on the other side of it."

Her eyes widened, and she caught herself. "My name is Orinleah, soon to be *faerhain*, of the Linharri Clan. We have the greatest forge in Norr. We supply armor to the royal army."

He cocked his head to the side with a smirk. "Impressive."

She reached out her hand, and he took it between both of his warm palms. Her face heated, and butterflies raged in her stomach. She cleared her throat. "Um." The back of her neck grew damp. "Are you married, Daghahen?"

He laughed. "I couldn't be so lucky."

"Well, I'm sure you do great honor to your family."

"I try."

Why was he still smiling? He'd be in so much trouble if her clansmen found him talking to her like this. She didn't make a move to leave or raise an alarm. Would it really be so bad if this attention continued? After they clasped hands, he moved closer to her, and she allowed it.

"Looks like you're lucky, though," he said, reaching over to brush a purple petal which had fallen from the trees off her shoulder. Once again, an improper gesture. His smile finally went limp when he ran his fingers across her collarbone. Her heart raced again, and he drew his hand away as she replaced it with her own. She pulled her collar tighter together. His smile vanished, and his eyes searched hers.

Though she trembled all over, she didn't raise an alarm. Fear wasn't exactly the thing causing her quaking. Remembering her basket of strawberries, she reached for it. When she moved, he frowned. But she didn't leave; instead, she held it out to him. "Are you also hungry?"

His smile returned with a heavy exhalation. "Thank you."

His voice… Though deep and grating, it drew her in, intensified her jitters. She watched him eat each one. He didn't eat many, as politeness dictated, and placed the basket on the ground.

"Will you tell me about the lands you've been to?" She tried to control her breathing and relax her spine.

"Of course I will, lass. Anything for the person who saved me today. I might've died of thirst."

He smiled deeper and touched his index finger to her forehead as if she were a child. His intoxicating attention made her smile nonetheless. He told her an amusing story about his childhood in Theddir, of how he used to play in the streets, and about the day he had helped some old human man find his lost coin purse. The man rewarded him with a magic button. It wasn't actually magic, but Daghahen accepted the reward anyway.

"I still have it," he said. "See?" From his pocket, he drew out an old wooden button, dark with age and scarred, a tool they didn't use in Norr. "The humans often use these to close parts of their clothing. Like this." He pointed to his shoulder, where his outermost mantle was fastened together with three similar objects.

The sun sank low, and Orinleah would have to go home soon. She grabbed his hand in both of hers and tugged. "Follow me. You can stay the night in my village," she said to his questioning expression. His smile vanished, and she longed for it.

"I can't. But meet me here tomorrow evening, and I'll tell you another story."

She made it her priority for the day to return to the spot. Long before sunset, he was already waiting for her. They talked for over an hour. He smiled and touched her forehead like he had yesterday, and told her a story as promised. And she listened to his voice, occasionally closing her eyes. She took his hand again and urged him to accompany her to the Desteer hall for evaluation. He refused and instead begged her not to tell anyone about him.

When she left him, instead of returning home, she banged on the door to the Desteer hall. None of the Desteer maidens had disrobed from their full regalia yet. Their hair hung long and loose, and their faces displayed pearly white paint with a purple stripe running across the eyes. They let her in and granted her an audience, noticing her state of energy and excitement. She asked them to grant her her *faerhain* ceremony early.

"No," the head maiden said, her voice flat.

Orinleah pressed them, but one couldn't argue with the Desteer after such a severe answer. "Why not?"

The maidens behind the leader were shaking their heads.

"You think we haven't seen a *farhah* in your state before? You are asking this favor because you want to get married quickly. You don't get married because you are in a momentary state of lust—you get married because you are ready to give your alliance, love, and service to a *saehgahn* for the rest of your life." Orinleah lowered her head in shame. "Go home and go to bed. Pray to the Bright One and tell Him all of your feelings. Repeat that until you fall asleep. When you awaken, the state you're in will have passed."

Orinleah ran outside after they dismissed her. She didn't go home; she ran back into the tangle of forest where she had left Daghahen. She found him lingering there, waiting and smiling. And she returned for several nights after. She didn't care how he disregarded her clan's laws. She wanted him.

Eventually, they were caught together in a bout of passion. The head Desteer maiden arrived with her father and the village elder with his rabble of sneering *saehgahn*, their faces burning red, blades in hand. But the head maiden kept calm and stern. As the roaring elder lifted his spear to skewer the foreigner, the head maiden grabbed the weapon's haft.

"Not yet!" she cried. The Desteer's pearly face paint glowed fresh in the soft morning sunlight; her black hair added shadow to her already grim face. Orinleah stood in her undermost gown, grasping her discarded garments to her bosom. Heeding the Desteer maiden's command, the *saehgahn* remained poised.

She approached Orinleah, who shrank under her shadow. "Choose," she ordered.

Orinleah didn't need an explanation. She didn't have to weigh the options. She stepped backward, shifting her eyes from the maiden to her father's distraught face as he dropped his bow and arrow.

"No!" he cried, but the elder restrained him and the maiden also put her hands on him to try to calm him.

Orinleah set her jaw, took Daghahen's hand, and allowed him to lead her away. She hadn't seen her father since. On the day she left, she must've already been pregnant.

Now walking through her old village, Orinleah and her son met a mixture of reactions. Few smiled. Most stared at her in confusion or wonder. Orinleah waved and smiled at an old neighbor-*faerhain* whose eyes darted away after meeting Orinleah's. Her mouth curled and slacked, and she retreated into her house. Orinleah tightened her hand around Dorhen's and moved on in search of her old house.

"Mother," Dorhen said, "these houses are funny."

"They're elvish houses, lad," she replied. "This one is where I was born. The inside is like a big circle. We sleep on the floor." As Dorhen stared at the building, his mouth dropped open. She pointed to the pavilion next to the house. "I used to cook in that kitchen. We cook outside in the clan village."

"Will we eat outside too?"

"Mmm-hmm, unless it's too cold or raining too hard."

He grinned. "I like being outside."

"I know you do." She tried her best to keep her smile for Dorhen's sake. The house hadn't changed at all in seven years. A nice blanket of green moss collected on the north side of the same old brush roof, and the chimney leaned a little like always.

She led Dorhen toward the pavilion. The wobbly clay cups she'd made while learning pottery hung from tiny hooks. A flat stone on the pavilion wall still showed a chalk drawing she had made at age twelve. This might not be her home anymore, but it could be again.

Her father, strong as ever, sauntered down the forest path with a bundle of wood on one shoulder. Orinleah took Dorhen's hand again and ran down the path to meet him. Strands of brown hair, the same color as hers, were falling out of his ponytail. She waited before saying anything. He glanced at her and dropped the wood. His mouth dropped open as he regarded her and Dorhen.

"Where is he?" he asked, his voice sharp as a snake's bite.

"Daghahen is busy," Orinleah said.

"Why are you here?"

"I…" Orinleah's eyes moved to the ground, and she choked back tears. "I want to come home." She dropped to her knees, leaned over, and placed her forehead on her crossed arms on the ground. She'd plant her face in the mud if it would be humbling enough. Reaching one arm to Dorhen, she tugged at his miniature tunic. At her prodding, he copied her pose, and they waited.

"You made the choice," her father said. She raised her head again. "And I pleaded with the Desteer long after you left." His furious voice rang at her like thunder.

When he stopped, she struggled for words. "But I—"

"You think I didn't have all the *saehgahn* rallied to slaughter him on the spot? We were ready, but the Desteer forbade it. It's over now." He squinted at her. "*You* made the choice. The Desteer silenced us and validated your marriage, though you were long gone."

Orinleah stood but stayed bent. Dorhen stood too, and she took his hand again. She paused to wonder why wisdom and love didn't go hand in hand. Why had she allowed herself to become a disgrace to her clan? Beholding her child's beautiful face and trusting eyes, she curled her hand tighter around his. He was worth all the trouble.

"Let's talk to the Desteer," she said. "And the elder!"

"Go talk to them all if you wish. The Desteer will tell you the same thing they told me six years ago."

She frowned and turned her face away.

"Orinleah," her father said, snapping her attention back. "Listen to me. The elder might grant you citizenship again, but *that one* can't stay." He pointed at her six-year-old child.

She cupped her hands over his ears. "Shh, how could you say such poison in front of him?" She let Dorhen go and stepped forward, clenching her fists. Her face twisted.

"You were in a hurry to be an adult—so be one. Listen. The Desteer will never let him stay. They don't know the origin of your husband. For all we know, he and your son might both carry the Overseas Taint."

The Overseas Taint was an ominous deviation in the Norrian bloodline, the main reason their customs forbade marrying foreign elves, and the reason her marriage to Daghahen had brought such trouble. But what a ridiculous superstition. Dorhen did not have the taint!

"He's my child. I know better than anyone, there is no shadow over Dorhen!"

Her father stared at her in silence for several moments, clearly aghast. "Is *that* his name?"

Her teeth clenched.

Her father's voice rose. "That name. The forbidden name! Who named him?"

"I did," she said.

"I know you're not so ignorant of your own people's customs. Or perhaps I'm wrong about everything! You let a foreigner court you, you ran away—before your *faerhain* naming ceremony—and now you've used the forbidden name and brought it among us?"

"Well, what could I do?" she asked. "I was so certain about this name." She felt faint as she recalled the incidents with the spirit in the forest and the strange frog Dorhen had caught. She desired to do right by her son in any way possible. By giving him his name, had she damned him instead?

Her father frowned as she worked her throat against a rising soreness. She wanted to see her mother, though how warmly would her mother receive her? She put her face in her hands, fighting some tears.

A strong male voice called from the west side of the forest, "Orinleah!"

A cold shock ran down her spine. *Daghahen*.

Her father scowled. Orinleah twisted around. Had he followed her? Was he angry?

Marching toward her in his tall, weathered boots and knee-length tabard from the human lands, Daghahen shot a wary glare at her father. Orinleah winced as he slid his hands around her. She had no one else to turn to. But since Daghahen offered his embrace, she took it, laying her head on his chest. He squeezed his warm, wool-clad arms around her and stroked her hair. She'd hoped to escape from this very *saehgahn* this morning. Now it appeared he'd come to her rescue. Orinleah's head clouded up.

"Who hurt my Orinleah?" he asked, his warm voice rumbling in her ear.

His fingers grazed the back of her hand and across her collarbone. He finished by touching his fingertip to her forehead as he often did. "Toss them behind you," he said, an old line adults recited to children when they faced a problem.

His gestures filled her with warmth and calm. She slipped her arms around his waist and sighed until he peeled them away.

"Now let's go home." He picked up their son. With Dorhen perched in one arm, he wrapped his other around her shoulders and guided her away.

"Daghahen!" her father roared from behind them. "Take the child but leave her!"

He didn't respond.

"Daghahen!"

Orinleah had no intention of choosing her old home over her son. When she glanced back at her father, her husband tightened his grip around her and they walked back home.

Daghahen returned to his practice for one more day and returned to collapse on their bed. The world around him disappeared for a while until he registered the sensation of someone prodding his back. He jerked upright and found Orinleah beside him. He sighed and lowered his head to rub his face.

"Orinleah," he said, and leaned closer to her. He took her face in his hands, savoring the sight of her. Her eyes darted between his. "I'm sorry. Listen..." He closed his eyelids as a filmy, hazy side effect from one of last night's spells pressed on them. He forced them back open, urgent to formulate a plan. "We won't stay here long. We're going to get away. Understand?"

"Why? What's going on?"

"Please listen. Trust me. Oh damn, I'm a fool. Orinleah..." He lowered his head, the door to his consciousness closing. Some of those side effects were murder. This was no time to sleep. Daylight showed through some cracks in the walls. He moved his hands from her face to her shoulders. "I'm going to fix it, all right?"

"I don't know what you're talking about anymore. I haven't understood you for a while."

His eyes closed again. Last night, the stars had warned him that Lambelhen drew close. The constellation of the Cloven-Headed Man, the one always attributed to Daghahen and his brother, had appeared straight across the sky, east to west, from the Open Door. The Gallows aligned between them, which always warned Daghahen about incoming danger. The Adoptive Parent, a constellation of a tall figure holding a smaller figure's hand, rose in the east behind the Cloven-Headed Man. Lambelhen might be out looking for Dorhen also.

"I'm going to explain it to you...on the road. Get Dorhen ready."

She reached toward his lapel, where one of his bloody bandages showed. He took her hand before she could inspect. "I'll explain it all to you very soon. You'll be better off knowing..."

He drifted off into a dream.

Dorhen sniffled and swallowed to make himself stop crying.

"From now on, you'll listen to Mother, won't you?" Mother scolded while she rubbed a cold yellow ointment on his hand.

"Yes, Mother. The frog, it was so pretty and shiny."

"But it was hot, wasn't it? I told you it needed several more hours to cool after coming out of the kiln. You didn't listen."

Mother had helped him make the little frog out of clay. She painted a special watery clay mix on it and pushed it into the fire after fanning it all day. Some cups she'd made went in with the little frog. When she pulled the clay things out earlier that evening, the frog had turned a beautiful, shiny dark green with little pink specks on its back.

"I worried about him all night, Mother."

She giggled. "It's a clay frog, *guenhighar*. He would've been fine. A few hours' wait was all he needed. Now look at your hand. You're an impatient *saeghar*, aren't you?"

"Sorry."

She wound a strip of cloth around his palm. His fingertips hurt too. They were turning white and puffy. "Don't be sorry. From now on, you'll listen to Mother. And you understand fire now, don't you?"

"Yes."

When Father came out of the bedroom, finally, Dorhen wiped his eyes on his sleeve. He didn't want Father to see him cry. "Father," he said, standing to meet him as squarely as he could while Mother worked on his hand, "can you take me fishing soon? I'm old enough now."

Father stayed busy, pulling an old sack from the trunk and going to the cupboard to shove all the dried mushrooms and spices they owned into it. Father didn't bother pausing when he said, "Of course you are."

"What are you doing?" Mother asked.

"I told you to get ready. We're leaving." He finally gave his attention to Dorhen. "We're going on a trip. There'll be tons of opportunities to learn how to fish when we're out in the wilds."

Dorhen threw his hands in the air. "Hurray!" Mother jerked his bandaged hand back down and continued wrapping his fingers tighter than before.

"We're leaving tonight," Father continued. "We'll be gone for a long time, so I'm counting on you to be tough. Let's see your arm."

Dorhen pushed up his sleeve and flexed.

"Perfect!" Father slapped his hands together. Mother took his hand back again. "But you'll get better. You'll work on yourself and be the best you can be. Won't you?"

Dorhen balled his free hand into a fist and raised it high. "Yes!"

"We can't leave," Mother said over his enthusiastic response. "I recently finished the new dishes. We haven't eaten today. And Dorhen burned his hand."

"*Saehgahn* have been known to travel with worse injuries, my dream. Go on and pack some extra clothes now."

"He's not *saehgahn* yet. It's getting late. We're not going anywhere until Dorhen eats. Let's talk tomorrow."

Father tied his best knife to his belt. "Tonight," he said.

"After he eats, he'll be sleepy. Who'll carry him?"

"Me!" He took a breath. "Trust me."

Mother bit her lip. "Fine. We'll leave tonight. But we're going nowhere until he eats, and we're out of everything. I'll need to dig some potatoes."

Father put his hand out really fast. "Stay. I'll go get some potatoes. You stay back and hurry with the fire and the water."

"I'll go too, Father." Dorhen tried to run forward, but Mother still held his arm and she squeezed it, holding him back. "Mother, can't I go?"

Her eyes grew big, and they shifted to Father and back. "Mmm," was all she said. She stood and marched toward Father, threw aside his tabard, and took the knife off his belt. "Without this, you can." Even though she said it to Dorhen, she stared at Father hard. Then she leaned down to look Dorhen in the face, and said, "I can hear from far, far away. If you need me, shout as loud as you can, understand?"

An excited tremor rattled his throat. "Yes, Mother!" He ran over to put on his belt and shoes before joining Father's side.

"Be quick," she said to Father.

"Exactly what I intend, my dream," he said back. "Let's go, *saeghar*."

"Wait." Dorhen returned to his mother's side as she sat alone by the hearth, pulling her shawl tight around her arms. "Don't be so worried, Mother." He kissed her cheek. Her eyelashes fluttered before she reopened them as he leaned back again. "I'll be fine. I can carry a lot of potatoes, and while I'm out, I'll scout the area. I'll keep you safe."

He turned back to Father. "Father, Father," he said as they went out the door, "look at my injury. I didn't even cry!"

At the place where the potatoes grew, Dorhen got to work digging his hands into the dirt like Mother had shown him long ago. He knew what kind of plant to look for to find a potato underground.

After digging the first one out, he said, "I'm gonna bring home a hundred potatoes. She'll be happy... Father?"

Father hadn't joined him yet. He stood motionless, staring at the barrier posts with the bird feathers and rocks dangling from them.

"Father?"

Father's hands shook. He rushed forward to inspect one of the broken posts. It leaned over with a split at its middle.

"Dorhen," Father said.

He waited for whatever Father would order. "We can fix it," Dorhen said.

Father lifted him and ran. The run jostled him all the way. He got dizzy after a while. The trees rushed past them and far into the dark distance over his father's shoulder. He'd dropped the potato he'd found, and now his hands dirtied up Father's yellow hair.

"Why are we running?"

Father breathed fast and didn't answer any questions. Talking was too hard to do while they ran anyway. The potato patch was kind of far away from the house, so it took a long time to run back, though not as long as walking.

Father was wheezing when they finally arrived. He stopped in the bushes before entering the yard and held Dorhen's hand firm, keeping him from running toward the house.

A soft blue light hung over the entire house like a draping sheet, making the whole house glow in the dark.

"No," Father whispered. "Dorhen," he said and leaned down, "stay here. Hide."

Father started saying strange words after he said to hide. He stepped over the twigs and through the bushes, saying those words Dorhen didn't understand. A few seconds later, Father's left hand glowed a soft pink color. Dorhen couldn't help but stare. How did he do that? Father approached the house very slowly and reached for the door. When he touched the handle, a bright wave of fire spread across the whole house from his glowing hand.

Father had set their house on fire.

Dorhen screamed and lunged out of the bushes. "Mother!"

Father leaped backward and landed on his bottom. His mouth gaped open, his eyes staring when Dorhen got close. Dorhen went to the door, but flames danced all across the wooden surface. The door handle burned like the clay frog, and he jerked his hand back.

"No!" Father yelled. He shoved Dorhen toward the bushes again.

"Father, what did you do? Why did you do that?"

"Hide, I said!" Father ran around to the other side of the house. The roof drooped for a moment and then caved into the house with a thunderous shout amidst the roar of the flames. It fell in with Mother trapped inside.

Before Dorhen could run toward it, another person grabbed his shoulder. The person who approached behind him was standing in a cloud around his feet. Long, long hair trailed all the way to the ground.

Mother had once told him older *saehgahn* grew their hair longer. This one's hair was blue!

"Who are you?"

The new person put a finger to his lips like Mother did on nights when Father came home late. The blue-haired person stretched out his hand. "It's not safe here. Follow me."

His voice was soft and soothing and louder in Dorhen's ears than the burning house. His shiny blue eyes made Dorhen stare. He tried to turn back to his house as it crumbled into nothing but a big bonfire with Mother inside—trapped inside like his frog in the kiln—but the stranger's eyes glimmered more.

"Take my hand, Sufferborn."

Once again, Dorhen tried to look at his burning house, but more voices, not his father's, shouted through the trees. "Get the child!" They wore red cloaks and held knives in their gloved fists.

"Hurry," the blue-haired stranger said, extending his hand toward Dorhen's chest. Dorhen tore his gaze away and viewed the scene behind him. The red-cloaked men were running toward him, one with a looped rope in his hands.

Where had Father gone? He wanted to call for Father, but there was no time. Before the scary people approached, Dorhen gave the stranger his hand. The cloud around his feet expanded and swirled around Dorhen too, hiding the hot, fiery chaos that used to be his home.

Chapter I
Her Sin

Sixteen years later...

M ay the One Creator forgive me... I sinned again."
A throat cleared and a voice resonated in the small wooden space on the other side of the grate. "Our Creator is patient. He will hear your confession and award his forgiveness."

"I did a bad deed... Well, it was good, I believe, but bad." Her voice choked off. Words whirled around in her head.

"Is that you, Kalea?"

"Yes."

"What will you confess?"

Twittering birds sang outside the thick walls. A cool spring breeze gusted through the open lattice window above her confession booth, flushing out the musty smell with fresh spring air.

Kalea cleared her throat. "I..." She twisted her canvas apron between her sweaty hands. "I'm sorry about one thing I did. Not the other."

"Hmm?"

She cleared her throat again. "I went to the market in Tintilly. They sent me for a bag of wool. But when I arrived, I stopped to look at books, hoping for one of the *Lehomis* books."

"*The Questionable Tales of Lehomis Lockheirhen* is forbidden."

"I know. And I'm sorry, but that's not what I have to confess..." She twisted her apron tighter. Better get it over with...

Kalea scanned over the vendor's collection for the telltale gilded arrow stamped on the spine. People rushed behind her, going both ways. On any trip to the market, she fought the temptation to look for one of those books. Her family owned one of the installments. Her father used to read to her most nights before bed about the handsome and funny elf named Lehomis who got himself into strings of hilarious mishaps and adventures. Her family only owned the first volume, so she had never found out if he lived happily-ever-after. She never got tired of hearing his early adventures, though, until her parents put her in the convent by

Hallowill Forest after her tenth birthday. Since it was a banned title, she could never take one of those books back to the convent, but how could a few moments' reading hurt if she found one right now?

"Ah ha!" a man's voice roared.

"I'm sorry!" She dropped the book she'd picked up. Novices were required to wear their allotted tabard and blue cloak when outside of the convent. Any superior clergy member could catch her looking at non-religious books out here.

"'Bout what, dame?" the bookseller asked, peering up from the book he'd been engrossed in.

Sighing, she twisted around. People were clustering in tight across the road, shouting and pointing. She pushed through the crowd to get closer.

One of the farmers working a table stacked with leafy green vegetables held a stranger by the wrist. Dressed plainly in a dark blue tabard, brown hood and mantle, and brown and grey leggings with worn shoes, the stranger stood about a hand taller than Kalea. He was long-legged and thin. Sweaty brown hair hung over his face, half-obscuring it. His teeth were clenched shut under his tight lips. Without cocking his head, he watched the towering farmer next to him. Bystanders were asking what had happened.

"A thief!" the farmer said. "Not only a thief, but a Norr elf."

Kalea put a hand over her mouth. In this town, numerous elves had been bound and dragged off to the jailhouse simply for entering town. Kalea hated it when these things happened.

"Ye know what happens to thievin' Norr elves bringin' their wicked sorcererin' here? Do ya?"

The elf squirmed and tried to pull away. The crowd swarmed in closer.

"Where did he come from?" someone asked.

"He's been walkin' around invisible," the farmer said, "using none other than sorcery right here in our decent town, until I caught his shadow disturbin' the look of the air. Not to mention he's a thief trying to steal my peas. And bad at his trade, to boot." The farmer swatted the thief's head, swishing his hair aside.

He *was* an elf! Pointed ears and all. Kalea had never seen one so close before. His smooth face glistened in the morning sun. His cheekbones were chiseled high; he was beautiful.

The townspeople shouted for the nearest guard. Kalea squeezed a little closer, reaching for her coin purse. If she could pay for the food he had tried to steal, the farmer might relax. The elf would still be arrested, but no one should get hurt because of this!

A rock whistled over Kalea's head and cracked against the wall behind the elf. He'd bent over to avoid it. When he lifted his head back up, his large eyes were glazed. The sweat on his cheeks sparkled and his eyes flashed a color no human could flaunt. He was young. Maybe he hadn't known how poorly he'd be treated here. Kalea's stomach knotted like a length of beads. The Kingdom of Sharr didn't get along well with the Sovereign State of Norr, and stray elves were prohibited in most places. They were usually imprisoned and ransomed back to their country, but this one might die before the guard could catch him if these people struck him hard enough.

Another rock flew. Kalea winced. She didn't see if it hit, but the crowd roared and raised their hands high. The elf squirmed, his eyes darting, unsure where to settle them. Another rock.

Kalea balled her fists. This shouldn't be happening. This could be one of the Creator's messengers in disguise, a hungry stranger. How could they do this? Yes, stealing was wrong, but they had regulated punishments for such crimes, like the pillory. She'd never witnessed this type of violence before; she'd heard about it in other places, but not here in Tintilly.

Working her way backward through the crowd, she retreated to a shady alley and tied her handkerchief around her mouth to hide her identity. She pulled her hood down tight. Keeping her head low, she traversed the crowded street again, unfastening her washing bat from her belt, which was used to wash the convent's linens. Good thing she had forgotten to leave it at the convent this morning. She gripped the old wood, smoothed and worn from generations of use. Inching closer, she settled her fingers into the grip grooves worked into the handle over the years.

A streak of blood trailed down the side of the elf's face from a nick on his scalp. Barking deep belly laughs, the towering farmer held the elf in place, inviting more rocks.

Kalea's teeth gnashed hard. She sprang. Yelling, she raised the bat and swung it. It crunched across the farmer's nose bone.

Her limbs moved before her brain could direct them. The elf leaned away from the bat's arc. Kalea teetered on one foot during the follow-through.

The farmer dropped the elf's hand, roaring with vibrato. Rocks stopped flying. Voices stopped shouting. The elf's mouth dropped open; his eyes met hers.

She grabbed his hand. "Hurry!" she said, and pulled him through the throng. He agreed, gripping her hand in return.

A jolt through her arm stopped her progression. The crowd had latched onto the elf, and he swiped back at them. When he jerked free, they ran through the rest of the market area, dodging many grabbing hands. One of the guards' voices thundered over the shouting crowd, alerting other guards to their direction.

Kalea and the elf made it to the next square, where folk walked around with their water buckets and handcarts. A swarm of children laughed, chasing a young dog who was determined not to let them have the stick in its jaws. She and the elf ran across this relaxed area, darting into an alley behind a hanging straw rug an old lady was beating.

To confuse the guards, Kalea picked the alleys she knew the best and took detours through cool, shady gaps between walls. They leaped over homeless beggars, ducked under soggy clothes strung between buildings, and broke through clouds of pipe smoke drifting from the mouths of layabouts. The guards' voices grew fainter.

They drew near the edge of the small town where the buildings thinned out, and the river became visible over a hill after a sprint across a grassy patch. Kalea located a shallow rocky section, and they traversed across, their hands still linked. They stepped into the river and the elf pushed past her to take the lead; both of them were ankle-deep. The icy water flooded her leather shoes and bit into her feet. Water seeped into the fibers of her skirt hem and slowed her down.

She glanced over her shoulder for possible pursuers. The waving grass in the field showed their footprints, which the guards might find as a clue later.

A barking dog jumped out from one of the tight spaces between the buildings. Kalea jumped and shrieked, causing the elf to lurch as well.

The dog stayed by the building, barking at them. Someone could show up at any moment.

The elf tugged at her hand. "Don't stop." If they ran fast enough, they might make it across the field to the forest's cover. The dog remained, barking, and Kalea glanced over her shoulder in panic.

He gripped her hand tighter and guided her over the entire rocky riverbed. Near the opposite bank, her foot slipped off a stone and she fell. He caught her with a strong arm scooped around her middle.

After the shock of falling wore off, she found his fingers pressing into her breast. In the next beat, he released her and continued to the bank. In such urgency, maybe he hadn't noticed what he'd done. And he had saved her from a sprained ankle or worse.

"Um, thanks," she said, wading after him, her dress soaking up more heavy water.

"Concentrate," he said.

They made it to the forest and kept running deeper into its fragrant pine atmosphere. Though he could've easily outrun and lost her, he matched her pace. She glanced back several times. The bright field glowing behind the dark layers of tree trunks faded.

Deep in the pines, a mile or so, they slowed and finally stopped. She collapsed to the ground, panting. The elf remained standing, surveying the area as if they weren't alone yet. They were. They were alone together in the forest.

Kalea threw off her hood and fumbled with the kerchief she'd tied over her nose, ripping it free and stuffing it back into her belt pouch. She removed her short novice's veil too, letting her hair out and savoring the cool air against her sweaty face.

The elf stopped pacing, and his eyes lingered on her.

She stood and tied her washing bat back to her belt. Through all that, she'd managed not to drop it. He didn't offer a word. He wasn't panting as hard either. The blood from his scalp trailed a line all the way to his jaw.

She met his soft eyes. "Did they hurt you back there?"

He shook his head. "I'll be fine."

She pointed to the glistening red trail along his face. "You're bleeding."

He wiped at the side of his face, his fingers trailing through the blood, and examined his hand. His expression didn't change.

She took her handkerchief out again and dabbed its corner on her tongue.

"May I?" She stepped toward him. He winced before allowing her to wipe the blood away. Afterward, a new red stain shimmered on the cloth's corner. Elven blood sparkled gold in the light, apparently.

"Um, that's better."

Her knees wobbled under his gaze. She stared back until the pine needles rustling in the breeze no longer offered enough noise for her comfort. "What were you doing?" Her words burst out as if on their own. "Don't you know how dangerous it is for elves in these parts?"

"I do now… I'm hungry. I haven't eaten in three days and I got desperate. Arius Medallus will punish me again for such a mistake." He lowered his eyes to the ground.

"Do you live in these woods?"

He shook his head. As her stomach knots vibrated with all sorts of new bubbles she'd never experienced before, she reached toward him again. Her fingertips grazed the wiry design stitched on his collar. He lurched backward. "That's pretty. Did your mother make it?"

"No."

"My mama used to make my clothes. She did needlework a lot. Joy and some other vestals taught me about sewing, but I don't get to do it much. I wash the clothes mostly."

"What are vestals?"

"You don't know what a vestal is? How many towns have you visited? Surely Tintilly wasn't your first. I mean, Norr has got to be weeks of travel away—though I wouldn't know, I've never been there. But I've studied maps. Vestals can be found anywhere close to a convent. We humans are very religious."

When she stopped talking, he didn't offer any words in return. He stared, as if still waiting for his answer.

"Oh, well, I mean, vestals are servants of the Creator. They're kind of like His brides." Kalea grasped her belt pouch, which jingled with the coins she'd been sent out with. "Oh no, I never got the wool they sent me to buy. You'd better leave. I have to go back to town—no, wait. I can't go back there, they might recognize me. I'll have to make up a story when I get back home. Please forget you saw me. I shouldn't be in the woods this deep. I'm not supposed to be alone with a man either."

"Agreed," he said. "I shouldn't have been seen by you either." He canceled his decision to turn away. "Can I ask your name, though? I promise I'll forget it right after."

Kalea put her hands on her hips. "Well, aren't you bold?"

"I never thought so before. Sorry." His head sank as he turned.

"Wait." Kalea stepped forward, opening her belt pouch, and pulled out a biscuit folded into another handkerchief she'd been saving for later. She unwrapped it and held it out to him. "My name is Kalea Thridmill."

He looked at the biscuit and then lingered on her eyes for quite a while. He took the biscuit.

"Kalea. Like a bell?"

"Pardon?"

"Your name is the sound of a bell ringing."

She crossed her arms. "My name means 'life-giving waters.'"

He shook his head. "Ka-*lee*-ah, see? It's a merry little bell."

"You haven't told me your name."

"It's Dorhen Sufferborn." He bit into the biscuit and winced at its hardness.

"What kind of name is Sufferborn?"

"I don't know," he said as he chewed. "Arius Medallus has been calling me that since…"

"If my name is a bell, what's Dorhen? Something that swings on a hinge?"

His smile dropped as he swallowed his current bite. "My name is something that rolls downhill into a valley."

Kalea cocked her head.

"But I like your name," he continued. "I'll *not* think of it whenever I hear a bell chiming."

"Good." She took in the sight of his face in one more visual swallow. His throat apple worked up and down as he finished the biscuit.

"Thank you for the food. And for helping me back there."

"You'd better get away from here, or they'll be coming with dogs through these woods. They hate your kind in these parts."

He drew his mouth tight and turned. She also turned to walk away, squaring her shoulders. She stole one more glance over her shoulder on the first step and caught him doing the same.

"Hurry now." She swiped her arm at him before walking briskly away.

"An interesting confession, Kalea."

"Father Liam."

"What is it?"

She breathed deep and easy now that her story was finished. "I'm confused."

"About what, child?"

"The whole thing. I committed a sin. I assaulted someone. I freed a thief... I saved an elf. I'm not sorry about it, and I feel guilty about not feeling sorry. I guess not being sorry is my second confession."

The dark silhouette of his head bowed. "You saved an innocent person who didn't deserve death."

Kalea swallowed. Her constricted throat held back her voice.

"How did you know he didn't deserve death?"

"I didn't."

"Exactly." The shadowy form on the other side of the grate leaned in closer. "The Creator's intentions are not told to us. We toss around a saying: He is mysterious. It's an easier solution to turn to than trying to puzzle it out. However, I don't condone what you did."

Kalea dabbed her eyes on a corner of her handkerchief. A dot of blood caught her eye, shimmering in the speckles of light through the grated ceiling of the little booth.

Father Liam continued, "It's no mystery that you *will* do penance, Kalea. But you may be experiencing some hint of the Creator's will. If this is the case, everything you did today was ordained, good and bad. Perhaps the elf would've died. I know how easily it happens. The Creator uses us to do His work—and not just clergy members like us. He uses everyone else too. Anyone He damn well pleases. We're doing his work, but no one said it would be easy or fun."

"So that means…"

"I don't know what it means. I assume you were wearing your novice tabard?"

"Yes, Father. I also wore my cloak." The novices wore regular peasant kirtles brought from home, as long as they met the dress requirements of modesty and simplicity. Kalea owned a light blue kirtle, and her chemise was made for housework. Strings had been sewn into the sleeves so they could be tied up high on her arms. Over their regular kirtles, the novices wore the signature woolen grey tabard with the "Creator's flower" stitched on the front. They would soon graduate to wearing the full habit with a long veil instead of a short one.

"Since many would've known one of our novices did this, I'll assure you that you're under the protection of the Sanctity of Creation. I'll send a letter to the bishop about the incident. Your identity will be kept secret nonetheless."

"Thank you, Father."

"Now I'll assign your penance. Take it faithfully as you always have. Say seventy Sovereign Creators tonight before you go to bed and another seventy in the morning. You'll do a shift volunteering at the hospital for a few days—"

"Oh, thank you!"

"I'm not finished… Tonight, you'll receive twenty lashes to your back."

"Yes, Father."

"And don't look for that book anymore."

"I won't, Father. Thank you."

"May the Creator utilize you in His vast network of plans, and may you accomplish your tasks. In the name of the Creator, our Friend, our God, you are dismissed."

Kalea stepped out of the confession booth, stifling a smile under her bloodied handkerchief, and began to sprint toward the stairway.

"Walk!" Father Liam said as he also stepped out, and she obeyed. Running wasn't allowed, except in the case of emergency situations. Otherwise, the vestals and novices were expected to go about their day with patience, full of prayer and contemplation.

On the way to the stairs, she passed the only door in the building painted red, Father Superior's office. It was a splash of color in an otherwise somber stone house. It sat recessed into the floor by a few steps.

The next floor up housed the personnel cells. Kalea tapped on the door belonging to Sister Scupley, the Mistress of Novices.

"Enter."

The Mistress of Novices came from a rich family and kept a lot of nice things in her cell. A large book collection sat crammed onto the shelves. A landscape painting hung above the mantel and a copper kettle dangled over the crackling fire. She owned a proper bed too, with a down mattress on taut ropes. The novices all slept on straw-stuffed floor mattresses in a large room.

The middle-aged vestal sat at her desk engrossed in an open book, the feather part of her quill waving above her hand. A fine porcelain cup of lavender and honey tea waited beside her with steam swirling into the air.

She didn't bother looking up from her work. "What is it, Kalea?"

"I have to do a penance when you have time."

She dropped the quill and cracked her knuckles before rubbing her baggy eyes. "Again, girl?"

Kalea lowered her head and spread her hands out by her sides. "It's worse than all my previous penances. Twenty lashes. To my back."

"Hmm." The sister's mouth drew thin as she eyed Kalea. She was under no obligation to tell how she had earned the lashes after going through the confession process, but some sisters in this convent could barely contain their curiosity—a downfall they, for the most part, kept in check.

"Well, I've been hunched over and smelling those ink fumes for the last four hours. Now is good."

The two walked through the corridor, their soft shoes and sweeping hems the loudest sound for a long distance until they passed a prayer room with a bell chiming in rhythm, followed by a murmur of recited prayer. One chime sounded at a time—not enough to spell out her name.

"Ka-*lee*-ah." Her own name slid through her lips with the air from her lungs.

Sister Scupley's eyes snapped her way. "What are you doing over there, saying your own name?"

"Sorry, Sister." Kalea dipped her head low and walked on with her lips clamped shut.

Lashings and self-flagellation took place in the basement where the thick walls were surrounded by earth and the heavy doors shielded the inevitable sounds from the peace and serenity of the world upstairs.

Kalea had never been one to shy away from doing her penance, at least after the age of twelve, but her heart rate did increase as she descended into the cold, silent underground. When Sister Scupley opened the heaviest door in the convent, its hinges groaned with each movement.

Ooooh-ren-boom! Kalea blew out a deep breath when it closed behind her. She'd try not to scream, but if it happened, no one upstairs would be bothered.

"You know the procedure," Sister Scupley said.

Yes. She'd been lashed before, but no more than groups of five. Some of them had been light switches to her arms or hands. This would be a new experience.

First, she knelt at the altar at the basement's heart. Bowing her head over her folded hands, she murmured, "Sin is inevitable." She reached for the little silver hammer on the table and tapped the bell once. "From Your generosity"—*ding*—"I humbly ask forgiveness." She tapped a third chime, bowed deeper, and rose. The prayer usually worked in calming her nerves, but this time it couldn't suppress the clamminess creeping across her flesh.

The groin-vaulted ceiling in this place bowed low overhead, sectioning off the basement into a series of tunnels with nooks set up for private prayer and penance. Kalea went into a larger wing with storage cupboards and ropes hanging from the ceiling.

She took off her veil and placed it on the bench, followed by her belt and her novice tabard. She unlaced the front of her kirtle and removed it. She folded it and placed it on the bench. Her chemise came off last, which she also neatly placed on the bench. Wearing nothing but her braies, she divided her hair and moved it away from her back as she approached the ropes dangling from the ceiling and put her wrists through their loops to help her stay in place.

The cupboard where they stored the various types of whips necessary for penance and flagellation creaked open. Kalea always averted her eyes from the selected penance tool, but this time she stole a glance at the thin leather whip with fringe at the end when Sister Scupley moved around to her back.

Trembling all over, she bit her lip. *Who cares about momentary pain against the life of an innocent? Throughout this ordeal, I'll thank the Creator again and again for having rescued him.*

Kalea closed her eyes and awaited the first lash…

Whack!

She gasped and her eyes sprang open again. The sting burst across her lower back and ran through all four limbs. A few seconds elapsed before the next one.

Pain roared through her like waves of evil spirits invading her body. By about the fifth lash, she forgot about thanking the Creator and cried instead. Thoughts of the elf dissipated too. She cried louder between each progressive crack of the switch.

Ten hits. She shrank away, attempting to tug one of her hands out of the loop.

"Stand your ground!"

Kalea planted her feet in a wide stance. Her body became heavy, and her knees buckled. She returned to slouching as the lashes continued. Soon she'd be hanging from the ropes. All her senses were smothered under a blanket of shredding waves. She whimpered between shrieks and her arms trembled, desperate to keep herself upright because her legs would soon give out. Tickling blood ran down the back of one of them. At the seventeenth lash, Kalea wailed, "Please stop!"

Sister Scupley delivered the eighteenth.

She sobbed. "I did it for the Creator!"

Nineteen.

"Keep standing!" the sister shouted.

The air stopped moving into Kalea's lungs. Her head lolled. Her vision darkened.

Twenty.

A familiar ceiling with huge, bowing cruck beams hovered over her. Everything between now and the twentieth lash blurred in the pulsing rage of pain dominating her memory. Bandages had been wrapped around her torso. Someone had tucked her into bed. Her eyes focused on the serene, enveloping darkness in the big dorm room where all the novices slept. The usual rhythm of many girls breathing filled the air. A sting ripped through her back as she attempted to move; she accomplished only a whimper.

She had done it. A smile spread on her face. She had saved a life and paid the price. Fighting to move her heavy arms, she wiped her eyes and put her hands together.

My dear, dear Creator. Thank You, thank You, for granting me the opportunity to save the life of an elf today. Or perhaps You wanted to test my bravery. If so, I accept Your test and any other challenge You want to send me. And I want the elves to have Your blessing, because I know they're Your children too. Thank You for setting me on my path—the path I'm meant to walk.

When she pictured Dorhen's face, sincere and smiling, her smile broadened. Her eyes fell closed of their own accord. Her thoughts drifted beyond her control. She had to recite seventy Sovereign Creators before falling asleep. Drowsiness pressed upon her eyelids, but she tried to say her prayers anyway.

Our Sovereign Creator, it is You who...almighty...in our lives... Your blessings...and in Your name...may there be... And please, I want to...see that elf again...

Chapter 2
A Crown for the Deserved

Twenty-two years ago...

With a gasp, Lambelhen yanked back on the reins. His horse, Daerbeth, shrieked and reared, nearly throwing him off its back. He dismounted, planting his expensive boots into the clammy mud. Throwing his cloak open, he reached for Hathrohjilh, the sword, and his hand found instead a cold shaft wrapped in a dingy rag. Lambelhen ran his eyes over a fireplace poker, the one Daghahen had used to stoke the fire. He gawked.

"How did that prick manage—?"

"Lam!" A red hood, flashing through the tall bramble, bobbed toward him. "Where've you been? The master is calling. We have to get to Carridax before the priest dies!"

Lambelhen gripped the poker tight and shoved it back into Hathrohjilh's sheath.

Lambelhen's fists and jaw squeezed tighter every time he had to lower himself to the floor for that stale-cocked old kingsorcerer, and now his bones might've reached their breaking point. The same old rocky smell of the Ilbith tower's stones wafted up his nose once again, cold and hard as always.

"My lord, please understand," he said to the old piss's pointed boots. "Hathrohjilh, the sword. You've no idea what I—what *we've*—lost."

One of those boots stepped on his hand and applied gradual pressure.

"*You've* no idea, pretty thing," the hard voice above him responded. Being the only elf in the entire faction had earned him that nickname, especially with Daghahen gone.

Lambelhen had worked hard with Dag for many years to get to this position in the Ilbith faction, but huddling on the floor and worrying about keeping other people happy or fearing punishment wasn't exactly the way he wanted to live his life. The spells he'd accumulated nearly fixed all his ailments, or at least kept them in check. He still had to work off his carnal lust every day, often multiple times, to stay level, and this place's free-sex policy with the servants allowed him his release whenever necessary. He couldn't leave like Daghahen had; he needed Ilbith. He needed to *own* Ilbith.

"My lord, I could raise this tower higher—I could make it soar, if only I could be allowed to go back for my sword."

"Didn't you hear me? I said no." The boot crunched down on his hand. His teeth ground together and squeaked in his skull. He held his growling voice in. "We're awfully busy, and I need you here, pretty boy."

"My lord…" Lambelhen paused to clear his throat. "My lord, the sword has powers I can't hope to unlock alone. If we can go back and—ahhh!" The boot ground down on his fingers, and a large, meaty fist grabbed his hair and jerked his face to meet a thick bearded one with the cold, empty eyes any kingsorcerer would have.

"Some lusty elf here doesn't respect the kingsorcerer's orders. I think he'll be alone in confinement, romancing himself tonight."

"No." He might've followed up with *please*, but Lambelhen had stopped begging long ago.

"Yes." The kingsorcerer ground the heel of his boot atop Lambelhen's hand. "Keep defying me, and your hands will be too broken to rub anything."

Lambelhen's forehead went cold, as it did when his anger peaked. His thoughts washed away, and a strange and dour consciousness he couldn't fathom replaced it. The pain in his hand also fled.

"Oh look, fellas, he's giving me the snake eyes now. We're all scared when you do that, pretty boy." He released Lambelhen's hair and his hand. "The hole."

Strong hands lifted both of Lambelhen's arms and carried him, feet dragging across the throne room toward the lower wing. Lost in a state of non-thought, his eyes lingered on the kingsorcerer until a wall passed between them.

Distant coughs echoed throughout the system of caves found under the Ilbith tower they referred to as "the hole." Iron doors were affixed to each little nook in the cave tunnels. The guilty waited out their time here, or waited to be beaten or gutted—whichever they had earned. Most people down here were servants who couldn't behave themselves. A few were prisoners from enemy factions, now resting between questioning sessions, while even fewer were Ilbith members.

Lambelhen had only visited this place from the other side of the door. Until now, he had played the perfect faction member and worked his way up the ranks using his practiced act. Losing his sword threw things off, and now he'd have to recover somehow. He'd have to recover *the sword* somehow.

His thoughts had returned to normal, and his hand throbbed. None of his fingers were broken, he found after testing each of them. His sore hand became the least of his concerns when his misty sweat and anxious jitters returned to greet him for a nice, long, miserable night like the days of his youth.

He rested the hand on his chest and leaned against the stone wall, beginning a chant he'd learned from sorcery practice to numb his body. Despite what the kingsorcerer had said, he couldn't simply masturbate the episode away; only real sex provided the relief he needed. Somehow, through keen skill and persistent meditation practice, he fell asleep...

And found himself underneath a soft, sleek body with draping mahogany hair dancing over his face, tickling here and there and obscuring the world around him. His clothes had vanished, and the cave tunnel struggled to keep its shape. The walls waved and changed colors, struggling to morph into wooden logs fused together with earth. A light pulsed as if fighting with the darkness, and even the floor beneath him half-shifted into a furry pelt or a woven rug from the cold rough surface it used to be.

His hands trailed up her narrow sides, running over jutting ribs and pale, delicate breasts toward her face. "Welcome back," he groaned, pulling her onto his penis, hiding it away in a fleshy, foreign land.

She bowed over him, teasing his mouth before seizing and sucking his bottom lip. She reared back, and the muscles around his cock clutched and pulled. She managed to coax a grunt out of him.

He panted and groped at any flesh his hands found in the confusion of exuberant movement. Finding and grasping her bucking hips, he helped her to move faster atop him, pushing in a few hard thrusts of his own.

She bent down again and pecked kisses all over his face. Loving kisses. Like she always did.

Wait...

He grasped her face. She moaned and tried to pull away, arching backward and jutting her breasts forward, but he held firm. He brushed her hair aside, focusing his eyes as best he could after their surroundings shifted back into the dark cave-prison cell. Her eyes were glazed and her mouth opened for a gasp simultaneous to a throbbing clench around his penis.

"Let go," she said through the hot, panting breath tickling his misty skin.

He ejaculated, but ignored the ecstatic pleasure. He leaned forward, practically sitting upright, squinting at her. "I know who you are now!"

Lambelhen jerked awake when a hand squeezed his shoulder. He lurched away. He hadn't noticed the hole in the wall the hand now stuck through before falling asleep.

"Calm down, my friend," a voice whispered.

"Whoever you are, I'm going to stick my thumbs into your eyes until I find your brain when I get out of here."

The hand retracted and the man talked through the opening, releasing the stench of his alcohol-laden breath into Lambelhen's cell. "It's me, Talekas. You're the elf, aren't you?"

"You stupid prick, do you have any idea what you've interrupted?" He wiped his forehead on his sleeve. Aside from the residual moisture, his sweating had stopped and his energy had replenished. The sexual urgency had dissolved already, even though it should've remained and taken him to levels of illness long into the morning after they let him out of here. One of *those* dreams had graced him again, one of those too-realistic dreams he had enjoyed several times in the past year.

"Good dream, huh? Sorry about that."

Beyond good. It was a healing kind of dream, and it always featured that same woman…

"Why did you wake me up?"

"Why else? I want to talk."

"I'm not interested." He rolled over and curled on the floor, ready to get a restful night now, thanks to the dream.

"I want to kill the kingsorcerer." Lambelhen raised his head. "That lumbering jackass has been asking for it for a long time. Lambelhen is your name, isn't it?" Lambelhen sat up again and pointed an ear at the hole. "I've had my eye on you. You're special, Lambelhen. Like a leader before he becomes a leader, ya know? I can sense these things. I know a lot, but I don't know it all. I need someone as savvy as me. With our combined efforts, I think we could do it."

"I don't share power."

"I didn't say anything about sharing. This is about you, my friend. I've got a disturbing notion that the jackass up there is going to run us into the ground. I mean, look at the place. It needs someone quick and intelligent to whip everyone into shape. We're the ruling faction, for crying out loud. You'd think we wouldn't have such money and resource trouble."

"Who are you?"

"I told you, I'm Talekas."

"No, what do you do, idiot?"

"I keep the books. I do lots of calculating. And we're not doing so well, Lam. I'm concerned. And my 'insolence' got me thrown in here. What are you in for?"

"I don't like hearing the word 'no.' I can't live in this place much longer."

"You're on the same leaf as me then. You and me is all it'll take."

Lambelhen rolled his eyes. "We'll need to win some allies."

"Allies? How long have you been in this faction, man? We don't need allies. We need our two cunning minds, the Ingnet's Tome, and some spell practice. If you want to be the next kingsorcerer, and I sure as hell would like you to be, you have to beat his protection spells and carry out a specific ritual. That's all. It's not even a magic ritual, it's symbolic. If done to a tee, no one will be able to deny you."

"How do you know this?"

"I keep books, lots and lots of books. This ritual is how it's done. We're not a ragtag group of practitioners who decided to form a faction, we're a unit written into the fabric of the netherworld and known by all of its dignitaries. It's not us who decides who is kingsorcerer, it's *them*. Are you with me, Lambelhen?"

He looked at his hands, soiled and still throbbing from the kingsorcerer's abuse. "Better yet," Lambelhen began, "call me Lamrhath."

Today…

"Send me," Chandran said, kneeling on the floor in the center of a blossom of star-patterned slates, an immaculate new addition to the room.

Kingsorcerer Lamrhath crossed his arms under his heavy robe, which was draped in gold chains with diamonds and rubies. "Are you sure?" His crown of many gold chains and gems glistened with fiery light. Two huge fangs from a long-extinct breed of scouel affixed to the crown stood tall like horns on his head.

"I want to prove myself to you. I'll do whatever you require."

"You've never met Daghahen. He's a greased viper and knows he's being followed."

"I'll go with your guidance, my lord."

Talekas, the Second, stood next to the kingsorcerer with his lists and his sharpened piece of charcoal. The office of the third-highest sorcerer stood empty after its previous occupant had gotten himself killed by blowing himself to pieces with a miscast spell while trying to destroy Daghahen. How could such an idiot get that office in the first place? Now it waited for Chandran to take it, so long as he could please the kingsorcerer. He'd worked many years to climb the ladder this far.

"Well," Lamrhath said, stepping forward. "You know the initiation protocol. You want to be the third?" He snapped his fingers, and a high-level red robe stepped forward with a small wooden box. "No one advances to an office without eating the heart of the fool stupid enough to lose the office. We all had to do it, myself included."

Chandran bowed his forehead to the stones. "I know the rules, my lord. Give me the heart."

The red robe placed the box on the floor before him. He opened it, and the thick stink of rotten flesh wafted out and taunted his nose. It must've been easy to retrieve the man's heart after such an explosion. It had been days since the accident, and now the heart's bright red had faded to grey. He lifted the slimy thing out. The bottom had gone soft and now wore a dusting of mold. Hints of blue were sprouting here and there under the meat's surface.

Lamrhath raised his arms horizontally to the sides. "Like the children of our beloved Thaxyl, we eat the hearts of our enemies. Begin, Chandran."

Chandran bit into the sour meat, which fell apart easily and stuck to his teeth. A chalky texture grated against his tongue, and the skunky mush slid down his throat after an eternity of reluctant chewing. Swallowing back a heave, he bit off another wad. Forcing swallow after thick swallow, he finished the thing, leaving his stomach churning and gurgling afterward.

Hugging his stomach, Chandran grunted out a few gags, tensed his jaw, closed his throat, and swallowed until the gagging reflex stopped. Lamrhath's arms stayed crossed, his mouth held straight. He didn't smile for anything.

"You'll do, Chandran. Go prepare your supplies."

He rose, bowed to a ninety-degree angle, and strode out, keeping his back straight. "Rayna!" he yelled to his thrall as she waited in the proper kneeling position. She jumped up and scurried behind him.

"Here, master," Rayna said, back in his humble chamber. She approached him with a waste bucket. "You can puke into this. I'll get rid of the evidence in secret."

He pushed the bucket away. "This is serious, bitch. I'm in the Third office now. I might become kingsorcerer if the two above me die. I don't fake my devotion to Thaxyl." He grabbed his heavy leather travel pack off the wall and threw it on the bed. "After this mission, my new rank will move us to a loftier chamber in the Chimera Tower."

She fell to her knees and kissed his boot. "I'm so lucky to have a master as capable as you."

"Get up." He rushed to the desk and scribbled a list onto a scrap of paper. "Go to the greenhouse and get these herbs."

"Yes, master." Pocketing the list, she ran out with her dark, wavy hair bouncing behind her.

Chandran opened his trunk to pack all the necessary weapons. He knew the small assassination tools best because he used to make a good living as a mercenary before sorcery entered his life.

"S'cuse, Chandran," a man's voice called. Rufus poked his head into the room. "Sorry to bother, but I just won a *big* shiny gold coin playing cards. Can I borrow Rayna again?"

Chandran unsheathed his lightest sword and doused a rag with polishing oil. "Find someone else to get you off. Rayna's going with me."

"You're taking her?"

"Yes. How many times would you like to hear it?"

"To the Lightlands?" Chandran sprang and swung the sword at him. Rufus reared back. "What's your problem?"

"Rayna is too talented to bother with you anymore. I've trained her well. She's not a whore for hire. She's going with me." Chandran sat on the stool and continued his polishing. "Maybe if you got off your fat ass and went out there, you could catch your own attractive thrall."

The servants living in the towers of Ilbith were free for the sorcerers to use and share, but they were also allowed to keep thralls taken from the little Darklandic villages scattered about the grasslands. Rayna had happened to be in the right place five years ago when Chandran went out on another mission. He never had been one to bother caring for others, but Rayna's bronze skin and long legs changed his mind a bit. She had protested plenty, but learned to like him after a good training regimen.

"Go away, Rufus." The man did so with a sniff.

Chandran opened a small chest nestled within the large one. Five holding spheres, glass balls preloaded with spells for quick use, rested upon the black velvet lining the box's interior, stuffed full with goose feathers. He moved them to his belt holster and included a few empty ones.

Rayna returned thirty minutes later with several drawstring bags bundled in each hand. "Pack for a long trip," he told her, taking the bags. She bowed without a word before kneeling beside the pile of hay she slept on and rolling up the threadbare blankets.

With their bedding packed, she slipped a brown leather corset on over her dowdy dress. He laced up the back for her, snapping the strings tight in his haste to set out. No matter who it was, Chandran's thrall would always wear this. He had ordered it specially made with close to one hundred pockets and sheaths hidden in the seams, so she always carried a whole arsenal for every job. Sweeping Rayna's hair aside, he placed the longest blade into her back sheath. Its handle was made small enough to hide under her hair. She loaded other lethal implements into her front pockets, anything from throwing darts to powdered poisons.

"Don't disappoint me," he said, lifting his own pack.

"I'll die first, master."

He exited the room with her on his heels. Downstairs, a handful of sorcerers would be casting expensive spells for the two of them. It took a lot of energy and resources to create a portal to the Lightlands—energy and resources spent for him. Chandran's moment to shine approached.

Chapter 3
Her Place

ee-ah-lee-ah-lee-ah-lee-ah!
The Mistress of Novices walked between the rows of sleeping girls, ringing the bell as she did each morning. At the wall, she stopped, knelt, and chanted the morning prayer.

Kalea and all her sisters rose from their floor mattresses, knelt, and did the same. Her back ached and stung all the while. After finishing the morning prayer, she commenced the one for her penance, seventy Sovereign Creators. She'd recite seventy more tonight before bed since last night she hadn't been able to hold her eyes open.

She dressed in her old blue kirtle for the day. Soon it would be replaced by the full habit. Novices could usually go on to be full Sisters of Sorrow at age twenty-five. Since she would turn twenty this year, she wasn't far off. She had done her best all these years to practice discipline, hone her skills, and be productive enough to prove herself worthy. No voices had spoken to her from the water for at least four years. Ages ago, she had proclaimed to her parents that the One Creator spoke to her through the water. They'd said they believed her, yet continued to shoot wary glances at each other. Back then, she had thought they'd sent her here as a punishment, but after a while it became clear that this was her place.

Over in the corner, Rose, a novice fifteen years old, struggled with her own kirtle's laces. "Rose," Kalea said, approaching her. "Where's Joy?"

"Joy can't help me right now, Kalea. She ran to the garderobe."

"Oh dear, is she feeling sick again?"

"She was hugging her stomach."

"Poor Joy. And poor Rose. Don't you know you can ask any one of us for help?"

"Sorry, I forgot."

Kalea took over her laces. As she worked, Rose studied her face with her asymmetrical eyes, one of which could not see as well as the other. A smile spread on her soft, round face. Her smile proved contagious. "What's so funny?"

"Nothing is funny. You look different."

"Well, I did a penance last night, and I have a lot of pain this morning."

Rose smiled deeper and shook her head. "I don't think so. You're happy. You're really, really happy."

Kalea giggled but winced at the twinge shooting across her sore skin. "How would you know?"

Rose put a chubby hand on Kalea's chest. "Follow your heart, Kalea."

Holding the smile, Kalea cocked her head. Rose beamed her everlasting innocent smile, and Kalea forced out another giggle and mimicked her, putting a hand to her chest. "Well, you follow your heart too, because that's good advice."

She tied the final bow at the top of Rose's kirtle and proceeded to help her put on her novice veil. "Let's get some breakfast in you, girl," she said with a wink.

She and Rose enjoyed a nice breakfast of oats in milk at the long table of novices. Today, she volunteered to help Rose stay tidy, wiping her chin and taking care of her dish when they finished eating. Their bowls had been filled half as full as yesterday. She said her goodbyes to Rose and wished her a lovely day before leaving her in the care of one of the elderly vestals, then went out to take yesterday's linens off the line.

Before starting the new washing load, she folded each gown and sheet into crisp squares. Joy rushed in, threw open the sewing box, and selected one of the garments in need of repair.

"Oh, Kalea, thank you for helping Rose this morning. I just got so…"

Kalea waved a hand. "Don't mention it. I know how you suffer." Joy's skin showed the pallor and clamminess of an illness she'd battled for years, some years more intensely than others. Kalea was a bit older than Joy, though she often felt like the younger one.

"Would you like another sewing lesson this afternoon?"

Kalea snapped a new sheet out on the rug and dragged one end over to the other. "I can't. I have a lot of laundry to catch up on."

"Well, I'll miss your company."

Kalea laughed. "For me, it's all about company. When it comes to sewing, I'm hopeless."

"No, you're not."

Kalea placed the last sheet on the neat stack and slid her hands under the lot of them. "See you later."

She passed the kitchen on her way to the vestals' wing, her stomach growling despite the breakfast within it.

"If I don't get a sack of flour and dried lentils, it'll be nothin' but onion soup for a while. I'm out of everything," the head cook murmured to her assistant novice. Similar complaints had arisen last week with lots of grumbling at the market. The pyramids of stacked produce on vendors' tables had seemed smaller.

From the kitchen, Kalea passed into the central hall with the red door. Father Liam headed toward it, giving her a weak smile while wringing his hands. He tapped on the door as Kalea walked around the corner with her stack of laundry.

A blue door marked the wing where the personnel lived. The main body of vestals each lived in their own cell in the building across the courtyard. Kalea would join them on their side of the complex after she finally took her vows.

A sense of serenity passed over her when in the personnel wing, a glimpse of what life would be like in the future. The little stained glass window at the end of the hall beamed soft, colored light onto the floor. It displayed a painted image of the Creator beaming on a mountaintop like a star, looking down at a city beside a forest, with a river running through both.

Tearing her eyes away from the bright, colorful image, she entered the first room, also with a blue painted door, and delivered the new sheet to the foot of the bed. All the vestals were in the prayer room at this time, where they usually spent two hours praying and reading the Creator's Word.

The next cell belonged to Sister Scupley, who would also be downstairs about now. Another novice, Vivene, stood in Sister Scupley's room, engrossed in one of her books. Vivene's broom stood abandoned against the bookshelf.

"Vivene!" Kalea said, plopping the stack of sheets down. "What are you doing?"

Vivene turned, putting a finger to her lips.

Kalea marched to her side. "I'm thinking you don't have permission to read her books right now." She peered at the illustrated book which had Vivene mesmerized and let out a gasp. She covered her mouth. An illustration displayed a man and woman in a naked tangle. Vivene turned the page to reveal the couple in a different position.

"What is that book?"

Holding the place with her thumb, Vivene showed the cover with its faint flash of an aged, gilded title reading, *An Exploration of Love in Three Forms: Poetic, Symbolic, and Carnal.*

"It's a manual about love," Vivene said, and Kalea frowned, gawking at the picture over the other girl's shoulder when she opened the book again. "Watch the door for me, will ya?"

Kalea whispered, "Put it away."

"Hold on." The ink drawings were a little crude; some took a moment to puzzle out what was going on. As Vivene turned each page, the positions got more elaborate, perhaps unlikely for real life, each one showing the man's...*part* entering the woman's body. A romantic poem or story came around every other page.

"Did Sister Scupley confiscate it from someone?"

"Nope," Vivene said. "I would've known about it if one of us owned it. She's kept this for years."

"Why?"

Vivene turned her eyes toward Kalea, cocking a smirk. Her eyes returned to the page. "Listen to this: 'My lady love, my lady love, my butterfly seeks the nectar in your quivering flower.'"

"That's disgusting!"

Vivene laughed, bending over the book as her finger kept the page marked.

"Why does the superioress have this?"

"Can you blame her? It's not as if we all chose to be in here. We were thrown in here because we were all deemed 'crazy.'"

"But I'm glad I'm in here."

"Good on you, K'lea, but for some of us, it can get unbearable. Don't you miss flirting?"

"I was too young to flirt when my parents enrolled me here. Are you saying you'd like to be married instead?"

"I don't know. Would you?"

Kalea averted her eyes and scanned the bookshelf. The rest of the collection consisted of religious musings, plant guides, and biographies of saints or their scribbled ecstasies. She hadn't thought much about marriage or if she should be on that path instead. She tried not to since she was already in here.

"I'm meant to be a Sister of Sorrow, Vivene."

"I've skimmed this book a lot," Vivene continued. "I've nearly memorized all the poses."

"Why?"

"Sometimes I think of them at night."

Kalea raised an eyebrow. Should she continue with the questioning?

"I guess Sister Scupley does the same. Ooh, no wait! Maybe she has a lover in Tintilly."

"Vivene. Stop, please. You have to confess about this."

"Well, I told *you*, didn't I?"

Kalea bit her lip. "I can't do this." She threw her hands up and turned to leave.

"There's something else in here I like."

"I don't want to know."

Vivene raised the book anyway, pointing to a page near the back. "There's love tales about elves."

Halfway to the door, Kalea stopped. Turned. And stepped slowly back over.

"Really great stuff," Vivene continued. "Listen to this. 'The female elf cries no louder than a whispering leaf under the careful tending of her husband, bottling up her passion lest the lonely neighbor *saehgahn* hear her and throw himself off a cliff to end his own loneliness.' Isn't that sad? It says most male elves have to be celibate. Like us, I guess."

"Yes... I guess it is a sad story."

"There's more. 'A vibrant young *saehgahn* leaves his homeland to seek adulthood in the human lands. There, he discovers the secret of love in the embrace of a townswoman or farmer's daughter, an act forbidden, but he is so appreciative that he leaves his mistress with a magical gift or blessing to brighten her life.'" Vivene's eyes slid shut as she paused to sigh. "Imagine getting a 'magical gift' from a romantic elf lover. Couldn't you just die thinking of such a wonderful...? Kalea, are you all right?"

Kalea shook out of her trance and caught herself staring out the window, bracing her palms across each arm. "Yes. Sorry. I'm listening. It is a pretty story. But you should put the book back and confess and never look at it again."

Vivene gave her a playful push. "Tch, indeed. And I won't find you in here tomorrow, thumbing through this?"

"No, of course..."

A door closing echoed in the hall.

"Put the book away!"

Vivene fumbled it back into place behind the row of ordinary books as Kalea lunged for her stack of linens, leaving one on the bed for the superioress. Swiping up the broom, Vivene feigned being busy.

With her stack in hand, Kalea turned toward the door, acting as if she were heading out, while an unsuspecting vestal strode past. Kalea exhaled, turned back to Vivene, and pointed a stiff finger at her before moving on with her chores.

At the river running through the forest near the convent, Kalea immersed each piece of today's laundry, laid a piece of sopping wet fabric against a rock, and absentmindedly beat it with her washing bat. The same bat she had used to free the elf.

Dorhen Sufferborn.

She reached into her belt pouch and retrieved her handkerchief, still stained with his blood. The stain had turned brown, but the gold sheen remained. She immersed that too.

The elf must be long gone by now. She closed her eyes and summoned his face to her imagination, already hazy since yesterday. The forest's pine scent wafted coolly around her on the breeze and the tall, stick-like swaying trees shielded the bright spring sunlight. In her imagination, she pieced his face back together and, once in focus, she thought about the feel of his hand on hers and the moment she slipped and he caught her. The forbidden touch he'd managed.

What am I doing? She snapped her eyes open again and plunged her arms into the cold water, where a small group of garments soaked in the little man-made pool sectioned off with stacked rocks. She resumed her toil, shifting them around. Winter had ended early, and new pointy shoots of grass pushed up through the red blanket of pine needles already. Her handkerchief floated in the water, its cold temperature perfect for removing stains, and she saw that the bloody smudge had lightened. Even her bandages from last night were renewed.

Watching the water, her eyes glazed and the light glinting atop the dancing liquid surface drew her stare as it always used to do. In the blurred shapes of reflected light, the elf's face assembled, smiling at her.

She growled and scrambled the water with her hand. "I'm not talking to you anymore, I'm a woman of the Creator now!"

She whipped a garment out of the water, slapped it on the rock, and thrashed it with her bat. Her arms were well-strengthened from doing this for so long, as willowy as they appeared. Beating her frustrations out with the bat had always been a soothing component to her day, leaving her free of tension and ready to fall right to sleep at the end of it. It also drew her focus away from the rhythmic dancing water. Though the water had always been the culprit to trigger her hallucinations, her superioress had specifically slotted her as washerwoman, as if facing the activity would cure it. Combined with intense prayer, busy days, and deep contemplation, it had worked...until now.

"I won't tell them," she said. "No one needs to know I saw it, just like no one needs to know I saw that hideous book." The inky image of a woman with her legs wrapped around a handsome man flashed in her head. She beat the clothing harder.

She'd lived here since age ten, and soon she'd finish her nineteenth year of life. A comfortable routine in the convent was all she needed to be happy. She loved her sisters, Father Liam, and Mother Superior; she enjoyed her chores, reading about the fabulous workings of the Creator and talking to Him, and visiting the hospital to care for the sick and feed the poor, and singing on Sundays—so many activities filled her time. She didn't need to…care for a husband. She could care for homeless children, she didn't need her own. A full life striving for perfection and holiness had been provided to her by her loving parents, who cared enough about her to pay to put her into the convent.

She stopped swinging the bat and bent over, panting. Dropping to the ground, she reclined atop the thick pine needles, which crunched under her head.

A spirit in the water. That's what it was. A spirit in the water had talked to her for as long as she could talk and kept showing up since, appearing in little rain puddles along the beaten path running by her house. She'd never been afraid of it. Her habit of talking to water used to cause a lot of problems in her family, though, and eventually led to her admission into the convent.

The spirit was nice, perhaps deceptively so. In her ninth year, it spoke to her so sweetly one day that she went into the calm river to get a closer look at it. She didn't remember actually seeing anything down there, but the time she spent submerged sent her parents into a roaring panic. Splashing. And screaming. Her father dragged her out so fast, her body created a tubular wave. His big hands pressed into her cheeks when he checked her face for life. He patted her back so firmly it hurt, but she was fine. She didn't even cough. A few months later, her tenth birthday had passed, and she watched her parents ride along the trail through the towering pine trees back home to Taulmoil, leaving her in the big squat house with the steeple and colored windows.

A tear trailed into her hair as she stared at the swaying canopy. She smiled regardless. Nothing in the world happened by coincidence; everything happened for a reason. She lived here because the Creator wanted her here. His will spoke louder than the water spirit's voice.

She sat up and sniffled, wiping her face. "Silly me." She crawled back to the water's edge, focusing hard on the laundry instead of the water's reflections.

The wind quickened and the trees bent farther over. She planted a hand atop her veil to keep it from flying away. The darkening depths of the forest attracted her eyes now. How far was she from the spot where she'd talked to the elf? Tintilly lay a few miles south and east from the convent. Their parting place must've been immediately east of Tintilly, considering the side of town they had exited. What had he been doing in town, especially if he knew he shouldn't be seen? Had he actually been looking for what that filthy book said elves sought in the human lands? To couple with a...? Surely not. He had mentioned he was hungry, a probable reason. Nonetheless, being hungry could be a truth standing beside another truth, that he was a "young *saehgahn* seeking adulthood in the human lands" and looking to "discover the secret of love in a townswoman's embrace."

A sharp tickle shot through her belly at the thought of that particular elf being the one in the story. How much religious contemplation would it take to wipe such a fantasy out of her thoughts?

She sighed and dunked her arms into the water again to retrieve the last few items. "I'm going to owe the Creator a lot of penance prayers."

Chapter 4
A Shield for His Fears

In the years since Dorhen's disappearance, Daghahen had walked across the continent and back as the spirits bade him. He never had achieved an audience with Hael, but he'd talked again to Thaxyl, offering beating animal hearts from which it drew a fraction of energy as a measly attempt to refill its store. A few offerings like that did much to gain favor from the desperate wisp which used to be a pixie. Thaxyl burned to be a powerful pixie again. In those moments when Daghahen allowed the wisp to draw energy from his own body, he felt it. The yearning sensation rising in his core made him bellow in discontent. There was no easy or quick remedy to such a longing. Is that what his brother, Lambelhen, experienced all the time in his desperation to achieve the final orgasm to end his never-ending hunger for sex?

Contacting Naerezek was out of the question. The dog-like beast of a spirit loved his brother; it would betray Daghahen to him, quickly ending Daghahen's mischief. But the three remaining pixies, Wik, Ingnet, and Hael, could possibly be bought. If he could gain certain abilities, or at least secrets, from them, he could defeat Lambelhen.

A long, rocky few years had slogged by, though he'd gained much. He walked tall along his way back from the Darklands after finding his secret weapon, a hollow glass ball containing the pixie Wik himself. He'd followed clues the stars gave him all the way to Hathrohskog, in the Darklands, where his path ended at its hiding place. He had degraded himself to a dark new extent to snatch it, but it was done. Now he needed to find out when and how to use it and why the stars thought it was so important.

He had spent the next few years traveling all the way back to the south side of the Lightlands, to the rock-strewn mountain terrain where the Sharzian kingdom mined its supply of gold. Lately, the sorcerers bustled there like a mating frenzy of rats. There he lingered, looking for the next clue, sometimes even asking the stars.

Picking his way along a winding mountain road, he stumbled upon a violent raid on a caravan and dropped to a huddle behind a wiry dead hedge. Daghahen's heart raced at the screams echoing off the canyon-like walls. There weren't many places to hide on this road, which snaked between two steep mountainsides. He had been planning to catch the caravan to ask them for food when it happened. The red-cloaked bandits set an ambush. The slaughter went on and would continue to completion. If the One Creator existed, no one would see Daghahen.

His mouth moved, forming some syllables before the words for Gariott's Blend came out. The spell worked with his tan-colored robes to make him blend into his surroundings. A haze crept over his vision to signal his casting success. He could still see his own body, but the bandits wouldn't be able to. Knowing the spell had reached full effect always took faith at first, and casting it as a veteran took trust, trust that he'd dissolved completely from their vision and didn't have a hand or wisp of hair showing.

Listening to the mess, he shuddered and reached for his shabby scarf, once a woman's turquoise-colored shawl but now his greying rag. He wrapped it around his head, to *feel* safe if nothing else. The red-cloaked bandits' laughter filled the mountain crevice as the screams quieted. Madmen like these murdered any time of the day that suited them, even at high noon like today.

Daghahen turned to look, peering over the dead hedge. These weren't normal bandits; they were sorcerers from his old faction, always inclined to attack innocent folk for their food and money. The victim-caravan flew royal Sharzian banners and kept several guards at each side. Its many wagons loaded with stacked crates and covered by tarps must be hauling preserved food rations for the towns. Other people in the group were regular traders, banding together for security. Though this assembly boasted a good company of swordsmen, they'd been no match for the Ilbith sorcerers.

Old Dag's luck. The Lightlands used to be a lovely place, a kingdom of valiance and honor, both when he had spent his youth here and later when he returned as an adult. But something had changed. The sorcerers ran amok now, in disguise when not flaunting their red cloaks or red bandannas or red leggings. They shouldn't have been able to cross Hanhelin's Gate, but they'd found a way. Even Daghahen could cross back and forth with his perfected system of spells.

All the caravan people fell motionless and the sorcerers roved over their goods, some dispersing to scout the area.

"I thought I spotted movement earlier!" one man called, and trotted toward the rocky nook off the road where Daghahen hid.

He sucked in air and tightened up like a scared child. The sorcerer searched around to his side of the hedge. "That was odd. Must've been a hare or lizard."

Daghahen held his breath and squeezed his arms around his knees.

The man ventured close, checking behind each available boulder. "I swear I saw somebody before we engaged," he mumbled, gripping his sword tight.

Daghahen winced when he stepped terribly close, a straw's width away from grazing his invisible form. He drew in long gulps of air through his mouth; his nose might've whistled.

Some poor trader's blood dripped off the man's sword. He shifted to one foot, surveying the road from this elevated vantage point, and the blade hovered right over Daghahen's shoulder. If he tried to scoot away, he'd disturb the dried flora, and there wasn't enough wind to take the blame for any plant movement. Any twig on the ground or dry hedge limb could also snap if he moved wrong.

A faint voice yelled from the road. "Hey! What are you doing? Get down here before someone comes along!"

"Right!" the man yelled back and whipped to the side, his blade narrowly slicing the air by Daghahen's cheek. He leaned over to avoid injury, risking any sudden plant movement or noise.

The man ran back down the bank between fallen boulders to the little road in the mountain crevice. Daghahen let out a sigh and turned again to watch the sorcerers ride away with their new wagons packed full of the people's food relief.

When Daghahen stood again, his spell wore off, and he loosened the rag from his face, letting it drape around his shoulders. His ratty hair flew free again as he made his way to the road to see the remains of the caravan for himself. The older wagons remained, although the sorcerers had taken all the animals, their hooves still audible down the canyon road. The rocky dirt crunched under his worn sandals; sharp pebbles stabbed his toes, which hung off the edges of the soles. He squatted by the first dead body, a hired guard, and pulled off his boots. The sorcerers hadn't taken everything of value after all.

After tugging the boots snugly over his nearly-too-large feet, he picked through the broken crates and dead peoples' pockets for any scrap of food. Nothing remained left behind, not even a crumb. The sorcerers would've taken anything edible, especially with the long overdue famine about to hit the Lightlands. He'd seen it in the stars last year when the constellation of the Choir of Weeping Children rotated around to face the Dead Tree. Today's event made certain that the sorcerers would aggravate the famine, if they weren't the sole cause of it.

A frown dragged his mouth down as he surveyed the scene once more. The gurgling of someone's bloody throat drew him to the far side of the wreckage. He left his scarf off his head. It wouldn't matter if a dying man saw his elven ears.

A fat man with a red beard leaned against a broken wagon. Its wheel had fallen off in the struggle and rolled off the road a ways. His hands clamped shut a vicious slice across his belly, the effort buying him a few extra minutes.

As Daghahen ventured closer, the man's chin worked up and down. His words were mostly air. "Helph…helph…" He wore a curious hood made out of pale, supple leather with the scratchy word "MERCY" inscribed across the front in whitewash.

Daghahen knelt beside him and tugged his hood down. A shiny bald spot capped the man's head, despite his bushy red beard.

"Helph…"

"Relax," Daghahen said. "Your troubles are over and the Creator's ravians will take you soon. I do envy you." A bland glaze washed over the fat man's eyes. He gasped for air now. "When you get to His kingdom, tell the Creator about the Lightlands' dire trouble."

Overhead, vultures were already gathering on the tiers of rocks. Daghahen reached out and pulled at the man's hood. It was attached to an elbow-length capelet. The garment's color would work well with Gariott's Blend, even as the sun continued to tan the new leather.

The fat man went limp, dead by the time Daghahen shook the hood free. He snapped it and studied it. No bloodstains. Unwinding his tattered old shawl, he put the hood and capelet on and placed the shawl over the fat man's dead staring face.

His stomach ached and growled, but he continued his trek, running down the road in fine new boots with a great new hood to protect him from the stars.

After sweeping to the end of the ruined caravan remnants, Chandran lifted an odd stringy rag off one of the dead men's faces, the only dead person with care paid to him. All the others sprawled around the ground, gawking as if shocked at their ill fate. This fat man had accepted his death.

"Master," Rayna called, popping up from behind one of the bowing wagons. "Our faction did this. I found a tuft of dog hair in this man's mouth."

Chandran didn't respond. He lifted the rag, filthy and grey with a few threads still displaying its original turquoise dye. He smelled it, pulling the scent deep into his nose. Pipe smoke. The pipe smoke scent told him nothing; everyone visited pubs and inns filled to the ceiling with pipe smoke. But another element accompanied it: sweat. Not like any sweat, though. Not like his or Rayna's. It was elf sweat. He hadn't found too many opportunities to study the scent of sweating elves, but this odor clung thick and potent, the way sweat collects in a man's clothes over time, but with distinct differences. It was the best lead he'd found so far. He stuffed the rag into his pack.

Around the dead man were boot prints, pressed deep into the dry, crumbly dirt as if this person's weight had lingered for an extended amount of time. A knee print had been stamped beside the corpse, confirming Chandran's suspicion that someone had visited this man before he died. Chandran stood again and called for Rayna. From the dead man, the boot prints trod the road going west, toward Logardvy and Tintilly.

The sky blazed orange when Daghahen emerged from the mountain path and approached a small town with a sign reading "LOGARDVY" with an accompanying illustration of a man taking a pickaxe to a large rock.

He entered an inn after flashing his coin purse to the owner and scrunched himself onto a bench at one of the long tables between a large, laughing drunkard and a cackling woman with a low, sweeping neckline. Resting his elbows on the table, he pulled his new hood low. They carried on their merriment, downing pint after pint, often talking loudly to each other. Neither minded him sitting between them.

"Ain't that right, mercyman?" the man yelled and laughed, elbowing him in the ribs.

"What?" he responded, but the man had already moved on to a new subject.

The barmaid leaned over the table from the other side between the other patrons. "You gonna pay for yer supper, mercyman?"

At first, Daghahen didn't answer, but when he braved raising his eyes, she was staring right at him. He pointed to his chest.

"Yes, you. You intend to pay? We ain't got no 'mercy' to share with a freeloader, mercyman. What's your answer?"

"Yes, of course. I have money." He drew his coin purse out once again and shook it.

"Now yer talkin' my language," she said with a sniff, and marched back toward the kitchen with an empty tray under her arm. A few moments later, she showed up with a bowl of stew and a tankard. He drew the bowl closer and pushed the tankard away.

"I can't drink this." If only he'd bitten his tongue instead of saying that.

The barmaid growled. "Bloody stink, I forgot about you religious types. What *can* you drink, your majesty?"

"Um. H-how 'bout some tea? Or at least hot water, if ya don't mind, darlin'?"

She squinted her eyes, a fist grafted to her hips, and stormed off again. She thought some religion kept him from drinking? And here he thought he'd blown his cover and announced his true race. Elves couldn't eat or drink fermented things, or they'd face death or at least terrible, horrible illness. He reached under his hood and wiped his forehead on his sleeve.

The hood. He had forgotten it displayed the word "mercy," which must be why folk had been calling him "mercyman" ever since he arrived. Must be a religious order. Regardless of what it meant, he'd keep it. Tonight it had saved him from being exposed. If his elven identity were found out in any one of these Sharzian cities, he'd be in trouble. Worse than being found out by a lord's guards, he'd also be caught by the sly sorcerers.

He let out the first sigh since entering town and dug into the lumpy bowl of stew. The salty gravy ran thick down his throat and into his empty stomach. It didn't take long to empty the bowl. He might've raised his hand for an immediate refill, but his coin wouldn't last long if he allowed himself such excesses. In fact, he'd be smart to pay for the stew and opt out of sleeping here. He had to save his money. Though a bed shared with a disgusting lout like the man next to him would be better than sleeping out there…under the stars.

When the barmaid returned, she placed a little clay cup before him. She'd brought tea after all.

"Thank you," he said, but she rolled her eyes and walked away grumbling about a tip. She'd get it.

Daghahen reached out and wrapped his fingers around the cup. Should he have ordered plain cool water instead? With the central hearth blazing and human bodies gathered in so close, perspiration beaded around his neck and under his arms. Nonetheless, the tea steam soothed his nerves.

He and Lambelhen had grown up in a place like this. Almost all of these inns were shaped the same. His old home was all the way on the other side of the continent, but it might as well have been this one. The ceiling soared above the ground and second floors, accessible via two staircases on each side ascending to a catwalk and the individual bedrooms. Only the wealthy could afford private rooms up there. Down below, the ground floor offered long stretches of rooms with rows of beds the lesser citizens were made to share, unless they traveled with their wives.

As Daghahen sipped the mug of bitter tea, a ratty grey scarf caught his eye. *His* scarf, bunched in the hand of a wild-eyed stranger. The stranger sniffed the thing and then roamed his eyes about the room from the shade of the overhanging loft. Daghahen ducked his head below his shoulders and chanced another look through one eye.

The stranger's eyes narrowed and darted this way and that. Under his heavy coat with bulging pockets, he wore no red garments to signify an affiliation with Ilbith, but he emitted the too-familiar aroma of salts and herbs any sorcerer carried around. He turned his head and made eye contact with a fetching woman standing behind him, and as she walked away, smoothly dodging drinkers and whores, he sniffed the scarf again before raising his nose for a whiff of the whole room.

The stranger's little friend disappeared into the kitchen. So many smells hung around in here, from the pipe smoke to roasted meat to alcohol and the body odor of the man next to him, the stranger would have to be using a spell to detect Daghahen's scent.

The stranger's woman returned from the kitchen, wearing an apron identical to the barmaid's over her flattering corset and wool dress. She went straight to the first table loaded with men, ignoring the one which hosted a group of chatty women. She leaned in low, looking hard at each one's face as she refilled their tankards.

Daghahen concentrated on his teacup again. "Damn." He grabbed the cup and placed it on the floor under the table. He had to be the only male patron in here drinking tea.

The woman moved to the next table full of men and looked at each of their faces. Eventually, she'd study his. They must be looking for an elf. No doubt they were sorcerers sent by Ilbith. He still carried Lambelhen's sword, after all. If she managed to get a look at his face, she'd notice the sharp, angular cheekbones and narrow jaw typical to his race.

The woman's friend toured the room too, flaring his nostrils. He drew closer to Daghahen than the lady would for a while. Though the hood and capelet had recently belonged to someone else, Daghahen could smell his own robes too easily.

Hissing through his teeth, he braced himself and reached for the woman to his left, grasped her head, and pressed his lips to hers.

"Oh, you hideous scoundrel!" She flung the remains of her tankard at him, dousing his robes in the fragrant ale. Any scent he could add to his ensemble would help.

"Thanks, darlin'." Daghahen rose and headed toward the kitchen for a discreet escape through the back alley.

After he passed the blazing central hearth, a drunk old man rose with his arms outstretched. "Hey, mercyman! How 'bout a dance? Don't you good folk answer requests?" He wrapped his meaty arms around Daghahen's whole frame. A woman with frizzy black hair cackled a stream of laughter at the two.

"No," Daghahen hissed. "Stop!" He wiggled until the man's arms loosened, but the drunk grabbed at him again.

"Give us a kiss for mercy's sake."

Daghahen ducked and slid to the side. The drunk's fingers caught his hood and pulled it off his head.

"It's an elf!" the black-haired woman yelled.

It was over. Daghahen dashed for the kitchen. Those two would be on his heels now.

Bursting through the kitchen, the cook yelled, "Marg! Where you been?"

Daghahen slipped behind the door before he turned around. From his viewpoint through the hinge gap, he saw the wild-eyed man and his pretty lackey shoot through the door. Daghahen held his breath, standing board-stiff behind the door.

"Who are you two? Get out, get out!"

"Didn't an elf come in here?" a sharp male voice hissed back.

"I see no elves. Patrons aren't allowed back here." Daghahen watched the gap between the door and the frame as two pairs of footsteps pattered closer and passed through.

"Close the door behind you!"

The two ruffians were gone, so Daghahen himself slammed the door to satisfy the cook and prevent himself from being discovered. He ducked behind the chopping block and crawled across the floor to the linen closet on the far wall. In the shadows, amongst stacks of fresh table cloths and spare aprons, Daghahen paused to rest his heart. How long could he get away with hiding in here?

Tap...tap...tap... The sound continued in perfect rhythm. The moon shone through the little window, and when his eyes adjusted, he reached his hands out. One hand grazed along the row of hanging cloaks belonging to the staff until it smeared across a soft, cold face. A woman's face.

Daghahen stifled his instinct to blurt out a "sorry." It wasn't needed because this woman had been murdered. He gasped instead and lifted his foot from the sticky puddle of blood under his new boots. Outside the window, a roar of voices was coming down the road with a glow of torches bouncing off the whitewashed walls of the buildings. It would be a better idea to slip out the back door before the noise reached the alley.

Chancing a peek into the kitchen, Daghahen saw that the cook was keeping busy dicing onions and cutting limbs off amorphous, skinned animal bodies. After a while, he checked out the door and shouted for Marg at regular intervals. The readied stew bowls were accumulating, and the barmaid could no longer serve them. Daghahen had to slip out fast before the cook decided to look for Marg in the linen closet where he'd finally find her.

After a few more minutes, the cook got so angry, he stormed into the dining hall. Daghahen finished his chant for Gariott's Blend and dashed out the back door.

"There!" a familiar sharp voice snapped. The man and woman had been waiting for him.

"I don't see where," the woman said, and the man slapped the side of her head.

"The door opened by itself!"

Daghahen raced through the alley with the stranger hot on his heels. A small explosion erupted with a flash of light—this man was indeed a sorcerer.

"See? There he is!"

"I see him now," the woman responded.

Damn! The flashes of light caused glimpses of him to show. Up ahead, the group of shouting people passed the alley; a large crowd surrounded a small group of skin-hooded men, jeering and threatening them. The glow of their torches would cancel Daghahen's spell; the spell generally worked better in daylight, but the crowd might be hiding place enough.

He flew into the mass of people, knocking a few men over, and wound around to enter the group of tan-hoods, pulling his own over his brow. These were mercymen—real ones, like the man he had taken his hood from. The mercymen walked with their open hands held high as some form of demonstration. Daghahen mimicked them, watching over his shoulder as the man and woman chasing him emerged from the alley and reeled at the flow of people, their eyes darting to find him. Soon he lost them in the throng of anger and flickering firelight.

After a long distance, he broke off from the mercymen and slipped into another dark alley. This one opened onto a new avenue with a few other inns. He took the inn at the corner and met the bouncer at the door.

"Out of here, mercyman! No handouts."

"I'm not asking for a—"

He shot a pointed finger alongside Daghahen's face. "Go!"

Five buildings down the street, some men were filing into a house with a red lantern. Daghahen weighed his coin purse and sighed. They would take all of his money. But a team of killers were lurking about looking for him, most likely for the troublesome sword he carried, and the stars glared overhead. He needed to get inside a building.

As he stepped in line to enter the alluring atmosphere, some of the men turned around and snickered. Daghahen kept his eyes low and his mouth in a frown.

"Does your kind go to places like this?"

"Sure," he said under his breath.

"I don't think so, old man. You must be lost."

"I'm just here for a room."

The door swung open and a brutish man waved an arm. "Come on in, fellas! Lookin' for a place to bury yer cocks?" The line began to move, and newcomers extended the line behind Daghahen. "I recognize you… Grathe, is it? Hey, Raul, welcome. Take off yer hats and loosen yer coin."

When Daghahen approached the threshold, the man pressed his chest with a rough, meaty hand. "Not you, grandpa."

"I need a place to shut my eyes."

"You wanna sleep? Go to an inn."

"Please, I've got lots o' money."

"Or maybe you're looking for a free bounce. You should already know we don't do free handouts."

"No, I have money—truly." He revealed his coin purse and shook it.

"Sorry, you didn't leave fast enough."

The man's hard fist connected with Daghahen's jaw and knocked him flat to the dusty road. Glittering stars spun in the sky. Force of habit made him shut his eyes, and the stars remained spinning inside his eyelids.

"This is for annoying me." The jingling of his money faded into the night air.

Daghahen pulled himself up and staggered to the nearest shadow, away from the laughing hooligans, trying to remember the words to the spell. In the darkness, he tripped over a heap of rubbish. A broken cart stood against the wall, and he crawled underneath it with barely enough room to fit his tall form. He yanked the hood over his face. Later, he'd try to scrape the paint off with a rock. But for now, the broken cart sheltered him. And so did his new mercy hood.

Chapter 5
Her Kindness

Kalea sprang up at the first ring of Mother Superior's hand bell—*lee-ah-lee-ah-lee-ah*. Hospital day! She said her morning prayers, dressed in her blue kirtle with the grey novice tabard, and flew out the big green door belonging to the novices' dorm. She walked as swiftly as she could get away with, her suede slippers scuffing across the slate floor. She bypassed the laundry room on her way outside, pausing to wave at Joy.

With her cloak on and hood drawn up against the chill morning air, she walked the long path through the forest toward town. The sun shone through the millions of crisp pine needles in the canopy, dappling light on the path and radiating on her skin, as if promising the return of summer heat.

Her favorite thing about the convent was its forest location. The tree line hid the hump-backed old house with the steeple and colored windows away as well as the Sisters of Sorrow as if by the Creator's design. They were all safe inside, though only partially cloistered. Established to protect disadvantaged girls in general, it also gave the well-functioning ones the opportunity to do work for the Creator in town, such as teaching the illiterate how to read and write, collecting donations, and helping out at the hospital to which she headed.

"Good morning, sister," various townsfolk said as she walked by. She returned the greeting with her best smile. The sun washed over Tintilly more than the forest, warming her under her heavy wool cloak and tabard. The smell of fresh-baked bread greeted her as it always did when she came here on duty, though when she approached the bakery, the bread was all gone. Her stomach ached for a slice after her thin breakfast—thinner than yesterday. Not that she could complain; some people ate less for breakfast every day than she did. Some people ate nothing for breakfast.

The squat little plastered buildings closed in tighter the farther she went, similar in appearance to the convent. The ancient cathedral had been converted to a hospital after the new one went up. It could easily be found by following the large, pointy bell tower looming over the shorter roofs.

She cut through various alleys on her way there and ducked under hanging laundry, like when she'd led the elf out of town. She crossed the same little courtyard with the well. Pulling her hood tighter, she cut through the market square. It stood empty because today wasn't a market day, but she proceeded warily anyway. Father Liam had assured her the Sanctity would protect her under its own jurisdiction, as it had already punished her for the deed. But what did that mean? What if any of the laypeople found out she had banged the farmer in the face with a washing bat and aided an outlaw's escape? She quickened her pace.

A stale, balmy air hit her when she walked through the hospital door, as it always did. Only once in a while could she volunteer at the hospital; she missed it in between visits. Huge windows emitted hot light, and a serenade of coughs and the raving voices of the homeless welcomed her.

A long string of linen-canopied beds stretching down the central aisle housed the sick middle class and wealthy people who could afford them. Otherwise, dozens of people sprawled out on thin beds of straw along each wall, practically shoulder to shoulder. The hospital didn't have enough straw for everyone. Many of the hospital residents were vagrants staying for a night, elderly people, and a few mentally ill.

She went straight to the kitchen and swapped her cloak for an apron on the wall.

"Been a while, Kalea," the cook said, twisting around as she stirred a huge pot of gruel.

"Too long, if you ask me. What shall I do first?"

"I've already got Annika sweeping the floor. Why don't you take some breakfast out to the residents?" She began ladling out small portions into chipped clay bowls.

Kalea pulled out the large wooden tray from the cupboard and placed it on the table so the cook could load it. About twelve bowls fit on the tray.

"Are these portions smaller than the last time I volunteered?"

The cook shrugged and placed two more on the tray. "Donations were light this month, in both dendrea and food."

"Oh," Kalea said. "Why do you think that is?"

"A famine's comin', according to the old folks."

"I see."

"Well, go on, girl!" Kalea lifted the tray by its handles, now much heavier, and pushed the door open with her hip.

On the other side of the door, the sultry air made her sweat. She turned to the right and lowered her tray to the people sitting on the floor, some coughing and pale, some elderly, and others scratching scabby boils on their skin.

"Hey!"

Kalea turned around. A middle-aged man in one of the beds had called her. "Yes?"

"Why are you serving them? Annika always serves us first."

"Sorry, but you'll have to wait. There's plenty to go around. The Creator rewards patience." What would this man say when he saw today's portions? Even the poor frowned when they received their bowls.

Against the wealthy man's moaning, Kalea moved along the row of poor people, unloading her tray. Along the walk back, an elderly man's hands shook violently as he struggled to hold the spoon and get any of the gruel into his mouth.

"Oh, you poor man." Kalea knelt beside him and wiped his mouth with the corner of her apron before helping him finish the rest of the bowl.

Finished with sweeping, Annika blew past Kalea and entered the kitchen. She passed her again coming out with the next load of bowls as Kalea went in. The cook had already dished out more gruel for the third round, these more shallow than the first. Taking the new tray, Kalea resumed delivering bowls to the hungry poor folk.

After that round, she collected the used bowls and took them back to the kitchen, where the cook huffed and sat down to wipe her sweaty hairline. Three bowls waited on the table to be delivered. Kalea put the tray on the table and unloaded the dirty bowls, staring at the three new ones.

"Do you need help with the next batch?"

The cook sighed and swept her eyes right to left. "That's it. There won't be another batch."

"What?"

"I told you already. We were expecting a load of food from the king yesterday. Didn't show yet… I should send a letter to the bishop. They might be swayed to sanction some donations for us."

"I'll tell Father Liam. He'll send a lot of us out to beg."

The cook threw her apron over her shoulder. "You won't get anything out of this town."

Kalea moved the three last bowls onto the tray and lugged them out to the main hall without the starch her shoulders used to have.

Her heart sank as she surveyed the people who'd already eaten. They could all use more. How could she ever tell the fourth person in line they wouldn't be fed today? She veered off to the other side of the hall, where no one had seen her yet. In this more open area, huge round columns supported the sky-high ceiling, and scattered people leaned against them as if they were massive trees. The hospital's priest currently made his rounds with the residents, reminding them to pray for the well-being of the hospital's donors.

How could Kalea choose who got the last three bowls? The first answer became obvious when she spotted a small child with tattered clothing and large, dark-ringed eyes.

"Here you go, little sir," she said. "May the Creator bless you."

She moved on, her eyes roving around the crowd for the next hungriest-looking person. A drowsy old woman got the second bowl before Kalea moved on toward the shadowy gallery at the other end where the sun hadn't angled yet.

The dark gallery was quiet, save for a cough here and there, and empty due to the cold absence of sunlight. When Kalea's sweat made her shiver, she turned to go back into the central aisle and spotted a figure curled in the corner who'd either frozen to death or was too sick to crawl into one of the sunbeams.

She reached out to touch his shoulder; a light spread of web-like blonde hair lay over it. "Sir?" One of his hands grasped the hood covering his face; his fingernails were a chilly blue. "Are you alive?"

As soon as her fingers brushed his soft leather mantle with the thin silken strands, he jerked upright, his flashing, pale blue eyes reflecting the soft light even from its odd angle.

She threw up her hands and shook them. "Sorry!"

His eyes darted around and returned to her. "It's all right." His eyelids drooped again and he rubbed them. "I was restin' my eyes, but I'll leave right now."

"Well, I should hope so. You have one of those hoods on. Do you mean to take a free breakfast away from someone more unfortunate than you?"

He waved a hand. "No. I swear, I merely needed a place to rest."

"Oh. Sorry about my rudeness. I don't see a lot of mercymen in here, but I've heard about how they extort hard-working innkeepers for free food in exchange for vague promises of 'mercy.'"

"Well, I'm not that kind o' mercyman, lass."

"Lass? Where are you from?"

"Nowhere! I mean, Theddir. I'm from Theddir."

"And so something happened that caused you to decide to join the mercymen, and now you're here, handing out mercy?"

"I give as much mercy as I can." The smile spreading across his gaunt, weathered face made Kalea's heart burn. He lifted his head some more, revealing the black-and-blue bruise around his eye typical of the mercymen. Superstition dictated respect for these zealots, but some could be so brazen as they wandered around demanding free food or a free bed that business people often had outbursts.

"I'm glad you're not here to take advantage. It's good of you to be so modest."

He leaned forward. "I'll get out of your way."

She put her hand on his shoulder. "Don't go. Here. You look hungry." She handed him the last bowl, and his eyes brightened and locked on hers.

"Thank you."

Kalea smiled. "You're in the house of the Creator now, and He has more than enough mercy for everyone."

"Thank you, lass. I needed that." He spooned small amounts of gruel into his mouth slowly, as if to make it last longer.

"You walked all the way from Theddir?"

He nodded as he swallowed. "Not in a straight line. I've been walking around for ages."

"As mercymen do, I suppose." He must've walked for years. Theddir was all the way across the continent to the northeast. The bottom hems of his robes and cloak were caked with mud, though it hadn't rained lately. It hadn't rained in weeks. It hadn't snowed either.

He practically sat on a travel pack wedged behind him. A wrapped, cross-shaped object stuck out of the top and leaned against the wall.

"Is that a sword?"

"Yes, but I don't know how to use it. It belonged to my father originally."

"Was he a knight? Or a guard?"

The mercyman leaned his head against the bricks and stared across the huge room echoing with distant voices and coughing. His smile had long faded. His empty bowl sat on the floor. "I'm looking for my son."

"Oh, really? How old is he?"

"Well, it's been sixteen years since I've seen him, so he should be an adult now. In his twenties, I think."

"I hope you find him."

"It might be too late… He's going to die."

"Oh my. Is he sick?"

"Yes. Or actually, he will be if not already."

She leaned forward to hear his gravelly voice better. "How do you know he's *going* to be sick?"

"I read it in the stars."

Kalea reared her head back, tempted to ask aloud how the stars could predict anything. "The Creator decides when we die," she said instead.

He smiled. "I'd like to be there for him when it happens. I owe him that much."

She reached out. "Give me your hands."

"Why?"

"It's important. Please." The mercyman eyed her hands before he obliged. "What's your name?"

"Ibex."

His hands numbed hers on contact. "Bow your head now." He did, and she commenced her prayer. "Our Creator, please help my friend, Ibex, to find his son. Please be merciful, and delay his son's death long enough to complete the reunion. Nonetheless, we always accept your judgment in matters of life and death. When it does happen, please accept his son, and all of us, into your loving embrace. Amen."

"Amen."

When she raised her head again, Ibex was studying her face closely with a bemused expression.

His voice withered to a whisper. "How can I repay such kindness, lass?"

Kalea leaned back. "You don't repay it. You walk in the Creator's light and help others to see it with you."

"I'm a mercyman… I'll remember you."

She stood up. "No need to remember me, sir." She took the empty bowl and walked away.

Kalea slogged through the rest of the day at the hospital, doing dirty chores and jumping in to help the residents remember to pray for the well-being of the hospital's donors—as they were all required to do. After about the first two, she took their hands and prayed with them instead for the Creator's mercy in the face of the impending famine.

Swapping her apron again for her cloak, she set out for the convent at dusk. She shot for the alleys to make the trip as fast as possible. She had spent extra time at the hospital and would soon violate her curfew. All novices and vestals were supposed to return before nightfall.

Midway through one of the last alleyways, the fiery sunset at the end snuffed out wall to wall. "'Ello, love," someone with a gruff voice said.

Kalea squinted, and her words slid out weakly. "Who are you? Father Rayum?"

"Don't you recognize me as no damn priest?"

She looked him over for weapons or anything he could be plotting, but his form was too dark against the backlighting.

"I been looking for you."

Her heart sped up. "Oh no. Are you…?"

"That's right, love. I'm the one you so wickedly assaulted. See what you did to my face?"

She shook her head. "I'm…sorry. I acted completely on impulse. I suffered a moment of confusion and weakness."

"I guess such a thing can be expected from you loony convent girls."

"We're not loony, sir, we're…"

"I don't care what you are."

She swallowed, and the difficulty hurt her throat. Her voice came hoarse after all the praying she had done with the hospital residents for the oncoming famine. "I did my penance." The gashes on her back throbbed now with the intensity of her heartbeat, making the events of the other day flood back into the front of her mind.

The man stepped forward, and she took a small step back. "How did you know it was me?"

"Oh, I asked around a lot yesterday. Though you covered your face, the witnesses and I worked together to deduce the tall, willowy novice's identity. Though a lot of you touched-in-the-head girls come here out of the woods, there's one in particular with such a small waist and graceful arms and silky brown hair like yours."

"Did you just mention my waist?" She darted a look behind her. "I told you, I did my penance, and the Sanctity of Creation will vouch for me. But what can I do to make it up to you, sir?"

"Kemp. Kemp Hydenman is my name. I heard all that. I been to the court yesterday, and your Sanctified people did vouch for you. But I can still think of a compensation you can offer to mend things between *us*."

As she paced steadily backward and he closed on her, the lantern light washed over his face. His eyes were both ringed in black, turning to purple by now, and his nose leaned to the side. The air struggled loudly through his nasal passages.

"I'll say it again, I'm sorry!" she said. "It was pure impulse. Blame it on mental illness if you want. I'm sorry about the evil thing I did to you!"

He stepped forward again, eyes beaming wide and vacant. Another step and he towered over her, his big, round beer belly jutting forward. "Gimme a few minutes and there'll be no hard feelings."

Kalea's stomach churned. "A few minutes for what?"

A greasy smile spread across his scratchy face. His rancid ale breath steamed out with each word he spoke. He must've drunk the whole night since yesterday's court ruling.

"Look at'cha." His voice drawled and croaked. "I'm glad it was you. There's something special about you. I knew it the day you hit me and broke my nose."

"I don't understand."

Kalea turned and sprang the opposite way. He grabbed her arm, and a painful jolt shot through it. He twisted it behind her using a massive amount of might to defeat hers. With a scratchy rope from his belt, he tied her hands behind her back and covered her mouth with his huge hand to stop her from screaming.

When he pressed her against the stone wall, his blatant sinful ways rubbed against her and he smiled, watching for a reaction. His hand reached around to her rear. She whimpered and squirmed, gasping for some air, but he didn't seem lucid enough to notice. Or care.

The force crushed her hands against the cold, rough wall behind her. This did no good for the gashes on her back. Her penance was complete. Was the Creator not satisfied with her lash wounds?

"If you scream again, I'll kill you," he said before removing his hand from her mouth.

She wept. "Please—"

His weight squeezed off her voice. She could no longer hope to scream. He tore the short veil off her head, allowing her hair to cascade around her shoulders. He shuddered and grabbed it tight in his fist and jerked, forcing Kalea to raise her chin. He licked her sweat, and she gagged at the feeling of the slimy tongue slipping across her throat and behind her ears. Meanwhile, his other hand mashed finger-shaped bruises into her flesh, squeezing any part of her he could grab.

"Enjoy it while it lasts, love. You'll thank me later—I know how frigid you God-lovin' loonies are. A mistake if you ask me," he said into her ear and grabbed at her dress to lift its hem.

Soon she'd live those drawings in Vivene's book, though she wasn't supposed to. The images flashed in her head, images of horror now instead of curiosity. A terrible sin against her Creator and her position in the convent. If they found out about this, they'd throw her out in the street. She'd become a new resident in the hospital if her parents didn't take her back. Losing her virginity would ruin her value as a bride too.

She mustered the strength to let out a short scream despite his warning. He grunted and pulled her hair more but slowed his advances.

"That's how you want to do it, huh?" Pinning her to the wall with his hand around her throat, he retrieved the fallen veil. "Pity. I wanted to hear you moan."

She fought to exhaustion, trapped between his body and the wall as he hastily wrapped her own veil around her head and tied it too tightly.

"Let's speed this along," he whispered, and loosened the drawstring on his leggings while lifting her dress again.

Despite the gag between her teeth, Kalea pushed out one more flimsy, will-driven squeal.

"I told you not to scream!" His meaty arm reared back for a heavy slap. Kalea winced.

The expected force was redirected to the side. Kemp toppled over and crashed to the ground like a dead tree. Kalea gasped for air through the gag, filling her lungs. Another person rose to a stand between her and Kemp, a familiar person with shoulders squared, fists tight, and a sturdy, wide stance.

Dorhen Sufferborn. He must've pushed Kemp over.

"Now I get it," Kemp said from the ground.

The elf stared him down, his reflective blue-green eyes afire with rage.

"You're still around. And now you wanna steal my screw."

Dorhen placed his left hand against the wall and held it there.

"I'll bet you've already had her before. The two of you meet in the shadows a lot, don't ya? A loony girl like her can't grasp the law against stealing, so how could she be expected to know the decency of keeping her legs together? Must be why she helped you escape. She knows you."

Sneering, Dorhen grabbed the man by the shirt, hauled him to his feet, and slammed his right fist into his face. Kemp's cheekbone shattered as if hit by a rock. As the large man reeled on his feet, Dorhen flung rocks at his face. Kemp wailed as a pebble hit his eye.

Where had the rocks come from?

Kalea leapt to the side as a small section of the wall foundation spontaneously cracked where Dorhen's hand had touched.

After struggling to his feet, Kemp balled his fists, tensing all the muscles in his arms. He swung. Dorhen ducked and followed through with an arcing kick, swiping his opponent's sore nose. Afterward, he slipped a deep side kick into Kemp's gut, sending him back to the ground. Before Kemp could rise again, Dorhen propelled himself forward and dropped a heel onto his groin. The man screamed and curled into a ball.

Dorhen grasped his own hair in a fist for an instant, then turned back to Kalea to untie her gag and wrist ties. "I must stop or I'll kill him! Arius Medallus said *never* to kill! People will be here soon anyway. C'mon."

No one lingered around in the next alley so they made a wild dash, stomping feet echoing through the narrow space. This time Dorhen led the way. Walls and objects became smears of vibrating colors in her vision. Every time she made a whimpering sound, his hand tightened around hers. As slimy as their sweating hands grew, he wouldn't let go. The frantic adrenaline kept her going. All she knew in each long minute was the memory of Kemp's breath and the hard feeling of his body crushing her against the wall.

Even when she began to slow, Dorhen kept her moving at full speed. When she attempted to turn a certain corner, eager to find a guard or someone helpful, he pulled her the other way with some other plan in mind. Out of her wits, she failed to note which route they took through town.

A tiny hint of relief crept over her mind when she saw the long grassy field and line of trees on the horizon: the protective forest which housed her convent.

They broke into the fields for a long desperate sprint toward the cover of the trees. Kalea finally gave in to sobbing as they reached the forest. She tore her hand away from his and ran off in another direction.

"Wait!"

She ignored him. The sun sank halfway past the horizon and a cool shadow crept over the land. She swallowed to loosen her throat, wiped her face, and chained up any more emotion wanting to pour out. Now where had she wound up? Clenching her hot eyes closed, she tried to picture which landmarks they had passed on the way out. Her memory was a tangle of fear and desperation.

Her voice trembled. "I don't know." She was lost. And that elf was out there, probably looking for her. She turned her head toward north and then west. Which way? She closed her eyes again as her throat tightened. Crying would help nothing.

"Kalea!"

She jumped and whirled to find the elf behind her.

"No!" she yelled, and took off again.

"Wait! You'll get lost!"

Oh no, he really is chasing me! "Stay away!"

The sun disappeared below the horizon, leaving behind a temporary residual orange glow in the sky and making way for the approach of a cold, heavy darkness that would soon bathe the forest in its brisk essence. If she wasn't lost before, she'd complete the issue now. She ran on through the dark, dodging trees she barely saw coming. She darted in different directions in an effort to confuse him. The pine needles crunched under her feet; surely he'd hear her from a long way off. Her panting turned into uncontrollable huffs and heaves. She pushed on until her lungs hurt.

Out of nowhere, a tree clipped her shoulder and her foot slid out from under her across the slick bed of pine needles. A sharp pain creaked in her ankle. She shut her mouth and listened. An owl hooted. No sound of the elf's footsteps. The darkness developed fully. A slight haze of moonlight lit her way. How lost could she be after her sprint?

She eased up to her feet, leaning against a tree, and tried her ankle. A piercing ache darted through it. She'd have to limp the rest of the way home.

Footsteps crunched behind her.

She turned as a cool light expanded and glowed like a huge, soft bubble in the night. After her eyes adjusted, a figure formed behind the light. The elf again! The light emanated from a tear-shaped object dangling from his hand. The soft glow revealed his face with a gentle smile.

He took a step forward. Kalea lurched, landing on her sore ankle. She moaned and nearly toppled over. Nonetheless, she limped on, trying to ignore the pain.

After today, she'd ask to join a stricter convent somewhere to be a fully cloistered vestal. She couldn't take the chance of getting raped by angry laymen or meeting some pretty elf somewhere who'd trick her into sleeping with him like in that hideous book. She'd worked too hard for her convent and intended to continue living in it. She owed the Creator her chastity for His mercy.

"Leave me alone!" she screamed over her shoulder. The light's pursuit slacked off a bit. Each fighting step increased the distance. With persistence, she covered more ground and, miraculously, the lantern at the convent's gate winked into existence.

Oh, thank You, thank You!

Before proceeding, she glanced behind her. No more blue light. She pounded on the rough door leading into the convent's yard. Its peeling paint flaked off under her fist. She would have to take a penance for arriving so late.

"It's me! It's Kalea!"

The door swung open with a whine. "Kalea?" Father Bersham kept watch tonight. "We were worried sick. Father Liam went out to fetch you at the hospital."

"I'm sorry, I got lost. I don't know how I…"

He took her hands. "You're freezing. You must've taken a fright. Come inside and get warm."

She clamped her mouth shut against the flood of frazzled complaints accruing in her mind's queue. She fished for the best phrase for a moment. "I have to tell Father Liam I'm all right."

"Don't concern yourself; get in there. I'll send Father Starm to tell him you've returned."

He guided her inside with a hand on her back. She checked again for any sign of the elf's light lurking amongst the rows of trees. Only darkness remained out there.

A sharp sting pulsed through her skin as Joy peeled back Kalea's bandages. They stuck to the raw gashes, and every little peel she made caused Kalea to wince. She hugged herself and clenched her teeth. She'd stripped down to her braies and bandages. The old sweat clinging to her in the chilly night air made her skin clammy. A few other novices filled the bath next to her, mixing boiling kettle water with cold buckets from the well. They darted glances toward her at every chance. The bath's heat touched her with welcoming wafts of steam.

The other novices left after filling the bath, hurrying to their evening prayers. When Joy finished peeling away the bandages, Kalea took off her braies and immersed into the steamy water with a sigh. After a good dunk to wet her hair, she leaned against the side, draping her elbows over the edge. Joy dabbed her sore back with a rag to clean the gashes before later applying the special herbal concoction they used for flagellation wounds. The tendons in Kalea's arms ached from all of Kemp's manhandling. The hot water soothed those and her stressed ankle.

She closed her eyes. "I'd like to sleep the night away in this water."

"It'll be freezing when you wake up. And you'd be all shriveled like a little shrunken muskrat," Joy responded as she worked.

Kalea giggled. "My Joy. She'll always be there to drag me back to reality." She hissed at the next dab of the cloth.

"We all want to know what happened to you," Joy said. "How could you get lost?"

Kalea checked to make sure they were alone in the room. A few candles were lit, illuminating the old tapestries which kept the room warm. They were woven with simple patterns of flowers and sun shapes.

"Didn't you use the path to get home?"

Which details should she tell?

"I'm going to have to talk to Father Liam," Kalea said, "but can you keep a secret for me?"

"Is it a confession-worthy secret?"

"Not exactly. I didn't technically commit a sin. But I'm scared."

"Why?"

"I don't want to go out anymore."

Joy stayed silent.

Kalea hesitated, and then said, "There's an elf out in the forest."

"A what?"

"An elf. A male one. I interacted with him on the day I got these lashes. He said he'd leave the area, but I met him again today. I don't know why he stayed around." She pressed her lips together. What all should she tell Joy? She wasn't obligated to talk about her sin after doing her penance, but there would be so many questions if Joy didn't hear the story.

"So did you...do something with the elf?"

"No! It's not like that. I'll tell you." So she inhaled deeply and told her the whole story of how she had rescued the elf at the market. Joy was her best friend anyway. If anyone could know about the bad deed she had done for the elf, Joy could.

"And then he showed up again today. He fought Kemp...for me."

"What a good soul."

Kalea sniffed. The room fell silent for a long time. "Indeed."

"Lucky he didn't leave the area, huh?"

Kalea lowered her chin to her folded arms on the edge of the tub. "Do you think...he rescued me today because I rescued him two days ago?"

"Yes, I do."

"But the whole reason for the incident today was because I rescued him earlier."

"Kalea, listen. You did a good thing two days ago. You rescued him because the Creator wanted you to."

Kalea tilted her head over her arms. "I'd hoped for that very thing."

"You don't need to hope. The Creator wanted him to get free, and you obliged to do His work. You took your punishment. The first act brought on another punishment in the form of an attack, but the elf was available to help you because you freed him first. And all of this was laid into the Creator's plan."

Kalea lifted her head again. "You think so?"

Joy's voice rose sharply. "Kalea!" She whirled around, creating a small wave in the quickly cooling water. "I'm surprised at you. How in the world could that have been hard? It was my first and easiest supposition. What would worry you so much about an elf who not only appreciated your help, but possessed enough kindness to return the favor?"

Kalea's mouth opened and closed before she could push anything out. "I *am* being silly, aren't I?"

Joy smiled and patted her shoulder. "You're overthinking it, and it's unnecessarily causing you bother."

"I'm shaken up after today. I don't want to go out anymore."

Joy stroked her hair. "I wouldn't either. It should take a while to heal from such an experience. I shouldn't have to tell *you* to pray. You'll be relieved when you do, though."

Kalea immersed her arms in the hot water; they needed it. Relaxing would be easier if she could lean back against the tub, but her wounds prevented it.

Joy put the rag and ointment bottle down, then fetched the regular soaps so Kalea could wash herself. Halfway across the room, she bent over and expelled a few rattling coughs.

"Are you all right, Joy?" Joy kept her back turned, wiping her mouth on her handkerchief. "Joy?"

"Yes. I'm fine." She grabbed a cube of soap, made fresh with the convent's grown and dried herbs, and placed it on the table beside the bathtub.

"You should go to see the apothecary at the hospital."

"I have. He's low on a lot of supplies. He's waiting on foragers who've gone miles away to find his most valuable plants. I don't know how long it will take."

Kalea reached her wet arms out, and Joy leaned into her embrace. "Poor Joy. Forget about me. I'll be praying for your health instead."

"I'm not worried," Joy said. "I trust in the Creator's plan for me."

Chapter 6
An Honor for a Saehgahn

Gaije jolted awake with a strong hand grasping his shoulder. "Wake up, *saeghar*."

"Grandfather? What are you…?" Gaije rubbed his eyes.

"Shh. Don't disturb your sister. Come on." His grandfather yanked him out of bed, shushing him again, and hauled him through the curving corridor toward the foyer and out the door.

"What about my shoes and shirt?"

"No questions."

A chill air hit him on the other side of the door. Summer wouldn't return for a few months, so the night wind still left frost behind when it came and went.

"Is it trouble? Humans?"

Grandfather didn't answer. The village remained sleepy; all the little doorstep lanterns glowed, but the sun would break the horizon soon. They bypassed the village center and the Desteer hall, locked up until sunrise. A glow or two appeared in its windows, winking as bodies passed by them.

Trees replaced the buildings, and what little light Gaije could see by waited behind him. Not much could be seen besides his grandfather's pale hand grasping his wrist. Gaije's bare feet moved from the beaten dirt to moist leaves and then into tall grass. The practice yards were located at the opposite side of the village, so they were moving into the wild forest.

"Am I in trouble?" Gaije asked.

"Depends on how you look at it, lad." He led Gaije around tall bramble, through tight thickets, and across ancient, caved-in crevasses bridged with logs. These crevasses and various sink holes found in Norr were created long ago during troll attacks.

Without his shirt, Gaije shivered in the night air. His discomfort didn't hamper his ability to cross the logs—he'd been doing it since he could walk. After crossing the deepest chasm close to the village, Grandfather waved a hand for Gaije to take the lead. He pointed into a small tunnel formed under a thicket with limbs and roots bowing overhead.

Grandfather whispered, "In there. You go first."

Gaije swallowed and obeyed, bending over to move through. A pale violet light glowed at the end of the tunnel, accompanied by a humming sound. Gaije desisted from trying to stay on his feet and planted his hands on the ground for a full crawl as the tunnel tightened around him.

"Grandfather, is this—?" Grandfather wasn't there when he glanced over his shoulder. Now alone, his teeth chattered for a different reason. He blew out a breath through puffed cheeks and continued forward, emerging from the tunnel into a clearing.

Glowing violet lanterns hung from tree branches in a perfect circle. At the center of the clearing, four Desteer maidens stood around a wooly ox pelt on the ground, humming the ominous tone, their expressions somber and distant. Each one wore a glowing stone on a necklace which cast a blue light across their faces, adding eerie shadows to their painted skin. The Desteer always strove to look like the same person, all wearing their hair hanging long and straight. Each one's face wore the same painted purple line running across the eyes, and the rest of their faces were doused with powdery white, even over their lips.

"Who comes into the Bright One's sacred place?" one Desteer maiden asked in a strong, commanding voice easily recognizable as that of Alhannah, the head Desteer maiden.

"Gaije Lockheirhen comes to the Bright One's sacred place," the other three maidens answered together.

"How dare he trespass upon the Bright One's sacred ground!" Her rhythmic voice rolled over tones like hills and valleys, similar to the way sermons were given, but a world more frightening tonight. "Shall he live tonight or die tonight?"

"He was called, he was called!" the other three answered. "And arrived on time to answer the Bright One's call. That's why he should live, he should live!"

The head maiden raised a hand in his direction. "Gaije Lockheirhen, you are called to service. Enter the grove and kneel."

Shivering more violently than ever, Gaije obeyed and took his place on the white ox skin. The Desteer maidens closed in around him, bringing a scent like lavender and charcoal. The leader confronted him head-on, arms crossed with her thick silken robes draping to the ground. Her hair must've been about knee length, almost as long as his grandfather's hair.

She frowned with her eyes squinting and continued her rhythmic speech, practically singing, though her volume reached ear-piercing levels. "A pathetic excuse for a candidate!"

"No, sister! He is fair—you'll see, you'll see. Look inside, please, and judge him as is just. His soul deserves as much!"

"If you insist, little sisters."

She reached out and slid her long fingers around his head and into his hair. Her eyes closed, and a cold tingle spread across his entire head from his eyes to the back of his skull. She shuddered, and he did the same when she took her hands away. He had never experienced *milhanrajea*, mind-viewing, before, but had seen it happen to others. Her hands left cold imprints of themselves along the sides of his scalp. He bowed over to catch his breath for a moment and shuddered upon rising again.

Every village owned a unit of Desteer, and each one required at least one maiden with the ability to evaluate someone's thoughts. If a village couldn't produce one, it was common practice to trade maidens with other villages, as in Alhannah's case. Who could say what or how much of one's mind *milhanrajea* might reveal to her? That was why all *saehgahn* were trained to practice meditation and discipline. This evaluation could lead to any kind of punishment if the Desteer maiden found something she didn't like—even if the elf in question acted fine on a regular basis.

"I saw his mind," Alhannah proclaimed. "This one is fair! I have glimpsed his soul; he is fair!"

The other maidens threw their hands up and howled before yelling, "I knew it, I knew it! We'll have another *saehgahn*! Praise to the Bright One!"

"Praise to the Bright One!" the head maiden echoed, and held a confident smile when she looked down at Gaije again, who gawked.

"Gaije Lockheirhen," she said. The muscles in her face relaxed and the slight hint of a smile graced her lips, but her eyes continued their efforts to bore into his as if her judgment of him still needed time. "Today you were called to service and you answered. And you are pure. And you are fair. And you are strong. And you are obedient. Do you agree to serve? You have a choice."

"Yes," he said, projecting his voice as much as he could, although he could only manage an average volume.

"Good. A 'no' could be arranged, but would've meant a dishonorable banishment or death after a deeper evaluation. Bow your head."

He did, and she raised her arms for a prayer. "Our Leader, the Bright One. This is Gaije, one of your *saeghar*. Tonight, You've called him and he has come to be Your servant, and a servant of the *faerhain*, and a servant of his clan. We are pleased with what we see and hope he will continue to please You. He is ready to begin his life. When he leaves here, he will take You with him, and there will be times when You are his sole companion. He will need Your guidance. Please don't abandon him when he is alone and when he faces temptation. For elves are born knowing

You, but sometimes they fall, and when *saehgahn* fall, they fall hard. They need Your strength."

She turned her attention to Gaije again. "Do you swear to keep the *saehgahn* code of honor, and to protect the females and the children and the weak, and to speak with honesty, and to kill the wicked, and to restrain your selfish desires, and to snatch up and bring stray *faerhain* back to Norr where they belong, and to kill any and all non-*saehgahn* who lay claim over them?"

Gaije's nod preceded a, "Yes."

"The world is cold, Gaije Lockheirhen." A rush of icy cold water splashed over his head, bouncing off his shoulders and running down his bare chest, stealing away his breath for a moment. A maiden behind him held the empty bucket. He gasped.

"You'll be alone. And the world is also cruel." She raised a hand, reared back, and laid an explosive slap across his face laced with an electric shock. A flash came before the sound—*crack!* Gaije fell backward and found himself a distance away. The bright flash imprinted on his vision, and for a while the negative residual image of her maniacal smile blinded him. He lay on his back.

"You'll feel pain, Gaije Lockheirhen," she said as he dragged himself upward. Her voice had gone flat and somber and now croaked after her yelling speech. "You came here a *saeghar*; you'll go home *saehgahn*. Bright One, be kind to Gaije on his *saehgahn*'s journey... You are dismissed."

Wasting not a second, Gaije collected himself, shivering. His head ached. His spinning, dim vision hardly mattered when he found the little thicket tunnel opening and scrambled through it. From there, he stumbled home through the tall grass and bramble. His stomach churned and he paused a few times to bend over; however, he didn't manage to throw up.

He reentered the Lockheirhen clan village and stumbled all the way back to his house, where Grandfather lounged under the kitchen pavilion by the oven's embers, as he usually did. His long, black hair trailed like a satiny onyx river beside him. He held his lit pipe in one hand, watching the smoke wander into the air like incense illuminated by the kitchen's lantern.

"How was it?" Grandfather asked.

Gaije's mouth opened several seconds before he answered. Grandfather didn't bother to look at him. "Awful! Is that how it always is?"

"I hear it's different for everyone. But always painful, yes."

Gaije hugged himself, shivering.

"Are you ill?"

"No."

"Then sit by the fire. Even if you are ill, it's not a good idea to go home crying for yer *aahmei* to serve you tea and tuck you into bed."

Gaije plopped down beside him, welcoming the caress of the oven's heat on his exposed skin. "So," he said after a deep breath. "I'm an adult now."

Grandfather finally smiled wide and slid his cat-like blue eyes toward Gaije. "Yep."

"Are you going to stop calling me 'lad' now?"

Grandfather laughed. "No, lad. But from now on, you can sit with me by the oven."

"Like an old, retired *shi-hehen*, lucky me."

"Shut up."

Gaije gazed at the stars twinkling in the sky as it grew pale, and Grandfather appeared to be doing the same now. "It's gonna be tough."

He sighed. "I know."

Grandfather's cheeks bunched into a smile in Gaije's peripheral vision. "Well, maybe not so much. Things have been pretty peaceful, haven't they?"

"Besides the raging boar incident years ago? I was little when that maddened creature rampaged through the village."

Grandfather laughed.

"You taught it a lesson. I was amazed."

"A good example of a slow day in the life of a *saehgahn*."

"Slow?" Gaije turned toward him. "When the boar refused to die with ten of your arrows sticking out of it, you jumped on its back with your little knife."

"Only four arrows. And I used an exceptionally large hunting knife."

"Tch. You wrestled it to the ground until you got all muddy. It spanned the length of a horse, and you rode it like one."

"You have a colorful memory, lad."

"I watched you gut it. All the blood. You smeared war paint on my face with it." Gaije couldn't contain his own smile at the memory. "And you hoisted it over your shoulders and allowed me to go with you when you dropped it off at the orphanage in Theddir."

"You have a clear memory too. Impressive."

"How could I forget? It's my favorite memory. I felt strong walking beside you. You were my hero." Gaije returned his gaze to the stars.

Grandfather remained silent for a while. He tapped his pipe empty and stuck it in his pocket. "I enjoyed having you with me that day."

"I always hoped you'd host my *caunsaehgahn* expedition. Do you think you could?"

"Well." He breathed a long sigh. "Would ha' been nice, but I can't leave these days. Someone has to take care of Anonhet. First lesson in being a *saehgahn*: we don't get what we want, and we shouldn't ask."

"Sorry I asked. Are you going to stay over tonight? You have a few hours left to get some more sleep."

Grandfather leaned forward. "Nope. You're *saehgahn* now. You guard your own household." He stood up, and his long mane pooled on the ground behind him. "I'll come over in the morning to get Anonhet, and to get my hair braided by your sister. And your father should be back by then too."

"You're right." Gaije also stood. "He'll be proud to hear I had my ceremony."

"He will indeed, lad." Grandfather reached out and slapped Gaije's arm. "I'm proud too. You'll be a fine *saehgahn*. I know it as surely as my name is Lehomis Lockheirhen."

After trudging in and collapsing on his bed, Gaije awoke a few hours later under the warm sun through the window and the beaming purple eyes of Mhina, his young sister.

"Grandfather told us what happened last night. Happy day, *saehgahn*."

Gaije yawned and turned his back to her. "Thanks."

Her tiny hands slapped his shoulder and shook him. "Wake up, wake up, wake up!" He groaned and pulled the cover over his shoulder. "Mother wants to see you. She's excited about today, about you. And also, Father is coming—did you know?"

"Yeah." Gaije dragged himself upright.

"Good. Now hurry and come out, don't go back to sleep. Mother's calling for you." She raced out of the room with her strawberry-gold hair waving behind her.

When he went outside, Grandfather Lehomis had already arrived and planted himself by the oven. Mhina was tying off his braid. When braided tightly, his hair reached down to his ankles. Gaije's mother, Tirnah, was setting places on the skin rug for the family to eat breakfast, fussing at Grandfather as normal.

"I wanted a night of peace, lass, peace and quiet and solitude. All you *faerhain* were fine with the new *saehgahn* in the house." Lehomis lowered his voice. "So show him some appreciation when he gets here, all right?"

"You had a job to do, Grandfather, and you left us. Right there in the wee hours of the morning. A few more hours was all we needed, and you failed, you lazy, pathetic excuse for—"

"Hey, lad, g'morning! There he is now, the new *saehgahn*." Lehomis approached and grasped Gaije's forearm with his strong hand in the proper greeting amongst males. He leaned in to grunt into his ear, "Help me out, will ya?"

"Gaije," his mother said, throwing her graceful arms out. "*Amonimori*, I'm so proud of you. Welcome, my son, to your new *saehgahn* life."

Her arms latched around his neck. She'd already let out some tears to dampen his cheek. Over her shoulder, Lehomis blew out a sigh, not noticing Mhina adding flowers to his new braid.

Tirnah pulled away and squeezed Gaije's face between her hands. "Let me see you."

"I'm the same as I was yesterday," he said. That wasn't true. Something different had become of him, and it wasn't a mere lack of sleep. There must've been something to that ritual. At the very least, a heaviness thickened the air around him and pressed down on his shoulders. It was slight, but enough to catch his attention. He really was *saehgahn* now. Finally.

More tears welled on Tirnah's bottom eyelids and she shook her head. "I can't believe it. Soon you'll leave me and you'll marry, and I won't have your protection anymore."

"You don't know that, Mother." He took one of her hands and held it in his. The sunlight radiated in her strawberry-gold hair, which matched Mhina's perfectly.

"Were the Desteer kind to you? How are you feeling?"

"Fine. I'm hungry, though."

"Of course you are. Now sit down, sit down."

Anonhet emerged from the house with a basket full of Gaije's dirty clothes. He froze and his hands turned clammy.

"Oh, good morning, Gaije." Her eyes roved over him once before retreating to the laundry in the basket.

"Good morning…Anonhet."

"Congratulations on your ceremony."

"Thank you." He reached out and jerked the basket from her grasp. She yelped in surprise at the sudden action. "You don't have to do that now." He dropped the basket. "I mean, please have breakfast with us."

She proceeded toward the picnic, gripping her wrist in her other hand.

When Gaije sat on the skin rug beside Lehomis, his grandfather shook his head, suppressing a smile. "You're gonna get your head cut off," he mumbled in a singsong tone as he reached toward the sweet roll platter waiting amongst bowls of honeyed berries, hot fish pastries, and candied nuts.

"What?" Gaije said.

"What?" Lehomis responded.

Tirnah reached over and slapped Lehomis's hand with a wicker flyswatter.

"Ow!" Lehomis shot a bright stare across the food spread at her.

"The new *saehgahn* gets first pick, Grandfather. Isn't that right, Mhina?"

As always, Gaije's little sister sat beside her grandfather. "Look, *Aamei*, isn't Grandfather pretty?" She held up his braid with the various colorful flowers adorning it.

Anonhet placed herself next to Tirnah and spread her skirt wide, as Gaije's mother was posed. Her hair, brown as the coat of a new fawn, tumbled over her shoulder like a silky vine. Her eyes were violet, like the majority of *faerhain*, but her irises were ringed in a dark blue shadow, and her bright violet skirt made them pop today.

In Gaije's father's absence, Lehomis was the chief guardian of the females in Gaije's household. Being underage, Gaije was merely a second-rate guardian who answered to Lehomis. Since Grandfather also had his own house to tend and Anonhet as a maidservant, they alternated week to week living both here and there. Because Gaije had been too young to take care of them, all the females accompanied Lehomis back to his house every other week. Today was special, as this would be their last breakfast all together.

As long as no one caught him, Gaije made a mental picture of Anonhet's image to keep. Since he'd been named *saehgahn*, he would soon go away on *caunsaehgahn*, a journeyman trip of sorts. And when Gaije and Mhina's father arrived, Lehomis and Anonhet would go back home to live a quieter routine on the far side of the village.

"Well?"

Gaije jumped, feeling guilty staring at Anonhet's skirt. Lehomis's arms were crossed high on his chest.

"Are you going to start? I'm starving."

"Sorry, Grandfather." He took the nearest sweet roll, and Lehomis scowled.

"What?" Gaije asked.

"You took the biggest one, you red-haired weasel." He snatched the next largest one and stuffed it in his mouth. "I shoulda dwown you in da bathtub when you were yownger."

Mhina finished eating first and resigned herself to leaning against Lehomis's side, twiddling the end of his braid in her hands and fanning it against her face like a paintbrush, until a donkey brayed in the distance.

"It's Togha!" she shrieked, and leaped to her feet.

Togha rode over the hill on that dark jenny-ass of his, with bulging leather bags hanging off each side of its rump. A fitting steed. Mhina ran toward him. After leaning over to hand a letter with a wink and a smirk to one of the young widowed *faerhain*, Togha snapped his attention to Mhina's approach. For an instant, he pointed one of his slanted eyes at Gaije, an eye grey like a frozen raincloud. Hair black as tar draped his head.

Gaije frowned and half-rose as his mother said, "What's the matter, Gaije? It's only Togha, come with the letters."

"Why's she so excited about him?"

Tirnah smiled. "You haven't heard her talk about Togha? Togha is her favorite these days." Lehomis wasn't smiling either. "She's going to marry Togha, she says."

"She can't marry Togha, Mother."

Tirnah giggled behind her swan feather fan. "Why not?"

"Because if the Desteer cuts anyone's head off, it'll be his."

"She's young, my son. Little *farhah* go through tons of choices for *daghen-saehgahn*. It's good practice for when she makes a real decision."

Up on the hill, Togha slid off his donkey and held a letter high, playing keep-away with Gaije's little sister. She bounced in place, reaching for it as he dipped the letter and yanked it back out of her reach again. She yelled and laughed and pulled on the old black poncho hiding his royal army tunic.

Togha's *saehgahn* naming ceremony had occurred six months ago. Immediately afterward, Lehomis sent him right over to the enlistment tent. As village elder, he also kept charge of Togha since his father had died before he was born. Within weeks, Togha reappeared in the village along his route, delivering letters as a new official runner and flaunting his new *saehgahn* status before any widow who'd look at him.

"He's such a stupid fool." Gaije settled down again and selected a bowl of honeyed berries from the array of food.

Anonhet fluttered her own fan briskly as she twisted around to watch the two at play. Gaije gobbled up the fruit, forgetting it had any flavor, and put the little ceramic bowl down fast before succumbing to the urge to chuck it at Togha's head.

Anonhet had also passed her coming-of-age ceremony not long ago. She had chosen the home over the Desteer hall, which meant she would now look at *saehgahn* in all seriousness and prepare her final decision soon. Unlike Mhina, she could make her decision at any minute. She held the power to change virtually any *saehgahn*'s destiny.

Gaije rose to his knees. "I'm going to get her."

Tirnah put her hand out. "Look at you, Gaije, so jealous and protective. You're already acting like a proper *saehgahn*." She leaned over to share a laugh with Anonhet. "Let your sister be. If there were anything dangerous about Togha, the Desteer would've seen it and acted accordingly. He wouldn't be in the service of the queen either."

Gaije looked to Lehomis for backup. He was frowning deeply, and quiet for one such as him.

Togha remounted the donkey and rode away as Mhina skipped back down the hill. "It's for me, Mother, look, look! It's from Father and it's for *me*!"

"How wonderful, my *guenhihah*. Now please tell me he hasn't been delayed."

Mhina untied the ribbon and unfolded the letter. A white flower petal fluttered out and landed by her bare feet. "Look what he sent me!" She lifted it over her head for all to see. She struggled through reading the handwriting. "'A gift for the…love-li-est *farhah* in Norr. This petal… fell…off the queen's crown. Don't tell her…I took it off the palace floor. I love you deeply and will see you…soon.'" She held the petal high again. "It's from the queen's crown, can you believe it?"

"Of course," Tirnah said. "He serves in the queen's guard, lass. He sees her every day. But he was discharged, and from now on will guard us instead."

Mhina pranced over to sit beside Lehomis again. "Look, Grandfather."

"Marvelous, lass. Don't lose it now. Keep it in a book—that's a good way not to lose a small thing."

"Good idea, Grandfather."

While the *faerhain* cleaned up, Lehomis went about the house packing his spare clothing and anything else he stowed there for convenience. Gaije sat on the spare bed assigned to Lehomis, watching him fold undershirts and tunics.

"Does Anonhet ever talk about Togha?" Gaije asked.

Lehomis stopped moving to aim a sharp glare at him. "No."

Gaije closed his mouth. It didn't mean she didn't think about him, which Lehomis couldn't have known.

He continued folding. "It gets easier, lad. I'd tell you what to do, but I think you've heard it a thousand times before—like all *saeghar* and *saehgahn* hear."

"Thoughts about love are forbidden thoughts," he recited.

"See? You remember."

"I'm talking to the wrong person. You've been married. And you wrote those books."

"The humans like those books. But you're right, I was married. Long ago. Now I'm in your boat. Talk about something else. Which direction will you go?"

"On my *caunsaehgahn*?"

"No, the next time you have to take a piss. Yes, your *caunsaehgahn*!"

Gaije shrugged and dropped his eyes to the floor. "I don't know. I guess I'll start walking and see where I wind up."

He avoided the stare Lehomis shot like one of his arrows. His grandfather's hands stopped moving, even though a few more garments waited to go into his trunk.

"Grandfather," Gaije whispered in the heavy silence, "does Anonhet ever talk about me?"

Lehomis reached out and grabbed Gaije's lapel, tearing his tunic clean out of his belt. "Do you want me to tie you to the post and beat you?"

Gaije's heart raced. Lehomis might as well have been his father; he'd always taken his discipline. The older *saehgahn*'s pale blue eyes burned into him. True, Gaije was being foolish, but his heart ached. Anything Lehomis delivered wouldn't hold a candle to what he already suffered. He and Anonhet were too close in age, for they had both received their coming-of-age ceremonies in the same year. Now she was ready to choose a husband, and Gaije had yet to overcome a ten or twenty-year journeyman trial before he could return home and be labeled suitable for marriage. Chances were best that when he returned, she'd already be married to an older, more accomplished *saehgahn* than he. Fresh young *saehgahn* were considered the most expendable and likely to live alone if they managed to survive life's duties. Along the journey of life, one could win honors and accolades. Those honorable *saehgahn*, with hair grown to their waists and sharp, knowing eyes, were the ones the *faerhain* chose.

"I'll say it again," Lehomis said, loosening his grip on Gaije's lapel. "It gets easier. But the first step is to stop thinking about it. Don't look at any *faerhain* longer than two seconds. When they speak to you, look no lower than their eyes."

What if he loved looking at her eyes? Gaije nodded to satisfy his grandfather. Lehomis released him, snapping his lapel to straighten it until Gaije took over the task.

"I still wish we could go together."

Lehomis sighed through his nose.

The fluttering of female laughter bursting into the house broke the silence. Anonhet's laughter stood out, causing Gaije to close his eyes. If Lehomis noticed his reaction, he'd take whatever beating he earned.

The front door banged open. "Gaije!" Anonhet's footsteps tapped in the circular corridor toward the spare room they occupied. Lehomis shook his head, glaring.

"Yes!" Gaije called back, rising.

"Gaije!" Anonhet burst into the room, and Gaije met her to deliver an answer.

"Yes?" he said.

She took his hands. Her smile widened around her teeth.

"Yes," Gaije said again.

"It's your father. He's back. He's just appeared over the hill. Come outside." She whipped around and ran out again.

Before darting out after her, Gaije glanced at Lehomis and found him frowning over crossed arms. Dismissing his grandfather, he ran on.

Tirnah ran right across the buttercup-speckled grass to greet Trisdahen, her husband. He dismounted a fine white horse with an exquisite saddle. He'd barely turned off the road when she approached and threw her arms around him. Lehomis followed Gaije outside to watch the spectacle.

Tirnah clearly didn't care she displayed such improper excited and affectionate behavior. She'd always been full of life, singing and dancing through her chores and laying kisses all over her children. Gaije's father knew her well and obliged her at least for today, returning the embrace and lifting her off the ground. Her dark green skirt waved on the breeze, and his herringbone braid, the standard Norrian military hairstyle, bounced around on his shoulder blades.

Turning toward the house, they came back hand in hand, Trisdahen's other hand leading the horse. Mhina hid behind Lehomis's legs.

Trisdahen's eyes landed immediately on Gaije. "I recognize that fiery bright hair—Gaije!" He lashed out a rock-hard arm and Gaije caught it, doing his best to match its hardness. Trisdahen's hair was almost as dark as Lehomis's, whom he took after.

Tirnah's hands stayed plastered to her husband's shoulder, and she patted him to get his attention. "Trisdahen, Gaije's ceremony happened last night. He's *saehgahn* now."

His father's eyes turned back to him, brighter than before. "Have I been away so long?"

Gaije said nothing, but kept his mouth wide and his gaze level with his father's.

"Congratulations, my son. What is your strength?"

"Archery."

He leaned back with his warm smile. "Like Grandfather. It would be swords if I'd had the good fortune to stay around as you grew. I want to hear all about you. Let's talk late into the night."

Gaije bobbed his head. "Yes, Father."

Tirnah waved a hand, drawing his attention to Lehomis next.

"And you know who this is, of course."

"Grandfather!" He grasped Lehomis's forearm as he had Gaije's and they exchanged tight, fearsome smiles with bared teeth as *saehgahn* customarily did. "You look exactly the same as you did when I became *saehgahn*. Amazing."

"My stories aren't lies," Lehomis said.

"I must say thank you. Actually, I can't thank you enough for your service to my family in my absence. Thank you, Grandfather." He stepped back and gave a low sweeping bow, holding it for several seconds.

"None o' that now, lad, stand up. I do it because I love them and I love you. It's all a matter of duty. Stand up."

Trisdahen gave him one more smile, this one warmer and more loving than that which *saehgahn* usually gave each other. When he turned to Anonhet, she curtsied.

"This is Anonhet," Tirnah said. "About eight years ago, soon after your last visit, she lost her family on a hazardous trek. Lehomis volunteered to take her in and keep her until her adulthood. She's his maidservant, properly. She became *faerhain* this year."

Trisdahen gave her the warm smile due to *faerhain* and bowed low. "My condolences to you for your loss, but I am glad my grandfather took up the honor of providing you his security."

"Thank you, *saehgahn*," Anonhet responded, bowing her head.

"And..." Trisdahen began, looking around.

"And she's down there hiding behind her grandfather. Mhina, step forward."

Mhina clung to Lehomis's leg, his braid in one of her hands. While Gaije remembered seeing his father on and off over the years as he grew, Mhina did not. She would soon turn eight, and about eight years ago Trisdahen's last visit had occurred. He squatted to be at her level, showing her his unrestrainable smile. Mhina stepped in front of Lehomis. Taking the end of his braid back, he nudged her forward and she ventured on cautiously, hiding her mouth behind her own hair.

For her, Trisdahen's voice softened the most. "Nice to meet you, Mhina. I heard much about you in letters from your mother."

She paused to reach into her largest skirt pocket. "I got your letter today from Togha. Thank you for the gift."

"You're welcome." He held out his open palms. "You'll get many, many more gifts from now on. And stories every night."

At the word "stories," Mhina checked Lehomis, whose face had gone uncharacteristically blank, but he gave her a nod. Tears streamed out of Tirnah's eyes so generously, Anonhet put her arm around her. Mhina stuffed the folded letter back into her pocket.

"I would like to hear your stories, Father." She placed her hands in one of his, and he covered them over with his other hand, the silent promise of protection a *saehgahn* could make to any female.

Lehomis turned back toward the house. "I should get back to packing."

Tirnah moved in and took Trisdahen's hands from Mhina. "I saved you a feast of breakfast. Come to the rug and eat. I'm sure you're hungry."

Trisdahen managed to convince Lehomis to stay a bit longer, and long after sunset the three *saehgahn* lounged around the fire on floor cushions in the central chamber, talking amongst themselves after Tirnah and Anonhet retreated to the back rooms. Mhina had fallen asleep on Trisdahen's lap, and he still absently stroked her hair in absolute contentment.

"Queen Kelenhanen," Trisdahen said, leaning over his sleeping daughter, "is also the Grand Desteer."

Lehomis's expression drifted into a stare. "How'd that happen?"

"She's remarkably gifted in Desteer talents, but there are also no other princesses or Tinharri cousins with Desteer talents. In fact, she hasn't got any sisters or female cousins at all. In this generation, the royal family has a shortage of females." His eyes darted from Lehomis to Gaije. "Do you know what this means?"

Gaije shook his head.

"Every single male family member will be ordained by the queen to tour Norr and select brides from the various clans."

"No," Lehomis hissed.

Gaije couldn't keep his eyes from roaming toward the corridor leading to Tirnah's bedroom, where she and Anonhet no doubt whispered secrets to each other.

"There's nothing we can do. Sometimes this happens," Trisdahen continued. Lehomis waved a hand, his eyebrows raised in passive agreement. "Their family will die out without marriageable females if the males remain single."

"So less of us will be chosen," Gaije said, and the two studied him sharply, the only one in the room who hadn't been married. Males were permitted to marry once, and those were a lucky few.

Lehomis patted Gaije's shoulder. "I've seen this before, lad, nothin' to worry about. They don't take wives unwillingly. They all have a choice. The difference is, in this situation, the males of the Tinharri Clan will be allowed to ask for our females' hands." His eyes trailed to the ceiling and he lifted his chin as if swallowing was difficult. "But then again, the same nonsense caused the Civil War of Two-hundred-and-two." He ended his statement, rubbing his forehead. "The *saehgahn* get mad about things like this. I guess I'll have to…talk to my rabble gently. Help them understand."

Gaije leaned forward into the tight circle they'd formed. "Help them understand what? That a bunch of silky royals from the Tinharri Clan will ride through our village, wooing *faerhain* we're not allowed to look in the eye for more than two seconds?"

Lehomis opened his mouth, but nothing came out. Trisdahen shushed Gaije.

"Lad," Lehomis said, "we have plenty of widows, and the Desteer are as eager to entice reproduction as anyone. If we lose a few, they'll pressure the widows to remarry. The Desteer might even take charge of political relations—in fact, I'm certain they will—and demand the royals take our widows instead. This is why we have Desteer. The *saehgahn* are hot-headed, like you, but the Desteer are quick and conniving."

Gaije huffed. "Having them take our widows would still leave some of us unmarried."

"Please, Gaije," Trisdahen said. "Don't repeat what we've said. Let Grandfather handle it. He's been around much longer than us."

The three fell silent, accentuating the sound of Mhina's steady breathing and the crackling fire. Lehomis stood and went to the hearth for a teacup, the end of his braid bouncing off the backs of his heels.

Trisdahen cleared his throat, but Gaije barely noticed, for his eyes were staring through the little archway toward the bedroom again, where Anonhet conversed with his mother. Would she talk about him at all?

"Gaije."

"Yes, Father?" He didn't mean to speak to his father with such gloom in his voice.

"There's more to say." He turned back to listen and found Trisdahen's face long, his eyes rounded. "When I said the queen is also the Grand Desteer, it's the reason for my honorable discharge." He smiled. "She took the throne a few months ago. As she acquainted herself with us, her new guard, she learned I was the only one married. She said, 'Why are you here, then?' Days later, she announced my honorable discharge. She let a few others go too because she's merging the White Moths with the White Owls. She didn't want any married *saehgahn* in her entourage."

Trisdahen reached into the pocket of his tunic and brought out a new folded letter. "She sent this to you, for after your naming ceremony."

Gaije opened it, revealing a huge swirling script that read, "HONORABLE SUMMONS."

"She wanted me replaced with a *saehgahn* equally as fine. You're being drafted."

Gaije's head went light. The rest of the words blurred in his vision, so he remained focused on "HONORABLE SUMMONS," his eyes tracing the dizzying lines over and over again.

"You'll go to training for a few weeks," Trisdahen continued, "and then you'll go to the palace and receive more specialized training for a year. After receiving your certification, you'll move inward and receive secret training. You'll be inducted into the cult of the White Owl, like me. You'll be kept on reserve, mostly being used when the queen travels. As those in her personal guard die or retire, you'll eventually be moved to her inner chambers. This is a great honor."

"What about my *caunsaehgahn*?"

"The training will be your *caunsaehgahn*."

Gaije rubbed his face. Lehomis knelt beside him with a fresh cup of honeysuckle tea and offered it to him. Gaije wanted nothing more than to grab the cup and throw it at the wall. He couldn't bring his eyes to look at his father anymore tonight.

"Drink this," Lehomis said, "and go to bed. We'll talk tomorrow."

Trisdahen slid his hands under Mhina's back and knees and stood. "We should all go to bed." He stepped toward the back rooms. "My wife is waiting, and I haven't seen her in eight years."

Lehomis pushed the teacup closer to him. "I'm taking Anonhet home. You're welcome to my house tomorrow for more tea. She'll pour it."

At least with his back turned, Trisdahen couldn't see Gaije's hands trembling as he took the cup.

Chapter 7
Her Guardian

I *can't go to the hospital again,* Kalea pleaded during her morning prayers to the Creator over and over. Her prayers were answered in the form of a heaping pile of laundry with some extra items from the more feeble and incontinent vestals—a normal part of doing laundry in the convent.

"Sorry, Kalea," Sister Scupley said. "I'm afraid you'll have to skip the hospital today. I'll send someone else in your place."

Kalea dipped her head to hide her face. "Yes, sister." Of course she'd miss the hospital, but yesterday had proved the danger lurking in town.

So she went to the courtyard, keeping a slow, contemplative step. She drew water out of the well. The water inside caught light from the sky and winked at her in its playful way after the bucket's splashing calmed. She tore her eyes away and focused on her task. She poured the water into the big cauldron, which waited over fresh, stacked firewood. Washing the clothes in a tub now, rather than out at the stream, might be better. She could stay locked behind the convent walls for safety. Somehow she'd have to dodge the chores which took her into town. A man who wanted to rape her lurked in town, and the forest hid an elf whose intentions weren't so obvious.

She lit a fire under the big cauldron with a rush candle bearing a flame from the kitchen and fanned the fire to boil the water. Washing could be a life's profession. Anyone could do the simple scrubbing and beating work, but not everyone possessed the deeper knowledge of the craft. Kalea had learned a lot from the senior washing vestal here, Sister Gani, enough to make a living doing it as a layperson. Sister Gani was in her seventy-eighth year, though, so Kalea could certainly take her place at this point.

At the end of the day, after the sheets and undergarments were hanging, waiting for the morning sun, she retreated to the dark corridors of the convent to the kitchen for supper. A long prayer of thanks and thoughts for the less fortunate preceded the meal, and then they ate in silence.

Kalea spooned her lentil soup into her mouth in tiny bites to make it last longer. Beside her bowl was set a trencher, baked small with a tiny portion of river fish. She used the quiet hour to thank the Creator a few times over for having this to eat at all, rather than brood about there not being enough of it.

The convent still stored barely enough grain and flour to make trenchers, which they used as plates for the few fish they'd caught in the river. The cook broke one of the trenchers into pieces for the lot of them to share, but the rest she broke for the poor who always waited outside for the leftovers. They didn't have many leftovers these days, but at least they could all get a bite of a trencher.

Kalea dipped her trencher piece in the water to soften it so she could take a bite. When she'd eaten it down to the size of a large coin, she wrapped the remainder in her handkerchief to keep for later.

During cleanup, the cook handed her the linen bag of trencher pieces, which clacked like wood when shaken, to pass on to the beggars who sat in the dying sunlight, lined against the outer wall of the convent. A few more than usual awaited; the sanctuary in Tintilly must also have minimal leftovers.

Before proceeding into their company, she peeked around the outer wall's corner to make sure Kemp wasn't among them, waiting for her like a badger among rabbits. No sign of him, just a load of good folk having to live more roughly than others.

"I'm sorry," Kalea said as she handed the first raggedy person a piece of trencher. "There's not enough for all of you." A beggar at the end of the line leaned forward to see past the rest of them as she talked and immediately leaned back.

"Here you are," she said to the next one. "May the Creator bless you." She moved down the line, emptying her bag and saying her lines. If she couldn't go to the hospital, at least she could tend the needy here.

The last beggar against the wall sat a good several feet apart from the rest. Kalea reached into her bag while he waited, twiddling his thumbs, his head hidden under a russet-brown hood. Kalea's hand found a dusting of crumbs.

"Oh dear, I'm so sorry," she said. "I've run out." She huffed and cast her pinched eyes over the beggar, biting her lip. How long would this famine last? She shook her head at the thought. It was in its beginning stage. She knelt beside him and opened her belt pouch for the portion of trencher she'd been saving.

"May the One Creator bless—whah!" She threw her hand over her mouth to prevent an oncoming shriek when he took his hood off. "It's you!"

"Dorhen. My name's Dorhen."

"I know. What in this world are you doing here?"

He grabbed her free hand. "Are you all right? Did he hurt you yesterday?"

Kalea closed her mouth, her cheeks heating up. His long hair hid his telltale ears from the rest of the beggars, who glanced over and returned to gnawing on their trenchers. "I needed to make sure you weren't harmed."

She jerked her hand away. "How did you know I'd be here?"

He leaned back against the wall, frowning. He must not have cared if the other beggars saw him. "I followed you last night," he said, pointing his turquoise eyes into the red-blanketed forest. "I wanted to see where you lived. And I wanted to make sure you got home safe." He slowly dragged his eyes back to hers.

She leaned in, forming her most serious expression to drive the point in. "I can't talk to you here. But listen: I can't talk to you at all. You have to go. Go on, as you said you would do before. You were supposed to forget about me." At the end of her statement, his frown drooped lower and his chest rose and fell heavily. "If you're smart, and I'm beginning to think you're not, you won't go back to town either."

"But yesterday, you—"

She raised her hand and then took his and slapped the ration piece into it. "Thank you for coming to my rescue yesterday."

She stood and rushed beside the line of beggars, back to the corner. Before turning the corner, she glanced back. He was gone.

Kalea took the busiest streets to the hospital the next day. Though she had insisted on the large pile of laundry to do, Sister Gani happened to be feeling up to taking care of it. There weren't many other arguments against going to the hospital she could use besides illness, and she couldn't fake a fever.

Before heading out, she paused by the confession booth. If Father Liam was in there, she could tell him about yesterday. But...the elf. Should she be going around announcing to anyone how an elf was following her? She'd get in serious trouble if they found out she'd been consorting with one, considering how sneaky and seductive they were known to be. If she lost her virginity in any way, voluntary or not, or if her superiors believed she had lost it, Kalea would never become a full Sister of Sorrow. Maybe if she told her superiors about the danger, they could send a priest to walk with her to and from the hospital. Or the Sanctity of Creation could take legal action against Kemp for his attack... But the elf. Kalea shook her head and walked away from the confession booth.

She sweat, even in the cold spring air, on her way to the hospital. The market opened today, and though she avoided the square, she did happen to pass by Kemp along her way. In the light of day, his hair showed dirty blonde. New, glowing bruises dotted his face. His eyes narrowed on her and he raised two fingers to his ears to indicate elf ears, following up with a shushing finger to his lips.

Kalea ran from the area, from the maniac's grin. When the large building appeared on the next street, she dashed for its double doors. They slammed behind her, and she leaned against them to catch her breath.

The hospital had emptied out a bit since the other day, especially of wealthy residents. On her way to the kitchen, she passed two men sitting against the wall, murmuring. One rested a rag on his head and the other chewed on an herb the hospital workers gave patients to relieve headaches.

"Did you see the Grey Knights in the square yesterday?" the man with the rag said.

The chewing man responded, "I didn't. Why were they here?"

"They're looking for a missing kid from their college. He's a Sharzian—got exceptionally pale hair and olive skin. A handsome thing, they said."

"Who is the kid?"

Kalea couldn't help but slow her pace to eavesdrop.

The first man dipped his rag in the water bucket next to him and returned it to his head. "I don't know, but he's important. They're offering money: six thousand silvers."

The other man paused in his chewing to whistle. "I haven't seen a full-blooded Sharzian since my trip to the coast. Them rich folk don't come out to the country too often."

"Peel your eyes, man. He'll be easy to spot."

Kalea moved on. Farther toward the back of the building, a frightful commotion echoed from one of the side wings. She wandered in that direction, bypassing the kitchen door out of plain curiosity.

A man's voice roared, stopping Kalea mid-step, and a priest's murmuring voice filled the pauses between screams. The corridor wound around and descended into a colder, darker underground atmosphere. After a distance, candle sconces lit the way. The hospital staff kept the dead bodies down here to wait in the cold air to be buried. A larger group than last time waited now, possibly some of the poor old folk she had helped feed on her last visit.

She walked between the rows of bodies covered by white sheets toward the back room, where the screams were exponentially louder. A half-open door showed a brighter light where several people gathered in the room.

Kalea nudged the door open a little more. The people stood gathered around a man on a bed. The smell of sulfur and vomit wafted out, and she coughed and hunched over, taking her face away from the open door for a moment. Lying on the bed, the man's eyes wandered wildly. He lurched whenever he got the chance, but two town guards stood by to restrain him.

"Tie his hands to the posts," Father Rayum said. "This will get worse as we progress."

Another priest went around the bed with a piece of chalk to the floor, drawing the flower-like circle of the One Creator.

"This pattern will keep other demons from getting too close and interfering with our rituals," Father Rayum told the younger priest next to him, an exorcist-in-training. Froth dribbled out of the possessed man's mouth.

"How could this have happened to him?" the lesser priest asked Father Rayum.

"It didn't happen recently. He could've been living with it for a while, sharing his mind with this demon. In order to cure him, we'll have to find out what type of demon it is. It's not a pixie, we know as much from his wildness."

The young priest shuddered as the possessed man bucked and screamed and slobbered while the guards finished tying him down.

"Thank the Creator it's a lesser demon," the young priest said.

"Indeed. Not only do pixies bring a level of sophistication, making the possession hard to spot, but it would mean death for this man. We'd have to burn him."

Also shuddering, Kalea shrank away from the door and closed it to prevent the noises from bothering the residents above. For the moment, she stood shivering in the cold air. As she walked back through the long rows of dead bodies, one of the corpses' hands moved under the sheet.

Kalea jumped. "Oh, Creator!" She lunged toward it as soon as the fright wore off. "You're alive!" Kneeling beside the person, she uncovered their head.

"Dorhen." Her teeth clenched and his name tumbled out as a growl. "You were following me again!"

He smiled, stretched out on the cold floor. "Sorry. What in the world is going on in there?"

She pointed her finger at his face. "Why? I want to know why. What do you want from me?"

His smiled dropped and he sat up. "I'm worried about you."

"You don't even know me."

"But still, I… Yesterday, you were…" He sighed and looked across the room, appearing much like he had yesterday evening with the beggars, as if he himself didn't know. But he knew. The answer hid somewhere in his slow brain, known or not, and Kalea would find it once and for all, as well as how to get rid of him.

"Listen." His eyes snapped back to her. "You're going to walk me home today." His smile returned in the dim light. His reflective eyes brightened, too. "And you'll answer, to the fullest, every question I ask you."

"Gladly."

"But don't let yourself be seen."

He nodded sharply.

"And if I get in trouble again, you'll protect me."

"Of course I will."

Her cheeks heated as she stood. "Hide yourself."

He reached back and drew up another hood—not the brown hood, but a blue one that also emerged from under his mantle. As soon as the blue hood settled over his head, he disappeared.

Kalea gawked and blinked. He really disappeared. The sheet over his lap remained hovering over thin air before flying off and falling into a bunch on the floor. Disregarding where he now stood or whatever he might do while invisible, Kalea went through the door to start her work.

There was no guessing where Dorhen lurked all day as Kalea did her rounds with the residents. She tried to push him out of her mind, but his eyes touched her like tickles of imaginary feathers in the air. Or at least her imagination did. Walking from here to there, or sweeping the floor, she caught herself looking into shadowy corners for the elf who no doubt waited for her to finish her work, no doubt ready and anxious to carry out her request. The image of his eyes brightening right before his vanishing trick stayed suspended in her memory.

Father Liam, who gave the sermons at their convent's sanctum, had once lectured on how eyes can say a lot. When someone was innocent, it showed in their eyes. The same went for the guilty, who might display a lack of light or life in their eyes. If Father Liam's message was true, Dorhen might be safe to speak with. She needed to be sure he could be trusted to walk her home without pulling some trick or attacking her once they got to the forest.

Eventually, she caught herself humming her favorite hymn, already forgetting her self-consciousness about the elf's eyes. She couldn't worry about his eyes as much as she worried about Kemp walking into the hospital, or the way *his* eyes had probed her this morning on her way to work. In fact, she no longer worried about him because an invisible guardian watched over her now.

At the end of the day, she hung up her apron, put her stern expression back on, and walked out the large double doors. She traversed the streets as if she were alone, mouth clamped shut, eyes locked forward in a prideful way. She wouldn't look at the ground to see if an extra pair of footprints stamped themselves beside or behind her, even when curiosity nagged her to do so.

As soon as she reached the quieter outskirts of Tintilly, she asked, "Are you there?"

A soft, deep voice answered back, "Yes," practically at her shoulder.

"I think it's safe to have our conversation now. Where did you come from?"

His disembodied voice responded eagerly, "I was born in Norr. These days I don't have a home. I walk around the Lightlands."

"Why don't you have a home?"

"Because Arius Medallus tells me to walk. He tells me where to walk, when to rest, and when to start walking again."

"Who is Arius Medallus?"

"He's like a father. I've known him since childhood."

"Where is Arius now?"

"His name is Arius *Medallus*, you have to say it like that." Dorhen's tone softened. "I don't know where he goes when he leaves me. I don't know where he is now."

Reflexively, Kalea checked her side, forgetting she'd only find thin air. She inspected the road again to make sure they wouldn't encounter any people who'd hear her talking to nothing. The Sisters of Sorrow got enough unfair assessment from laypeople. She didn't need to strengthen their belief about the vestals being a bunch of "loony" girls.

"So why does he tell you to walk? And why don't you have a home? Can't you live in Norr?"

"No," Dorhen said. "I'm forbidden to return to Norr. Arius Medallus warns me how humans can harm, so I can't stay in any human place either."

"Well, he's right, basically. Elves are outlawed here because of an old war. They still don't like elves. And yet here you are."

"You think I'm not smart."

"Yes, in a way." She tightened her jaw. Perhaps she shouldn't have said that, but it had come out too fast. "I mean, you saw what happened when they caught you stealing. If I hadn't been there, you could be dead."

"I'm glad I did it."

Kalea stopped walking. Dorhen appeared beside her, his eyes fixed on her. He stood about half a head taller than she. His straight brown hair hung heavy despite the gentle breeze, framing his face, which showed no sign anywhere of a five o'clock shadow. His fingers lingered on the blue hood inside his ordinary brown one. He dropped his hands to the sides. His stare was too much.

"Be invisible again." Kalea walked on. They weren't out of town yet. Footsteps pattered to catch up to her. When she glanced back, he had disappeared again. "Now I want to know why you're still here. I remember clearly that on the day we met, you said you weren't supposed to be seen and you were leaving the area. You haven't."

"I don't want to."

"Why?"

"Because of you."

Her cheeks warmed up again. She stroked a lock of hair lying on her shoulder to cover any indication of her embarrassment. "What's so special about me?" She batted her eyes and turned her face away from the sound of his resonant voice.

"I don't know… I couldn't get you off my mind after first meeting you. I tried. I walked a good ten miles away. I came back. And I'm glad I did—I found you again in town when you…when that man…"

Kalea sighed. "Look. I helped you out at first, and you helped me in return. Can't we call it even? Don't you have to move on because of Arius Med—Med…"

"Medallus… Your words make sense, Kalea. They were my words, too. But look, here I am. I'm worried about you. What if that man attacks you again?"

"I don't know. I'll have to tell my superiors about him. But when I tell them, they'll also know about you. Kemp will tell everyone about you even if they don't squeeze it out of me. You have to leave this area and forget about me."

"I can't."

Kalea sighed again, and her hands balled into fists at her sides. "You are *not* smart."

"I know I'm not."

"So… What? You're going to follow me around forever?" She yelled the question, and then remembered to keep quiet.

They drew near to Tintilly's west-side entrance. The town, though growing in size, didn't have a wall surrounding it like the larger cities near the borders. The sleepy town sat nestled in a rural area, close to other small towns in the heart of the Lightlands. They had been established during a long peaceful period which hadn't warranted any walls. But times would soon change. The famine would cause a rise in hunger, leading to anxiety, leading to desperation, and on to crime, both organized and chaotic. New bandit gangs would form, and these little towns would need more security. The roads between them would become even more dangerous than they were now.

"I can walk you to the hospital and back. I won't let anyone bother you."

"That's the stupidest thing I've heard all day. They'd catch you eventually."

He grunted softly, and her words echoed in her head like a rake against a stone wall. Her comment was reflexive. It might be the perfect time for a personal guardian, as long as he was honest and genuine.

"Okay, listen. I can't make you leave this town. If you must follow me, do it without being seen. And if you get caught, we don't know each other. I can point a finger at you as easily as I can at Kemp."

"Of course." He stayed quiet as they walked through the gate, past the town watchmen.

The road wound up and around the rolling hills and into the towering pine forest on the horizon. A long way into the field, Kalea said, "I have more questions before we get to the convent."

"Yes." He appeared beside her, attentive as ever.

"I'm going to be blunt." She shifted her eyes to him. He practically walked sideways to keep his attention on her. "Is there anything you expect from me?"

"No."

"So you won't talk to me?"

"Not if you don't want me to."

"All right. Anything else?"

"Like what?" he asked.

"Like for instance... You're not going to try to seduce me? Or attack me like Kemp did?"

Dorhen's face went long, his mouth opening and his eyebrows rising. "No, I would never...!" His eyebrows turned downward. "You think I would...?" Kalea looked away and opened her hands wide. "I told you, you don't even have to talk to me."

"You've made it hard not to talk to you already."

"Well, I'll stop, starting now."

"Not until I'm done asking you questions."

From then on, Dorhen walked with his eyes forward and his mouth tight. The bridge of his nose stood out strong, the tip pointing forward as if to say wherever he was going, he meant it.

"Isn't there a girl-elf you have back home?"

"I don't have a home. And I don't know any other elves." He said it without looking at her.

Kalea's shoulders deflated. "Sorry I asked. But I *had* to. When you're a woman, you have to worry about who is nice and who's not. Especially when you're at the fertile age and unmarried. Especially again if you want to be inducted into the Sisters of Sorrow." Kalea frowned and shook her head, watching the path winding into the trees ahead. "Wicked men like Kemp think the best way to get their pleasure is with a virgin. They'll take any chance they can find to deflower one."

"What is that?" His voice lost its strong edge. He slid his eyes toward her but didn't keep them there.

"What's what?"

"The Sisters of Sorrow."

The tension building at the back of her neck at the thought of having to explain to him what a virgin was vanished. "It's a religious faction for women who aren't good for marriage because they're mentally ill. Our parents put us in the convent to give us the best life possible for our unique situations. Once I'm a full sister, I can have a lot of privileges and do a lot of good for the community."

"What is *mentally ill*?"

"It has a lot of variations. Basically, it has to do with a person's mind being unhealthy. I'm called mentally ill because from a young age, I used to get distracted by the water. I could see faces in it."

Her throat closed up. She'd never been sensitive about her problem before, but a new hurt sparked, possibly because the problem had recently returned. She thought she'd been cured. It might prove to be a greater problem than previously expected. "I've always seen these faces. It's one face, I mean. Actually, it changes, but I know it's the same person. If it can be considered a person. I used to get so mesmerized. It made me feel safe."

Dorhen grabbed her arm and put himself in front of her, forcing her to meet his eyes. The shock filled her core with a turbulence she couldn't quite place. His strong hand gripping her arm sent a jolt of carnal excitement through her abdomen.

"Kalea."

Gaping, she slapped his hand away. "Don't grab me! Don't touch me!"

she yelled, not caring if anyone heard her now.

He raised his hands by his head as she turned away and rubbed her arm, willing the tingles to leave her core. That must've been elven magic. With the use of magic, he *did* mean to seduce her! If not today, eventually he would. He'd keep feeding magic into her until she believed the idea was hers. That little taste of it was strong. Good thing she hadn't gotten locked into his eyes when it happened.

"Leave me alone!" She took off at a run.

"Kalea, wait!" He ran after her. "I'm sorry! I didn't know!"

Her heart pounded in her ears. She whimpered as she sprinted, frantic not to let him grab her again. Once in the forest, she huffed as the path inclined up a gentle hill.

"Help!" she cried.

His voice echoed behind her, "Please stop!"

She didn't. When the path leveled off, she ran on against all exhaustion until her lungs struggled to fill. She grabbed a tree beside the path and used it to stay on her feet as well as propel herself to the next tree. At the area where the ground sloped into a valley beside the path, her foot slipped on the pine needles and she tumbled down.

Dorhen gasped from the road above. "I'm coming, don't move!"

She rolled a long way, and by chance didn't hit any trees. When she slowed to a smooth stop at the bottom, her breaths came short and weak and her vision darkened. She fell asleep. Her eyelids fluttered open again to a soft breeze fanning against her. The orange sky beamed behind the treetops.

A distant man's voice, not Dorhen's, called from above, "Kalea!"

She couldn't call back in her heavy daze. At least she could breathe again.

"Oh no." Dorhen's voice resonated beside her. Strong hands scooped her up, and her head flopped against a warm chest. A warm, masculine scent tantalized her nose, and his long hair tickled across her face as they moved. They traveled upward at a dizzying pace. Kalea reached her hand around his neck for stability.

"Don't worry," he said softly over her face. "I'll get you home. I know where it is now." Kalea closed her eyes and endured the movement, inhaling his scent.

When she opened her eyes again, she was curled up at the gate of the convent. The sun had set completely and Dorhen had disappeared with it, replaced by Father Liam standing over her. He carried her all the way to her bed in the dorm.

She awakened to the bright sun beaming through the windows.

"Good morning," came Father Liam's voice. He sat on the floor beside her mattress.

"Father? Where is everyone?"

He twisted around to survey the large dorm room full of empty, made beds.

"Oh, they're all at their afternoon prayers about now."

Kalea stirred, and he placed a hand on her shoulder. "Don't get up so fast."

"Why did I sleep so long? I have things to—"

"Not today, child. You had another fright last night. I assume you got lost again and panicked, though you did make your way back when you collapsed at the gate. I don't think you were there long before I found you. Kalea."

Still a bit dizzy, she eased back onto her pillow. "Yes?"

"I told them you won't go to the hospital anymore. Twice getting lost is too much. And we're all too busy to send you girls in groups or escort you."

"That's probably better. I'll miss it, though."

"I know."

"Maybe I can go again after a while."

Father Liam smiled. "We'll talk about it." He stood. "Stay in bed today."

"I can't." Kalea worked back up to her elbows. "I have to do the laundry. Sister Gani can't do it all herself."

"I'll let you sort it out with her. But listen, Kalea." She paused in her struggle to regard him. "Go slow. Sister Scupley said you were dehydrated and hungry. So stay here. We'll get some food and water in you before you try anything else." He pointed at the pitcher and cup beside her bed.

"Yes, Father." He turned for the door. "Wait, Father."

Words she wanted to say whirled around in her head and aligned to come out: *Kemp attacked me the other day. An elf attacked me last night, and now he's following me. He won't leave me alone. He cast a spell on me.*

"What do you need, Kalea?"

Her hand still hovered in the air from when she called him. "I…" … *have many feelings about the elf, and I don't know why. His name is Dorhen. I can't get his name out of my head.* "Um. I don't think…" …*I can be a vestal.* "I don't think I can get up. I think I'll stay in bed today."

Father Liam's smile broadened. "It's recommended. I'll get you some soup."

Kalea's pounding heart drowned out the sound of his footsteps. She began to sweat with the onset of nausea. It was merely dehydration. She hadn't gotten many drinks of water yesterday while she worked at the hospital. Her hands shook. She pushed herself up on one hand to drink from the full cup of water left for her. She lay back down while the ceiling spun above her.

Every time she closed her eyes, Dorhen's turquoise stare flashed in the darkness. Why couldn't she tell Father Liam about Dorhen, especially after he had grabbed and cast his spell on her? Nonetheless, her problem appeared to be solved: she didn't have to go to the hospital anymore. But how long would the spell last?

She opened her eyes to let the bright, spinning ceiling flood her vision and wash away the image of Dorhen's face. It didn't work. His smell rushed back to her memory to make things worse. She'd have to tell Father Liam about him soon, or the elf would never go away. He had said it himself: *I can walk you to the hospital and back. I won't let anyone bother you.*

"But why?" she murmured aloud. She was a novice Sister of Sorrow. She couldn't love him back, if that's what he wanted, love spell or no love spell. Lying flat, she put her hands to her aching heart. She sat up again. Doing work should help her focus, or this sickness would kill her.

After eating the lentil soup Father Liam had brought, she staggered out of bed, dressed, and staggered outside despite the novice and elder vestals' protests. Some good vigorous work would fight the spell. She splashed her face with some cold water from the wash tub. It helped a little to energize her.

"Kalea. Stand back and lemme—"

Kalea pushed Sister Gani's hand away as the old vestal attempted to take one of the garments soaking in her tub. "Please, Sister, I need to do this. Why don't you go rest?"

The old woman stood, wringing her hands. "Someone's gotta watch you, girl."

Kalea forced a smile. "I'm fine. Look at me. I'm just glad I didn't have to go to the hospital today. I missed washing."

Sister Gani's baggy old eyes narrowed as she turned to study Kalea. "All right. Well, shout if you feel ill again."

"Yes, ma'am. I know they'll hear me from the kitchen."

Sister Gani hobbled away, wiping her hands on her apron. Kalea could finish the last load and hang all of it up to dry, which Sister Gani couldn't do so well with her frail body.

At least this peaceful work gave her plenty of time to think. She could talk herself into telling Father Liam about Dorhen. There weren't many ways she could think to get rid of him herself. She could scream at him, but he was so persistent about staying around, screaming might not work. Whatever screaming she had done yesterday hadn't worked. No other choice beyond telling her superiors presented itself.

It didn't take long to finish the washing and move on to the hanging. She stopped to rest every few moments; all the bending and standing did no good for her dizziness. A few more sheets and she'd be done. Supper wasn't far off, and she didn't want to be late for getting more food into her stomach, as little as it would be.

In her eagerness to finish, she grew lightheaded after several rounds of stooping and standing. She stumbled with a faint moan and teetered.

A pair of strong hands steadied her.

"Father," she said, sighing, "I wasn't overexerting myself, I swear." Standing on her own feet again, she turned to thank Father Liam. Dorhen stood there instead. Too woozy to scream, she gasped and tried to leap away. When she stumbled, he threw his arms around her waist.

"Don't be afraid, relax," he said.

"How did you get in here? We have a wall around this place for a reason."

He retrieved the little stool and placed it inside the walls of hanging sheets before guiding her onto it. "Sit down," he said, keeping his voice low, though it retained a sense of authority. He remained visible for now, and sat on his knees before her, his eyes large and concerned. "You must think I'm a scab by now."

"I've been planning to tell them about you."

"Please don't." He raised his hands, palms out. "I don't mean to scare you so much. What can I do to make you unafraid of me?"

"You can start by giving me a straight answer. Why do you keep coming back?"

He seemed reluctant to answer. "Because of you, Kalea."

"What is it about me?"

"Your hair. It's…brown. And the sound of your voice makes me want to come closer to you. There's something about you…" Kalea put a hand to her chest as she listened. "I'll be no trouble, I promise."

"Didn't you say Arius Medallus makes you walk?"

Dorhen closed his eyes. His throat apple bounced as he nodded. "I'm finished walking."

"Has he returned?"

"No."

"What would happen if he returns and beckons you and you don't obey?"

"I don't know. I've never wanted to disobey him before. Not to say I haven't. I have, and when I get him mad enough...he has ways of... putting images in my head, I can't even..." He closed his eyes and swallowed again.

"If you want to stay around so bad, you could consider training for the priesthood." The ridiculous idea made her smile, and she covered her mouth. "But you'll have to cut all that hair off and have a tonsure instead."

"Yes. I'll do it. I'll do anything to be near you." He bowed his head to the ground as if she were a queen sitting on a throne.

Kalea scowled. "I was joking. You can't join the priesthood solely to be near me. That would be wrong." Nonetheless, she laughed as the image materialized in her mind: Dorhen in a robe with his ears sticking way out to the sides, uncovered by any hair, and a big shaven bald spot on his pate.

She carried on laughing for a bit, and he peered up through his eyelashes. Tears streaked his face. His eyes were cloudy with moisture, hopeless. He offered no more words. Kalea's laughter died, and her smile followed.

"You really mean it." He did nothing more in response. She couldn't laugh anymore, even if she wanted to. "What can I do? You're an elf—and a male, and I'm a novice vestal."

He remained staring at her—pleading with her, his tears still running and his hands planted on the ground. Apparently, he could produce no good solutions to his strange dilemma.

"Well," she said, "you do make me feel safe when I know you're near."

He raised his head a bit more. "I do?"

"Yes, I must admit. Sometimes." Doubting thoughts crept in after her statement. It didn't make sense. Though the statement was true, his grabbing her yesterday, paired with the notion that he had cast spells on her, battled the paradoxical feeling.

He blinked as he drew in a long breath. His tears had stopped.

"Dorhen, I have a quandary."

"What's a quandary?"

"It's a problem." She crossed her arms under her breasts. "Did you cast a spell on me?"

He shook his head. "I don't know any spells."

"So how do you turn invisible?"

He tugged his blue hood from inside the brown one. "It's a spelled hood. Arius Medallus made it. Otherwise, I can't do any magic."

"I see. You seem fond of me though."

"I am." He bowed his head again.

"Stop doing that. It feels wrong. You should bow to the One Creator and no one else." He raised his head again but remained planted on his hands, faithful as a dog. "What kind of person is Arius Medallus if he can make a magic hood?"

"He's a fairy at the level of fairy-major."

Dorhen and the waving sheets around them blurred in her vision. Her voice trembled out. "What did you say?" Her dizziness returned.

"Kalea," Dorhen said, "I didn't only come here to grovel at your feet. I have to tell you an important thing before you banish me from yourself forever."

"What have you to say?" Saving Dorhen had been the wrong choice. He'd bring fairies and demons into her safe little world. He could endanger the whole convent! Her breath caught, ready to let out a scream. They'd call the guard and have Dorhen hauled away, and then Kalea could get on with her life once and for all. No more love spells to plague her with him gone.

"You're not mentally ill."

She canceled her impending scream. His eyes brightened again, and his cheeks were drying, but his eyelids were still red. "What?"

"I thought you should know. You're not mentally ill. I see those faces in the water too. It's Arius Medallus."

"You're trying to fool me."

He lurched to grab her hand but canceled the action, instead grabbing air and clenching his fist. "No, I'm not. Arius Medallus shows up full-body for me, but sometimes he appears as a face in the water. He's a water spirit. He's not harmful. This means you're not mentally ill. You're normal."

"I wouldn't call seeing spirits normal."

"Call it what you want. You have the gift of being able to see him. I understand most humans can't see beings like him. Not so easily, at least."

"So..." Kalea pointed to her chest. "We have Arius Medallus in common."

Dorhen bobbed his head rapidly like a child would. His smile returned after such a long absence.

Kalea frowned deeper. "This isn't good."

"Why not?"

"Why not? Because we can't trust stray spirits like fairies who fly around causing mischief."

"You're right. But Arius Medallus is special."

"How?"

"He rescued me from danger."

"Is that why you wander around with him? Where are your parents?"

His smile wilted. "My mother's dead. My father murdered her. He set our house on fire and she burned up in it." Kalea covered her mouth with both hands. "If Arius Medallus hadn't been there to spirit me away to a safe place, my father probably would've killed me too."

Dorhen's eyes dulled as he recounted his past, as if he'd already cried plenty about it and couldn't cry anymore. The turquoise fire in his eyes had been doused into black holes by an old emotion harbored deep inside. He waved a hand at whatever horrified expression she was making. "It's all right. It happened a long time ago."

"How long?"

"I was about six."

"Oh, dear Creator."

"I'm twenty-two now and have come a long way. Arius Medallus taught me how to survive in the forest: how to catch fish, and which plants and insects are safe to eat. He also made this magic hood. He knows I can't settle anywhere outside of Norr because I'm an elf. He keeps me walking in circles around the Lightlands, altering my path every season."

Kalea wiped her eyes, restraining any more tears. "I'm so sorry."

"Don't be sorry. I can survive. Arius Medallus chose me. And you being able to see him in water means he chose you too."

"For what?"

"Who can say?"

The sun was waning, and voices at the door murmured to each other before calling, "Kalea, are you all right?"

"Yes!" she called back. "I'm finishing up. I'll be in soon."

"Supper's about ready, girl."

"Thank you, Sister!"

She turned back to Dorhen and grabbed his hand from where it rested on his knee. He paused in awe to watch their two hands in contact.

"Dorhen," Kalea said, "tomorrow I'm going to wash my loads at the creek. Do you know where the dam is?"

"Yes."

"Good. Meet me there."

Chapter 8
A Companion for a Mercyman

After managing to avoid looking at the stars for the last few days, Daghahen toiled with the holding sphere containing Wik, which he'd brought back from the Darklands after painstakingly searching for it over a five-year period. After some well-made bets in various pubs, he'd restored his coin purse enough to buy a room for a few nights at an inn for some imperative privacy.

At first, the sphere appeared to be nothing but a beautiful black ornament in his hands, but the more he handled it and became familiar with it, the more familiar it became with him.

"Can you talk?" Daghahen whispered, testing the thing, certain that it possessed an awareness of some kind.

He was answered by strands of slight vibrations running through his nerves from where the orb touched his hand. It was a start, and the more he touched and tapped it, the more it responded. He tried new ways to agitate it—to provoke it into speaking or communicating by some means. He put it in water, in direct sunlight, and when he held it over a flame, a horrid, sand-like hiss rushed through his head, nearly making him drop it.

You fool!

After placing it on the inn room's stained straw pillow where he always rested it, Daghahen paused and looked around. "Hello?"

No one had entered the room. Turning back to the holding sphere, he squinted and reached out to touch it again.

Damn you!

He jerked backward and fell on his rear. It did talk! Climbing to his knees, he placed his hand on the orb and asked, "Are you the pixie called Wik?"

A gentler sound like sand sliding down a slope ran through his head. The pixie must be using his own nerves and energy source to communicate telepathically. It wasn't hard to imagine, knowing that pixies came with the ability to enter people's minds in general. Wik wouldn't be able to possess anyone now, since he was trapped in the glass.

He tried again. "I took you out of that witch's trunk. Can't you speak to me at least? Are you Wik?"

What else would I be, little elf?

Daghahen knew as much, but confirming the information never hurt. This was one of Ilbith's coveted five, Wik himself. Daghahen had already talked Thaxyl's energy away, and now talking might glean something from this one. There was always a chance a new pixie would yield new answers. Wik held more value than Thaxyl; he was still at the level of pixie. He carried on an economical system for circulating his energy, apparently more economical than breeding a hybrid race of heart-eaters to gather energy for him. No, Wik liked to possess mortal people. Pixies were the only fairy type powerful enough to perform pixtah, the feat of possession. Some favored the practice more than others, but Wik existed by it.

This foreboding creature spent its time floating around in the shadows, looking for its next host. When it found one, it lived in the human or elf's body, using it like a suit. It leeched the person's life force away until no more remained, or until the host body was destroyed by other people. Until then, the new being which stepped forth from the combination of the two, always called Wikshen, enjoyed a lavish life of violence and debauchery.

Alternately, Wik could be caught in a sphere, and this had happened more than once. Darklandic lore mentioned that whoever the sphere was broken closest to would automatically be possessed. If Daghahen wanted to share Wik's power and use it to kill Lambelhen, all he'd have to do would be to break the sphere. But nothing in his calculations made clear that it would be a good idea. Daghahen wasn't the one. Besides, there were other uses for this item, the most valuable item in Kaihals.

"Good. I knew it. Now, there are things we must talk about."

I owe you nothing, little elf.

"Not even for a bargain?"

So let me out and we'll bargain.

Daghahen smiled and shook his head. "We'll have to do our bargaining before that happens."

The sand sound grazed his eardrums. It sounded so real, as if there should be sand spilling into the room whenever it happened.

What do you want?

"I want to kill my brother."

Pathetic. I'll not join with a shriveled toad like you. Find me a better host.

"That's not what I mean."

The sand rushed again, and Wik's voice became faint. *You haven't enough talent...*

"No, not me!" he yelled. "I have a sword, Hathrohjilh. Do you remember that name?"

The sword is useless. Throw it away. I am all you need. The sword only brings you trou...

"What?" He shook the orb and put his ear to it. The effort didn't help. "Wik!"

The sand ran in long drifts through his head, sometimes separating into indiscernible syllables.

"What do you mean?" He shook it again to no avail.

Keep walking.

Afterward, all the sounds and vibrations stopped.

Those two sly sorcerers had been following him the whole week. Actually, one was the sorcerer and the woman was his thrall: a talented lass who could be a sorceress if she'd entered the faction by some different way. Instead, the man had somehow captured a woman he found beautiful, tamed, trained, disciplined, and used her, and now he had brought her here to help with trying to capture Daghahen and the burden he carried on his back. He had seen this process before when he, too, practiced sorcery ages ago. It was one thing for a woman to be born into the servant class of Ilbith, or even to be captured, chained, and put to servant-like purposes. It was a more disturbing concept for a person to be trained as a personal thrall against their will and set to walk free of chains, assisting and carrying out complex missions for their sorcerer-masters, as if participating of their own will.

Today she wore a wig, blonde to cover the thick, black hair which usually cascaded down her shapely form. Daghahen recognized her from yesterday, when she'd pretended to sell stolen twisted bread off a stick in Tintilly's market.

Now she shimmered in her blonde wig and dancer's skirt, wearing the same dark-colored corset she always wore, this time glittering with all manner of glass baubles dangling around her neck and falling into her cleavage. Swaying her hips, she moseyed right over and perched herself next to Daghahen as he sipped his tea at a table in the biggest inn in Tintilly.

A medley of pleasant scents rushed up his nose, particularly clove and vanilla. She leaned right into his space, hovering her chin over his shoulder. "Care to show me a little *mercy*, mercyman?"

He glanced at her before shooting his eyes across the room for her master.

"Sorry," he said. "I got all my money stolen in the last brothel I visited."

"I'm sure you have some left, my sweet sir."

He smiled toward his half-empty cup. "Nonetheless, you don't want to dally with me, darlin'. You might catch my melancholy."

She let out a pleasant, musical laugh and batted his shoulder. "Pardon my manners. I forgot the protocol. I believe I am supposed to perform a charitable act for you before you can show mercy to me."

Her hand found his leg under the table, but he snatched it, brought it up, and kissed her knuckles. She flashed a bright smile. Her eyes were painted with black and lavender.

"Your manners are faster than my desires."

He flashed a smile back at her. "You should go find someone else." He studied her eyes for a long, serious moment. She read them. "To tell the truth, I don't like talking to women in this setting."

The musical pleasantry chimed in her voice. "Why not?"

"There's so much sadness in my past. I used to talk to girls like you a lot. Got them good and hot for me before sending them upstairs to meet me in my private room."

One of her eyebrows popped up. "What happened next?"

He cocked his head back to his cup and sniffed. "Upstairs, they found a different me. I hate to talk about it."

"Aw. You poor, weary soul." She smoothed a hand along his cheekbone.

"You really don't get it, lass."

She straightened her back and pushed her bosom forward. "I think you misinterpreted me a moment ago. When I said I'd do a charitable act for you, I meant I should buy you some food. You look hungry." She waved her hand in the air to the barmaid. "A bowl of stew!"

Daghahen ground his teeth. Where was her master hiding? No doubt she'd find some quick moment to poison his food when it arrived. He couldn't take the chance of letting her near it. Not for an instant.

"You're so kind, lass." He kissed her hand again. She smiled, and he smiled back. No telling if she knew his special talent. He summoned his quickest reflexes for what came next. Holding her hand, he touched her palm with his finger, whipped it to her collarbone, and then to her forehead, touching her between the eyes. "A pretty thing, too," he said simultaneously.

When he relaxed again and dropped her hand, she sat staring, as if struggling to register what happened. Her pupils swelled as she stared into his eyes. Success.

"Isn't that better?"

"Oh, yes, my love." The barmaid placed the stew bowl on the table as the thrall hugged his arm. She buried her face into his hair and kissed his neck.

"Ah-ah, not yet. Hold on." He uncoiled her spindly grasp from his arm and brought her attention to the food. "It's on me. Go ahead."

"Thank you, my love."

"You're welcome." He braced his elbow on the table, smiling at her, and then surveyed the room while she ate. He kept the smile pasted on his face. "My dear sweet maiden, who's the man you were traveling with?"

She flashed her eyes up, hastily swallowing a large bite of potato. "Oh, my love, he's nothing, I swear. His name is Chandran. My former master, but now I serve you. I promise. If you'll let me hold you tonight, I'll be yours forever."

Daghahen waved a hand. "I know, I know. What does he want?"

"He wants the sword you carry. He also wants to take you back to Ilbith, but if he can get the sword at least, he'll be satisfied with your death. But I'll *never* let that happen to my love, my love, my Daghahen."

"As I expected. You know my name?"

"Yes. It's the most beautiful name in the world."

"Thanks, lass. It means 'guardian.'"

She nestled against him, pausing her eating. "Well, I will guard *you*, my love, with my life."

He sighed. "I know." He rubbed her back. "Finish your meal before it gets cold." She obeyed. "Tell me what Chandran is planning here tonight."

Goggling at him over her bowl, bright-eyed and eager to please, she said, "He knows what room you rented. He's hiding there now. He wanted me to drug your stew to loosen you up. I was to accompany you upstairs, making sure you got there, where he'd assassinate you."

She reached into her bodice and pulled out a tiny drawstring bag. "Here's the sleeping powder." She opened all sorts of hidden pouches encasing throwing darts and daggers.

He hissed, "No. Please, put it all back. Don't let anyone see them."

"Oh, sorry." She loaded her little assassination implements back into their compartments. "I thought you should know all about me and what I own. All you have to do is ask, and I will protect you."

He motioned to the bowl, now almost empty. "Well, you should know I don't want to be killed by Chandran, and I don't want him to have my sword. Got it?"

"Yes, my love."

"What would you have done if I didn't want to eat the stew?"

"Used my best seduction techniques on you to get you to take me upstairs."

"Why do you have to go upstairs with me if he's already there?"

"He wanted you to be in another state of mind, whatever that might be. He also needs me in there to help him cast the difficult portal spell to get home."

"To Ilbith?"

She nodded. "We were going to work together to subdue you and complete the spell. He can't do it alone—not to cover such a distance."

"I see." Daghahen blinked. They wanted to drag him all the way back to Ilbith. "What if I didn't want to have sex with you? What would happen?"

"He has a few extra plans. He might've decided to hide under your bed and stab you while you slept. And in the most extreme case, he wasn't going to let you leave the building alive. He made me ward all the doors so you couldn't walk out of here. They're spelled especially for you. If you pass through either one, it will electrocute you to death. I also have these poisoned darts I could've used to kill you, in case you decided to stay here in the hall all night."

"Oh, how dreadful," Daghahen said. "I'm trapped in this place."

"I know, my love, but it'll be fine."

"How in the world will I get out of here alive?" He took her tiny hand in his and rubbed his thumb along the back of it.

"I'm so sorry."

He patted the side of her smooth face. "Forget about it. I'm grateful you told me these things."

"Yes, anything, my love." To deepen her infatuation, he rewarded her with a kiss to her forehead. She took it upon herself to peck kisses on his cheek, trailing to his mouth. He allowed a little of that. If Chandran happened to spy them, he'd be pleased to think her plan went well.

By the time Daghahen peeled her mouth off his, her chest heaved up and down. Her plump lips parted to breathe. She cradled his hand and pressed it to her bronze collarbone, covered with a few glittering necklaces.

"Can't we slip away for a bit of privacy, my love?" She laid her head on his shoulder and brought his hand to her lips to kiss each of his fingertips.

"Only if you can help me leave this place alive." She reached under his hood to stroke his hair. "No, no, no." He took her hand away and secured his hood.

"Please forgive me."

"Think hard now… What's your name?"

"Rayna."

"Rayna, are the windows warded too?"

"Yes, I had to be thorough."

"What would you say is the best way to leave?"

She blinked her eyes slowly, staying fixed on him. She stroked his arm with her graceful hand, no doubt wishing she could do more. "It would take some effort to dispel the wards on the doors, though they'll wear off after forty-eight hours."

"I can't stay here that long. Is there any chance you missed a window somewhere?"

She shook her head, her eyes relaxed as they gazed into his. "Obviously, I couldn't get into all the guest rooms to ward their windows, and the window in your room is not warded. We saved our energy on that one because we'd both planned to be in there to prevent you from leaving."

He reached out and stroked her face with the back of his hand. "Well then, I suppose I'll have to go out through there, pretending to be seduced by you."

"Leave Chandran to me. And let me be on top—I'll protect you with my body."

He rose, grabbed his pack with the sword attached from under the table, and offered his arm. She took it and they ascended the stairs together, locked in each other's eyes, smiling. This lass and her talents could prove valuable to have around. He wouldn't need to worry about the extra mouth to feed because she was so capable. She could probably bring many extra ideas to the table when it came to finding food and dodging the sorcerers. And all he had to do was relinquish his body to her every once in a while. Nothing in this world could ever redeem him enough to deserve a lover or any loving companion, but at least he'd treat her better than any of those horrible sorcerers.

He relaxed his face and put a drunken smile on it. "Stay sharp," he whispered, hooking his arm around her shoulders.

"Of course."

He nudged her into the dark room first as they stumbled together, laughing. Chandran should be wise enough not to kill his own thrall by mistake in some foolish ambush.

Daghahen dropped his belongings by the bed, snatched Rayna's face in the dark, and kissed her mouth. She sighed through her nose and moaned. She didn't have to do any acting here. He didn't egg her on by touching her body, although she snaked her hands under his tunic hem to find the strings attaching his leggings to his codpiece.

He guided her to the bed. They couldn't get too far into it. He needed his clothes on for the escape, but Rayna's actions were very real, and her induced state of arousal would cloud her judgment; she needed him to help her stay sharp. If he decided to keep her in his company, the infatuation state would eventually wear off, and she would have already committed to the relationship by then—similar to the natural way for lovers. Daghahen's initial spell helped to get the infatuation phase going by way of intense arousal.

He lay on the bed, and she crawled on top of him with a noticeably eager speed, hiking her skirts and perching herself right on his pelvis. She bent over him and continued the kiss. He guided her hand to her bodice, where she hid her arsenal of lethal instruments, just to make sure she remembered her duty. A blade grazed against squeaky leather; whether it was her blade or Chandran's was anyone's guess. She rubbed her body against his and groaned.

Concentrate, Rayna! If only he could say it out loud. He'd never find the mood for his own arousal in this hazardous situation.

Rayna sat up straight, arching her back, leaving Daghahen exposed beneath her. She rubbed against him all the more. Her hands were hidden down by her thighs and her bunched skirts, no telling if she had any knives ready to defend him. No sign of Chandran either. A blanket hung over the window to block out whatever moonlight might have revealed a third person in the room.

A rope looped and tightened around Daghahen's neck. His attempted cry was squeezed off under its scratchy grip. Growling, Rayna sprang off of him. A man roared, and the noose slackened. Daghahen freed himself from the scratchy rope, which snapped a little spark when he dropped it—a spelled rope, but Chandran couldn't complete the casting.

Daghahen sprang off the bed and tore the fabric off the window to flood the room in soft, blue moonlight. Rayna's friend, the wild-eyed man, clutched his own neck while dodging her strikes. After another strike, he reached out and slapped her hard. Rayna dropped to the floor with a clatter.

Chandran glared at him next. Daghahen leaned over for the sword fastened to his pack. Pulling the knot in the twine, he shook off the sword's wrappings so the blade could flash in the moonbeam. Chandran's eyes widened in fear or lust—it was too hard to tell which.

Daghahen swung the sword in a nice, light arc. It was incredibly easy to handle, curling back on the rebound as if ready to rejoin his hands and make another attack. Its ease of handling unnerved him.

Chandran leaped backward and fiddled with the doorknob. The fool had locked it as Daghahen and Rayna were carrying on. Glass shattered behind Daghahen as he lunged.

Chandran fell through the door and into the glowing firelight of the merry inn, narrowly missing the blade. The people gathered on the catwalk shouted and scattered when Chandran crashed out, bleeding from his neck.

Daghahen slammed the door, locked it, and turned to Rayna. No longer sprawled on the floor, she had broken the window panes and secured Chandran's rope to the bedpost.

"That's my girl!" Daghahen said.

He tied the naked sword back to his pack, hoisted it, and climbed down the rope after Rayna. In the alley below, she took his hand and guided him away from the inn.

In the pine forest, immediately west of Tintilly, Daghahen and Rayna stopped to rest and she let her dark, flowing hair tumble down. She'd lost her wig in the struggle with Chandran. Daghahen preferred dark hair to light. When he studied hers long enough, a sharp pain stabbed his chest.

They built a small fire, for the persistent winter chill lingered in the new spring air. He opened his robe lapel wide and allowed her to huddle in its warmth beside him. The gesture would excite her, no doubt, but who was he to deny her some comfort in the cold night? He could finally let his hood fall since the stars were smothered by thick, rushing clouds as well as the protective pine canopy.

Rayna couldn't be satisfied only to stay warm; her hands roamed all over him. Her lips stamped wet little kisses anywhere she could get them. He stared at the fire, happy to fill his eyes with its burning light and avoid any accidental glance at the sky, clouds or no clouds.

He avoided looking at her too. No matter where her hands managed to wander, he couldn't quite find the heart to touch her in return.

Eventually, he smiled, kissed her forehead, and said, "Let's go to sleep."

"Do I not please you, my love?"

"You do." He took her down to the ground with him and made sure to tuck her snugly into his robe. She nestled close to him, putting her arm around his body, her head under his chin.

"Goodnight, my love," she said.

He closed his eyes and sighed. He hadn't enjoyed the privilege of sleeping like this in sixteen years.

Chandran's neck pulsed with pain. In his and Rayna's inn room, he stitched his wound closed by candlelight—a task Rayna should've done for him. But this cut was that whore's own work. Why? What had the shriveled old elf offered to sway her away from years of training and rewards? His forked tongue must be a smooth one too. Chandran had emerged now and again to check on them while they smiled and pawed at each other in the dining hall. Something that pointy-eared bastard said to her had made her turn on her master.

Early the next morning, he trudged through the blanketed forest where their thin trail led him, and detected wood smoke on the breeze. Hiding amongst these straight, pole-like pine trees would help little, so he took extreme precautions, treading gingerly and keeping his distance.

There she was. Rayna slept, wrapped tightly in Daghahen's cloak on the ground, alone beside a pile of charred, smoking wood. Daghahen wasn't around.

Upon waking, Daghahen tucked his cloak around Rayna as she slept sweetly and headed off to find the creek he'd heard babbling in the night during their trek through the forest. Rayna should appreciate some fresh water when she woke up.

He fastened his codpiece back in place after a long morning piss and hoisted his pack again. He trusted Rayna as much as he trusted his tried and true infatuation spell—not merely a spell, an ability he'd been born with—but it couldn't trump the comfort he got from keeping the sword in his possession at all times.

When he found the creek, he filled his waterskin and splashed his face. If he was to even think about indulging what she wanted of him, he should do it the right way—and bathe first. But they had no time for tumbling now; they had to get far away from Tintilly and Chandran. Too many sorcerers cluttered Wexwick, so he'd turn them around and head back to Gaulice.

Along the way, he could pick flowers for Rayna. He could do some proper courting protocol first. A little protocol should make him feel better about the whole thing, and then…and then…

He glowered down at the reflection of the pale, wrinkled face framed in frizzy blonde hair in the water. Practicing sorcery again had rotted him, inside and out.

He laughed. "You hideous fool. *Saehgahn* can't marry twice." He swiped his hand across the reflection, and it scrambled into thousands of little blotches of colored light. Drawing up his hood, he started back to their campsite with his pack and his full waterskin.

A man with dark reddish hair straddled Rayna's form. Strangling her. His eyes wide and teeth gnashing.

Angry bile boiled in Daghahen's stomach, but he resisted his *saehgahn* instinct to charge forward in search of violent revenge. He jumped behind a tree, the thickest one near him, squeezing his eyes closed and clenching his teeth. Rayna lay motionless, already dead. The Creator only knew how long Chandran would indulge in his sick task before finally stopping.

In a whisper, Daghahen began the words for Gariott's Blend. *"Ernah, pah, toh gah. Lah ti oungeh…"* As soon as he finished, he rushed off.

Goodbye, Rayna.

Chapter 9
Her Charity

Hoisting a hefty basket of linens on her back, Kalea trekked out to the stream where the water had been dammed for washing. Should she call Dorhen's name, or would he already be there waiting for her, invisible? Though she had convinced herself to a degree that the stranger in the forest didn't mean any harm—for now—she'd have to watch for the other stranger who did: Kemp.

What a nice thing it would be if she really could have Dorhen as her invisible guardian. She couldn't deny the idea was more than a little intriguing. An hour of every morning was spent reciting practiced prayers, and when she wasn't absentmindedly running through them, her mind's voice slurred into prayers about the elf. Was he good? Could she trust him? Was it a sin to have been speaking to him so much? Other times of the day allowed for her own composed prayers, and she couldn't stand to wait for those opportunities. She needed answers.

"Vivene," she whispered to the mischievous novice as the two stood side by side during their biweekly choir practice. Vivene looked over, and Kalea buried her nose in her hymnal.

"What?"

"*Shh!*"

Vivene frowned and glanced around. Practice hadn't started yet. All the novices were taking the opportunity to chat up the sanctum while they waited for their choir leader to arrive. "What already?"

Kalea opened her mouth and stopped short of the first word. She grabbed Vivene's sleeve and ushered her down the choir steps to the darkest corner behind a column.

"What?" Vivene said again. Kalea leaned in close to her, wringing her musty old hymnal in her hands. "Hurry and say it, or you'll need a new book."

Kalea took a deep breath. "What else does the love manual say about elves?"

A huge smile full of crooked teeth spread across Vivene's chubby face. "Who wants to know?"

"Please… You said you had the book memorized. What else does it say about young…*sae*—what's the word?"

"*Saehgahn*. It's like 'say' and 'gone.' And the book doesn't tell much. What do you want to know?"

"Anything you've gleaned about them."

"Why so urgent? Oh, my holy shitty shoes!"

"*Shh!*" Some other girls standing on the runner between the pews leaned over to view the two.

Kalea slapped Vivene's arm, but the girl ignored it. "Your face is all red. I don't believe it. Does Joy know? I'll bet you told *her*."

"Can you please answer my question?"

"I'm going to ask Joy after this, you can bet."

"Please! Tell me before someone comes over here."

Vivene waved both her hands, one holding her own hymnal. "All right, let's see." Vivene tapped her chin and smirked. "What was it like?"

"What was *what* like? I didn't do anything."

"All right, all right. I'll tell you what I know, and I'll even keep an eye out for more material. But later tonight, I want details."

"Hurry, before the sister gets here!"

"Fine, look. The book is just a bunch of romance. It paints them as loveable heroic types. And sad, they're usually sad for some reason—I guess because of what it says about their culture forcing them to be celibate."

"Do they really ask women for…for…um—*that*, in exchange for a gift or service?"

"Well, no. *Saehgahn* have an air of melancholy about them. They don't expect earthly pleasures, at least in these stories. The women are eager to 'get to know' them because the *saehgahn* are inhumanly attractive."

"Do they cast any love spells on the women?"

"No. But let's remember there's not much reading material in the book."

"Does Sister Scupley have any other romantic storybooks?"

"I haven't found any."

"In the stories you read, were the elves…particularly protective?"

"Oh yes, very. Their protective nature makes a great loveable attribute. Typical heroic story stuff."

"So they don't have any tricks up their sleeves?"

"Nothing like that from the elf stories. Tell me, what's his name?"

"I'm not saying anything else."

"This is so great. We have to talk in private tonight. I can tell you all about what to do with him, if you know what I mean."

Kalea shushed her again, and after a gentle shove, ran back to the choir steps and began warming up her voice. "La *la*—lo *li*!"

Vivene joined her like before and leaned over to catch her eyes again, but before she could whisper any prying questions, the door opened and the sister strolled in.

If Kalea's turquoise-eyed elf could write, she would tell him to write Vivene a letter of thanks. Otherwise, anything might've made Kalea change her mind about entering the forest today. Dropping her basket, she knelt by the water. Was he here yet? She could call out to him, but her throat closed up.

She drank some stream water from her cupped hands. Acting aloof might be best. She opened the lid on her shoulder basket and pulled the first shift out.

"I came like you asked."

Kalea jumped and nearly shrieked. She twisted around to find Dorhen standing behind her. "Don't sneak up on me!"

He huffed as she turned back around and tended her laundry. He dropped into a squat beside her. She kept her face straight and focused on her work, swishing the linen around in the water. In her peripheral vision, he untied a handkerchief and held it out to her over both hands. A bunch of wild strawberries were gathered in its center.

"What've you got?"

He bowed his head, still extending the berries. "I'm sorry for everything I did wrong." *Saehgahn* truly did offer gifts. When she didn't take them, he raised his eyes to inspect the situation, and extended them a bit closer. "I found these for you."

Kalea sighed. "Thank you." It *was* a nice gesture. She shouldn't stay mad at him over such small reasons for long, especially if this meeting was to learn more about him. And her stomach continued its groans after today's tiny breakfast. She took the handkerchief. "Will you eat some with me?"

"They're for you."

She ate one, wincing at its premature bitter flavor, and held the bunch back out to him. "Nonsense. Humans share food with each other. Share it with me."

He shifted closer to her over the grass. Maybe she had been acting a little crazy as of late. When he took one off the pile, she said, "I'm also sorry about being harsh. I hope you can understand my worries."

He swallowed the strawberry, also making a face at the sour thing. "I can."

"Sit down. We have a lot to talk about."

He did, crossing his legs and folding his hands together.

Kalea leaned over the water to scrub the garment against the rock. "Have you seen Arius Medallus since we talked yesterday?"

"No," he said, watching her hands work. "Have you?"

"No. And I don't want to. I've worked hard for ten years to keep the visions away."

"You should ask him what he wants."

She paused to look at him with an eyebrow raised. She could've snapped a haughty reply, but she stopped herself, remembering her manners. Come to think of it, she'd never thought to ask "the face" anything before. "I don't talk to demons."

Dorhen showed no reaction to the comment. "Can I join your community in there?" he asked, and Kalea burst out in laughter, though she felt no mirth.

"Only women can be in the convent."

"I've seen men going in and out."

"Yes, but those are priests. They don't directly join the convent, they get assigned personnel positions by a bishop in a large city with a cathedral."

Dorhen's mouth cocked as if he were sucking his teeth. "So if I became a priest, I wouldn't be able to go in there of my own will?"

"No."

"Tch. I wouldn't want to be stuck behind those walls anyway."

Kalea twisted the garment, and a rush of water escaped its fibers. "Well, they work fine for us mentally ill girls. It's a safe place for us to live."

"You're not mentally ill." His brow narrowed. "And there are no safe places to live."

"You see?" Kalea said, wagging her finger from him to herself and back. "This is what I want to talk about. You have some interest in me, and I think it's the kind of interest I can't entertain."

He crossed his arms. "What kind of interest do you mean?"

"Why don't you tell *me*? Take a good guess." She would construct the conversation any way she could to avoid using difficult carnal words.

He averted his turquoise eyes.

"This is what I'm talking about. You want something from me, but you won't even say what it is."

"I would like to be near you."

She took her attention wholly off the laundry now and gestured animatedly with her hands while she spoke. "But you can't. All right? I'm going to be a vestal. I can't be friends with you. My life is about work, prayer, contemplation, and praising the One Creator. I'm not allowed to talk to laymen—or lay-*saehgahn*—too intimately, if at all. As I said, I *can't* entertain your interests."

"And I've already told you, you don't have to talk to me—but I will be here. I'll live out here, right by your home. And I'll protect you."

That hotness crept into her face again, and she snapped back to the laundry in the cold water.

"Kalea." He reached out for her shoulder, and she shrugged away. He scooted closer. "Would you like to know what my life has been like for the last sixteen years?"

"Yes," she said in total honesty, fixated on the laundry.

"It was like being dead, though I could still walk. A strange existence. I walked and walked, practically sleeping through it. My head stayed cloudy. There were times when my survival depended on being quick and alert, but most days my body walked on its own, drifting through forests and cities and farms. I was unseen and felt every bit of it. Being unseen and unheard was the aim, the model life Arius Medallus designed for me. I fell easily into the routine. And lost my soul." His eyes flared. "I watched my house burn and collapse with my mother inside."

Kalea's hands hovered over the water, dripping. His last statement made her stomach rattle and echo up to her bottom lip.

"I miss her."

"I'm so sorry." Half of the word "sorry" choked off. She pressed her wrist against her mouth to try to stop the quivering. She couldn't imagine such a thing happening to her own mother. Right now, her mother lived safe in Taulmoil, in a warm house with her father, writing Kalea letters at least once a month. "Dorhen, you and I can pray for—"

"When I saw you, something happened to me."

"Huh?"

He leaned toward her, hardly blinking. "Something changed. When I saw you, I woke up. I left the area but quickly returned. I wanted to hear your voice again. Though I promised not to remember your name, it kept ringing in my head as if you were calling—"

"Did your mother honor the One Creator?"

Dorhen's voice caught for a moment as she forced him to change the subject. "I don't know."

Kalea bit the inside of her cheek for a moment. "What was she like?"

His eyes spaced out. "Beautiful. If your One Creator created anything, He created her. She had brown hair. Like yours. Her voice sounded soft and sweet. She used to get her hands all dirty and make things with clay. She'd step into the water and splash around with me when I was little."

A genuine smile spread across Kalea's face. "She sounds lovely." Dorhen offered no response. He studied her in that serious and curious way of his. "But she never told you about the One Creator?"

"I don't remember."

Kalea dropped the next garment into the pool. "And so you walked around the Lightlands for sixteen years. What's Arius Medallus like?"

"Strict." Dorhen's eyes perused the forest on the other side of the stream. "My childhood ended right there at age six. I learned a lot from him, but my cloud started around the same time."

"Oh. You poor thing."

"The nightmares came too."

"Nightmares? About your house burning?"

"Not quite. Well, at first, sure. But they shifted into stranger territory."

"Like what?" She put her attention on him again; the linen gown swirled in the water on its own.

"There's old women around me. They make me sleepy, but I never quite fall asleep. My arms and legs go numb, and they hold me down with large, twig-like hands. When I can't fight back, they cut open my chest and reach their hands inside. It's cold. I can't figure out what they're searching for."

Kalea listened long after he stopped talking. The stream babbled on and the pine needles rustled in the breeze.

"That's the nightmare I have the most."

"I know what you need to do." His head jerked her way, and his eyebrows rose. "You came to me for a reason, so I might be able to help."

"Really?"

"Yes. You say you don't remember your mother teaching you about the One Creator?" He nodded. "And how about Arius Medallus?" He shook his head. "First, we'll pray for your mother's soul." She wiped her hands on her apron and sat facing him on her knees. "Have you ever prayed before?"

"No."

"Copy this pose." She put her hands together. "Now bow your head. If you were to join the priesthood, you'd do this a lot. Listen closely: Our One Creator, please look after Dorhen, Your new follower. And please keep the soul of his mother..." She raised her head. "What was her name?"

"Orinleah."

"Please keep Orinleah's soul safe in Your care for all eternity. Bless us all. Amen... Now say 'amen.'"

Dorhen parroted the word.

"There. Now how do you feel?"

With his head still bowed, he looked at her and smiled. "Good."

"It's a start, but we have a lot of work to do. When I met you, you had committed a sin. The sin follows you, but you'll release it by confessing. You should establish a regimen of regular confession and keep it for the rest of your life."

"What if I don't do anything else wrong?"

"Oh, you will. We all do, so get used to it." She cleared her throat. "You said you 'walked in a cloud' and you've experienced dark dreams."

"Yes."

"These are symptoms of a heavy heart. Or perhaps an empty heart. People who don't have the One Creator to fill their hearts have empty holes in their hearts."

Dorhen glanced down at his chest.

"It even appeared as a literal symbol in your nightmare, so this must be the case. But your condition is easy to fix. We'll do your first confession. Normally, we have private booths and a priest to hear our confession, but right now we don't have such luxury. I'll have to fill in as your confessor."

She stood and went over to sit on the nearest large rock at the edge of the water. "Kneel before me." He did so. "Turn your face that way and I'll look this way. We don't make eye contact."

"Now what?"

"Now say, 'May the One Creator forgive me because I have sinned.'"

"May the One Creator forgive me because I've sinned."

"Good. Now you can tell me what you did wrong recently. The day you stole at the market is an easy one."

"Okay. Well. Several days ago, I got so hungry I went to the market and I stole a fistful of peas against Arius Medallus's order, but I didn't get to eat them—"

Kalea cleared her throat loudly. "Now stop. And now I say, 'One Creator bless you. Your confession has been heard and you are forgiven.' Now you must say...um, ten Sovereign Creators."

"What're those?"

She regarded him as he stared across the stream. "You can look at me now. It's a recited prayer. Since I assigned ten of them to you, you go away and say the prayer ten times in private. It's a penance, which is a punishment. After you say them, you'll be absolved. You should feel better too."

"I don't know the words."

Kalea stood and stretched her back. "Not a problem, I'll write them for you." She picked up the straightest pine twig she could find, cleared a spot in the red pine blanket, and wrote the first word.

"I can't read that."

"Oh, sorry. I'll be clearer."

"No, I mean I can't read." He was standing now, his face bland.

What'll I do with him? Bringing Dorhen to the One Creator will be harder than I thought. We have a lot of work to do.

"Understandable. You have been living in the forest with a fairy, after all. I can teach you."

"You mean it?" All of his front teeth showed in the wide smile spreading across his face. All of them were perfect except for one long, pointy one on the side, grown beyond its twin on the other side. His face was adorable when he smiled.

"Yes, I meant it. Come closer."

He practically leapt to her side to see the bald patch of earth she'd made for writing. She drew the first alphabetical symbol. "This is an A. It makes the 'ah' sound…"

She rushed through the alphabet with Dorhen, and then rushed through the rest of her laundry. "Try to remember any symbol you can. We'll go over them again tomorrow," she told him before she sprinted away with her basket of wet linens.

In the courtyard, she released yesterday's hanging laundry to clear space for the new wet load. Sister Scupley stomped through the door.

"There you are! We were going to send someone out for you again. We insisted you not go to the stream today."

Kalea stepped away from the soggy hanging linen and curtsied. "I'm sorry, Sister. There were some stubborn stains on the linens. I'm fine now, though. Please don't worry about me anymore. I didn't get woozy at all today."

"Well, good. Hurry and finish here. Father Superior needs a new set of linens for his room."

"Yes, Sister."

After hanging the second-to-the-last garment, she lifted the remaining one out. A white object dropped out of its folds and clacked at the basket's bottom. "Hmm?"

A jagged white ring glowed in the shaded wicker space. She lifted it out and inspected it on her open palm. A string of pearly seashells—a bracelet. The novices couldn't have jewelry in the convent; she would know if it belonged to any of the others. They certainly wouldn't have let it fall into the laundry basket.

Dorhen. Jitters returned to her core. A brief, skeptical laugh burst from her throat. *Surely not… He did. He dropped this in the basket for me to find!*

Unable to contain her smile, she shoved it over her hand and turned her wrist around to see it twinkle in the sun. She would have to hide it. Jewelry was prohibited here. Vestals were supposed to practice modesty and poverty. Once upon a time—as in five minutes ago—she had agreed with that virtue. Now, something about it, a gift from an elf…or a boy at least, made her heart fly.

Dorhen.

Leaving it on her wrist, she untied her chemise sleeves, which were gathered up around her upper arms, and pulled them down into their long and straight positions.

She dropped off her hastily folded sheets and visited Father Superior's chamber last. The office with the red door sunken into the floor also served as his bedchamber.

Her knuckles stopped an inch before hitting the painted wood. A guest was with him. It wasn't Father Liam's voice.

Father Superior said in soft, muffled tones, "We'll have to rotate personnel, so please, could you give us a few days?"

"However you want to do it."

"They'll be well taken care of, you say?"

"Of course. The famine won't reach our region. We get more than enough rain for our crops, and our resources are numerous."

Though they murmured to each other, their voices echoed loud enough through the key hole. She tried to peek through it. A hand rested on Father Superior's little tea table in the faint glow through the window.

"They'll have a bit of a shock at such an abrupt change, I hope you know, due to being placed into a non-religious institution."

The hand's fingers drummed on the table. "Father, you misunderstood me. Our institution is very religious."

"Excellent. We're settled then. I'll get back to you on the day. But when you come, be quick. It's the green door in the west building. It'll be locked, but please be as quick as you can."

Green door? The novices' dorm?

"Have some more tea, Mr.…."

"Tal. Mr. Tal."

"Yes, of course, Mr. Tal." The sound of tea trickled. "H-h-how much can you—"

Father Superior's guest hissed through his teeth. "Oh, dear. This is awkward."

"What is, Mr. Tal?"

"You're asking for an expensive movement here, which will require two castings. It's such a long distance. I'm afraid I'll have to ask *you* for some gold, however much you can spare."

Father Superior cleared his throat. "As long as this alleviates some of the mouths to be fed in this establishment, it'll be worth it." Coins jingled. "I have thirty on me now."

"I'll take them." The coins chimed again with a snap as a hand snatched the whole purse. "Though I'm afraid I've no time for another cup of tea. Thank you for your time, Father."

"And you, Mr. Tal."

Chairs scooted on the tile floor, and Kalea scrambled away from the door and hid around the corner. She waited. And waited. The red door never opened.

At the supper table, Kalea couldn't eat. Vivene shot sly glances at her and smiled, always on the edge of bursting into a laugh. Nothing was funny, especially not the secret Vivene now knew. She could easily be the one to get Kalea into deep trouble if she carried on with her nosiness.

Sister Scupley reached over and smacked Vivene's hand with a wooden spoon.

"Owww!"

Sister Scupley gave her a harsh, "Shhh!" They weren't allowed to talk during supper.

Kalea's stomach churned at the thought of the apparent changes about to happen around here. Which of them would be sent away? And which personnel? She propped her head on her palm and stared at her lentil soup. Next to her, Joy had already finished her little drop of soup. The convent was in trouble. The people within it were in trouble.

Kalea slid her bowl over to Joy, who popped her head up and turned to Kalea. Joy's face had gone pallid. She needed the nourishment more than Kalea did. Joy's mouth dropped open, and she pointed to herself. With a smile, Kalea pointed to the bowl. Gawking at her, Joy slid it the rest of the way and dug in with her spoon.

Chapter 10
Her Body

At the breakfast table, Kalea took one bite of her oats and slid the bowl over to Rose, who sat tearing up while staring at her already empty one. A smile brightened her innocent face when Kalea's offering scooted into her sight. Kalea touched one fingertip to her lips—a hand gesture to honor the One Creator, showing a single finger to indicate Him, and kissing it to indicate love. Rose gave the gesture back to her.

On that single bite of food, Kalea went about her morning chores, her afternoon prayers, and on to afternoon laundry hanging. By the midafternoon hour, her stomach roared and she braced a hand on the wall when another dizzy spell overtook her.

A deep familiar voice resonated beside her. "Are you all right, Kalea?"

"Dorhen, you're not supposed to be in here."

He appeared beside her as the hood fell off his head. "You weren't at the creek. I thought we were going to meet and say the alphabet today."

She released the wall and balanced herself. "Oh. I forgot."

"You don't look good. Have you eaten?"

She turned back to her basket of soggy linens. "No. I'm fasting. It's a ritual we do once in a while to honor the One Creator."

"Well, stop it. You've gone pale."

"I can't. Don't you know there's a famine?" He grabbed a linen out of the basket and copied what she did with it. "You don't have to do that."

"I don't think you can handle it on your own."

She clenched her teeth. Should she be offended or happy for the help? She was too tired to decide at the moment. He had certainly become bold about appearing in open spaces where he might be seen. In this area, the cover of the hanging sheets provided them some privacy, but that wouldn't stop Sister Gani from coming to check on her.

"Kalea," he said with his voice high and inquisitive.

"Hmm?"

"You should leave this place."

She cocked her head toward him, holding her current garment high. "You're joking. Tell me you're joking."

"I'm not. Staying here is a bad idea, especially with a famine. There are other places we can go where food can be found more easily."

"*We?*"

"Yes."

When should she tell him some of the novices would be sent away? What would he do if she turned out to be one of them?

"You want me to go away with you?"

"I'm good at surviving in the forest."

"So together, we'll eat a bunch of tree bark?"

"I'm being serious."

She clicked her tongue and went for the next garment in the basket. "You just don't understand."

"What, your willingness to starve in here because no one's bringing in any food for you?"

"But I'm going to be a vestal."

"And?"

"And vestals have a duty to—"

"To the One Creator?" He smiled.

"What's so funny?"

"Nothing. I sat outside the window of the big room and listened to the man talking about the One Creator."

"And what did you hear Father Liam say about Him?"

"That the One Creator created everything. This earth." He stamped his foot. "This rock. Those trees out there."

"And what else did you hear?"

"It's not what I heard afterward, it's what I thought. The world in there was created by other humans." He pointed to the building behind her. She frowned and glanced back where his finger pointed. "You insist on staying closed up in your world made by humans, and yet you want to praise and honor the One Creator, who created much more out here. Why not come outside with me and enjoy all of it?"

"Because I live in there where it's safe."

He grabbed her hand, and she held in a scream. His eyes sparked brightly over his joyful and mischievous smile, like any elf from any fairy tale she'd read. "Come out with me for one day."

"What will we do?" she asked as she inspected him all over for any indication of baseness she could find. This could be the invitation to her downfall.

"We'll go to the creek and splash around. We can catch frogs."

"What?"

"If you follow the creek downstream a few miles, it runs into a cave. A big one. The sun shines into the cave and makes amazing lights on the walls. And it echoes. We can go in there and yell. We can sing!"

Kalea blinked her eyes, looking at his warm hand grasping hers. The excited light in his beaming eyes spread to her lips in a smile. She forced the smile down. If she allowed the smile, it might escalate into a laugh. A laugh might escalate into her squeezing his hand back, and then maybe a hug, or she might take his other hand and twirl with him and laugh some more and say "yes."

The jittery sensation rose in her abdomen. Had he cast the spell again? Or was this…was this what happened when people fell in love like in the stories?

She took her hand away. "No." She said it softly; no need to get riled up and make him feel bad again. His smile faded. Though the picture of the two of them dancing hand-in-hand was nice, it wasn't her destiny. She belonged in this convent as a Sister of Sorrow, not in a lover's hand, a husband's house, or an elf's forest.

"Sorry," she added.

His hands dropped to his sides. His smile was obviously forced.

"Since you're here, though, let's go over the alphabet again. And we'll do another confession."

"Sure." With his posture deflated, he followed her to a deep corner where the wall adjoined one of the convent wings. She took the broom leaning against the wall along the way.

"I'll go slow to help you soak it up." She turned the broom over and used its handle to draw an A in the dirt.

"That's A," he said.

"Very good. What sound does it make?"

"'Ah.'" Beside it, she drew the next symbol. "That's B. As in 'bucket' or 'barrel.'"

She paused to wonder at him. "I didn't expect you to remember all this. Our session yesterday was so brief. Can you remember the—"

"C as in 'cart.' D as in 'danger.' E as in 'everyone.' F as in 'fight.' G as in 'girl.' H as in 'heat…'" He went through them all, speaking rapidly. He stopped at Q, remembering the symbol, but unable to put it to a word.

"As in 'quick,'" she said.

"Thank you," he replied, and went through the rest of the alphabet, stopping again at X.

"This one is hard. I'm not good with words starting with X, but it's the third letter in 'next.' I'm impressed with you, though. Were you practicing all night?"

"I remember all the symbols you taught me. I applied the sounds you taught me to words I knew. Am I right about these words?"

"You are." She studied him for a moment.

"What else?"

"Um." She shook out of her little trance and said, "Next I'll explain how the letters work together. You said the word 'cart.'" She wrote "cart" in the dirt and explained each letter and how it worked to make the word possible.

"And that's it. That's reading. If you can remember each letter and the sounds it makes, you can read any word. If you find a long word, you can sound it out to figure it out for yourself." She underlined the word while pronouncing it.

"How do you write 'Kalea?'"

Hiding her smile, she wrote her name in the dirt.

"This one's my favorite. It's beautiful."

Kalea cleared her throat and kept her raging amusement suppressed. "And this is your name." She marked out the letters of his name, and he shook his head.

"It's hard and somber. But yours is curly and playful."

Her giggle drew his eyes. "Your name isn't somber. It's soft, gentle."

He smirked.

"So, then…do you grasp reading now?"

"I think so. I'll look at words I find and try to practice on them."

"Dorhen."

"Hmm?"

She lowered her chin but tried to maintain eye contact. "We can keep meeting. I'll help you practice reading and teach you more about praying too."

His sweet, bright smile returned.

Still holding the broom, she focused on her two hands grasping its handle. She resituated them.

"That reminds me," he said, reaching into his largest belt pouch. A few leather pouches hung from his belt, implements of his traveler's lifestyle. He pulled out a book. "I found this this morning. I thought you could read it to me."

A sleek golden arrow winked at her from the book's spine. Her mouth dropped open and rounded. "A *Lehomis* book? Where did you get this?" She narrowed her brow. "Did you steal it?"

"The shiny arrow caught my eye. When I opened it, there were more pretty pictures inside."

"Dorhen, I'm not allowed to read *Lehomis* books…"

He showed her a hand-colored woodcut somewhere in the middle of the book with jagged, splintery lines illustrating Lehomis with his long, black braid running along the curve of his spine, grasping a shy woman's hand and shoving his face closer to hers. The woman gave a coy smile and his mouth gaped in a longing frown. The ears of the woman in the picture were rounded—a human. Dorhen's smile curved under glowing eyes. Lehomis was an elf, and his affection was aimed at a human woman in the picture.

Kalea shook her head. "I don't know what to say."

"Will you read it to me?"

She sighed. "You'll read it to *me*. What do you say?"

"Fair enough."

"Put it away. We can't read right now."

He obeyed. "Kalea," he said as she bent over to pick up another wet garment from the basket, "How did you get in here?"

"I told you. I'm mentally ill. My parents sent me to this place."

"But you're better now, aren't you? Especially since now you know you don't have a mental illness."

"We don't leave when we 'get better.' It's not a hospital, it's a convent, and we are a faction of religious women. And are you arguing with me about leaving again?"

Biting his lip, he glanced at his soft leather shoes. He always dressed like a human. He must've told the truth about not visiting Norr since his childhood. "I want to know things about you."

She clenched her teeth at the thought of talking about herself in depth with him. She'd demanded he answer any and all of her questions about himself—it wouldn't be fair to refuse to answer his questions about her.

"Where did you live before you came here?"

"Taulmoil," Kalea surrendered. "It's a few days' ride to—"

"To the east, I know."

"Have you been there?"

"Yes, many times. Even when I was little. Maybe we came close to each other in the past and didn't know it."

She smiled and continued with the laundry. He also took out a bedsheet and hung it beside the chemise she was hanging.

"No," she said. "Don't let it have any folds or it'll take longer to dry. Straighten it out." She leaned into his personal space, using her free hand to adjust his sheet while holding up the other side of her garment.

"Sorry." His voice hummed warm in her ear.

"You'll get it. Is this the plan? Helping me hang laundry now?"

"If you wish it. I'll do anything you ask."

She shook her head. "You'll get caught."

"Kalea, what's your favorite food?"

A snort escaped in her laugh. "Frog legs."

At his silence, she turned to check on him. His face had gone long. "Why?"

"They're good, and they're plentiful too."

His mouth dropped open. "That's awful. Why would you eat them?"

She laughed out loud. "What's the matter? Do you have sympathy for the frogs?"

"I love them."

She couldn't help but turn to study his sincere and sorrowful face. Her heart warmed. "You're kind of"—she lowered her voice—"sweet sometimes."

"Hmm?"

"Never mind." Another light, feathery laugh escaped her throat. "I won't eat anymore frog legs, how about that?"

"Actually, I'd have you eat anything. You're so fragile-looking. When I met you, you were full of energy, enough to swing that stick and run with me all the way to the forest."

"Well, things are changing, and I'm afraid it'll get worse fast." When she looked up again, he was frowning. "You want to nag me to leave again?"

"I believe it would be better for you. Give me the order, and I'll help you get out of here."

"I can't." The two words slid out as a breathy whisper. Why couldn't she leave?

"Do you still have a mother?"

The question jarred her out of her thought. "Yes. My mother is alive."

"Is she in Taulmoil?"

"She is. And my father."

His eyebrows narrowed at the last part. "Don't you miss her?"

"Sometimes." Kalea returned to her work again.

"What is she like? She stitches clothes, you said before."

"Yes."

"What else is she like?"

"A hard, no-nonsense woman who would have preferred a boy. My father is gentler. I used to love to sit on his lap by the fire and he'd read me the *Lehomis* book..." She stopped talking when Dorhen's face went long in surprise.

"You had this book?" He motioned to the pouch where he'd stashed it.

"Yeah. I adore Lehomis."

Dorhen grinned wide. "Now I know your favorite book. And I happened to find one. I have good instincts, you'll learn about me."

She giggled. "All the more reason to run away with you, huh?"

His smile retracted to the closed-mouth type, but his soft eyes implied she was correct.

Noting the sun's angle, she clicked her tongue. "This isn't good. The evening prayer hour is coming and I have to finish this laundry. Quick, let's do a confession before I have to go back in. Someone could also come out here to fetch me for any reason."

Several new walls of sheets hung with the others now, and at the heart of the complex, Kalea sat on the stool. Dorhen knelt before her like he had yesterday. "I'm going to make you a good follower of the Creator if you insist on seeing me every day."

"Yes," he said, "anything for you. I'll do anything."

She cleared her throat. "If you remember most of the alphabet after one run through, can I assume you remember the confession opening?"

Dorhen cleared his throat and began, "One Creator, forgive me because I've sinned."

"What have you to confess?" Kalea settled her eyes on the treetops over the convent wall as he pointed his face the opposite way. The wind whistled. She waited. A few moments passed before she peeked at him. He frowned and squinted. "Have you anything to confess, child?"

"I don't think I've done anything sinful."

She couldn't stifle her smile this time. "You must've done something. There's always something."

"I don't know. I've stolen food before the day we met."

"Well, that's something. But what else? Did you steal the book?"

"I bought it, unless it's a sin to buy it."

Kalea squinted and fought the urge to look at his face for signs of deception. "How did you buy it?"

"I was in town, blending into plain sight with my ordinary hood on. An old man's handcart turned over when its wheel broke. I was standing close and reflexively caught it. A few of his pottery pieces fell off, but no major damage occurred. I did my best to hide my face, but he was so happy he handed me a copper right out of his coin purse. Keeping my face low, I went straight to the market to find a present for you, and the books were there. This one stood out to me."

"I see. I'm glad to hear of your kind deed."

A flush of pink came to his cheeks with the grin her words caused.

"No one got suspicious of you?"

He shook his head. "No. It was fine."

"I believe you. Now let's get back to confession. Think about it hard."

"I still don't know."

"Let's see… Have you entertained any unclean thoughts?"

"What kind of thought is unclean?"

"Don't look at me." He snapped his face away. "Most men have unclean thoughts; it tends to be a universal downfall of theirs. Women can have them too, but they're also pretty susceptible to jealousy and gossip."

"But what's an unclean thought?"

"You don't know?" She caught herself looking at him. When their eyes met, she snapped her gaze away. "It's…well…you know. It's thinking about women and having lustful desires for them."

"That's unclean?"

"Shh, not so loud. But yes. Unclean thoughts lead to unclean actions… I said don't look at me." His head whipped away again in her peripheral vision. "So would you like to confess any unclean thoughts?"

"Not really."

"Well, at least you're honest about that. But in confession you have to. Don't worry, I won't judge you. As your confessor, I'll be as professional as can be, and I'll assign you a penance, and then you'll be absolved. You'll feel better."

"Are you sure I'll feel better?"

"Yes."

His hesitation continued. A quick peek at him revealed his bowed head and his white-knuckled fists grasping the hem of his tabard.

"Could it be so bad?" she asked. "Because more extreme sins require more extreme penances, like lashings. But if it's a paltry unclean thought, you don't have to worry. You'll just have to recite prayers."

"Lashings?"

"Surely you know this word. Lashing? As in getting whipped on your back."

Another few seconds of silence passed. "Did that happen to you?"

The neatly healing lash wounds on her back burned after a sudden flare of pain. "What are you talking about?"

"Did you get lashed? On your back?"

Kalea's heart accelerated to pounding in her ears. Dropping her professional confessor's demeanor, she turned to him. He remained staring at the ground, gripping his tabard hem.

"Did you get lashed after we met?"

"Dorhen…how would you know?"

"Your back. It was all ripped up. Red and raw. Did it hurt?"

"How did you see my back?"

"Does it still hurt?"

"How?" She clenched her own fists to keep a hold on her panic.

"I saw you in the bath."

"When? How?"

He paused to swallow, avoiding her eyes. "On the night you were attacked and you ran from me, I followed you all the way to this building. They took you through the gate, and I couldn't slip in with you. So I climbed the wall."

"I don't believe it!"

"I'm sorry. I didn't want to lose you. I got in here and looked for you. I waited in the shadows…over there." He pointed generally toward the corner at the other end of the courtyard. "Until I heard a girl say your name. It echoed above me."

He must've meant Joy.

"And?"

"I climbed the wall again, and from there I stepped onto that awning. I walked across there and stepped onto the adjoining sloped roof. Your voice sounded in the open window above it." He pointed to the window belonging to the room with the bathtubs. "The window stood halfway open."

"Why?"

"I wanted to find you." His eyes met hers for an instant and sprang away. "I didn't know you'd be naked in there."

"And then what? You watched me? Why did you watch me?"

"I couldn't help it."

"How much did you see?" Kalea's fingernails stabbed into her palms.

He shifted uncomfortably. "You were talking to your friend. In the bath. As she rubbed something on your back. I worried about you. I saw you wince and I felt pain for a moment too, like scratches raking across my back. I resisted the urge to go in."

Kalea's throat closed up and a shiver rattled her entire body. "What else did you see?" The words escaped through her clenched teeth.

"Your warm skin. It had steam swirling off of it. And you stood up. I couldn't look away. Your long hair trailed down your back like ribbons of wet silk. And to your front where it…clung around your breasts, flashing hints of flesh when you moved."

"Enough!" She shot to her feet too fast and fought an oncoming faint. "Get out!" She pointed to the wall. He rose too and put up his hands. "Climb back over the wall and leave, or I'll scream and we'll turn you over to the guard!"

"But you said confessing was good and I could get absolved!"

"This is different." She sat again and crossed her arms. "I said that *before* knowing you were a pervert."

"You said we all do things wrong."

"It's still different."

"How?"

"Tell me what happened after."

"I climbed off the roof and went back to the forest."

"What next? Did you have unclean thoughts about *me*?"

"That's not what I'd call them, but to answer your question…yes, after getting over the nausea of knowing you endured such pain."

She stood again and thrust her palm at his stomach. "Leave! Don't ever come back!"

She moved too fast and swayed to the side, precariously keeping her footing. He exhaled at her strike, but collected himself fast enough to catch her and ease her back onto the stool.

"Kalea, I'm sorry." His voice cracked. She batted him away with flailing arms. "I didn't mean anything by it. I want forgiveness. I want your forgiveness…and the Creator's."

Kalea bowed over on her seat to try and get her vision back. She panted. Her head spun and she grasped it in both hands. "I can't believe you saw me. You saw me." The sighs puffing out of her lungs turned to sobs.

His heavy breathing became apparent when she covered her face with shaky hands. His feet stayed planted on the compacted earth before her. "Are you still standing there? I told you to leave me."

She raised her head again, knowing how red her face must be. He stood with his hands limp by his sides, frowning.

He ripped open the buttons on his outer russet mantle and threw the whole thing to the ground. Underneath that, his blue hood showed as a scarf-like drapery about his shoulders. He took off his belt and threw it down. He untied the laces on the sides of his outer tabard and threw it onto the forming pile.

"What are you doing?"

He untied the laces which kept his undershirt closed at the sides, drew it past his narrow but muscled shoulders and off his tight, sinewy arms. He threw the undershirt aside.

"Stop it! What are you doing?" Only the blue hood and a vibrant white stone hanging around his neck on a leather thong were left on his upper body.

"I'm going to let you see my body so we can be even. It's penance."

"That's not penance!"

"It's fair," he said as his hands moved to his mismatched brown and grey leggings to untie the tight, bulging codpiece which joined all the pieces together.

"Don't!" Kalea rose again and lurched for him.

He dodged and continued to work through the undressing process.

The codpiece came off.

By the time she had grabbed his wrists and pushed him against the wall, he wore nothing all the way to his knees, where he'd peeled down his leggings. Nothing at all.

She pinned him there and paused long enough to process what had happened. His pulse hammered in his wrists under her grip. He stared at her, as serious as she'd ever seen him. His blue hood remained draped around his shoulders. Smooth, milky skin glowed below it with no hint of body hair anywhere. She saw a stomach with a soft composition of hills and valleys—an artful mingle of bone and muscle. His protruding ribs pumped up and down. And his penis dangled in the open air for Kalea and all to see, plump and colored rosier than the rest of him. A thick vein ran the length of it. A gathered bit of skin pinched together at its tip.

The warm smell of his flesh registered. She caught herself staring at it, trembling delicately with each beat of his heart. Her eyes trailed back up, over all the smooth elven skin, over his intricate ab muscles, his ribs, then stopping at his deep turquoise eyes. He offered no words. He waited instead, rosy lips pouting.

Kalea swallowed, but her mouth had gone dry. "What if someone comes out here?"

He answered in a voice both deep and serious, "That's why I left the blue hood on. Can I have your forgiveness now?"

"Only if you put your clothes back on." She released his wrists and stepped back. She thought to turn her back, but she'd already seen him in great detail.

No hair grew on his legs either, she noted as he pulled the skin-tight leggings back over them. The codpiece dangled off to one side, and he pulled it over and fastened it to the other side, doing a little dance to situate his genitals within. His eyes lingered on her with a dark intensity while he dressed. Not resentful, more like he wanted to know her impression, or if he'd obtained her forgiveness. He next put on the white linen undershirt, overlapped its lapels, and tied them in place at the sides.

Her mouth poised on the edge of speaking as she watched him. She might've offered some words, but they kept getting lost under the rhythm of heartbeats in her ears. She dropped to the stool.

"Are you all right?" he asked, his voice running hard. He pulled the tabard over his head and made sure the blue hood was accessible through the neck hole.

Her voice slid out as a whisper. "Yeah."

His voice. The sound of it, so dark and deep brought back the nervous jitters which wracked her body and carried hot tingles through her belly and flared up her thighs. She tore her eyes away at last, but longed to return them. When she did, his eyes were still boring into her, demanding an answer. He'd never come across so...mature before now. He even seemed taller than before.

"Kalea," he said.

"Yes?"

"I'm sorry." He stood over her, no groveling this time. "I'm sorry a thousand times. Have I redeemed myself?"

Her head bobbed. "I forgive you."

Chapter 11
A Cake for the Courier

Mhina hummed her favorite song, the one about Grandfather's magic bow, as she patted the little cakes together. Gaije and Grandfather called them "power cakes" because the ingredients of oats and other good things gave them energy to practice longer. The tea kettle whistled on the stove under the rustling of the leaves in the wind. Holding her shawl tighter so it wouldn't blow away, she left the cakes on the tray and hurried over to the kettle.

"Mhina, what are you doing?" Mother asked, coming out of the house along the stones embedded in the earth.

"Being a good *faerhain*, Mother." Mhina resumed her humming as she prepared to grab the kettle handle with the rag.

"Hold on! You'll burn your hands. What are we doing here?"

"We're making a lunch for Togha."

"For Togha?"

She handed the rag to Mother. "Yes. I can't bring a lunch to Gaije anymore."

"You can take a lunch to your father as he trains the horses." Mother poured the hot water into the tea kettle Mhina had loaded with the raspberry tea from Mother's collection of canisters.

"But you already do that. You also were the one who made the lunch for Gaije. But now Gaije is gone and Togha and I will be together someday, so why not start now? I also need to learn how to cook. Right now, I only know how to make power cakes. Can you start teaching me already?"

Mother laughed into her long sleeve. "You're a better *farhah* than I was. I didn't learn to cook until I was twelve."

Mhina returned to her cakes and bundled them together in a handkerchief. "Even Grandfather has Anonhet to make his lunch. Togha will have me."

"Well, all right. It can't hurt to make a lunch for Togha. He is one of our *saehgahn*, after all. How do you expect to deliver this tea to him, though? Is he going to sip from the cup as he rides around on his donkey?"

Mhina reached over and took the waterskin off the wall. "I have it all figured out."

Mother's face shifted into a new smile before another laugh erupted.

During the part of the afternoon when Togha usually rode through, Mhina waited for him where the road curved, unable to keep her smile away. A yelling voice and a bray sounded in the distance, and around he came, running with the donkey keeping pace beside him. The corners of his black poncho waved like a flag.

With the waterskin and tied handkerchief hanging off one arm, she raised her other and called, "Togha!"

His mailbag bounced with each of his steps. She raised her voice louder and called again until he finally noticed her. He raised an eyebrow after coming to a halt with his donkey.

"Togha, can you stop for a minute?"

Gritting his teeth, he looked behind him and snapped his head back. "Yeah, let's go down the road farther."

"If you insist. I brought you some lunch. Can you stop and eat it?"

His gorgeous grey eyes finally landed on her things, and he grinned. "As long as we can eat it in a quiet place with no one around."

"Of course, but not my house, my mother will talk over me. If my father is home, he'll talk over her."

Togha nodded rapidly. "Sure, let's go."

In a small clearing off the path from her house, Togha tied Haggis's reins to a tree. Haggis was his donkey's name. Mhina took off her apron, which the females usually wore to protect their treasured *hanbohiks*, and spread it on the ground.

"So," Mhina began, "Gaije went off to the army about a week ago. Has he sent any letters to me yet?"

"Nope." Togha sat beside her spread apron, upon which she laid the handkerchief and untied it to display the cakes. He sighed. "Power cakes, huh?"

"There's tea in this waterskin." She held it high and shook it.

Smirking, he reached out and took the skin.

"So what happened back there?" she asked.

He hurried to swallow the hot tea, seeming surprised at its temperature. "Nothing. I mean…they think I was ogling a *faerhain* too long. The Desteer were yelling at me."

"One of the widows again?"

"Yeah. Can you do me a favor?"

"Of course!"

"Tell 'em you saw the whole thing. I did *not* do whatever they say I did."

Mhina cocked her head, gazing at his beautiful face with raven-black hair shimmering in the shady grove. It had barely grown past his shoulders as of yet. He'd only been *saehgahn* for several months. Only full *saehgahn* could grow their hair past their shoulders.

"But did you do it?" she asked.

He stuffed a cake into his mouth and shook his head, his eyebrows sinking low.

"I believe you, *saehgahn*."

He managed to smile despite the wide bulge of food in his cheek. He was still beautiful. She laid her face on her hand, watching him.

"Togha, why do you always wear that old black poncho?"

"You got a problem with my poncho?"

She shrugged. "No. But I could make you a new one. A bluish one to accentuate your eyes. I'll spin the wool and everything."

He looked over the power cakes to choose which one to eat next. "Well," he began in that short-voiced way of his, "I wear this poncho because it was my father's."

Mhina rounded her mouth, saying, "Ooooh, forgive me, *saehgahn*."

He smiled sweetly. "You know he died right before I was born."

"I do." Her own smile weakened. "I'm sorry you never got to meet your *pawbhen*."

"It's okay."

She continued, "I just met mine, and we're best friends already. I never thought I'd meet him in the first place."

Togha leaned forward, extending his hand when she got a little teary-eyed. "Don't cry. It's nothing to cry about."

She took his hand and squeezed it.

"You don't see me cryin'."

A laugh pushed past her tears. "I would hope not." *Saehgahn* were never supposed to cry, ever. That's why she would do all the crying for him. As his wife. "I'll bet your mother gets lonely since you joined the army."

"Perhaps not, since I've been delivering letters almost every day."

"My grandfather has been checking on her a lot since then. Two days ago, he cleaned her chimney."

Togha leaned back. "Is that so?"

Mhina nodded. "Why doesn't she get a house-guardian to protect her and do those kinds of chores?"

Togha's eyes had spaced out. "Maybe she will."

"Oh, guess what, Togha, I'm gonna learn how to cook," she said.

"That's nice." He reached for another cake.

"So, you know, the lunches will get better. I'm going to bring one to you every day."

He cocked his head. "But sometimes, I don't come near enough." He bit off a bite of the next one.

"I know," she said. "I'll meet you at the front of the village where you usually enter."

His chewing slowed. "Sounds good, but…"

"But what?"

He looked around them even though they were completely alone. "Mhina. There might be some days when I don't come back."

"I know that. Sometimes there aren't letters to deliver here. But I can make your lunch anyway, and if you don't show up, my father will enjoy it."

He shook his head and opened his mouth; instead of talking, he crammed the rest of the cake into it. "It's good," he said with a full mouth.

Chapter 12
Her Dreams

After the incident in the courtyard, Dorhen plagued Kalea's dreams throughout the night, beginning with a return visitation to the incident in which he had taken off his clothes.

She woke up in a sweat before each dream concluded, her heart fluttering. She'd drift off again to find him standing over her, shielding her under a long dark shadow, or standing behind her, his arms embracing her as she fell back into him.

"I'll keep you safe," he whispered into her ear.

She turned to embrace him back. And soon they melded into a tangle, kissing, groping, and exploring. Dorhen acted far less ashamed to bare himself or allow her to touch him than she was at first. And with her shy demeanor at the beginning of each dream, he never pressured her. Their exploration advanced on the terms of her own curiosity. He didn't frighten her like Kemp did either. He remained patient and warm, always promising to protect her.

She gave in to her curiosity each time, wrapping her arms around him, tasting his flesh, breathing his name, and accepting his own attempts to touch and kiss and pin her down under his long, sinewy body. To an onlooker, they must've looked like the couple in the love manual...

The...love manual? Vivene.

"Wait," Kalea whispered into his hair as steam drifted off their bodies. He didn't respond; he was losing himself. "But I'm a...vestal candidate."

They'd stripped to their smallclothes, he in his undershirt and she in her chemise. The forest setting around them danced into a blur. She pushed back on his shoulders before he could take them into the next phase—that daunting phase she'd always wondered about but never imagined she'd experience. She still hadn't. A headache developed, and she groaned.

"What's wrong?" he asked.

"This isn't real." She rubbed her eyes. "I don't know what this is..."

When she opened her eyes again, the trees morphed into lampstands like the ones in town, and the ground became a marble floor like in her convent's sanctum. Some of the spaces between the trees became stained glass windows.

"This doesn't make sense."

Dorhen sat back on his knees, watching her with concern on his face. Steam rose off his skin to mingle with the cool air. His hair hung in damp clumps, the ragged tips brushing his collarbone. The morphing scenery caught his attention too.

She rubbed her face again and…

She woke up in another sweat, back in her bed in the dorm. Dorhen had vanished. That dream again. Every time those dreams took place, she couldn't tell it was illusion. She felt every fingertip he traced across her skin. Even in the waking world, the hot, residual fingerprints stamped her body. The effect was stronger this time: her body ached and her heart pounded. The dream always ended before they could complete the sexual process.

Her eyes widened, staring at the ceiling rafters. Dust glittered in the sunbeams through the windows. Those dreams were too real. Proof of their realness pulsed physically through her. What was happening to her? Whatever it was, it wasn't supposed to be happening.

Within hours, she stood down the hall from the confession booths. Her feet had stopped.

I have to do it! Her foot refused to make another step. Demons. Demons must be holding her feet, preventing them from moving forward. If she couldn't confess, she might go to hell for her unclean thoughts. Even now, awake, when she thought of Dorhen, her heart pounded. To touch him again…his hair…his face.

She clenched her fists. *I'll never be a vestal if I can't get past this illness!* Maybe he really had cast magic on her. What if he carried a contagious disease? He was plagued with unclean thoughts, and now he had passed them to her. She'd never imagined how difficult this condition would be. All her life, she had followed the rules laid before her: keeping faithful, vigilant, and constitutional. Vestals were bid to think of the Creator as soon as they woke up and last before falling asleep.

Now, one particular incident had occurred, and her long-refined discipline failed. All of a sudden, keeping to pure thoughts proved difficult. Dorhen had moved into her mind, made himself her last thought, frolicked with her imagination all night long, and managed to push himself past the Creator in her thoughts upon waking.

A sob squeezed up her throat and the tears started. She leaned her forehead against the wall and cried.

She never made it to the confession booth; instead, she rushed to the sanctum before Father Liam's weekly sermon. His words drifted through her head as weightless and temporary as a firefly's glow. As soon as every syllable ended, she forgot what he'd said.

"I have an announcement to make," Father Liam said after the proper length of pause following the sermon's end. "What I am about to tell you… Don't be alarmed by it. Some changes are underway."

Separated into their grouped pews, the novices and vestals all murmured until Father Liam raised his hand.

"Changes are not a bad thing," he said. "They can be a blessing. As you have seen in your own food portions and possibly around town, a famine is about to happen. As it has always done, the Kingdom of Sharr, its people, and we the Sanctified will carry on with strength and dignity.

"Sometimes the One Creator tests us. He uses us to help people in need. He is filled with pride and joy when He sees how well we come out on the other end of our trials. Some people don't survive, and for those people…the Creator welcomes them with open arms, a feast, music, dancing, and a love we could never ever possibly imagine—until we experience it, of course. We must pray for the dying, that they may be prepared to go to Him."

Kalea's mouth hung open as she listened. Her consciousness did not miss any of these words. Would he talk about what she already heard through Father Superior's door?

He continued, "I thank you, vestals, priests, and novices, for your patience and understanding. The Sanctity of Creation…does what it can, and you all will find that some extra duties will befall you. In the meantime, as I said, a few changes will happen. The bishop is rearranging staff again. And this convent, as it struggles financially, will experience some drastic changes." Father Liam lowered his head and raised it again, his face straight. Not the hint of a blush or the twitch of an eyebrow could mar his serious expression whenever he meant to keep calm. "Some of the novices are being rotated to other places."

The whole novice section roared with a loud flutter of whispering, hand gestures, and girls moving to their seats' edges.

Father Liam raised his hands. "Be calm. You'll all be fine. A visitor from the bishop came to Father Superior the other day. It will be a change, but it's all right."

The girls settled down. Kalea's heart raced. Though she'd heard the news from the earliest rooster, it was all too sudden. In her years living in the convent, she'd always known she'd stay here. Never had word passed around of the vestals or novices being rotated. The personnel, yes, but the actual residents, no! But it was like Father Liam said, they were moving into hard times. His sermons were often riddled with references to people from long ago enduring trials and suffering. The thought of her going through a similar time felt too real.

"If you are scared or concerned, as always, you should pray. Pray often. Sometimes prayer is all we have. You are dismissed."

As the mass of people rose from their seats, mingled a bit, and eventually drifted out of the sanctum, Father Liam took a seat next to Kalea on the pew.

"Your face was so vacant today, Kalea. Is everything all right?"

"Oh, hello, Father," she said, perking up. She'd barely even registered his presence. "Yes, it's fine."

"Are you worried?"

"A little, I must admit. Father, what about our parents? Were they informed?"

He leaned forward and laced his fingers together. "The *novices* will write letters to their parents, I'm sure. As of yet, the *vestals* aren't going anywhere."

"Why are you talking like that?"

A smile crooked his mouth. "I have some pretty wonderful news, if you'd like to hear it."

She gave him the best smile she could. "Yes, I would. What's—what's the news?"

"Well, you've impressed me and the superioress these last few years. You're a model novice, hardworking and faithful. We did a lot of talking, and with your upcoming twentieth birthday, we've written all the documents to expedite you to the promotion of full Sister of Sorrow."

Kalea huffed and waved her hands. "I don't believe it." She almost threw her arms around him, but instead did the more proper gesture of grabbing his hand and squeezing it. "Thank you, Father!"

He chuckled. "I thought you might be pleased. We're making preparations, and your vow ceremony will take place on your birthday. Congratulation on your marriage to the One Creator." He took her hand again.

"Thank you." She slipped her handkerchief out of her pocket and wiped the moisture gathering at her eyes. Its fabric still displayed a faint stain on its corner: Dorhen's blood.

"Are those tears of joy, or are you bothered today?"

"Father... Um, what do you know about elves? Are they wicked?"

"You're worried about the elf you saved last week?" He chuckled again when her face pinched with emotion. "First of all, stop worrying about him. You've been forgiven regardless of the elf's morals and intentions. And to answer your question…" He closed his mouth and studied her. "You know something?"

"Hmm?"

"Long before you were born, when I was young but old enough to have been placed in my own parish, the town guard caught some elves, comparable to the incident you witnessed and disrupted. Except these elves weren't stealing, they were travelers passing through. Two males, a female, and two children."

"They were innocent, and yet they got arrested?"

Father Liam bowed his head. "Attitudes were and are bad, aren't they? Anyway, the female was married to one of the males, I believe, but I didn't know if she had any relation of any sort to the other. A struggle broke out, much like you saw, and the husband took a fatal injury. He lay dead by the end of the havoc."

Kalea's eyes burned and she sniffled.

"The other…*saehgahn*, they call themselves, was bound in ropes while the female and her children complied with being led into the courthouse, where they were locked behind the wooden defendant's grate. They took the remaining male into the stronger, more unpleasant jail under the guardhouse. Curiosity overtook me, but I also considered it my duty as the Creator's servant to investigate these foreigners for myself."

"And what were they…?"

"Well, the male in his damp dungeon cell might as well have been a wild animal. None of us could interpret his language, which hardly mattered because he'd gone mad. He raved and slammed himself against the bars until long bruise lines appeared on his arms and shoulders. The guards gave up on communication and got to teasing and laughing at him instead. By the time I arrived, I couldn't calm him enough to try to make sense of his language."

"How did they treat the female and children?"

"They were in a warmer atmosphere, and they were fed well. She did her best to answer our questions, though we didn't have any resources to decode her language beyond an old *Lehomis* book the local sheriff owned. I convinced the manor lord to send a message to Norr about the elves.

"While we waited, I visited the female and her children daily. The two children were boys, all smiley and curious, both under the age of nine. The younger one couldn't have been older than four. We grasped hands through the wooden bars. I brought carved wooden horses for them to play with. Their mother smiled at our interactions. She always sat several feet to the back, on her knees—an astounding display of discipline I'd never seen from a prisoner before.

"My visitations grew longer. I pointed to the little horses and said the word 'horse.' The children repeated it and memorized it. They promptly pointed to other objects and demanded more words, and I gave them.

"I brought the Creator's Word and read passages to them the next day. They listened and loved it, and surprised me by reciting some passages back to me from memory.

"And then one day, a miraculous thing happened."

"What?" Kalea asked. She hung on his every word, temporarily forgetting about her worries.

"The mother spoke to me in Lightlandic."

"How long had she…?"

"About a month, they'd spent locked up. But she could speak well enough. Brokenly, but I understood her. And her children spoke Lightlandic too."

"What did she say?"

"She asked about the surviving *saehgahn*. I chose the simplest words I could, explaining his condition and his non-compliance. She asked for him to be placed in the same cage as she. I asked why, and then she reached her hand through the bars.

"Feeling a little too enamored for my profession, I took her hand eagerly. She was the most beautiful creature I'd ever seen… She said 'please.' What could I do? I knew they'd never put that wild animal in such a low security cage as hers. I convinced the guard to put her and the children into the damp, dark cell with the *saehgahn*."

His eyes perused the sanctum as he shook his head. "When she descended those steps and into his sight, he went into another rage. She broke away from the guard and ran to the cell, spouting fast Elvish words to the male. They couldn't get the door open fast enough.

"She soothed the male, cooing soft foreign words and stroking his matted hair. He checked her face for any sign of abuse. She showed him only serenity.

"He checked the children next and ordered them all to sit at certain spots within the cell. They obeyed him. The children took their ordered places and sat quietly while fiddling with their little toy horses, and the male planted himself at the front of the cell, now sitting stern and disciplined like the female.

"Let me remind you, he wasn't their husband and father. He had been their neighbor back in their village, the female told us. But because he was male and she female, he took responsibility for their safety."

"Did they get to go home together?"

"They did. All thanks to the clever female, who managed to keep the peace and translate the male's speech, things went more smoothly. In an orderly fashion, they boarded the caged wagon and were ransomed back to their country when the time came."

Kalea waited a moment to let the story sink in. "Your story was… kind of romantic."

"I thought so too."

"So basically, you're telling me…"

"What I've learned from the story is that elves are extremely smart and deeply passionate in their relationships with each other and in their approach to duty. To answer your question, I don't think elves are wicked. I think they're quite honorable. But I also think they are and will be misunderstood. Their customs are a world different from ours; in fact, they're a whole different species."

Father Liam's story replayed in her head all the long day as Kalea went about her routine. Even though Father Liam didn't know her real problem, his story at least soothed her mind a bit so she could function, focusing on something besides Dorhen and her sisters' impending departure.

During one of the prayer hours, she begged the Creator to alleviate her illness and to detach whatever demons had grabbed onto her body to manipulate it. She also asked Him to wipe thoughts of Dorhen from her mind and help her return to thinking about Him instead. Eventually, she'd try to make her way back to the confession booth and rid herself of her unclean thoughts for good. A lot of prayer and contemplation awaited her with her destiny now laid out. She'd take her vows and become a full vestal in merely a week.

For the rest of the day, she avoided going outside.

The next day, Sunday, the young choir group gathered to sing praises to the Creator by evening candlelight. All day, she avoided going outside, instead finding lots of chores to busy herself with inside. She hadn't seen Dorhen since the day he'd stripped naked in front of her, and she'd been practicing a new discipline: whenever the image of his warm body and pleading eyes emerged from the shadows of her consciousness, she recited a short practiced prayer and forced thoughts of Dorhen away in favor of the image of her favorite stained glass window, the one showing the Creator standing on the mountain as light itself. The trick worked, so she could finally focus on her chores. Keeping Dorhen out of her dreams had turned into another problem.

Hundreds of candles illuminated the sanctum in the evening hour, and the pews were filled with the rest of the convent's residents, the full vestals, as well as the townspeople who'd come to worship and hear the expert harmony of the young girls' voices.

Kalea swept her eyes across the crowd. She couldn't spot Kemp, thank the Creator. His absence made it easy to relax and enjoy the music.

Though far from being the best singer, Kalea enjoyed this activity more than most others. When she sang, she often felt the ecstatic presence of the Creator join her side. Tonight, they wore their fine silken choir robes with swirling stylized vines to form the Creator's flower. Their voices rose and fell like waves. Deeper-voiced girls hummed like the Creator's earth, and higher-voiced girls soared and frolicked like plants and animals over the earth's crust. Kalea hit her high notes perfectly tonight. Her head went light with pleasure, never mind her empty stomach after giving away her breakfast and supper again today.

"Glor-rious! Glor-rious!" She croaked on the end of the second word when she saw a person moving about the room behind the audience. Dorhen! He'd gotten in somehow; perhaps he'd merged with the flow of the incoming crowd. And now he'd taken his hood off and traversed the shadowy gallery to the side of the audience. He stopped and leaned against one of the columns supporting the gallery arches, watching her, his mouth partly open.

"Ahhh—ah, ah, ah, ohhhh," she sang her next part.

Dorhen's eyes lingered, unblinking. When he did blink, he did so slowly. He must've been listening for her voice, picking it out from the rest of the singers. He listened for a long time, leaning his head against the column, often closing his eyes.

When the song ended, he slipped through the doorway leading to the kitchen wing. The choir finished their last song, dispersed, and took seats in their pew section to listen to Father Liam's evening sermon.

Before everyone was seated, Kalea snatched a candle off one of the side tables and slipped through that door herself. No telling where Dorhen had gone. Her feet tapped loudly on the slate floor of the dark kitchen. The door to the cellar stood open a crack. She might've missed it if her pace were any more brisk.

She stepped down the small set of steps to the sunken door and went through, closing it behind her. The cellar opened its black atmosphere around her candle.

"Dorhen," she said in a hard voice.

"Yes."

She went around the corner and found a blue glow, like the one he had flashed the first night he chased her through the woods. His necklace, which he'd taken off and hung on a hook on the wall, supplied the glow.

She moved forward until her warm candlelight mingled with his cool blue light.

"Why are you in here?"

He reached into a bag he'd brought along and produced a bundled cloth. Unwrapping it revealed a decent-sized trout skewered on a stick, roasted and still warm. Her stomach roaring, she put the candle on an empty barrel, took the fish, and sank her teeth into its crispy skin, which slid easily off the warm meat.

"I won't share this one with you," he said. "Your cheekbones are starting to stick out and your eyes are darkening. Why weren't you outside today or yesterday?"

"I was busy preparing for the ceremony."

"Well, from now on, make time to come outside. I'll bring you food."

She stopped chewing. "What?"

He pointed to the fish. "Eat. I said I'll bring food from now on. You won't have to worry about starving."

"I was *fasting*!"

"Call it what you want, but you won't be doing any more of it. I caught this in the river earlier, and I'll catch another one tomorrow. I'm going to make sure you eat."

Kalea couldn't argue with him while she so desperately scarfed the food.

"Though I'd prefer you leave with me. We can go to a place where we don't have to worry about food."

She dropped the stick and fish skeleton on the floor and licked her fingers. She leaned back against another empty barrel because the temperature change from the room above this one and her hunger had caused her a dizzy headache.

"Nonetheless," Dorhen went on, "I don't care what you want to do. Stay here if it's so important. I'll stay too, and make sure you eat."

She shook her head. "Dorhen."

"What?"

She swallowed, and he stepped toward her.

"You're going to tell me *no*? You're going to refuse help? You're going to refuse reason? Kalea." He took her wrist, for she was too slow to dodge his hand, as gentle as he was. "I want to take care of you. Let me provide for you... I want to protect you."

Her heart raced.

"Kalea." He moved in closer. "Let me protect you."

He tugged off her novice veil and released her hair. The veil dropped to the floor beside the fish skeleton. "Please," he whispered into her hair and lingered there, breathing, his lips touching her skin. His fingers combed through her hair on both sides of her face.

She trembled all over. He did too. She was sitting on the barrel now, relaxed, her knees apart. Her back arched the moment he laid his hand against it. His warmth radiated through her layers of clothing. His lips trembled when they grazed across her cheek to meet hers. Soft. Kalea groaned, partly in fright, partly in euphoria. He pressed his lips firmer and took her bottom lip between them. Moist.

She put her hands on his shoulders. She could push him away or pull him closer. Before she could decide, he slid both arms around her waist and drew her off the barrel, pressing her against his body. He hugged her and stroked her hair.

"I don't like having these thick walls between us."

She pushed away. She did it before he could decide to take the situation further. On her own feet again, she swayed and braced herself on the barrel. She owed this bout of dizziness to his bold action.

"Get out of here," she groaned.

When she raised her head again, a look of shock stopped him cold and his hands shook, partially raised.

"Did you not like it?"

"No." A sob escaped her throat. "I don't need your protection. I don't need your fish. I don't need *you*! I'm going to be a vestal. That means I'll be married to God!"

He leaned over and took the glowing stone off the wall. He held it out to her, his lips trembling, open as if to speak soon.

"No more gifts!" She struck it, and it skidded across the floor. She let the barrel go and stood on her own feet again. Dorhen had become a shadow form standing in front of the distant blue glow. "If I see you once more, I'll call the guard and tell them about the elf who's harassing the novices!"

She took her candle and left him standing in the dark.

Chapter 13
A Gem for the Jeweler

Roaring waves crashed against rocks unseen down the long drop of the cliff. Daghahen's toes hung off the edge. As brightly as the moon shone, he couldn't see what jagged formations awaited below. The wind rushed around him in front and then hooked around behind as if to tease him. One strong gust, misplaced foot, or second of dizziness would finally end it. His hood blew off his head, and he didn't bother to pull it back on. He'd already seen the stars tonight.

A smile curled on one side of his mouth, and his eyes went to the sword in his hands. He pushed aside the musty wrappings. Highlighting the gleaming surface was no problem for the full moon. Hathrohjilh's peaceful dead face glimmered in cold blue, the shining points dancing along the sculpture with every movement.

"What a strange fellow you are," he said to it. He cast his sight into the endless realm of blue and black with the dark caress of the moon against the ocean and sky. Such a calm, dark scene for such noise roaring below him. He pulled the fresh salty air deep into his lungs.

"Well," he said to the sword. "Time for us to part, you scamp." He held the whole thing out horizontally over the cliff. "Go trouble someone else for a while. We'll meet again on the other side, I'll wager."

Stop, you fool! What are you doing?

Ibex again.

"I'm doing the wiser thing," Daghahen said. "How am I to acquiesce those"—he pointed upward—"with this thing bringing all manner of scoundrels into my hair? I've got a dismal amount of hair left as it is."

Throw it away, and the sorcerers will have it by Sunday.

"Then I'll go with it, so at least my misery can end."

Even if you were so brave, they'd still have it.

Daghahen huffed and his arms dropped to his sides, still holding the sword in one hand. "You're right. It may still kill Lambelhen… I'm no swordsman, though."

He observed the stars again. With each progressing night, their formations tightened. Their latest news was grim, but it didn't involve the sword. The orb containing Wik had been the new item in question.

Somewhere, sometime soon, he'd have another reunion with Lambelhen.

Looking up, he pointed to one of the constellations and then traced his finger in an arc to the horizon opposite the ocean. North, maybe northeast, but only by a smidge. "How far will I have to go?"

Ibex didn't answer. Behind him, a salty old inn was nestled in between the rolling hills of Wistara. He trailed his eyes across the stars again, squinting at the odd way the Wooden Tortoise was poised over the roof of the inn, as if it crawled across the thatch. He'd planned to spare a few coins to sleep there tonight, but something…useful might also be found inside. The major problem with the stars tonight was the upside-down orientation of the Cloven-Headed Man, especially when he had spied it through a hole in a passing cloud during an earlier hour, bringing back the eerie memory of spying Lambelhen through the peephole at his old cabin twenty-two years ago.

Daghahen's ability to collect messages from the stars was extensive, though unwanted. Even their relation to odd things like clouds, birds, and twilight colors communicated messages to him. He didn't want to run into Lambelhen yet. He wasn't ready. And he certainly couldn't encounter him while holding the sword, so he had developed the temptation to get rid of it, or hide it at least. But Ibex was right, as always. It still might play a part. He stepped away from the cliff's edge and refastened the sword to his bag. Then he made the short hike around the little hill to the inn.

Rayna was a whore for the worms now. Chandran traveled alone through the pine forest, though he hung onto her clothes and her wig. He could look for a new thrall while out here chasing that scaly elf. The kingsorcerer hadn't been joking about him being a greased viper. Daghahen had even undone years of Rayna's training within one evening of flirting and kissing. He dodged Chandran's traps several times more along an eastward arc across the Lightlands.

Eventually, Chandran found himself north of the Wistaran peninsula, close to its border, at an inn on the coast which bustled with all manner of travelers. This humble inn didn't have a courtyard or stable, just a large front door with a wanted poster nailed to the wood, leading straight into the dining hall. Chandran stepped past the glaring bouncer at the entrance. The inside bustled, as expected, with the worst riffraff in the area. He strained his eyes for the telltale hood. At least the idiot's choice in fashion helped Chandran narrow down his search criteria.

Over to the side, a musician strummed on a mandolin, making horrid little piercing plucks here and there and missing notes other times. The bystanders started throwing food at him, and he raised a hand, mushy potato caked in his hair, with apologies and "Let me try again" speeches before going back to it. The food throwers laughed and allowed him to continue as if he was worth at least the comedy.

Chandran's armpits and neck moistened with sweat soon after walking in; many bodies heated up the place in addition to the big, blazing hearth in the center of the room. Summer would arrive in a few weeks, which meant an increase in travel due to all the fairs and pilgrimages the warm seasons ushered in, providing better environments in which Daghahen could hide. He might disappear in the crowds that would bleed away afterward.

A cheer escalated in a corner opposite the bad minstrel. Another, louder cheer waved across the crowd. A few seconds later, another arose. Someone must be on a winning streak at cards. Chandran pushed his way over. He could stalk the winner to find the right moment to supplement his own finances. Daghahen had worn him thin for the last week.

At a little round table, two people squared off in a dice game; Highest Score was what they played. Each person rolled two dice simultaneously in cups, then slammed the cups upside down, and the person with the higher number won. The players added more to the pot whenever a tie occurred.

He'd found Daghahen. Some daft young man squared off against the raggedy elf hiding under his hood. He had to be cheating the game. The smirk gracing his thin-lipped mouth flashed each time he tilted his head. Thin strands of silver-blonde hair wisped out of the hood and trailed down his back through its open end.

The players hit another tie, and the crowd raised another loud cheer. Each added another coin, dropped the dice back into the cups, shook, and slammed. Daghahen won again. A huge cheer. He scraped the other man's money across the table toward his growing pile. Another man snatched the chair as soon as the loser rose.

Chandran squeezed closer. Nestled into the corner behind Daghahen's chair sat his travel bag with Lamrhath's sword swaddled in rags, leaning against the wall.

Daghahen added yet another fistful of coins to the pot, and with it dropped little pearl earrings. Other, more elaborate objects were already in the pile, like little marble figurines and a delicate red glass box, empty because it in itself held value.

The new opponent reached into his pocket and pulled out a large gold coin, holding it high between his fingers. He slapped it on the table. A big smile spread across Daghahen's face. His shoulders shook too, though the loud room muffled his laugh. Chandran crossed his arms.

Clack! This opponent slammed his cup loudest of all. He lifted it. The dice showed nine.

"Beat that now," he said, leaning back and waiting.

The elf kept his bony hand flat atop his cup. He rose halfway, waving his free hand with an outstretched index finger. The crowd quieted. His index finger met his lips and they hushed all the way. He sat again and put both hands on his cup. Slowly lifted it. Ten.

The crowd roared, and the opponent's face turned bright red. He stood and cocked his fist, but the men behind him grabbed it and pulled him away from the table. They all laughed, and the next man seated himself on the empty chair.

Daghahen stood up. "Not you," he said and peered across the shoulder-to-shoulder crowd. Chandran dipped his chin to shield his face under his own hood.

Daghahen's pointing finger passed over many faces. He couldn't help but think of one of the constellations he'd soon follow, the Pointing Young Man. He hadn't been "young" for centuries, but a powerful connection tethered him to that constellation.

He settled his pointing finger on a man with dark hair and a scruffy face who must've been forty years old at least. Daghahen had spotted him as soon as he approached the table to watch the spectacle, lugging a large, box-shaped thing upon his back under his cloak. The accessory made the man appear comically like…a turtle.

The man's smile dropped as he uncrossed his arms and pointed to his own chest. "Me?"

Daghahen waved him over, and the crowd parted for him.

"I don't have much, old man," he said.

"I'm sure you have something."

The scruffy man sat down and ogled the glittering pot of spoils. He dug through his pockets. "Why not?" He sighed and slapped four silvers and six coppers onto the table.

"There ya go, lad."

They both dropped the dice into the leather cups and shook.

Clack! The scruffy man peeked and revealed his number, grimacing. He'd rolled four.

Daghahen lifted his cup with a gripping slowness.

Two. A round of sweeping hisses went over the crowd before they cheered and rattled the scruffy man's chair. Some playful slaps to his head disarrayed his hair. He checked again.

"Really?" He let out a laugh. "I don't believe it, no stinkin' way!" He laughed again as he reached over to scoop Daghahen's pile over to his side.

Daghahen crossed his wrists on the table, a smile pasted on his face.

"Are you okay, old man?" his opponent asked, leaning forward and trying to see under his hood.

"Of course."

"Are you..." The scruffy man lowered his voice. "Are you an *elf*?"

He made a slight laugh. "Now, now, that's not polite, lad."

"You are," the scruffy man whispered. "What tricks are you playing here?"

"No tricks. I lost it all, didn't I?"

"Yeah."

"Remember now, *mercy*." He bowed his head and ran a finger across the front of his hood. He had already tried and failed to remove the word from the hood's leather surface by scraping a rock over it. The stubborn stains appeared a bit weathered now, but the word remained as legible as always. Daghahen was still a mercyman.

"Whatever, old man."

Daghahen motioned to the cups on the table. "Let's try again. Let me redeem myself a bit so I can pay for a room."

"I don't know..."

Daghahen put up his two hands, palms forward, showing his filthy woolen gloves with the fingers cut off. "Don't bet it all, please, sir. Enough for a room will be fine for me."

"Fine by me." The scruffy man picked out a silver half-dendrea and a few coppers. He slid the coins to the center of the table.

Daghahen eyed them while scratching his chin, faking his hesitation. "Hmm."

"What, not enough for you, old man? It's more than enough for a room."

"No, I'm just thinkin', how 'bout this?" He leaned way over to his grimy, mud-spattered travel pack against the wall and untied the sword. He unwound its bindings, revealing the pristine, shiny surface to entice the man. He was sure to expose the long rain guard between the blade and crossguard, showing the sculpted naked figure.

The scruffy man snorted. "What am I looking at? An elven sex token?"

He placed the sword on the table. "Elves don't have sex tokens, young man. This is a terribly powerful *saehgahn* who died long ago."

"You think I wanna see his cock 'n' balls every time I get into a fight?" The man laughed, and those around him laughed, too.

Daghahen gave a toothy grin. "I said he's dead. We aren't born with any clothes and can take nothing to the afterlife with us either, now can we?"

The scruffy man shrugged. "Looks expensive. And it's a bit short, even though it has the drooping crossguard of a claymore. Is this ornamental or what?"

"No, it's a fine sword for fighting, light and balanced. And it has special secrets to share with you, if you have the patience to unlock them. Put your ear here…" Daghahen leaned over and hovered his ear over the nude figure's face. "Listen carefully, and he might whisper to you. What's your name?"

The scruffy man gawked at him for several moments before he shook himself out of his trance. "Bowaen. I'm a jeweler, and also the best swordsman in Gaulice." He held out his hand, but Daghahen ignored it.

"Bowaen," he said, "better not let anyone take this from you. Don't let anyone buy it from you either. It's more valuable than money."

"Why would you bet it?"

"I need a room. I'm so sick of sleeping on the ground." He told only half the truth. In reality, he hated the stars outside so much, one hundred roofs to separate him from them would be too little.

"Okay. You're crazy, but okay."

Bowaen dropped his dice into the cup, and Daghahen did the same. He had switched to his special dice, weighted to show their lowest number, for this opponent.

The cups rattled. *Clack!*

Snake eyes. Bowaen deflated in his seat.

Daghahen slammed his cup down and lifted it with flourishing hands. Two. A tie. The whole room fell silent. He shrugged.

Bowaen grabbed a few more coins off his pile of winnings and added them to the pot; Daghahen added three coppers.

They rolled. *Slam, slam!*

Bowaen rolled a three.

Daghahen raised a finger and did another flourish with his arm to excite the audience. Lifted his cup. Two.

The crowd roared, some tousling Bowaen's hair while others aimed laughs and jeers at Daghahen. He stood and leaned over to collect his pack.

After scooping up his winnings and tying the sword to his belt, Bowaen caught Daghahen's arm before he could walk away. "Get your room." He placed a few silver dendrea in Daghahen's hand.

Daghahen smiled, a genuine smile. "Bless you, lad."

Chandran stalked closer, squeezing a hidden knife within his pocket. He would have enough time to stab one of them; it should probably be Daghahen to ensure he no longer foiled Chandran's plans. This new man might be easier to kill later with the elf out of the way.

The mercy hood whipped off, throwing Daghahen's secret into the open air. Chandran froze. The man who had lost the large gold coin had returned with the bouncer and grabbed Daghahen's hood. The crowd began shouting and pointing.

"See? I knew it! It's a damned bloody elf! He must've been cheating!"

The old elf's thin hair couldn't hide his large, pointed ears. Even after enjoying quite a thrilling game of dice, the crowd yelled and pelted bread ends and greasy bones at him.

"What're you doing here, elf?" the bouncer demanded with a strong hand on his shoulder. Chandran and Bowaen both stayed back and watched.

Daghahen shifted his voice remarkably into that of a feeble old character. "Only what the rest of these good folk are here to do, sir."

"I'm afraid you can't stay here." The bouncer yanked him away, dragging him through the bustle toward the cool night air outside the open door.

Chandran kept his feet planted and his eyes on Bowaen. Though Daghahen was a terrible nuisance, the sword was what he'd been sent to retrieve. Chandran was now tasked with finding a way to get it from its new owner by whatever means, sneaky or murderous.

Chapter 14
Her Vow

The dreams hadn't stopped. Kalea took a walk through the forest in her chemise, without shoes. She walked until the soft light of dawn illuminated the mist and dew. The pine needles prickled her feet with a sensation all too real, along with the wet, shimmering walls passing over her in the low, drifting cloud.

She walked until she found Dorhen, huddled against a tree in a ball of somber misery. She placed her shaky hand on his shoulder. She must've broken his heart last night with her cruel stupidity.

His dull eyes acknowledged her. They didn't catch the dim light like they usually did. He didn't smile either. He didn't speak. A frown drew his face long. His eyelid rims might've been reddened, but it was hard to tell for sure in the cloudy morning light.

She fell on him, her arms wrapping around him, her chin resting on his shoulder. He didn't hug back.

"Why are you torturing me every night?"

She opened her mouth for a counterquestion and a sob burst out before the words, "Oh, Dorhen!"

She put her hand on his head. She knew the texture of his hair under her hand from the dreams alone. She'd never ventured to touch him on her own in the waking world, not even last night when he had given her the perfect opportunity.

"I…" She pulled back to look at his face.

His frown persisted. He *scowled* at her.

"I can't do it." She stroked the side of his face, handsome as ever, regardless of his anger. Especially while angry. As an elf, he didn't have the ability to grow a beard, but he had hair resembling soft, smooth sideburns growing along his face in front of his ears. She couldn't control her quivering lips, but she had important things to tell him. Maybe her body language could speak for her.

She kissed him. He didn't kiss back.

"You don't understand the struggle I have," she said, forcing the words out. "I want to tell you…"

She kissed him again. He gradually gave in and kissed her back. And to the ground they went again like in the dreams. He lay on the ground and allowed her to lean over and pull his undershirt open to trail kisses down his neck and chest. The smell of his skin, she'd missed it.

"What do you want from me?" he asked in the same lifeless voice, willing to partake, yet playing a dead weight.

"I'm sorry," she said, taking her lips off his navel. "If we could talk…" She moved to resume her task but popped her head up again. Lying flat with his arms out to the sides, he stared at the tree canopy. "Do you not want to…?"

"It's not about my wanting. I live to serve you. So take what you want."

"Dorhen." Her hand was poised on his codpiece laces, eager to rip them open like he had let her do in the dreams. The bulge under her hand hardened, which she had been fascinated to see in those dreams.

She took her hand away. Isn't this what he wanted? The trees around them crumbled like sand sculptures. The light faded. Dorhen faded.

She woke up. Another dream? In fact, in the recent strange dreams, she awakened each time at the moment when something confused her, usually the real-yet-surreal feeling of the situation. As always, her blood roared and tingled with yearning. She would remember the dream and its acute sensory detail for a good long time, but like normal dreams they'd fade.

I have to talk to him.

She got out of bed, dressed, and put on her novice's veil.

"Good morning, Kalea!" Joy said, walking by with some extra strength in her gait.

"Good morning." Kalea gawked at her confident stroll out the door. Giving up her food to Joy at supper must've been paying off. Kalea's balance and energy had also returned today…thanks to Dorhen, who'd been sweet enough to catch and cook that fish for her.

She beat her sisters to the kitchen for breakfast, like she had been doing for a few days, and grabbed her own bowl of oats before it could be served. She divided her portion between Joy and Rose's bowls and washed her own. Skipping breakfast, she went straight outside to do the laundry.

At the stream, she scrubbed the garments, beat them with her bat, and frequently lifted her eyes to scan the forest for Dorhen. Would he bring another fish?

"Dorhen," she said after an hour. "Are you there?" No answer. "Dorhen!" Her voice echoed a long way through the trees.

A new kind of nausea churned her stomach as she returned to her work. Her scrubbing became absentminded and her arm weakened while using the washing bat. The chore of scanning the stretch of thin forest for Dorhen distracted her from her real duty. He wasn't there. No feelings of being watched either.

Back in the courtyard, she hung the laundry as Sister Gani chatted away about Kalea's upcoming vow ceremony. With the old woman's voice babbling on and on in the background, she watched the corners and shadows for signs of him.

"I'm gonna keep washing clothes," she said when Sister Gani asked what her area of expertise would be as a full Sister of Sorrow. A lot of options would be laid before her. If she favored singing, she could join the full sisters' choir group. Or she could teach reading, writing, and religion to the children in Tintilly. She could learn how to paint and add fantastic murals to their convent. "Washing is what I do best."

She slogged off toward the study hall, where she practiced her writing. She sat at the long table amongst several full vestals who studied and wrote, and opened her prayer book beside her journal to copy the texts. She absentmindedly dipped her quill into the inkwell and failed to run the tip over the edge to eliminate excess ink. Terrible-looking pools of ink ran from the quill here and there, and some of the blotches ran together, obscuring the sentences into gibberish dancing around under her stare.

She blinked her eyes, and the movement stopped, leaving her with blotted shapes so wet they ran and mingled with each other until a face appeared, composed from the dark and light areas of the mess she'd made. The face smiled at her.

She slammed the book closed, splattering dots of ink onto the table. About twenty veiled heads popped up and stern old faces turned to glare at her.

"Sorry, sisters," Kalea said, "my hand slipped." The veiled heads bowed again over their own prayer books.

An hour later, she stood in the seamstress's room getting measured for her official habit.

"I'll do the best I can," the sister who specialized in sewing said. "Your ceremony has been ordered at such short notice. No guarantees it'll be finished in time, but at least you'll have it by the end of the..."

Kalea stared out the window with her arms held out to the sides. Dorhen had lain on the ground in the same pose in her dream this morning, his face so drawn and resigned.

Take what you want.

"Kalea!"

She jumped. "Yes?"

"Put your arms down."

"Oh." She dropped them.

"I also said there might be an extra habit in the closet you can take. I'm sure it's too big, though. Put it on and I'll pin it on you."

"Yes, ma'am."

She managed not to dream about him the next night. And when she rushed out to the stream with her loaded basket, calling for him, he didn't show himself. He didn't show in the courtyard either; he remained absent during all the long hours she spent alone. She went to supper, relinquished her food, prayed, and retired to bed.

No dreams. She woke up. Prayed. Relinquished her breakfast. Went to the stream with a light load against Sister Gani's protests that there was no need, and spent the time alone. Dorhen didn't come. She returned. Relinquished her supper—though she did take a bite because by now she felt faint off and on. Prayed. Fell asleep.

The third day since last seeing Dorhen. She awoke. Prayed. Washed clothes. Prayed. Gave up her supper. And then the time came to rehearse her rituals.

"Are you listening?" Father Liam asked.

"Hmm?"

"Are you listening, Kalea?"

"Sorry. Yes. What were you saying?"

He motioned to a cushion they'd set before the altar. "You'll sit here all day tomorrow in contemplation, and the ceremony will happen at dusk. Let's go over your speech…"

After rehearsal, Kalea crept down to the cellar to see if Dorhen lurked around there. Once again, she brought a candle swiped from the One Creator's altar to see in the dense underground shadow. Her fish bones still littered the floor, pillaged by ants, some of which continued the feast, but he must've collected his glowing stone necklace before leaving, because she found no sign of it near the wall racks where it had skidded after she rudely batted it out of his hand.

"Dorhen," she whispered. It was worth a try. She waited in the silence for his voice or any indication of movement. A breath, or clothing shifting.

Nothing. Nothing except her own heartbeat.

What have I done? He's really gone this time. She put the candle down and stood by the barrel. The place where he kissed her. Their first kiss.

She hugged herself; she hadn't thought to bring a cloak to cover her arms.

"Dorhen," she whispered again, "I'm sorry." She closed her eyes and kept them closed, as if he'd appear at her will whenever she opened them again. "I changed my mind. I don't want to be a vestal… I want to be a woman."

She opened her eyes again slowly. The illuminated floor around her stayed empty. No shadows to hint at someone joining her in her orb of light. No blue light appeared to merge with hers.

She pulled the veil off her head. "I mean it." She untied her belt and dropped it to the floor, followed by her grey, open-sided novice tabard. "Would you like me to go further?"

She sat on the barrel and waited. She leaned back on her hands and opened her knees. "You're a stubborn boy, you know that?" She closed her eyes again. "I wouldn't have come here if I wasn't positive you'd follow me…that you've been stalking me."

She opened her eyes again. Still alone. She closed her mouth and listened. She listened as hard as she could.

Clack-clatter!

She jumped and shrieked. A rat ran along the wall in the faint outskirts of her candlelight. She huffed out the air she'd sucked in.

Back upstairs, Kalea sat in the bathtub and closed her eyes as a handful of other novices recited prayers over her in honor of her becoming a vestal. The bath had been prepared for this special occasion with spices like jasmine and clover, and dried rose petals floated on the water. Several extra candles lit the room, standing tall and stiff like the pine forest outside.

Sister Scupley led the ritual, reciting certain lines and periodically dipping a cup in a bowl of blessed water to pour over Kalea's head. A shock of cold hit her scalp and separated into various cold streams on the way down, contrasting with the steamy water engulfing her body. Whenever needed, Kalea added her own words to the chanting, having memorized them for the last two days.

After the chanting, she stood up in the bath and allowed two other novices to rub fragrant, sacred oils all over her body: a cleansing ritual to prepare her for her symbolic marriage to the One Creator. During the oiling process, she recited more lines she'd practiced. The lines were in an ancient language. For the most part, she had no idea what she was saying except for a vague impression after reading a translation earlier.

The words were still drivel spilling out of her mouth.

Her eyes kept flicking to the window: the one Dorhen had confessed to peeping through to watch her bathe last week. Glancing at the window turned to staring during her recital. The other novices' hands slicked across her body, around her legs and over her breasts. The window. She settled her eyes there.

When they finished that portion of the ritual, she lowered back into the tub and dunked her head. The novices finished their chanting with an *amen* and a curtsey, then filed out of the room one by one. Sister Scupley left first, and Joy hung around last to help her dry off. Kalea didn't speak to Joy after the chanting ended. Joy knew, like they all did, about this sacred ritual in which Kalea should be in deep contemplation. Better if they didn't talk. On a normal evening, Joy would've sensed her mood, and Kalea might've spilled all of her pent-up thoughts and confusions at the other girl's prodding.

As Joy rubbed her with the towel, Kalea focused on the window again. The black glass showed reflected candlelight and her own naked body in a foggy, warped abstraction; nonetheless, she pierced it with her eyes, trying to send a silent message to whoever might be looking through from the other side.

After the bathing ritual, she tucked herself into bed and spent a long while awake in the dark. Her last night in the novices' dorm. Her last night as a novice. Her last night to change her mind. Where would she go if she did change her mind? Nowhere. She couldn't go back to her parents—they were the ones who'd decided to put her in here. She was *supposed* to take the vows. Her destiny had been laid out for her.

She closed her eyes and couldn't keep the images of Dorhen away. How casually he'd strolled into her life and wrecked everything. And now, on the night before her initiation, the One Creator turned out to be the last person she could focus on. If she concentrated hard enough, could she see Dorhen in another dream? The thought of trying made her stomach twist into knots. It was wrong. She owed the Creator quite a bloody lashing to her back for those lustful dreams.

She woke up at the first grey light of dawn through the window, before Sister Scupley entered with the bell that shouted her name. A light rain pattered on the windows. The other novices helped her dress in a white ceremonial gown with layers of robes. They combed her hair and put a lace veil over her head.

Enswathed in a sea of veils, all neat and pristine underneath, she and a handful of novices walked, procession-like, into the sanctum, where she took her place on the cushion. The novices stretched out a long, white, silken sheet and put it over her head; its mass engulfed her. Today, she'd sit underneath it all day long until the hour of her vows arrived.

Beyond the silken outer veil's film, the novices split into two groups and proceeded down each side of the room, lighting all the candles in the sanctum. Afterward, they left her alone in there. They'd check on her regularly, but for today they moved all prayer and sermon sessions to another space.

Kalea sat alone with the rain sounds, waiting for her god. A cool grey light from the outside mingled with the warm orange glow of the candles. She had skipped breakfast and gone straight to preparing herself for the ceremony. At least today, the cook would prepare a nice plate of food as a symbolic wedding meal she'd eat alone, in the spiritual presence of the Creator. Eating should rejuvenate her a bit. In the meantime, she'd sit here for ten hours, keeping as still and straight as possible. She could shift her position once in a while, but the trial would be murder on her joints and muscles nonetheless. The best way to handle it was to meditate, to lose track of time.

She closed her eyes and listened for Dorhen, like she had in the cellar last night. It was difficult to believe he'd left her, just like that… Could she blame him? Thinking about it made her choke up, so she thought about the pleasant dreams with him instead. Those thoughts made her body speak back.

She opened her eyes. In addition to listening, she could watch for a glimpse of him. Filling her eyes with other things might help to alleviate the erotic thoughts persisting on plaguing her mind.

An hour…or two hours passed before the side door clicked and opened. Soft footsteps tapped toward her.

Joy leaned into her sight and whispered, "Do you need any water?"

"No, thank you," Kalea whispered back.

"All right. I'll be back in another two hours. I'm jealous, I'll have you know." Kalea smiled in reaction to Joy's giggle as she practically pranced away.

The rain pattered—the first rain in about two months. Maybe it would help alleviate the famine. The sanctum glowed with soft orange candlelight wavering against the blue morning haze from the windows. This place shriveled in comparison to the cathedral in Carridax she'd visited at age fourteen when Father Liam had taken the girls on a pilgrimage, but it boasted its own pleasant and simple charm. The thick wooden cruck beams holding up the ceiling were carved with clover-shaped holes, and the stained glass windows were colorful and happy on a sunny day. She used to think she could live the rest of her life here, visiting this room daily…in the past.

She focused hard on the room, widening her awareness for any hint at all of an invisible guest. Minutes passed. Thirty of them. Sixty of them. Who knew how many? She watched.

Joy returned. "Two hour check. Would you like a break?" She meant a trip to the garderobe.

"Yes, please."

Kalea's bones creaked as she worked up to her feet. Joy drew the outer veil off her head, folding it over. Kalea stretched out her legs and flexed as many joints as she could remember she had. Joy helped her all the way through her break. She accepted a drink of water, and Joy covered her again when they returned to the altar. Back to meditation.

Kalea scanned the room, opening her senses and her most acute visual awareness. *Where are you? Come back already, you stubborn elf.*

She focused as best she could through the thin silk. Along the left wall, the candle flames bowed over and whipped back as if someone walked swiftly past. She froze. Could it be him? It might've been a draft, though all day the candles had been calm. It was today's first anomaly in their behavior. It had to be him!

"Dorhen," she whispered, "if that's you, please let me know." She waited. No sign came. "I have to talk to you…"

She listened for any change in the vibrations. The rain tapping against the windows and pattering down on the roof filled the silence, covering any mild scuff or breath. Why did the rain choose to fall on a day like this?

"I'm sorry, Dorhen. I don't know if you were in the cellar listening to me last night. I'm sorry. I'm sorry I've been cruel to you. I'm sorry I turned away your generosity." She bit her lip before taking a deep, shaky breath. "I've been having dreams about you. In the dreams, we came close to making love. This happened two nights in a row and several times on the first night. I was afraid of the concept of…making love. But I'm not anymore, thanks to you."

She sniffled. *I'm telling such intimate thoughts to thin air.*

"You saw how I was attacked that day. You saved me. I didn't know why you cared, since you were a stranger. Nonetheless, the attack made me afraid of you too. I thought you'd try to take advantage of me in a similar way, and that would be a problem for my process of becoming a vestal. I have to be a virgin to be a Sister of Sorrow. I was scared to trust you, that's all. But you know what?"

She surveyed the room, searching for any more waving candle flames.

"I was told by other people to become a Sister of Sorrow. *They* chose my destiny, not me. And I thought it was the best thing for me too. I never thought I could be happy as a wife, and also be a faithful servant of the Creator. I can." She wiped her leaky eyes on her long sleeve.

"I love you, Dorhen... It's more than that: I want you for myself. It's a selfish and willful plight. Those dreams I had of us carrying on—I loved them. I want you. I no longer want to be a vestal. I want to teach you more about reading. I want you to catch fish for me and protect me. If you could please...come back, I'll gladly walk out of here with you. Please."

A sob escaped her throat and she swallowed the rest of them, wiping her eyes on her sleeve again. "If you're punishing me, I deserve it. I deserve whatever I get."

Keeping count of the hours proved too hard on such a dark, rainy day. Eventually, the windows darkened and the rain gained in weight.

If Dorhen indeed spied on her and listened to her speech, he didn't care. He must be rejecting her pleas. He probably wasn't around anymore; he would be a long way down the road now, leaving her where she belonged, in the choking dust of his past.

There was no blaming him for leaving her; she'd acted so neurotically toward him all these days. She genuinely was crazy. She belonged in here. Hopefully, her dreams of him would continue through the years, to help her through her difficult life of loneliness. A suffering kind of life, masked under the honorable title of celibacy.

When the hour of her vow ceremony arrived, cold sweat beaded under her layers of silk. Her eyes darted around the sanctum for an elf who'd rescue her from her marriage to the One Creator. An imaginary elf. Maybe she'd imagined him the whole time due to her mental illness. The rain pounded, and thunder added to the miserable mix. Her hollow stomach groaned. She grew woozy. When it came time to give her speech, the words were lost in the hurricane that used to be her mind.

"My honor...is...solely—I will honor You with all my heart, um..." And the rest of the speech sounded about the same. Once in a while, Father Liam whispered words to help her along, his eyes wide and his lips parted, awaiting every word she could manage to push out. She made an absolute fool of herself.

When she finally said the last word, "amen," she sighed and fell to the floor for a low bow to the Creator, as rehearsed. She crawled up the little steps to the altar's dais and kissed the floor sectioned off by a rope around the altar. This space was accessible for the faithful to tend the altar without stepping past the rope onto an exquisite woven rug reserved to be trod upon by the Creator Himself. Tears dampened her cheeks by now. She let them out without being too mortified because crying in the presence of the One Creator was a normal thing to do.

She crawled backward to her designated spot and stood again so Father Liam could wrap the official cincture around her hips, a woven belt with a silver-plated Creator's flower medallion at the front.

Next, he turned around and took her official vestal's veil off the little table of objects and held it over her head. "On this sacred evening," Father Liam recited over a sharp crash of thunder, "I hereby announce Kalea Thridmill, by honor of the One Creator and His—"

A crash boomed through the sanctum. The novices screamed and scattered. Kalea fell during the raucous tremor. The ceiling caved in, roaring in a barrage of slate shingles, wood, and glass from the skylight. She saw each piece suspended like a messy mobile, frozen in time for a second before disappearing. Darkness followed as the wind and rain snuffed out all the candles. A cold, wet splash doused her robes.

"Everyone be calm!" Father Liam shouted. "Be still!"

In her starving state, the excitement made Kalea dizzy again. Her chest rose and fell uncontrollably. Someone tripped over her feet and screamed in pain—a novice. All the novices in the convent must've been shrieking.

Sister Scupley commanded, "Calm!" and some of the voices finally hushed.

One of the older vestals came through the door from the kitchen with a lantern. The new light revealed a gaping hole in the ceiling and rain pounding over the pile of rubble which had once been the roof and part of the skylight. The rain pouring in filled the area with mist, soaking Kalea's clothes. Sharp sounds marked pieces of glass falling from above.

"Is anyone hurt?" Father Liam called. "If someone is on the floor, make sure they're all right." He stepped over to Kalea. "How about you, Kalea? Are you hurt?"

"No. I don't think so."

He took her arm and pulled her up. Her weak hands twitched and trembled. "That damn roof has needed service for a while, but we haven't had the funds!" When she stood on her own, he made his way to the raining pile of rubble. "Bring the light!"

Kalea moved closer too, dragging her dress over the broken glass and wrecked pews. The vestal with the lantern went about, helping other women to relight some of the candles.

"Bring some light! Hurry!" Father Liam dug through the wreckage, overturning heavy ceiling beams. "Oh, dear Creator."

"What is it?" Kalea asked, stretching her neck after her dress snagged, ignoring the ripping sounds as she pulled it.

"Oh no, please, Creator." Father Liam's voice dipped low.

As Kalea drew closer and the candles gathered together at the rubble, Father Liam knelt and stroked the hair of a novice who had been unfortunate enough to be standing too close to the collapse.

Joy.

He wiped her soaked hair away from her face. She stared into oblivion.

Kalea gasped and covered her mouth. "Oh, please." Her voice shook. She gnashed her teeth and soon put a wad of her sleeve between them. "Is she…?"

Father Liam was already reciting death rites over Joy with his hand on her forehead.

"Amen." He closed her eyelids.

Chapter 15
Her Choice

Kalea's initiation ceremony had turned into Joy's last rites. With the sanctum ruined, they set up a bier in one of the study halls. The vestals cleaned and anointed Joy's body. They didn't ask Kalea, the newest vestal, to participate, to which she sighed in relief and stood back to watch helplessly as they finished Joy's presentation. Kalea's best friend lay in repose for now, and tomorrow would begin the funeral arrangements.

Today, Kalea donned her official vestal's habit; the seamstress-vestal had managed to finish it in time. At the breakfast table, she sat with Rose, who laid her head on Kalea's shoulder. She could barely tell Rose was there from under all those layers: a long veil and wimple, a gown and scapular, and a triangular red mantle over her shoulders bearing the symbol of their faith.

In the flurry of Joy's death, the focus had shifted away from Kalea's initiation and a couple of her rituals were postponed, so for now her hair hid under her headpieces. Though Father Liam had informed her she was official, she had yet to do the shearing ceremony to cut all of her hair off. She wouldn't be in a hurry to do that ceremony anyway.

After folding a stack of sheets in a laundry room devoid of Joy's chatter—her stool left empty and cold in the corner—Kalea did her rounds, delivering them to their various cells. Father Liam was stuffing his spare linens into a trunk when she entered his cell.

"Father," Kalea said. "Are you going away on business again?"

His eyes snapped to her and he gave a weak smile. "Kalea," he said. "I didn't hear you come in."

"When will you be back?" She placed the linen stack on his bed.

"I have to tell you something." She shook her head. "We personnel, we're not set in place permanently. You know that very well. I even announced the personnel rotation."

"You're leaving?" *No. Not now. He can't leave now.* "You didn't specifically say *you* were leaving!"

Father Liam shook his head and placed a stack of books in the trunk. "This is how things are. You're twenty years old now. You can make it without me."

"But I can't… But you can't leave so suddenly."

"It's not that I'm leaving; I'm being rotated to a parish in Sharr."

"In Sharr!"

He shushed her. "I'll write to you biweekly."

"Father."

He took his attention off his packing and placed his hands on her shoulders. "Listen to me. Although you still need a few rituals to complete your confirmation, you must wear the habit anyway. And I've got your new cell all prepared for you in the east building. I want you to sleep in it tonight. Things change. It's the way of the world, of life. Now Joy is gone, and I will be too. And you, too, will be gone, off to your new cell, to your new life as a Sister of Sorrow. It's a new chapter, nothing to fear or mourn."

Kalea sniffled and forced back the tears. "If you say so."

"All right." He turned back to his task. "Go on and take a look at your cell. I made sure you got a good one. And I put some of my books in there to start your collection."

A short, weepy laugh burst from her throat. "Thank you, Father."

"Don't mention it."

Kalea put off her trip to the stream to watch as Father Liam loaded his trunk onto the little hired cart and sat next to the driver. With a whip of the reins, the spotted white horse jolted forward. Father Liam twisted around to wave at Kalea and most of the other convent residents. As soon as they disappeared behind a bend of shrubs and pine trees, Kalea rushed back inside, swallowing repeatedly to loosen her throat, and grabbed her shoulder basket full of dirty linens.

At the stream, she opened up the basket and dropped the bloody rags used to clean Joy's body last night into the cold pool of water within the piled stones. Watching them float around in the dammed water's gentle flow, she let her gaze drift across the dancing sunlight on the water's surface. No faces today. She wouldn't look for Dorhen, though. If he'd listened to her speech yesterday, he must not have cared.

As the bloody rags swirled, she took a step back. Another. Then her feet moved in consecutive steps. She walked. She followed the river. Her head felt numb. When the stream grew shallow, she traversed the wet stones and meandered into the forest. Her mind remained devoid of any thought. She lost most feeling in her body too.

A thin mist drifted through the forest. After yesterday's rain, the world had withered into a soggy grey rot. Once in a while, a sparrow song whistled in the distance to bring her back to reality.

Am I still walking? Or am I dreaming again?

Though she should stop and try to retrace her steps, she couldn't. Her feet kept moving, crunching over the dead pine needles. The light expanded in the distance. A clearing? The trees thinned out as she drew near it. It wasn't a clearing, it was a cliff, or at least a minor drop-off after a patch of fresh spring grass.

Right there in such an odd place stood a well, an old one. Nowhere in sight, here or down the cliff, was any house or settlement to make use of the well. It must've been ancient, outlasting even the remnants of the settlement that had once used it.

Not much could be seen from here. Though the cliff stood tall, the giant pine trees on the ground below surpassed its height. Kalea approached the well and placed her hands on the cold, damp stones. It no longer had a roof. Its water level reached high, probably from rainwater collected over centuries of clogged brush.

A cold gust of air drifted up and caressed her face. She reached for her veil and pulled it off, followed by her wimple, to enjoy the cool air. Her hair tumbled down around her shoulders. She watched the surface of the water again.

You should ask him what he wants, Dorhen had said about Arius Medallus.

"I could use some guidance now," she whispered.

The well water showed nothing beyond her reflection in its still, mercurial surface. The whole forest was calm and silent, as if resting. No wind stirred the trees, and the wisps of mist dancing with each other made for the only movement in the atmosphere. That same sparrow whistled once in a while, the solitary sound the forest offered.

When the stone well made her hands cold, she took them away to rub them, glancing up to catch someone standing in the forest.

"Dorhen?"

The first bit of a smile in a long time touched her lips, though tears gathered in her eyes. She ran to him.

He kept his arms by his sides and a frown on his face regardless of how eagerly she ran, stumbling over a root and spreading her arms. He took a step back before she reached him, and she threw her arms around his middle before he could slink away.

"Where've you been?" She'd lost Joy and Father Liam, but maybe she hadn't lost Dorhen yet. Though she'd turned him away several times, snapped at him, and lectured him, she had grown accustomed to his presence, invisible or not.

His arms dangled over hers. He hadn't said anything yet.

"What's the matter?" she asked.

"I'm afraid."

She pulled away. "Why?"

"Because I don't know if you're going to be cruel again."

She raised her hands. "I'm sorry for the way I treated you. I truly am. Where've you been?"

"I went away as you ordered."

"But you were so persistent about meeting and befriending me."

"And I overstepped myself, causing you to lash out. Which you were right to do."

She reached out and took his hand. It shook. "I wasn't right. I overreacted—several times. I want to talk. I have much, *much* to say!" She closed her mouth and regarded him. "If you're afraid of me, why are you here now? Why did I not see you in the convent?"

"I stayed out of the convent because it's your domain, and you didn't like me there. I'm here now because I thought it'd make sense to say goodbye."

"Oh." She embraced him again and laid her head on his chest. "Dorhen, I've needed you. Awful things have…" His heart hammered under her ear. "A horrible accident…"

"Are you married to God yet?"

She lifted her head. "Hmm?"

"You're dressed different. Are you off-limits yet?"

She squeezed tighter around his torso. "That's what I want to talk about."

"So, are you?"

"Yes. But I'm changing my mind." He peeled her arms off himself. "What's the matter?"

He yanked his face away from hers, and she moved around to catch his eyes again. "The matter is you're off-limits now."

"I'm not!"

He stormed over to the well and threw his attention into it. She joined him by his side. "I don't know how to explain my problem. But what the hell, you get mad at me at the drop of a leaf anyway. I've nothing to lose anymore."

"Let's talk about it. I want to talk for a long time. We can sort it out."

"Go ahead, I've nothing to lose! Would you like another confession while we're at it?"

"Please calm down."

He stopped talking, and so did she. She watched him closely.

"I've done my best," he said. "I couldn't take my eyes off you when

I first saw you. I sought you out, sought out your voice. I made myself available for you. I kept watch at the convent's gate. To protect you—it's all I wanted to do. Did I want you for myself? On a few occasions, yes—and I'm sorry. Did I have *unclean* thoughts? Yes—and I'm sorry. But did I also feel hurt and responsible when you were looking all faint and pale and starving?" He finally turned to look at her through pinched eyes.

"Why did you feel responsible for that?"

"I can't say why. I just did. Like a force of nature. It was up to me to make sure you ate. To make sure you were healthy and happy. I don't know why. I heard you each time you told me we couldn't be in contact. I wanted to find a balance that would allow me to provide food and protection, but I also could've resisted talking to you. I was willing to respect your religion and your wishes. And then…"

Kalea waited a few agonizing seconds. "And then?"

"I had dreams."

"You—you did?" Kalea's core rattled, the jitters returning to her stomach.

A deep frown formed on his face, and he avoided her eyes. "They were so real. More real than this." He wagged his finger from her to himself. "This is surreal, if you ask me. But the dreams…"

She attempted to finish for him. "Were…torturous?"

His eyes widened on her. "Yeah." He stared like he used to, but more bewildered. "I felt I was crazy for a moment, experiencing these…dreams. Out of my mind and weak. So I'm sorry. I'm sorry I acted—"

"Shhh." She put her hand on his shoulder and then reached for his hair. He closed his eyes as she slipped her fingers into his weather-bedraggled mahogany locks, the same texture she remembered from her too-real dreams. "Don't be sorry anymore. I can't blame you."

He opened his eyes again. "And now you're married to the Creator. How am I supposed to compete with your god?"

"I want you to take me away from the convent."

He blinked. "What?"

Her hand slid to his shoulder, noting its firmness. "I've changed my mind. A horrible accident happened last night, and I can't live there anymore. Also, Father Liam went to a parish in Sharr."

She placed her hand over her mouth when her lip trembled. Taking a moment, she swallowed. "It's not the same. Nothing is. I have to leave, and I need *you* to protect me out in the world."

He clamped his mouth shut as if to stifle any counterarguments. She took his face between her hands. His eyes misted over. She put a soft kiss on his cheek, right beside his mouth, and ran her fingers through his hair.

"I never chose to be in there. I'm not supposed to be, and I know it now from deep within me. Will you take me away, Dorhen?"

He nodded a few times before opening his eyes. He swallowed, and when he opened them again, a tear fell out of each. She put her arms around his middle again and he hugged back this time, squeezing. He sniffled with his face buried in her hair.

It all came back to her. The dreams had become reality. None of this—his warmth, his breath steaming against her neck, his firm chest pressing against hers tighter by the moment as he squeezed, the spring water scent of his hair against her nose—none of it was new. She'd known these sensations several times in her dreams. She knew this person, had acquainted herself with him, had touched him, seen his body, seen him cry, and had already become dependent on his company for the sake of her own comfort.

His words came almost as a groan. "I'll do anything you ask."

Not to mention the vibration of his voice. Though he was young, an innocent and tender twenty-two, his voice hung deep in the air. It soothed her to the core. It made her want to forget about her insistent worries, her mental illness, and her loneliness. With his eagerness to please, he'd speak if she asked. And she *would* ask him. For the rest of her life. She'd continue teaching him to read, and then he'd read to her. Those moments couldn't come soon enough.

Resting her face against his shoulder, her nose along his neck as the wind blew his hair over her face, she said, "Thank you."

She crept her hand up his back, under the side of his tabard but over his undershirt, which clung to his damp body. Her fingers caressed the intricate sculpture of his muscles and shoulder blade—all familiar shapes. His heat remedied the chill in her hand.

"Dorhen," she said. "I'm the one who is sorry." It might be proper to look him in the eye for this statement, but she'd rather not lose the contact of his body. "I'm sorry." He remained silent. "I can tell you my whole ridiculous story in as much time as you'd like to take, but I want you to know I'll be easier from now on. I promise. And if you'd like to establish a…union with me, then you can also ask of me whatever you like. I'll be helpful, patient, steady, whatever you need me to be."

She took her hand out of his tabard and trailed her fingers along the side of his neck behind his hair. His heart hammered faster against her breast. He shuddered and took her hand out of his hair.

"You still don't understand," he said. She pulled away to look at his face. "It's not about what I want." He locked his eyes on hers in the gravest stare she'd seen yet. "I live to serve you. Will you let me?"

Now her heart was beating to match his heart's speed. She couldn't speak yet, trapped in the whirlpool of his greenish eyes.

"Yes, Dorhen," she finally said, her voice coming out strong. "I'll let you serve me."

His serious eyes blinked, and another set of tears ran down his cheeks. It was an odd request of his, but so important that he'd weep at her agreement?

Dorhen's tears were contagious. She covered her mouth as if a sob would emerge, but she smiled as her tears ran. "Is that good enough for you? I said yes!"

A smile broke through on his weepy face, and he scooped her again into a hard embrace, as if to tell the world he'd not let anyone in to harm her. Inside was their own private space.

She giggled as more tears ran out and soaked into his clothes. He planted his mouth atop her head, breathing with heavy jubilation and coiling his long arms around her as far as they'd go. His rib cage trembled against her as he both laughed and cried, his tears soaking into her hair. She trembled hysterically as she laughed and laughed until she had to pat his arm for release. She needed air.

His face glowed red and wet by the time she pulled away. Hers must look the same. His smile spread wide, as if he'd lost the ability to close his lips. That long tooth of his showed on the side. The contact wasn't lost; he retained her hand, wiping his face on his other sleeve. She did the same with her linen habit sleeve.

She reached out and took his other hand, hardly satisfied with holding one at a time. "All right now, let's talk. Where are we going first?"

He dipped his head to wipe his eyes on his shoulder one more time. "Wherever you want. Do you want to see the ocean?"

A new smile quirked on her lips. "Yes. I've always wanted to see it. I want to see everything with you." She laughed. "The ocean. That reminds me. Was this your doing?" She showed her wrist, still wearing the shell bracelet she'd found in her laundry basket.

He nodded, this time displaying a warm, calm, and genuine smile. "I couldn't resist any opportunity to give you a gift."

"I noticed." She lowered her chin. "And I never got to thank you for it."

She placed her hands on his chest and pressed a warm kiss to his lips, reliving the same soft texture she'd known in her dreams. After it ended, he reached for her hands and she pulled away coyly, though she wanted nothing more than to grace him with kisses and praises. She ached to let go of all the restraint she'd practiced in the convent, but if she didn't practice a little of it now, they wouldn't get very far. The longing look in his eyes and parted lips in the brief instant she denied him her hands confirmed that there was indeed a dance to this interaction. But she didn't know the steps. Vivene's love manual must've been written about it. Too bad it was too late to learn anything from that book.

Leaving him in that longing state amidst the cold, pine-scented wind, she turned and walked in a circle, partially to let him look at her from other angles. "I can't believe I'm going to be a laywoman. I never dreamed I would ever leave the convent."

"You're making the right choice," he said.

She took his hand again, this time more casually. "Lead the way."

"Hold on."

"What?"

Though it should take a while for his—and her—momentary pleasure to wear off, his expression shifted into something more sober. "Let's go back to the convent."

"Are you serious?"

"We'll need rations."

Her smile wore off. "I thought you said you could thrive in the forest?"

"I can, but you did meet me after I stole some food. It's wise to have rations with us. We're lucky we're setting out in spring, but it'll get hard later."

"You're right, I'm sure." She put her hands up in surrender. "There's the famine. The farmers will be producing less. The towns could become chaotic."

"True. We're going to find some place where we can better eke out a living. We might even find our way to the Darklands. Wherever living happens to be easy."

"But the convent doesn't have much food in store."

"Find what you can. Anything will help. Also, you'll want to put on more sensible clothing. Bring a blanket. Bring anything useful."

She shrugged. "I can do that. But don't you have a blanket?"

"I have a bedroll," he said, and raised an eyebrow. "Should we share it instead?"

Kalea burst out laughing. "Not so fast. I'm sure I can find a spare blanket to bring with me. It could take some time to gather these things. We'll need a rendezvous plan. I'll take the rest of the day to pack my things and smuggle away some supplies. Then I'll slip out at night while everyone sleeps."

His expression lost the rest of its delirious warmth and took on a businesslike mien. "I'll be waiting for you outside the convent walls."

"I'm so excited, I'm shaking!"

He smiled and extended his hand. Picking up her discarded headpiece articles, she took his hand, and together they walked back to the convent.

Sliding her palm slowly across Dorhen's in her reluctance to let it go, she finally broke the contact as they stood on the protruding river stones. On the other bank, she collected the laundry she'd abandoned earlier and hurried back to the convent. Since she had never gotten to wash it, she hid the load in a corner of the courtyard behind a stack of firewood. She dumped the bloody rags and kept the basket to use for her travels.

Before heading up to her new cell in the east building, she hurried into the west building to the room where Joy lay in repose. They'd decorated the room in Kalea's absence with vines of ivy draped along the bier, and Joy wore a wreath of snowdrops on her head, gathered from the garden they kept in the convent. Many candles lit the room—the whole thing bore a similar appearance to Kalea's contemplation ritual from yesterday. Although in this case, the heat from the candles mingling with the fragrant crocuses arranged all around the body helped to mask the rising smell of death.

"Hi, Joy," Kalea whispered as the attending vestal left the room, leaving her alone with her best friend. Kalea dropped the basket and sat on the chair beside the bier. "You look beautiful. The Creator should be pleased."

She leaned forward and lowered her voice to the level of a hum. "I have more to say than goodbye. I have to tell you a secret." She couldn't contain her smile. "I'm leaving. I decided not to be a vestal. I'm in love with the elf, and I'm leaving with him. I'm honestly happy. I needed to tell someone. I love you, Joy. Be happy in your new life too." She leaned over and kissed Joy's forehead.

After murmuring a traditional prayer for the dead, she left and ventured across the courtyard into the east building where the vestals lived, and where her new cell had been arranged for her. The doors were painted blue in this building. It was even quieter than the west building strove to be, even as vestals scurried about and gathered in little prayer nooks built into the corners.

"Oh, Father," she said with a pout, standing in the first private space she'd ever owned, either at the convent or at home. He'd given her a room with a stained glass window, a little one composed of simple shapes to make the Creator's flower pattern within a U-shaped frame, but a magnificent sight in her opinion. A large wooden bookshelf, like Sister

Scupley's, took up one whole wall. He'd left five books behind on it; she would've spent her lifetime filling in the rest of the shelves. There was also a writing desk and a standard bed with ropes tied across the frame. The straw mattress waited on the floor, folded over, with a fresh set of sheets and a quilt folded on top.

Among the books, one with a golden arrow on the spine had been placed. "Father, what have you done now?" She opened it to the middle where a picture showed Lehomis hiding from a group of angry bandits. This was the one she'd grown up with, the first installment. "I don't believe it."

She placed the book at the bottom of her basket, rolled the quilt tightly, and squeezed it into the remaining space. Any food she could find, she could tuck snugly into the quilt's center. She placed the mattress across the bed ropes to sleep on for tonight. She would sleep under the sheets and leave the quilt in the basket.

Back downstairs in the central hall lying between the two buildings, she raided the pantry and cellar. She found some salted fish and a wedge of cheese to smuggle away. She also managed to find her blue kirtle in the laundry room, waiting to be washed and donated to the poor later. Tonight, she'd dress in it before starting her new life with Dorhen.

At bedtime, she couldn't bring herself to sleep in the empty, unfamiliar cell. Over the years, it would've been filled with books, her prayers and contemplation, and perhaps a potted plant. In this hour of complex emotions, such as Joy's loss and her own new beginning, how could she ever fall asleep alone? Surveying the empty cell, she shook her head. She left her packed basket behind and went back to sleep in the novice dorm for one more night.

They hadn't removed her bedding yet, thankfully. A few of her belongings remained, like the washing bat she'd forgotten to take outside two days ago. Her little chest of drawers still stored some of her handkerchiefs and her pocket-sized prayer book.

"Kalea?" Vivene said when she sat on her old bedroll. "What are you doing here?"

"I…" She averted her eyes. "It's lonely in my new cell. I miss Joy. I can't sleep alone right now."

Vivene laughed, but also dabbed her eyes on her own handkerchief. "You're such a soft-hearted ninny."

"Thanks, so are you." Kalea rose and hugged her.

"I never got to say congratulations. Congratulations."

Kalea smiled as a blush warmed up her cheeks. "Thanks, Viv."

She undressed to her new chemise and lay down on her old bed, curling up her knees. She pulled the old blanket over her shoulder. One by one, the girls blew their candles out, filling the dark air with a familiar smoky scent.

Her heart danced as her brain skipped from thought to thought. What was she doing? Existing in a surreal space between two lives, that's what. The vestal and the laywoman. Not only a laywoman—she was about to become an outcast woman who'd chosen to make a life with an elf. They wouldn't be able to settle anywhere, either in Norr or Sharr. They might have to keep Dorhen's perpetual routine of traveling around the continent. Perhaps they'd use the routine to eat well year-round. For each season, they might stop in a region which flourished in that particular season. She couldn't walk forever, though. Eventually, she'd get old...

Get old. Something she'd never thought of, concerning Dorhen. She'd be old in a few decades, but he wouldn't. Elves were said to live up to four hundred years. What would he think of her when her hair turned white and wrinkles appeared after a mere forty? Would he still love her?

No, stop it, Kalea! She'd talked herself out of too many good thoughts already. *Worry about it later.*

Excitement as well as nervousness wracked her body. She would never be able to sleep, even if she wanted to. Around midnight she would creep out of this room, get her packed things from her cell, and slip outside to meet Dorhen.

Some time passed, and gentle breathing and snores started here and there. Soon. She turned over, and there must've been some pollen in her nose from the viewing room because she let out a loud sneeze. "*Hac-choo!*"

Click.

Burying her nose in her sleeve, she paused to listen. What was that sound? Some feet shuffled in the hall behind the door. She raised her head and listened some more. Nothing.

Squinting her eyes in the darkness, she lay back down. More snores and soft murmuring joined the orchestra of sleeping girls. This was how she was accustomed to sleeping: in a noisy room. As she closed her eyes, the soothing noises made her drowsy at last.

A hum ran through the floorboards, snapping her out of her sleepy daze. When she opened her eyes, a flash of light bombarded them unprepared. She gasped and shielded her face. The other girls awoke and reacted similarly.

The light settled into a sliver hovering in the air before expanding into a U-shaped hole. Firelight bloomed on the other side of the hole, and then men with torches ran through and jumped onto this side—the novices' room.

The humming hole gaped at the far side of the chamber from where Kalea's bed belonged. She froze and gawked.

One of the men tripped over a girl on the floor and cursed. Another man pulled her up roughly by her arm. More men poured out of the hole, and each pounced on the first girl in his path. Screaming filled the dorm to its arching rafters. Girls jumped from their beds and scrambled around, causing the men to chase them. Male voices yelled and cursed and growled.

"Come here, bitch!" One grabbed Vivene's hair and yanked her backward.

Kalea jumped up and grabbed her washing bat, the best weapon available in here.

The men kept coming. Around twenty of them entered before the portal finally closed. When it did, two men wearing red cloaks and jeweled red gloves commenced a string of strange words. They drew symbols in the air with their gloved hands. Each held a long, golden rod and tapped the ends on the floor throughout the chant.

Kalea stayed against the shadowy back wall as long as she could before one man spotted her. She hit his head with the bat. He yelled and grabbed at it, but she spun away and rebounded for another hit. Then another.

He fell. She must've knocked him out. She couldn't defeat all these men, however.

She kept low, making her way along the shadowy wall toward the door. A man lunged for her, and she darted away, sprinting for the door. She pulled the handle, but it didn't move.

Locked. They'd been locked in!

Returning to the back of the room, she screamed Dorhen's name. He supposedly waited outside for her. He'd said he had always watched the convent. She screamed it again. Hopefully, Sister Scupley and the remaining priests would hear all the commotion inside the convent. But Dorhen…he would hear her. The thought of his nearness gave her an irrational sense of confidence. She would have to make sure he heard. The large windows were too high to access. Glancing around frantically, she considered items to throw at the window. She couldn't risk throwing her washing bat at a window and losing it.

She lifted her chest of drawers, which spanned about as wide as her shoulders, and threw it with all the strength she could gather. Glass shattered and rained all over the floor.

"Dorhen!" In addition to her shouting, he should hear the chaos through the open window now.

Girls sprawled on the ground, kicking at the grabbing hands and bleeding from their noses.

"How's the bloody portal comin'?" one man shouted at the men with the jeweled gloves. They ignored him and continued their chant in a hasty rhythm.

Vivene writhed on the floor, being hog-tied. Kalea ran over and banged the man's head before he could finish knotting the rope.

"Somebody catch that bitch!"

Kalea sprinted. "Dorhen!" She ended his name in a squeal, dodging some hands.

She roared in disgust when she made it to the farthest corner and found one of her friends with her hands tied behind her back, pinned to the floor, being raped. Kalea cocked her washing bat and hit the man as he worked his hips.

Bang! Some wood behind her took abuse.

Hands grabbed Kalea's hair in her hesitation. "You don't like that? Well, guess what!"

Bang!

The man slammed Kalea against the wall. The washing bat parted from her hand.

Bang!

She screamed and thrashed as he seized her hands and fought them out of the way, using the rest of his body to suppress her. His erection poked her hip, just like Kemp's had done.

Bang-crack!

"Hold still, bitch!" Using her hair, he forced her to stand straight against the wall, her head smacking against the stone. Stars whirled around in her vision, blinding her. In her daze, he ripped her chemise and tore at her braies underneath. So much for being a chaste and pure Sister of Sorrow.

Right as he forced her legs open and aligned himself between them, he dropped her. The jolt knocked her lungs empty.

Dorhen had broken into the room!

He bashed the man's forehead against the wall beside her. Lifting Kalea from the floor, he ordered, "Stand!" She shook and swayed like a newborn deer.

"Take this." He handed her the washing bat. With a hand on her shoulder, he guided her toward the door, pausing to punch a charging man with that mysteriously superior elven strength he'd also used to fight Kemp. Near the door, the gloved men's golden poles spouted sparks from their gleaming surfaces.

Dorhen took her hand again right as she spotted poor sweet Rose, also squirming and crying under a violent man. Kalea pulled away and struck him with her bat.

"Kalea!" Dorhen shouted. In her achy daze, she couldn't swing as hard anymore. Dorhen pushed her aside and grabbed the man as he lunged for an angry counterattack, then threw him into the wall. "Get to the door!"

Kalea grabbed Rose's hand and helped her up. Dorhen pushed her forward and stopped again to fight off a sneering man with a knife. Kalea turned and hit him as Dorhen seized his knife hand and the two wrestled.

"Go!" The hit dazed the man long enough for Dorhen to wrench the knife away and stab his neck.

They made it to the door. By then, word had reached all the men of an elf in the room. The gloved-men's golden poles flared bright, blinding them for an instant. A string of lightning stretched from the top of one pole to the other, and another hole appeared in the air between them.

Kalea and Dorhen were about to step over the wreckage of the heavy green door when someone grabbed his hood and yanked him backward. Dorhen shoved Kalea over the wooden obstacle, and she tumbled into the hallway.

"No!" she yelled. Three men now wrestled with him. "Rose!" The girl wasn't there. She must've been grabbed without Kalea's notice. "Dorhen!"

He punched one of his three attackers with an unreal level of strength. "It'll be all right!" he yelled back. Another man grabbed him from behind. "Meet me at the well in the forest!"

She clenched her teeth and sucked air through them. *I can't leave him!* She would wait here to make sure he got free.

But another man came stepping over the wood shards. "Think you can leave, you little whore?"

Dorhen lurched forward, grabbed that man's shirt, and hauled him backward. "Run, Kalea!"

She did.

The old well in the forest wasn't as far away as it seemed. Yesterday, she'd walked erratically until she stumbled upon it. She knew how to find it now, since Dorhen had walked her back from there. She sprinted straight to it, splashing across the stream and over the pine needles with bare feet.

As soon as she found it, she hid behind it in case someone happened to follow her. In the grass, she panted and retched, covering her mouth to stifle the sounds. She leaned against the well. Her feet took on a stinging numbness in the chill air, and her teeth chattered in terror. Periodically, she peeked over the edge to try to see Dorhen coming through the forest, though he might be running while invisible.

She returned to sitting and waiting, her stomach churning. The hours rolled on. She slumped over to lie on the grass until the sky began to lighten. Dorhen still hadn't joined her.

Using the well for help, she climbed to her frozen feet. In the dawn light, she could see herself. Her crisp new vestal chemise sported a long rip from its hem to her belly button. Her braies remained intact, although they'd been damaged and loosened.

She paced. Looking toward the forest again, now visible in the brightening sunlight, she chewed her thumbnail. Why didn't he come? He couldn't have gotten lost, not the elf whose domain was the forest.

She let out a shaky moan. "Dorhen."

The higher the sun rose, the less she could wait any longer. Kalea went back to the convent.

Chapter 16
Her Ecstasy

By the time Kalea made it back to the convent, entering on tiptoe, the halls were silent and empty. Creeping along, her hand trailing the wall, she ventured into the shadowy corridor to the novice dorm. No screams, no voices, not even the softest footsteps stirred the stagnant air.

Her foot hit a piece of wood, and it skipped across several slate tiles. Ahead, the dim morning glow illuminated the wrecked doorway. Green-painted shards of broken wood still obstructed the portal. No one moved within the large room beyond it.

"Dorhen?" she called.

No answer. She stepped over a scrap of wood and around the largest piece. She paused. The doorknob on the largest piece appeared...melted. Most of the metal was gone, revealing the original hole bored through the wood.

The grey morning sun showed the room devoid of life. A jumble of bed mattresses and linens and overturned chests were strewn about the floor, disordered and abandoned.

Where did everyone go? Dorhen?

She stepped over the mess, scanning the floor until a bright twinkle winked from under the spread dirt of a broken potted plant. She dropped into a squat and brushed the dirt aside. It was a pale stone.

"This is Dorhen's," she said to herself. The stone he could make glow at night. She turned it from side to side, and a blue flash shot across the cloudy white surface in the light. "A moonstone."

Shaking her head in doubt, she scanned the room again. They were all gone, Dorhen with them.

She squeezed the moonstone in a fist and rushed out into the hall. "Dorhen!" she called, and then changed to calling for Sister Scupley. The vestals in the other building should wake up soon. Her padding feet echoed through the empty halls. Never mind their numbness.

She went into the sanctum. "Father Liam—oh damn! I forgot."

A huge pile of wood, slate, and glass still heaped at the foot of the altar in the sanctum. No one had found the time to clear it away yet. She shook her head and frowned, placing the moonstone around her neck.

An eerie mist was rising from the floor and rubble with the introduction of the sun. So much moisture damage would happen to the furniture, and it would take a fortune to restore the roof.

There are no safe places to live, Dorhen had once said. He was right. That elf was wise, and she had been too blinded by her institution to see his logic. In here, they weren't even safe from the damned ceiling. Not to mention magic doorways with raping men charging through…

Unable to look at the travesty any longer, she turned away, but stopped at the uncanny sight of a person in the mist. He remained visible after she blinked her eyes and squinted. With a gasp, she stepped forward. The brightening sunlight bouncing off the airborne mist droplets created rainbows, and as the rainbows crossed each other, the image of a robed figure was created.

Kalea went lightheaded as her mouth dropped open. "My Creator! My Creator!"

She ran forward and dropped to her knees at the foot of the rubble pile. She could see Him from this angle too. He wasn't merely an illusion. She bowed her head. She would have kissed His feet, but she couldn't find them; they weren't apparent in the shadowy rubble.

"My Creator," Kalea said again, too humble to raise her eyes.

"Look at me."

She obeyed. How could she not?

"I'm not the Creator. In fact, I'm weakening by the moment, so pay attention."

"You're not? Who are you?"

His veiled head bowed over her from his towering height. The veil concealed his face except for a hint of bone structure that appeared whenever the soft air pressed the ethereal fabric against it.

Kalea's heart froze. The figure's smooth, long hair cascaded past his shoulders. Blue hair. She stood up and stepped backward, ready to shield her face from whatever the spirit would do to her.

"What's the matter, my girl? Don't you recognize me?"

"Where did he go?"

"You mean Dorhen? Dorhen is gone," the figure said, his voice loud as if in her head. He made no movement.

"Wh-what have you done with him?"

His shroud whipped softly in a rhythmic frolic. "Brought him to you. But now he has ripened." A hand from within the robes tossed something red. A pear. She lurched and caught it in her cupped hands. As soon as it touched her skin, it wrinkled, its vibrant red distorted to a queasy black that continued to shrivel smaller and smaller, leaving nothing behind but the stem. "It can be in your hands now." The spirit's hand disappeared into his robes.

Kalea's mouth hung open as she shook her head. "I think he's been kidnapped. Where is he now?"

"I tried, my girl. I used the best of my collected energy to bring the Sufferborn up, to groom him, to clear his slate. Despite my work, he was flawed and let his guard down. I'm set back, and now he's useless to me."

Kalea dropped to her knees again. "I want him back. Don't you understand? I love him! Please tell me where he is."

"Your pleas are like a surge to my essence. Is it your wish to have the Sufferborn, then?"

"Yes, please!"

"Out of pity, I would grant your request. Pity and longing. And though there are other things I could do for you, you want *him*. A foolish thing I did, to think I could use him as I'd planned. Fine." By now, his image had faded under the sun's diligent work in drying the mist and dew. "It's in your hands, but his days are numbered now. Remember my words and act fast before he falls into oblivion, never to be seen again even by the few who have seen him."

The figure stepped forward, and though her good sense told her to shrink away, she couldn't. A nagging curiosity and desperation for answers kept her attention plastered to the specter. She held her eyes open, resisting the urge to blink for fear he might vanish before she could learn something.

"Where is he?"

"He's north. Take the road north. As you walk, search for a weapon like this one."

He raised one arm, unfurling a wide grey sleeve from which he unsheathed a sword. Its shining blade glistened like silver from pommel to tip. Heavily decorated, its swirling reliefs and human-like figure lying on the Y-shaped cross section demanded any onlooker's attention. He flipped it over in his hand to show the figure's absence on the other side. Instead, the word "HATHROHJILH" was inscribed on the blade. The illusionary sword disintegrated, and he showed his empty hand before letting the sleeve fall back over it.

"Stay close to this sword," the figure said. "It goes toward the Sufferborn. If you find him, stay close. Don't leave his side."

Kalea teetered on wobbly legs. "What happened to him?"

"There's no time. Here," the figure said, "don't forget this." From his sleeve, he revealed her washing bat. She'd lost track of it sometime between last night and now.

Kalea tiptoed closer. She reached out, and he dropped it over her open, trembling palms. Veins of its rough old wood grains now shone like silver, clustered brightest along the handle.

"What did you do to it?"

"Keep it close to you. As you should stay close to him."

Her eyes scanned the figure, tracing over his obscured face. She moved closer, clutching the bat's handle. "Who are you?"

"Because you charm me, I'll tell you we are without names. Those who aren't born are not given names. But as some have seen me, I have been called 'Raining Cloud.' By the Norrian tongue, the words are 'Arius Medallus.'"

She repeated in a whisper, "Arius Me*dallus*…"

Venturing close enough, she lashed toward his draped veil. Her hand entered a shower of mist. The wind blew into the sanctum, scattering the droplets creating his image, and he vanished.

With his image gone, his voice spoke once more in her head. *Walk fast. Dorhen's time is over. But you may see him once more if you wish. Until then, pray hard he says 'no' to Wik's enticement.*

Kalea stood alone again, clutching her washing bat, now glittering in the sunbeam. Snapping out of her gaping awe, she rushed outside to the courtyard and through the door to the east building, shooting past sleepy vestals on their way to the dining room.

"What in the world are you doing?" one asked, but she ignored the woman. They hadn't heard the attack from their quarters.

An older vestal caught her arm in the hall. "Kalea, what in the world are you doing, walking around practically naked? The new priests might see you when they arrive!"

"Sister!" Kalea replied. "Where's Sister Scupley?"

The old vestal wrinkled her nose. "Don't you remember? She left with the novices last night. They're being transferred to another institution to alleviate us in this famine."

"Transferred?"

"Don't you remember? Father Liam wasn't the only person who transferred."

"The novices were attacked in their beds!" Kalea shouted.

The woman's mouth dropped open. "What?"

"Marauders raped and kidnapped my sisters, and my elf is missing too!" Kalea yanked her arm away and stormed back to her path, shouting more of the news. "There was an attack! Listen to me!"

Veiled women stepped around corners to gawk at her.

"We were attacked!" She didn't stop to answer questions, but walked on, showing her bruised body and torn chemise to anyone who would look. "Go to the novices' dorm and see the remnants of your so-called transfer!"

The vestals took her up on it, rushing toward the door to find out what she ranted about.

In her new cell, she opened the wardrobe and found a few hand-me-down habits. She sneered and shook her head and put on her old washing chemise along with the blue kirtle; it fit her body slightly looser now because of all the meals she'd skipped. With her basket already packed, she could make a hasty exit. She tied her bat to her old leather belt, donned her cloak, and slung the basket over her shoulder.

Big, wide eyes on faces framed in identical veils stared at her as she strode back through the convent, allowing her leather shoes to scuff along the floor at any volume they chose.

One vestal returned from the west building yelling, "Deceit! Deceit!"

Stupid, clueless old bags. They lived on the far side of the convent from the novices, the two groups hardly interacted, and they had been deaf to those long minutes of violence that befell their own people. They were two different classes. The novices all waited to make that leap into the higher class. Kalea's chance had come early; otherwise, age twenty-five was the customary age to become a full vestal.

And hapless Father Superior... He was up to something. Who knows, Sister Scupley might've also been involved in the planning. Or maybe she had left the convent in blissful ignorance like Father Liam. If only he knew what had happened to the innocent girls he had helped raise...

Perhaps she shouldn't be so angry at the vestals; today would make them wiser. Several of them noticed her laywoman's clothing and asked about it. She didn't answer. She wouldn't take the time to answer questions about the raid either. She offered whatever answers she could get out along her way outside.

"They lied to you," Kalea told one woman. "Maybe Father Liam lied too. I don't know, and I don't have time to wonder about it."

She walked out the door, cloak on, basket hanging off one shoulder, and washing bat at her hip. If anyone tried to stop her, she'd fight.

Chapter 17
A Trip for the Lost

"Come here, dear boy. Lay down your head." The smiling old crone held out her sinewy hand.

Dorhen shrank back, but did he have a choice? She and three others held the only light in the dark forest. A cold, misty breeze grazed his back. His decision didn't matter. Several hands shot forward and snatched his arms.

Were they hands or branches? They might as well have been branches for their chilling scratchiness. Three crones' faces glowed in the soft light, but the grabbing hands suggested more people. It was hard to tell.

Their skull-like witch faces moved around the light source in the onslaught, casting moving shadows over pronounced cheekbones and smiling, crooked teeth. Wispy hair in various shades of grey and white waved about.

The bony hands caressed his face and moved down his body. Other hands eased him onto his back on a bed of moist, decaying leaves. More branch-like hands secured his arms until he couldn't move and tore his shirt open to continue the caress. Two, three—six or more hands searched his sides, sliding against the flow of his ribs.

One hand found his sternum to inspect where the bones were weakest. He relaxed under the chilling, yet soothing touch. Right after his eyes closed, they sprang wide again as his skin opened up beneath the drag of a fine blade.

Murder.

No, it wasn't murder. The knife didn't plunge between his ribs; it sliced with thoughtful precision. The other hands inserted their fingers into the incision and pulled his flesh open for the hand of the crone in charge to squeeze into his body.

His temperature dropped as the sudden freezing presence explored upward, bypassing his lungs. A surge of blood overflowed and spilled down his sides to make room for the foreign object. The chill took him over in an instant. He wouldn't survive despite the old crones' intention.

The light faded.

He had never gotten to live the life he wanted, but for some reason it didn't matter. An odd sense of fulfillment calmed him. He had served his purpose. Still. What a shame he couldn't have enjoyed his life for a while at least.

Deep in his chest cavity, the hand found his heart and grasped it in a frozen fist. He screamed in numbing agony.

His scream continued into the waking world as usual. That dream again. His vision didn't return quite the way it should have, and his head floated with the lightness of dandelion seeds on the wind. The shapes rushing past him remained blurred and oddly colored with deep purples and piercing yellows. He couldn't focus his eyes. Deep, rumbling sounds rolled across him in long heavy echoes, pounding on his head. Voices. At least the ache had lifted off his chest from the nightmare, always so real…

"HE DOESN'T HEAR NOTHIN'."

"BUT HIS EYES ARE ALL FLUTTERY NOW."

Dorhen groaned.

"See? He can hear us."

The blur of vibrations caused by sound and…movement began to separate and settle. A steady roughness dragged up his back. Dim firelight focused in his vision, showing wooden ceiling beams passing over him one after another. He was being dragged, dragged by his feet. Hands appeared behind him and scooped under his arms.

"Down some steps we go, boy-o."

A few dizzying jolts indicated the change in direction. His stomach churned. Unable to warn anyone, and with no energy to lurch away, Dorhen couldn't do more than turn his head to spew all his stomach contents out.

"Ah, shit!" A hand dropped one of his shoulders, and it banged against the edge of a stone step. He moaned weakly at the painful shock.

The other man laughed. "Hey, you've been on opium before, can't blame the kid."

"Yes, I can."

During their pause, the man behind him must've used the edge of Dorhen's dragging tabard to clean his shoes. The vomit's warmth seeped through his clothes.

Dorhen blurred out of consciousness until some slaps landed on his face. "Are you done skipping through fantasy land? We've gotta talk to you. Eh? What's your name, boy-o?"

Dorhen closed his eyes and leaned over. Had he been sitting up?

"He's not done yet. Let him sleep some more." The man's voice alternated between deep underground and high in the air.

"What mixture did you give him? He *is* an elf, after all. They respond differently to the recipes than men do."

"Nightshade was in it; it was one of our strongest recipes."

"Overkill for an elf, I'd expect." The man clicked his tongue, and it sounded like a slap straight to the center of Dorhen's face. "You better hope he lives through this trip. Let's try to straighten him up and get some answers out of him. The lord will be here from Ilbith tomorrow, and he'll want to see our catch."

"Do you think…? Could it be *him?*"

"Who knows? I can't get over where we found him." Laughter stabbed through the room and bounced off each bare wall one hundred beats over. "How long do you think he'd been visiting those little vestals?"

"You dirty boy." The laughter continued and a tousle on his head stirred all his hair follicles like needles. "This one right here. He's special. I think we caught a rare fish last night, though he managed killing three full-fledged sorcerers. This fish might be worth it."

"Considering that alone, the little bastard is special. Look at ya, you little fornicating, murdering rapscallion!"

They laughed, and the piercing noise churned his stomach again. He didn't vomit, though; he blacked out.

To avoid getting lost in the woods, Kalea followed the path down to Tintilly to access the road going north. The market was open today, so the streets were clogged with villagers and farmers. Kalea squeezed through the crowd, reaching for the little bit of money she had stashed away over the years, most of which her parents had sent with her upon entering the convent.

The tables had been picked clean and the farmers were already leaving, shouting back at the tense crowd and shooing them away with wide, arcing arms. The sun had yet to reach its apex, and not even a scrap of stale bread was left for Kalea to buy for her journey.

She gave up and headed for the north exit, where a lot of the farmers' wagons were already filing out.

"Are you going north?" she shouted to the first one to pass her outside the city where the trees huddled in close to the road.

"No, dame! I'm turning off east at the second fork."

"I'm going north, madam," the wagon driver rolling in behind him said, pulling on his reins. "Need a ride?"

"Oh, bless you!" Kalea replied, already rushing to the back of the wagon. "I can pay, rest assured."

"No problem, dame, I trust you." Four other men were already riding in the wagon bed. She sighed and dropped her basket near the back, where she could dangle her feet off next to one of the men.

"Better sit closer up front," he said, pointing toward the driver. "The roads've been roughed up by the rain."

"Thanks, you're right about that." She stood up in the wagon bed and lifted her basket.

"Where ya headed, ultimately?" The driver twisted around and took off his wide-brimmed straw hat. Dirty blonde hair clung to his temples with sweat. His nose leaned to the side. "Where's yer elf-lover?"

"Kemp," Kalea squeaked, and swallowed. She lunged toward the back of the wagon again and dodged the men's grabbing arms.

"That's her, fellas. Get her!"

The man sitting on the end grazed her arm, but she leaped away and landed on the ground. She fell and rolled, bending her weak ankle wrong. Sparing not a second to worry over it, she dashed into the forest where the wagon couldn't follow.

"Come on!"

Kalea sprinted forward, her basket bouncing wildly on her shoulder.

"Beware the elf!" Kemp called to his friends. "He's strong, so when he shows, we've gotta overwhelm him."

Kalea pumped her legs. She'd hoped they wouldn't chase her on foot, as foolish as that hope was. If only she did have an elf to run to. Her and Dorhen's disturbance of the town had left it unsafe for her, and after the incident at the convent, she truly had nowhere to go, except for Taulmoil, where her parents lived, but no. She wouldn't go home. She couldn't forget about that elf.

The men's voices grew louder, but she couldn't chance a look over her shoulder to see how close they drew.

Keep running. Just keep running. Who was she kidding? She would run out of stamina soon, and her old ankle strain ached.

She whirled to her right, darting behind a tight cluster of pine trees. Her foot skidded on the pine needles. She tensed her legs and focused on not falling, for if she did, it would all be over. She launched forward, but the men's voices increased in volume. They didn't pant as heavily as she did.

She whirled around another bunch of trees, this one with the additive effect of thick shrubs, budding with fresh new leaves. A hiding place would be imperative soon. If she kept running, they'd catch her.

She used the cover of the greenery to traverse the gentle slope of earth. There might be hope for her if she could make them think she had gone a different direction. At the bottom of the slope, she slowed and looked around for an idea. Her chest heaved, gasping for air.

A trickle of water echoed nearby, and the voices sounded from above. "She went down there!"

Kalea took off again and ran until she found the creek at the bottom of another slope. She used to wash clothes in this same creek; this part of it wove between lifts and falls of rocks and sloping earth, picking up speed as it went deeper, until the sound of rushing water echoed as it flowed into a cave.

Following the rushing current, she spotted a hole in the ground on her side of the stream. Similar, nearby crevasses were taking in water to supply the echoing noises. This opening was narrow, but so was she. She stepped into the water and crammed her basket into the hole, then herself. She couldn't move fast enough, because as soon as she squeezed into the opening, the voices rang above her.

"She crossed the river!" Kemp said.

She gnashed her teeth and wiggled to get farther in. If she wedged herself in too far, she could eventually drown if the water level rose—a better fate than being caught by these men.

She pushed her basket farther. Apparently, the crevasse went deep, because the basket continued with each nudge. The men walked right over her, their feet kicking rocks and pine needles over the opening in front of her face.

Please, Creator, don't let them cross the water and see me!

"No sign of the elf yet," Kemp said. "When you find him, catch him alive. The man at the pub promised a great reward for us to bring him in."

"She's been using the slopes to hide," one of the men said. "Let's go this way." The group tromped away along the stream.

She nudged her basket again, and it dropped. *Smack!* The sound came after a second. She should be able to fall the same distance with no injury. She inched along. Water trickles echoed in the distance; it must be a good-sized cave. How perfect it would be if she could hide here until the men quit their search...as long as any late-sleeping bears didn't mind.

She squeezed inward until her feet found open air. She worked them forward so they could touch the ground first. Could she pull herself up onto the same ledge to squeeze back through later? Too late to change her mind.

Her eyes adjusted easily to the dark, thanks to several more openings allowing in beams of light which darted across the space. No bears.

Water trickled into a pretty little pool with reflected blue-green lights shimmering on the wall. A brighter light toward the back suggested a better exit. Shouldering her basket, she traversed around some jagged rocks and down several tiers until she landed on a dirt floor.

Her heart skipped at the sight of a charred spot with a pile of ash. Someone had built a fire in here. No sign of anyone now, though, no belongings or food scraps to be found.

Kalea dropped her basket before noticing the marks in the dirt. A, C, E, F, and G. She covered her mouth. A stick lay on the ground next to the scrawled letters. The ground had been stirred in a few places and more letters drawn on top of the stirred earth.

"Oh, Dorhen," she whispered. To the side of the practiced alphabet, her name had been spelled out. The K was drawn prominently, and the following letters had been brushed over and redrawn a few times.

He really loved me. She pressed the back of her wrist against her mouth. Shaking her head, she dropped to the ground beside the graffiti and put her hand over one of the symbols, gently so as not to ruin his work. "I'm going to help you."

He might've made this cave his permanent home if she had agreed to let him support her life in the convent. This must be the cave he had wanted to sing with her in.

She sniffled and leaned her head against the large rock beside her. "I can't believe this has happened."

She closed her mouth, remembering to be quiet. Her lip quivered, and she swallowed and took a few deep breaths to keep from crying. She couldn't sit idly for long. Dorhen was out there somewhere, and he needed her.

Ruffians or no ruffians, she stood and shouldered her basket. Ahead, more accessible holes gaped with stabbing light beams. Before exiting, she glanced around for any belongings, or possibly a travel pack, he might've stowed here. Nothing. Maybe he hid his things somewhere closer to the convent so he and Kalea could make a faster escape. No time to go look for them.

A gentle waterfall splattered outside, but she emerged on dry ground. She followed the stream, unable to hear any voices over its babble. They must be gone.

By the sun's position, she did her best to find north. She picked a direction and departed from the water after filling her belly with a good drink of it. She went back to walking across the thinning pine needles. In this area, the pines grew scarce and were replaced by poplar. Her feet trod through leaves and tall, green grass now.

She hadn't been out of the cave for more than a few minutes before Kemp and his lackeys charged up from another slope.

"There's my girl! Come here, sweetheart. Haven't found your stud yet?"

When she ran again, her legs felt thick and heavy, not ready to exert such effort so soon. "Leave me alone! The elf is gone!" she shouted.

"We thought if we gave ya time, you'd come out of there with him. Boy, I'd like to snag him even more than you. You know what he did to me on my way to your convent to hear the choir?"

So Kemp did *mean to come to my convent with the townspeople.*

"He attacked me. It must've been around midnight when I woke up. Your little creature gave me a good wallop that evening. I've still got a knot on my skull."

Dorhen had attacked Kemp to keep him out of the convent—to protect Kalea? That was also the night he had kissed her and she yelled and told him off. Kalea moaned.

The stream wound back into view again, and she dashed for it. Splashing into the chilly stream, she plunged past her knees. The firm current pulled on her skirts, trying to sweep her away. She waded across with all her strength and was approaching the steep bank on the other side, hauling her heavy basket, when Kemp and his men stepped in.

"What the hell?" they yelled behind her before she took off on the other bank.

"Creator preserve me!"

Kalea turned around. Discolored hands were reaching out of the water and grabbing the five men's clothing. The men were splashing and kicking and falling over as the hands grabbed and pulled them under.

Kalea froze. Kemp's crooked-nosed face showed fear, and he reached toward her frantically for help now. Blue, grey, and green clawing webbed hands reached up and pulled down. Sometimes ten of them appeared at once!

A head, slimy with matted clinging hair in a greenish hue, blue smiling lips, and big, wide frog eyes emerged to smile at her as if quite pleased with itself. The hands dragged the first man under long enough to drown him, and he bobbed back up to float on with the current. The hands continued furiously with the rest of them.

Into the water they went, until they all were released to float after their friend. Once all of them were dead, the frog-eyed spirit retreated underwater, eyes open as it immersed and disappeared from view.

The sound of the babbling water returned to its peaceful steadiness after the screams echoed away. Sharp needlepoints stabbed up Kalea's legs and spine. Her throat constricted and she gasped for air. Should she murmur a prayer for the men's last rites or pray for her own safety from that demonic…thing in the water?

It was over now. No more Kemp. She could travel in peace. Shaking her head, she turned and continued her northward route. Hopefully, she wouldn't have to cross any more water.

Chapter 18
An Heir for the Kingsorcerer

Dorhen awoke to the same men murmuring off in the corner. He didn't move at first. Let them think he was still asleep.

"Tomorrow, he said," one of the men answered the other's question. "He's being delayed another day, the usual type of business. But I told him we found an elf, so he should come as soon as he can."

They glanced over, smiling at Dorhen, who kept his eyes low enough to look closed. He couldn't chance a peek at his clothes, but he still had Arius Medallus's blue cloth on under his brown mantle, swathed around his neck as always. Warm and secure, it was a treasure to keep him safe. The knife and supplies he always wore on his belt were gone, but they wouldn't have known to take his blue hood.

"How long have we been looking for this kid?"

"Has to be fifteen or sixteen years."

"That long?"

"Yep. I was positive the kid had died ages ago, eaten by a bear or frozen as soon as winter caught him—it's what shoulda happened."

The other man snorted. "But our lord's been so certain we should keep looking, and it got easier when we secured this manor. But yeah."

"Well, this one seems the right age. And brown hair. He had to have brown hair, which this one does."

Dorhen chanced a peek at them. They leaned over the table, one man carving lines into the wood with Dorhen's knife while the other stuffed pinches of soft bread into his mouth and talked around each puffy wad.

Dorhen reached up and yanked the blue hood over his head. His hands disappeared. He rolled silently to his feet.

"Where'd he go?"

Dorhen bolted toward the set of stone steps they'd dragged him down hours ago. His vomit remained pooled on one of them, and he slipped on it.

"Ah ha ha, I see!" The men gave chase.

Dorhen jerked and jiggled the door handle, but it was locked. As the men ascended the steps, he leaped off and collapsed to his knees on the floor below. His hood fell off upon landing.

"There he is!"

His muscles weren't quite ready for vigorous activity yet, though his vision had sharpened again. Pulling his hood back on, he sprinted to the back of the room, where fishy-smelling crates were stacked to the ceiling in the cold atmosphere. The table offered no weapons; the one man retained and brandished his knife. No other doors were available, and the two men widened their stances and extended their arms, guarding the one at the top of the stairs.

"I got him," the older of the men said, and retrieved a small sack of flour from the heaping pile in the corner.

Dorhen summoned his best sneaking skill and tiptoed his way around them as they listened and watched with the flour sack poised.

The younger of the two turned. "Behind you!"

The older man flung the sack. It exploded, releasing a white, choking cloud into the air. Dorhen's coughing didn't matter; he now wore a good coating of flour to announce his position.

The men tackled and overpowered him, struggling until he found himself tied up, standing stretched with his hands held high above his head by a rope secured to a timber ceiling beam. They'd already taken his belt, but now the men took it upon themselves to probe deeper.

"How did you do that, boy-o?" The older man forced the brown mantle over his head with a series of firm tugs and jostles. After giving it a thorough look-over, he dropped the mantle and tugged off the blue hood next.

Dorhen stuttered in panic, "N-no!"

The man paused to smile. "Oh! Heh heh, I see." His eyes brightened. "He's got some secrets. Let's see what's so special about this pretty scarf."

Dorhen groaned as the man unwound the blue swath from around his neck. As soon as it left his person, the whole thing turned dull and crumbled through the man's fingers as heavy brown chunks.

Now scowling, the older man smelled his hand. "This is horse shit!" He slapped the soiled hand across Dorhen's face. "What the hell kind of trick are you playing on me, boy-o?" He smacked him twice more.

Clumps of manure littered the floor. Dorhen gawked at his once-magic hood. Even he hadn't known that would happen. Arius Medallus had made it for his use alone. Hopefully, his moonstone wouldn't turn to horse dung if and when Kalea picked it up.

Kalea.

He never should have dropped the moonstone for her. Better if she forgot about him and stayed safe. Maybe she'd go home to her parents when she realized he was gone. Settling on that thought soothed his troubled mind.

But he hadn't actually seen her escape. For all he knew, she might've gotten caught. No. She got away and returned to her home to live happily with her mother. She was safe by now. And as soon as he got out of here, he'd find her house and join her there. Her family home was in Taulmoil, she'd said. He was strong with lots of stamina; he could bargain with her parents for his physical labor to let him stay.

The two men eyed each other. "This ain't simply some journeyman *saehgahn* lost in the human lands," the old one said to the young.

He turned to Dorhen and wiped his filthy hand on Dorhen's white undershirt. "Listen here." He grinned close to his face. Dorhen wanted nothing more than to look away. He hadn't been exposed to such close human contact besides Kalea before. "I bet I know your name. Is it Dorhen?"

Dorhen tried to keep his face straight, to mask his secrets, but it proved impossible. He huffed and darted his eyes away, only to have them drawn back to the man's smug stare.

"I thought so. We've got 'im, Jerick. We're getting a pretty big reward when the kingsorcerer gets here."

He snapped out a laugh and slapped two open palms on Dorhen's chest with enough force to make him swing. He grabbed Dorhen's face again and squeezed his cheeks. "Where you been, you little bastard? Bah, you know what? I don't care. You know how much you're worth to our kingsorcerer?" A grin spread across his greasy, pock-scarred face, and the sour air seeping through the smile stank up Dorhen's personal space.

"What do you want with me?" Dorhen asked.

His answer came as another slap to the face. "A major rule in this community is no questions. Got it? Because the fact is, you can ask questions all day long, but we'll do with you what we want to do. That's how it is. Now, I suggest you obey. Don't try to escape again, or we'll clobber you real good."

"Spare his face, Harn. The kingsorcerer will want to see him."

Harn squeezed Dorhen's cheeks again as if he were a child. "Right, we wouldn't want to ruin this pretty thing up. So instead we'll mess up other parts of you."

Harn punched Dorhen in the stomach and he groaned, unable to lean over and hug himself. He tried to gasp for air but couldn't. His lungs ached when they finally filled, and his stomach gurgled with nausea. Nothing remained in his stomach to vomit, so bile oozed up his throat instead.

"The girls," he managed to croak out despite the man's warning. The image of Kalea's terrified face in his last memory rattled a sob through him. He had to find out if she'd escaped or not. "What did you do with the convent girls?" He strained to lift his lolling head.

"More questions. Wrong!" Jerick handed Harn a horse crop, and he proceeded to whip it across Dorhen's stomach. "I'm a patient man, boy-o. I've got all night to help you learn your etiquette. The kingsorcerer comes tomorrow, and he'll expect you on your best behavior.

"We're going to untie you now. Once again, don't try to escape. Embarrassment is all you'll accomplish. This place is well-warded and hidden far away from where we took you."

They cut the rope, and Dorhen crumpled into a heap of shaking limbs on the floor, bending over to cradle the raw streak across his stomach. Jerick tugged his shirt off so Harn could deliver a set of loud, burning lashes to his back.

Eventually, they left him alone to compose himself. He put his shirt back on gingerly over the new raw lacerations on his clammy skin. To his surprise, they fed him a steaming hot plate of cabbage and mutton. And when he satisfied them with his good behavior, they tied his hands, grabbed his arms, and guided him upstairs into the manor where several roaring fireplaces soothed his chilled bones. Plenty of other men wearing red tabards and tunics traversed the halls muttering eerie chants or sat beside the fireplaces, turning to gawk as Dorhen passed.

Everywhere they went, Dorhen stretched his neck in search of Kalea, or at least any of Kalea's friends. Last night, maybe two nights ago, the sorcerers had dragged him through the sparking portal, then continued going out and in again, collecting the fighting girls. They were screaming. Dorhen fell, and two or three girls fell on top of him as the sorcerers threw them through the magic doorway. He got lost in the confusion of thrashing limbs and sharp fingernails for a time, lost in the screaming.

He made his way out of the pile and was caught when a sorcerer noticed him. The hole in the air closed abruptly, stealing his slim chance to run back through. He fought. The sorcerers yelled for something called a hookah.

An object hit him in the face, purposefully or not. He fell. He might've fallen on a girl. Two sorcerers tackled him while he was down. One pinned him as the other strapped a leather mask to his face.

The leather was warm and smoky. A long hose attached the mask to another object. The smoke smelled like flowers and made him lightheaded, but he couldn't take the mask off because they had also tied his hands during his daze. He breathed a lot of the smoke, and afterward things didn't make much sense anymore.

Now, as he walked with Harn and Jerick, he searched that chaotic memory for any indication that Kalea had also been thrown through the portal onto the pile of squirming bodies. He shook his head. She would've called his name if she was. He also would've picked out her protesting voice among the others—unless they had knocked her out. The thought of the sorcerers doing that to Kalea made him grind his teeth and work his wrists, straining the bindings around them.

Crack! Jerick whipped his back, and the leather strap stung his arms too. "Don't try to escape," he snarled.

Dorhen wouldn't try now. First, he'd make sure Kalea wasn't here.

A certain wing housed a series of apartments. "No getting away now, boy-o," Harn said as they walked through the long hall of doors. "If you can shut your mouth and walk, I'll take your bonds off you. Like I said, no point in running. This place is locked up tight and crawling with brutes worse than me."

Dorhen offered his hands, and the man proceeded to free them, then he followed them to the end of the hall of doors, where another staircase took them up. They stopped at a certain door with a large, dark splotch of damage across it.

"The kingsorcerer sent word ahead of him," Harn said. "He liked hearing about your spirited fight the other night and about your fornications with the vestals. He wants you to be comfortable. So this room is yours, tidied and prepped for your arrival…brother."

"Brother?" Dorhen said, and quickly winced. He didn't get another slap.

Inside waited a wooden frame with ropes, a mattress rolled over to the side, a basin, and a small fireplace. Some other sort of basin with a lid over it stood on the floor in the corner. No windows.

"Nice, huh?" Harn said. "The rest of us have to work for years to gain a room like this, you lucky bastard. You really make me sick, you know that?"

Dorhen stepped inside. The walls were wood paneled. Dead trees, but trees nonetheless. As soon as he turned back around, Harn shoved a finger in his face.

"Once again, behave." Harn shook his head and combed his fingers through his grey hair. "C'mon, Jerick. Let's go eat."

"I need a screw," Jerick murmured as he exited the room first. Harn slammed the door behind him, and a lock clicked.

Despite the lack of windows in the dark, musty room, it must've been the next morning when the door opened. A man's laughter startled Dorhen awake, and he jumped to sit up. He'd curled up on the mattress spread out on the floor, and slept on and off for an unknown amount of time. At the sight of Harn, he relaxed and rubbed his eyes.

"What'll I do with you? How feral are you? Don't you know the mattress goes across the bed ropes?" Harn wiped the corner of his eye with a knuckle and shook his head. "Mercy."

Jerick appeared beside him and also laughed. "What an idiot. Putting the mattress on the bedframe keeps the draft and the cockroaches away, you fool."

Harn turned to his companion. "Well," he said, "who tells the kingsorcerer?"

Jerick raised his hands by his face. "Knob that in the head. His audition is still going on."

Harn's mouth dropped open. "All night?"

Dorhen went to the basin to rinse his face, and turned back around to listen to their exchange.

"Indeed. He has more than a load of convent girls. A gaggle from Wexwick arrived too, some of them talented prostitutes."

Convent girls?

Harn snorted. "Wish I were an elf. Mine can hardly stand for one round anymore." He turned to Dorhen. "You people are a filthy bunch, aren't ya?" They both laughed. "Anyway, the kingsorcerer 'specially said to tell him when the boy wakes up. Do we take it to heart?"

"Of course we do. But he'll be angry if we interrupt him at the wrong minute. If we can't get the words out fast enough, a mighty pain will befall us."

The two of them paused to look at Dorhen.

"You hear our dilemma, boy-o?"

Dorhen shrugged.

"Let's send *him*," Jerick said, pointing.

"Eh?"

"Let him walk in and announce himself."

Harn smiled, holding his eyes on Dorhen. "Boy-o, follow us. The lord will be happier to see you than us right now… Well, he's happiest seeing something else, but the fact is, you've gotta tell him you're here now, because his audition could last all day."

Dorhen looked from one man to the other. "What are you talking about?"

"Follow us and you'll see." Harn grabbed Dorhen's arm, digging his meaty fingers into the muscle, and guided him out of the chamber.

They didn't go far before pausing at the mouth of a longer, wider corridor. Harn pointed. "See that line of girls before the large double doors?"

Dorhen nodded.

"Go in there and tell the *saehgahn* inside who you are. He's the kingsorcerer."

Dorhen took slow steps forward as the two men lingered behind, whispering. His awkwardness intensified to some sort of numb, out-of-body sensation as he approached the line of women waiting outside the double doors. He had never walked around in a crowded place without his magic hood, or at least a regular hood, before. Everything about his identity was out in the open now. No one seemed to care about his elven heritage, though, besides Harn's odd comment about wishing to be one.

Some of the women in line wore gowns similar to the one Kalea had worn on the night of her convent's raid. Dorhen's heart hammered and nausea boiled in his core at the thought of what these girls had gone through. Such violence had come right into the place Kalea slept. Though their hair hung long and silky, recently combed, their complexions were ashy, and they wobbled and swayed in their stances.

He reached out to the one at the end of the line, about to ask if she was all right, but another's chestnut-colored hair caught his eye. His heart skipped and dropped to the floor.

"Kalea?" He rushed forward and grabbed her shoulder. "Kalea, did they hurt you?" He spun her around.

It wasn't Kalea who returned his attention with a dead stare. The girl swayed, eyes dull and droopy. Whatever they'd done to Dorhen to make him weak and incoherent, they had done something similar to Kalea's friends. Her eyelids closed and struggled to open again. It wasn't Kalea. Sighing, he surveyed the other hair colors—no others matched Kalea's. She had escaped. She had to have escaped.

As he stared, wondering what to do now that he'd found the other girls, a woman standing next to him whispered, "You're an elf too." This one didn't sway or blink dizzily. Her pretty painted face made him stare for a few extra seconds. Thick rings of soot outlined her eyes to make them look bigger. Black hair tumbled over her shoulders and curled about her face. Between a short bodice and a low-hipped skirt, her exposed stomach shimmered with silver chains running across her navel. At a second glance, there wasn't actually a bodice to cover her, only rows of frisky beads dangling over her breasts. This wasn't a convent girl, perhaps one of those "prostitutes" from Wexwick.

"What's going on here?" he asked.

"An audition," she said. A few other women like her throughout the line were smoothing their hair, wiping their faces, or dabbing color on their lips. "We all got invitations to come here. Except those young ones back there… They look like they could each use a jug of rum." She giggled behind her ringed hand.

"Audition?" Dorhen stumbled around the word.

The woman batted her eyes. "Yeah. We hear the king in there is ridiculously rich and he wants some mistresses. Wish me luck, won't you?"

Dorhen nodded once despite not fathoming what was happening. He bypassed the rest of the women and braved a few more steps into the dark room beyond the open door. A soothing blue light accompanied by the ambient glow of candles lit the space. Soft noises alerted him of the people in the room.

His feet stopped and didn't seem to want to move again. A carved wooden lattice dividing the room came into view, behind which most of the candles glowed. Two figures interacted back there. Smooth, feminine legs were kneeling on the floor before a standing figure who panted in deep, heavy pulls. Dorhen couldn't make out much more.

When his foot scraped on the wooden floor, the standing figure's head shifted and a pair of yellow eyes appeared, reflecting the light and glaring like a venomous snake. A feminine voice sighed before the standing figure moved, leaving her on the floor to wipe her mouth against the back of her hand. Dorhen squinted to make sure that wasn't Kalea.

An elf came from around the divider, tightening the strings on his leggings. He wore a loose black robe with red trim. His blonde hair danced in wavy locks over his shoulders, vibrant in color, yet a bit oily. He studied Dorhen with those piercing yellow eyes.

"I was told to announce myself." He paused to swallow. "I'm Dorhen."

The other elf's voice grated out, low and breathy. "Of course you are." He strode closer in a wide arc, surveying Dorhen up and down. "Who else would you be?"

Dorhen worked his jaw, looking for an answer.

The blonde elf stopped several feet away and dragged his gaze over Dorhen once more. "You are mature. How old are you?"

"Twenty-two."

"*Saehgahn?*"

Dorhen worked his mouth, unsure what to say.

"Have you been through the ceremony? Do you even know what…? Where have you been?"

Dorhen clamped his mouth shut. Afraid to withhold information from this one, he chose the most comfortable answer. "The human lands."

"Obviously."

"Why am I here?"

The elf squinted. "Try not to ask me questions. You're here because I've been looking for you. This is a small outpost, but soon you'll go home with me to the Ilbith tower." At Dorhen's silence he continued, "It'll be a transition for you, but such is life."

"Why are you looking at me like that?" Dorhen asked.

"Do I stare, lad? Pardon if I'm having trouble grasping what's happening here. That I am actually looking at...*you*. I knew it was you before you told me. You look unmistakably like *her*."

"Who?"

"Your mother."

Dorhen's throat closed up, but he wanted to ask again.

"Do you remember your mother, lad?"

Dorhen nodded, but changed to shaking his head. "Who are you?"

"I'm your father's brother. My name is Lamrhath. And you are... Dorhen...aren't you?" He surveyed Dorhen yet again. "You have your father's nose, but everything else resembles her." Lamrhath reached toward his face. "Your eyes have the telltale green hue, and your brown hair—like a damned tree trunk."

He laid his hand upon Dorhen's cheek. His fingers smelled strongly of a fascinating scent Dorhen couldn't place.

"You knew my mother?" Dorhen whispered, and Lamrhath removed his hand.

"I knew her. I met her the day you were born. She was weak and frail because you caused her a lot of pain when you came out of her."

Dorhen paused in whatever he would say next and aimed his gaze at the floor. An ache crept into his throat.

"We'll talk more of her later."

Lamrhath put his arm over Dorhen's shoulders and guided his attention to the woman he'd left on the floor, sitting on the rug, waiting. Though long, her soft-looking hair could not quite conceal her nakedness. It wasn't Kalea, he knew by the feminine layers of fat on her belly and legs. Kalea's body was gaunt because of how much she "fasted."

"Dorhen," Lamrhath said, "you and I are the only *saehgahn* here. We two are superior. And you are my kin, so I have special plans for you. I've no children, so you'll be my heir. My young lad, I heard you like to sneak into convents, and that made me laugh." He gave a smile. "Few things can."

Dorhen frowned. "What do you all think I...?" He stopped himself before finishing the question.

"Come out here," Lamrhath continued. "These girls were chosen for my audition. You may know some of them. I know this place is strange to you, so pick one to keep you company tonight. Don't be afraid. They're not allowed to refuse."

As soon as they stepped into the corridor with Lamrhath's arm draped around Dorhen's shoulders, the women's primping motions moved faster for a second before their hands fell into neat order by their sides or behind their backs. Too many eyes. Dorhen averted his own.

"Don't be shy. The flashy ones know all about this business. Which one takes your liking?"

Dorhen struggled to find a way to refuse. "I'll be fine alone tonight," he said after a moment of awkward silence.

Lamrhath's next word came as a spirited snap. "Nonsense."

"I *haven't* ever had a woman."

Lamrhath stopped and narrowed his brow. "You're a virgin? Then why were you caught when…?"

Dorhen tightened his lips. He would tell no one about Kalea.

Lamrhath sniffed. "We'll talk all about you later. But listen to me. You'll find out what we do here soon, and I'll tell you now it's hard. We hardly sleep, and as soon as night falls, we'll be knocking at your door to join us in our ritual. So while you're here, you'll learn to channel your exhaustion away by methods other than sleep. It's a process granted to us by the great and powerful Naerezek. Do you know of him?"

Dorhen shook his head.

"You'll learn. And tonight, you'll be initiated into his arcane faith. A lot of our rituals can get…rough. If you don't lose your virginity in your own chamber, I'm afraid you'll have to lose it on the ritual floor with all of us watching. I expect one option is more embarrassing than the other. The choice is yours…"

Lamrhath regarded Dorhen's lost expression. One of his golden eyes twitched. "How about this? I'll pick a docile one for you because that's the impression I'm getting about you. So go on then, you're excused."

Sliding his hand from around Dorhen's shoulder, Lamrhath gave him a firm shove.

Intuition told Dorhen to walk briskly at his dismissal. He wanted to look back and gawk at the intimidating character but abstained. Lamrhath's hateful voice raked his memory, and Dorhen couldn't get away from him fast enough.

A few hours later, as Dorhen paced in his claustrophobic little chamber brainstorming escape plans, the door creaked open and a short, slim blonde woman wearing a long wool robe slipped in. She dropped a bag by the wall and leaned against the closed door and smiled. This one hadn't been standing in line.

"What do you want?"

"I'm Selka. They sent me. I'm supposed to help you relax. Is it true you've never done it before?"

"Done what?"

"Had sex."

His face flamed with heat. "No."

Her smile curled wider until her teeth glistened in the candlelight. "Aw, that's so cute." She let her robe fall down around her bare shoulders. She wasn't wearing anything underneath. "I mean, look at you. You're so tall and…mature. It's hard to believe. How old are you?"

"You can go." Dorhen pointed to the door.

She stepped closer. "Don't be shy, sweetie. We can practice as much as you want. I'm considered an expert at this."

When he dodged her hands, her attention turned to his mattress on the floor. She put her robe back on her shoulders and bent to gather it up.

"First we put the bed together." She paused to regard him staring at her. What could he say to get out of this situation? "I suppose you like the floor better." She dragged the mattress out a bit and spread it, smoothing the blanket and fluffing the straw pillow. She plopped down and patted the spot beside her. He didn't move from his stance against the wall.

"You look troubled. What's wrong?" Selka stood up and approached him. "Sex isn't just carnal. It's also about lovemaking, which is tender and emotional. We can touch each other. Here…" She gathered her long flaxen hair in a large lock and extended it. "Feel my hair. I recently washed it."

He tucked his chin and kept his hands firmly by his sides.

She cleared her throat and let her hair drop. "Talking can be a big part of it too. So talk to me."

"I'm not supposed to be here."

She reached for his shaking hand. He'd never considered himself to be particularly large, but his hands were giant compared to her slim, graceful ones.

"Aw." She patted the top of his hand. "Neither am I. But here we are… I've never been with an elf before. Well, except for the kingsorcerer. And he wasn't nearly as nervous as you… Then again, I guess he'd done it a thousand times before he met me."

She pointed a new, more intrigued smile at him. Her eyes were also enhanced with soot and a powdery blue pigment. Her lips were stained bright red. "You're different than him, though."

"Those girls out there were attacked and kidnapped!"

"Sit down, sweetie." He pulled away. "You need to relax." She extended her hand toward his face, and he dodged.

He pointed to the door. "You have to leave."

When he retreated to the wall again, hoping she'd go away, she approached behind him and put her hand on his back. His eyes watered, and he growled at the spark of pain she ignited.

"Did they whip you?"

"Yes," he said through clenched teeth. Keeping his back turned from her, he wiped his face with a shaky hand.

"Hold on." Her footsteps padded away, and the sound of her rummaging through her bag followed. "I can tell you're one who is like an onion; I'll have to peel away the layers to help you relax, starting with your physical wounds." She swirled a bottle containing a thick substance and gave a bright smile. "Sit on the mattress and take off your shirt."

He paced to the other end of the room and faced the wall. The fiery burning in his back intensified. A cold sweat doused his temples and upper lip. He buried his face in his hands and receded into the corner to wait for her to leave.

"This isn't happening."

"What isn't happening?"

What in the world was he doing here? Sixteen years he'd spent living in the fresh air, eating wild strawberries, blackberries, freshwater fish, and sleeping under the stars. Every other spring, he'd made his way to the southwest side of the Lightlands where the pines scented the breeze. So many times he'd brushed right past Kalea and not seen her. His life had changed forever when he did meet her. He'd known her face and her scent and her voice for a few sweet days, although time didn't matter when it came to her. Her uncanny presence had attached to his soul. It belonged there. Finding her had been like a puzzle piece falling neatly into place. Wherever she dwelled, so would he. That handful of days had filled him with dreams and fantasies and her laugh. He'd found his place. His purpose. And then all of it...all of a sudden...had disappeared in one night.

"Why are you shaking?" The voice cooed, soft and tender like the hand touching his arm. Like Kalea's voice.

He kept his eyes clenched and hidden. He couldn't take the chance of it not being her.

The hand tugged the back of his shirt up. "Let's see now. Oh, dear.

It'll be fine, though. Hold still."

The sound of a tipping bottle *glunked*. A cold wetness spread over one of the lower lash marks on his side. The cool put the burning out. After a long sigh, he took control of his breathing. He still didn't want to open his eyes.

"There might be too much light in here for relaxation," Kalea said, as if reading his thoughts. She blew out the candle, and the fire in his wounds quieted a little more. She tugged on his arm. "Come sit down, or you'll never relax."

He stumbled through the dark until his foot found the mattress on the floor. He sat hugging his knees as she pulled his shirt up around the back of his neck. She turned the bottle again and added more coolness to the screaming gashes on his back.

"A few of them have torn open, but most of them are red and irritated. This salve will also clean the open wounds so they'll heal better."

It must've been the same salve Kalea had used on her lash marks in the bath. Though the darkness enshrouded his vision, he held his eyes closed to keep out the unfamiliar surroundings. Images of the convent raid returned to him in the dark, however. Being drugged up on that flowery smoke they'd forced him to inhale had obscured his past, his present, and his physical awareness. His mind was clear now, and those memories and concerns had returned.

"Those girls…" he said, unable to keep the weepy sound out of his voice.

She shushed him softly. "You're all right now."

Anything Kalea told him must be true. After her hands finished covering his back with the cold, oily liquid, they went into his hair to massage his scalp.

"You're safe now."

"Kalea," he whispered.

"Yes," she whispered back.

Tingles ran from each of her fingertip points. He sighed again, and his shoulders slackened. From behind him, she pecked kisses on his cheek and traced them along his neck. Goosebumps rose on either of his arms, depending on which side of his neck her lips touched. Her hands grazed around to his chest and stomach.

"Lie down," she whispered in his ear. She put his shirt neatly down, and he obeyed. "Careful, try not to rub the salve away on your shirt."

When he lay flat in surrender, sore and too tired to move anymore, her hands went to his codpiece and fiddled the laces loose. He could've slept easily, but the touch of slender fingers sliding around and caressing his penis filled him with both a new alertness and an intensified relaxation. All his blood traveled downward in thundering pulses.

In a trembling whisper, he said, "I thought the lashings came after the unclean thoughts."

A gentle little laugh rang in the darkness, though it rang flat. Was it still Kalea? Her laugh should sound like fluttery music. Her scent was different too. Thinking made his head hurt, though. Every part of his body except the part she handled went limp. He lay helpless in a medley of exhaustion and tingles.

"No more talking," she responded. "You have to let me do my work, or they'll beat me later."

"I won't let them." He found her hair and ran his hand through the soft locks.

Caught by surprise as he stroked her hair, he sucked in a breath when a pair of lips kissed down on the tip. He exhaled over a long moment to savor the texture of her soft tongue playing around his foreskin. The lips slid down the length of the shaft and up again, squeezing, sucking.

His other senses fluttered away in the dim atmosphere of the last remaining candle. Shadows danced over the walls with its turbulent flickering. He let it all go. The warm radiance of his inner furor spread to every limb. Is this what it was like to be touched? An enchanting blend of relaxation and excitement he'd waited a long time to experience. He used to assume he never would.

When he opened his eyes again, the tree canopy bowed over him. Kalea was there, like in his dreams. Lying limply, he let her do with him whatever she wanted. A smile touched his lips. He melted into a drift of euphoric darkness.

Chapter 19
A Hole for His Heart

The knife plunged into his flesh. The other hands swarmed in and peeled the flesh open for the prominent hand to delve in. Dorhen screamed at the cold shock...

And woke up sweating on a stale mattress. Candlelight flickered on the wall in a small room with warm, salty air.

"There you are. Have a bad dream?"

He jumped at the voice of the blonde woman wearing a robe—Selka. She sat by the little fireplace, trying to ignite some logs. "You were so tired," she said, tossing more kindling twigs in. "You suffered a small delirious panic attack, but after a good blow you fell right to sleep. You were out for a full hour. When you're ready again, you can practice on me. Shouldn't be long now before their ritual starts."

Dorhen squinted. "What do you mean 'blow'?"

She burst out a flat-toned laugh and strode over, a smooth, naked leg sliding out of the robe with each step, and tousled his hair.

"You are so cute. I'm starting to like you."

"Never mind. I think I understand." The bile overflowed in his stomach. What had he done? This might be something Kalea would make him confess about. Of course, it would get him in boiling trouble with her, and his preference not to tell her battled with his desire to oblige her every request, as it usually did.

"You're already sitting more loosely. Glad I could help." She returned to the fireplace.

Leaning on his elbow, he pulled the blanket over his chest. His undershirt stuck to his back with the salve. "What's the ritual you mentioned?"

"One of their routine things."

"Why do I have to go?"

She raised her eyebrows and gave a breezy smile. "What do you mean *why*? You're going to learn sorcery." She poked the little burning twigs with a stronger one.

"Learn sorcery? I can't."

"Why not?"

"Kalea won't have it. She'll never talk to me again. Besides, I have to get back to her."

The woman played the name on her tongue. "Ka-lee-ah. You were calling me that earlier. It seemed to make you feel better, so I played along."

"Oh, God." Dorhen buried his face in his hands and curled up on his side.

"It was cute. Is she your sweetheart?"

He didn't answer. Instead, he rose to his feet. The front of his leggings hung open, letting the chilly air shock his genitals, so he refastened it and double-knotted the strings. He strode to stand over her.

"You're going to tell me how to get out of here. Does this place really have magic wards?"

Looking up at him, her smile dropped and her eyes narrowed. "Think again, sweetie."

"About what?"

She shook her head with a dark glare in her eye that made a shiver run through him. "They've got you now. Just like they got me." She had made that comment before.

"Tell me how to get out of here."

Her mouth tightened as she stood. "If I do, they'll skewer me and make me a prop in their rituals!" She shoved him. "Don't get me killed!"

Dorhen fell onto the naked bedframe's corner post and remained leaning on it, his hands up. She stared him down with an intensity he didn't want to challenge.

"I won't get you killed," he said. "It'll be all on me, I promise."

She threw a pointed finger. "I've worked hard to gain the position I have now. I even work in the kingsorcerer's chamber. You won't ruin my life, okay?"

"Okay."

She sank back to her knees to continue with the fire. "When I'm done here, I'll get you some supper and then I'll teach you how to please a woman."

He knelt beside her. "What are they going to make me do in the ritual?"

She glanced up, her lips pouting now. "I don't know. But they sent me to teach you about sex, and if you don't show them you learned something, they'll beat me up good. That's their way." She leaned in and blew on the embers until a flame blossomed.

Dipping his chin nearly to his chest, he murmured, "They disgust me. I won't participate."

"I think you will."

He grabbed her wrist as it moved for more kindling, and she froze. "Tell me something useful about this place. Anything. I swear they'll never find out."

She glared at his hand grasping hers and jerked away. She stood. "I'll be back with your supper." She slammed the door behind her.

A locking sound didn't follow like when Harn and Jerick had left him alone in here. The fire crackled in the little stone-lined hole in the wall, filling the room with a portion of its smoke. All he had left of his possessions were his leggings, shoes, and his undershirt. Selka's bag sat abandoned by the door. He threw it open and rummaged for anything he could use as a weapon. All he found were bottles of different colored smelly oils, some extra candles, and a book.

He attempted to sound out the words burned onto the leather cover. "C-coi-tu-s, Coitus…Mm-a-g-mag-nificenzuhhh…"

Giving up on the strange, foreign words, he opened it to the middle and found drawings of men and women not wearing any clothing, intertwining with each other. Suddenly hot and clammy, he flipped several pages until he found a drawing of what she had done to him with her mouth an hour ago.

Dropping the book with a grimace, he turned to the bedframe and tried the post. It wobbled. He yanked on it, tugging it out of the joint which connected it to the crossbeams with the ropes threaded through. He braced his foot on the crossbeam at the foot of the bed.

Crack-crick! The more he pulled, the more it cracked and the looser it became. *Crack!* He fell backward on the last jerk with a broken bed post in his hand. Its thickness required two hands wrapped around it.

He practiced a few heavy and awkward swings. It would have to do since it was the only weapon this room offered. He returned to the bag to stuff the largest oil bottle into the fold of his tied shirt and went out the door. Trying to remember which turns they had taken on the way to his new room, he traversed back through the halls.

A man stepped around the corner wearing a threadbare red mantle. "What are you—?"

Dorhen bashed his head with the wooden post and rushed forward. Not looking back to inspect his work, he flew down a set of stairs he remembered walking up…unless it was the opposite stairs they'd taken.

The house stretched on before him. Fancy carved panels lined the walls, though aged and damaged. Some were stained black as if this place had caught fire years ago. The wicked burn stains sent a cold shiver through him and emerged from his pores as misty sweat on his palms and sides. The smell of his house burning with his mother inside returned to his nose after all those years. With an increase of his heart rate, he rushed on.

The corridor wound around for a long way, offering many doors. A sculpted wooden archway announced a curling stairway descending again. That…might be right. As long as he could find the ground floor, he could find a way out. Although climbing out a second story window wasn't a bad idea either…

"The elf is out!" someone cried.

From the dining hall, a handful of scowling men dashed, red robes flowing around their feet. One pointed a finger, and the other three drew long, glinting daggers.

"What are you doing, new brother?"

"I'm leaving!"

The nearest one with a long dagger charged, but Dorhen kept his eye on the others.

Whoosh! He swiped his club wide across the others after side-stepping the first dagger-wielder. The three men tumbled and climbed to their feet again, none of them injured.

Dorhen sprang backward and ran the way he had come, managing to disappear into a complex of corridors branching off from the central hall. He found a dark room with a desk holding potent, inky bottles and quills. No windows, though. He ducked behind an ornate bench against the wall.

Voices were rising, alerting all the manor residents to his violence. "Get the hookah!"

Not the flower smoke! He couldn't let them use it to daze him again.

As he watched the doorway from his hiding place, a candle glow rushed past with a group of men. As their voices faded, Dorhen took the chance to slip out behind them. He couldn't hide in one place forever, or they'd eventually find him in a thorough search.

Hoisting his club, he exited the room and sprinted down the hall; his soft leather shoes aided in running quietly. He navigated a set of dark, winding corridors with the help of the moonlight shining through windows.

Another set of voices approached from behind. Throwing his free hand into his shirt, he fished for the oil bottle, which had made its way around to his back. Pulling the cork with his teeth, he dumped the bottle's contents onto the floor and darted through the nearest door.

A woman shrieked, startling him in the dark.

"Please don't," the woman said. Dorhen squinted until his eyes adjusted to the room's dimmer lighting. "I recently pleased one of you. I need time before I can do it again."

It didn't take long for the angry footsteps to echo in the hall on the other side of the door. Dorhen put his finger to his lips, hoping she could see it, and shushed her.

She whimpered. "I've been here a wretched two weeks. I can't—"

He lurched forward and jumped onto the bed where she sat nestled into its sagging straw mattress, then snatched her, causing her to yelp until he put his hand over her mouth. The voices in the hall were too close now. He shushed her again. Silent sobs rattled her in his arms.

"Shut up," he whispered. It didn't help, and he was forced to squeeze her tighter. She was naked under the sheet bunched around her middle. He'd apologize later.

The voices and footsteps herded in beside their door, and some angry grunts and yelling erupted when they slipped on the oil pool he'd made. Their odd sounds made the naked woman quiet herself, though she hiccupped in his embrace.

At the highest point in their noisy crescendo, Dorhen released the woman, pushing her aside and leaping off the bed and out the door. He left the door open because her crying might provide more distraction.

Vaulting over a man who cursed and collected himself from his hands and knees, he sprinted past some other stunned men, who were wiping their oily hands on their handkerchiefs and dusting off their soiled red garments. He headed through the corridor in the opposite direction.

"Hey!" a voice yelled behind him. "Was that him? Little bastard!"

Groaning at his bad idea, Dorhen ran on, around the curving corridor and down a few gently sloping landings with carved steps.

Without a moment to think, he took the first available door leading to a warm room with a soft glow. A kitchen. Large pots boiled, letting off cabbage-scented steam. A haunch of meat steamed on the stone slab, ready for carving.

A woman gasped at his intrusion. Selka!

"What are you doing?" she shrieked.

Dorhen shushed her and ducked beside her, behind the central hearth with the largest cauldron.

"I don't believe this."

Kneeling beside her, he took her tiny, graceful hand and kissed it. "Please," he whispered. "Help me. Help me."

She studied his expression. He kissed her fingertips. "Please."

The voices echoed through the corridor toward this room, and Dorhen shut his voice off, using his eyes instead to win any kind of support he could from this woman. This woman whom he didn't know, but had already shared such a deeply intimate moment with. Her lips pouted. He only needed her to tell the men she hadn't seen him.

Footsteps tapped outside the door. Dorhen shook his head slowly at her, his mouth opened to form the word *please*. He caressed her palm with his thumb. The door hinges whined open.

She screamed and pulled her hand away. "Aiiih! He's got me! He's attacking me! Help! He's bewitching me with elven magic!"

She ran across the room and covered her face. The men stormed forward and seized Dorhen, tossing his club aside. As they dragged him out, he locked his eyes with Selka. Her face rebounded from her fake fear, now showing blankness.

They dragged him through the tallest set of doors he'd seen yet, into a large hall where people smoked and murmured by a roaring fireplace. At the center back of the room, an array of red velvet and shimmering gold draperies spilled from the ceiling and pooled on the floor behind a chair where a crowned figure lounged with one knee up.

"Hello, Dorhen. You're early. Did you have a good lay already?"

It was Lamrhath. He didn't bother to turn his eyes; instead he kept them focused on a man standing in front of a wooden rectangular panel, smearing pasty colors on its surface to make Lamrhath's image. Lamrhath kept still, posing one hand on his bare abdomen and the other on the side of his face.

"How did Selka do? She's the best chamber mistress in this outpost, you know. Only the best for my little heir."

The men let go of his arms, and Dorhen stood on his own. He stepped forward. "I want to leave."

Lamrhath turned his eyes to Dorhen. "Why?"

"You took me against my will. I don't belong here. I live in the forest."

"Excuse me. You interfered with our official business."

"What official business? You attacked young girls!"

Lamrhath dropped the rest of his pose, and the man with the brush and colors exhaled and sat on a stool beside his panel.

"If you weren't exactly who you are, you'd be dead right now, you follow?" Lamrhath leaned forward. "Those girls were promised to us, and we merely arrived to collect our dues. But you showed up—a bizarre surprise—and killed three valuable people. You deserve a slow death."

Dorhen swallowed and stepped back again.

"But you happen to be the famous Dorhen! Dorhen! *Dorhen*! A name I hear daily! Dorhen! I have plans for you, *Dorhen*! You're alive because of your name. I have a great reward set aside, *Dorhen*! If you want it, you'll follow orders. If I send you out for sage, you'll bring it. If I send you out for gold, you'll bring it. You'll say the chants I ask you to say. You'll cast the spells I assign you. You'll fuck whom I ask you to fuck! You're on a road to great things, and all you must do is obey!"

He leaned back again and continued the glare. Dorhen had always assumed he had no family, but this was his uncle. For an uncle who'd promised him rewards and greatness, he displayed an awful lot of hatred.

"How have you heard my name so many times?"

Lamrhath curled his lip into a sneer. "And there he goes, asking questions."

A fist hooked around and punched Dorhen's stomach. He curled over and fell to a kneeling position, determined to keep upright.

"I've been kind to you. You're my kin. I welcomed you. I promised you a reward when we go home. I also sent my best chamber mistress to your room. And you want to leave?" He sighed and rubbed his forehead. "I thought you'd be thrilled. You lived in the dirt before I brought you here. We work hard, but we also enjoy luxury, as you can see. I can't believe you'd be so rude to your loving uncle."

Dorhen clenched his teeth and shook his head, trembling as he returned to standing straight.

"This is awkward… Dorhen, we have a policy. Well, it's a program actually. Sometimes we get recruits who don't quite know how things work. So we put them through the program to help them learn. Normally, these recruits go on to be servicemen, but you're still my heir, rest assured. You'll be kingsorcerer one day. Do you understand the meaning of this?"

Dorhen kept silent.

"We're making progress. Our faction, Ilbith, will own the Darklands soon, and we're easing our way into the Lightlands to better gather their available resources in gold. As kingsorcerer, I'll be the most powerful person on the continent, and if I should die, you'll take my place. Don't you want that?"

He worked his response out, determined to stay strong. "No."

"See?" Lamrhath threw a hand out. "This is what the program is designed for." He waved a pointed finger across the room. "Put him through the program. Oh, but first he must be officially initiated. Let him take the test, and then give him the sacred mark."

The men grabbed Dorhen again and wrestled him, limbs thrashing, toward a table. A man opened a splintery wardrobe, mismatched with some of the cushioned and gilded items in the room, and brought out a small iron cauldron with a linen cloth bound around the rim. Untying the twine and removing the cloth allowed a rancid smell to waft out of the cauldron and churn Dorhen's stomach.

Lamrhath descended his throne and approached the table. "This'll be interesting," he said. "We give this test to many people to find out how they can be of use to our establishment."

Dorhen wanted to ask what was in the cauldron, but he couldn't force any words through the nausea. His answer was provided by the liquid's dark red color, which showed as they poured some into a smaller stone bowl. The stink churned and spread farther during the pour. Dorhen covered his face and turned away, heaving. Nothing came out, but that could change.

"Pay attention," Lamrhath said, stepping closer. Another sorcerer grabbed Dorhen's hand and held it over the table. "We call this the Sacred Wine of the Hound. It's made from a mixture of animal and human blood, and blessed by Naerezek in our rituals. Naerezek teaches that everyone has a place in society, and they must all be sorted. We use this sacred potion to see your worth, and in some cases, your potential magical ability. Many a valuable new sorcerer can be discovered this way.

"Now, Dorhen"—his voice lowered to a hiss, his eyes bright—"put your hand in the blood."

Shaking his head, Dorhen pulled away. The sorcerer holding his hand jerked it forward again. Other sorcerers joined in to control his arm. It stank like death, like sour meat in the sun! If he touched it, he'd throw up.

He held his breath, growing sluggish as they fought against his muscles. His hand drew closer. He could barely see the bowl anymore as they pushed forward to dip his hand in.

"Stop struggling!" Lamrhath said.

A thick, slimy liquid splashed out and engulfed his hand. They'd won. Holding his hand in place, they all stared as the blood suddenly moved. Bubbles. Hundreds of small orbs rose and popped at the surface, churning up more of the noxious smell.

Lamrhath's mouth dropped open as he stared hard at the ever-rising bubbles, as if the blood were boiling. "Is it not hot?"

It wasn't hot, but Dorhen couldn't answer either way. He held his mouth with his other hand. Even the texture, sliding and squishing against his immersed hand, pushed him closer to illness.

"I've never seen it do this before in my life." Lamrhath's eyes shot to Dorhen. "Let him go."

They finally released Dorhen and he fell backward with his own force of resistance. On the floor, he hastily wiped his hand on his leggings. The smell didn't let up.

"What type of magic do you know?" Lamrhath asked, coming to stand over him.

"N-n-none!" Dorhen responded, still trying to wipe the stench off his skin.

"Tell me now, and I'll consider letting you take a bath. You can change into fresh clothes too."

As tempting as that sounded, he couldn't produce an answer that would please his uncle. "I don't know any magic." Gagging and choking on hopeless grief, he tucked his smelly hand under his arm and leaned forward. Now the stink was trapped in the fibers of his leggings. "I don't have magic. I don't."

Lamrhath's lips drew thin and his eyes narrowed. "All right. There's a possibility that some rare talent dwelling inside you, dormant for now, was detected by the blood potion. You're more valuable to me now than you've ever been, my little heir. We'll work with you to discover your secret. As you've been learning, cooperation earns rewards. All you must do is listen and obey. Can you do that?"

Dorhen didn't answer. Of course he wouldn't cooperate—he had to get out of here and find Kalea. He gasped and buried his nose in his sleeve.

Lamrhath grunted at him. "Oh, grow a pair. You'll get used to the smell of the potion. In fact, you'll be administering it to others in time."

He turned to the other sorcerers. "He needs full initiation. Now give him the mark."

The sorcerers seized him again and dragged him to the opposite side of the room where the fireplace blazed. They clamped a set of cold shackles around his wrists.

"To minimize your struggling," the stoutest sorcerer with a deep voice said.

Dorhen fought and kicked and wriggled anyway, until they grabbed his feet and carried him closer to the roaring fireplace. The heat baked his skin a long way before they stopped.

A man put a long iron pole into the flames.

"If ya don't stop kicking, we'll put the mask on ya," the man holding his feet said.

Someone laid out a wide plank and they placed him on it, stretching his bound wrists above his head and securing the chain on a hook at the far end. Other men tied his feet together and fixed them over a hook at the opposite side. Fastened down to the board, stretched out, he was helpless. The man standing over him drew a long, shiny dagger like he'd seen earlier; the flames reflected off its polished surface.

His nightmare was coming true. They were going to cut his heart out! Dorhen lost control of his breathing. He might've been crying. He might've wailed. But the intense heat dominated his awareness like the inside of a kiln. Burning, the way his mother had burned in their flaming house.

This was supposed to happen. This was how he'd die. He had never been meant to live like normal people, to live in peace beside Kalea as her protector and provider. She'd told him there was a hole in his heart. She hadn't known how right she was.

The man with the dagger balled Dorhen's shirt in his fist and sliced through it. Dorhen tensed up. He clenched his eyes shut and gritted his teeth. He knew precisely how much this would hurt. He began to hyperventilate.

No blade touched his skin. He opened one eye, unwilling to see it happening, but the anticipation would kill him if he didn't.

The man with the dagger stood again and sheathed it after only cutting open Dorhen's shirt, exposing his entire naked torso. For an instant, relief graced him, although the fire's heat seared, causing his skin to bead over with sweat.

To his right, a man kneeling at the hearth stood up, holding an iron pole with thick gloves. The end of the pole glowed bright orange. Another man kneeling at his left chanted monotone words in another language. He dipped his hand into a small bowl and brought them out glistening with amber oil in the light.

He put his oily fingers at the base of Dorhen's ribs, where the witches always cut in his dream. They still meant to cut him open! Dorhen wriggled frantically. The man continued his chant and drew a pattern on his chest with the oil.

The man with the hot iron stood over him, and Dorhen screamed, "No!"

A menacing smile brightened the iron-bearer's face as he waited for the one with the oil to finish his chant. The bright, glowing end of the pole curved around into several loops to form a design.

The man with the oil drew a line running through Dorhen's navel and then another going over his face to his hairline. He stood and stepped aside for the other man, poised for the press.

Dorhen thrashed. Hands came in to keep him steady. The man aimed the glowing iron at the spot where the first one had drawn the oil pattern and didn't hesitate to land it on Dorhen's skin.

At the last instant, Dorhen wiggled to the side and screamed. The brand pressed against his side, searing through his flesh, melting the skin upon his rib cage. Dorhen's screams echoed off each tall wall. His raw flesh stuck and ripped as the iron peeled away.

"Shit," the man with the brand said. "You little puke!"

He kicked Dorhen in the side with his booted foot, knocking his wind out. The brand had missed the oil pattern target. But it was done. The flesh-melting heat and short, uncontrollable gasps consumed Dorhen's consciousness.

Lamrhath approached as his vision faded, his mouth straight and solemn. "Welcome to Ilbith, little heir."

Chapter 20
Her Escort

Kalea's stomach growled as she thumbed through her coin purse, counting one last copper dendrea. Hoping she and Dorhen would be foraging for their dinners, she hadn't expected to have to rely much at all on her little fistful of savings. After a week of trudging her way toward Gaulice, it had nearly run out.

She unwrapped the salted fish from the convent's larder and took a bite, only to find it as satisfying as a fistful of salt. She spat out the first bite and leaned over the stream to rinse the salt off the rest of the fish. The effort hardly helped. Memory provided her with the image of seeing preserved fish soaking in buckets in her convent's kitchen. There was no time to soak the fish for several hours. She made do, eating the salty thing as best she could and making sure to refill her waterskin before leaving.

She quickly ate through the rest of her food stolen from the convent in the following days and whittled her money away at a springtime fair in a field, purchasing a few squares of hardtack to gnaw on for the next few days.

Deep in the forest, she wandered, lost until she stumbled over a hedge and onto a road with deep ruts carved into it among a mess of traffic footprints. It led her right into Gaulice, the next town up from Taulmoil. She'd skipped Taulmoil, her hometown, to avoid a confrontation with her parents or any neighbor who might recognize her.

In Gaulice, she sat huddled in a corner in some pub. The bouncer glared at her as she awoke from a nap. She hadn't bought anything yet anyway. She pulled herself to standing with a hold on an empty chair and gathered her basket and cloak.

The bouncer stomped over to her, his boots rattling the floor. She searched for a clear path to the door. As he moved to block her way, two Grey Knights from Wistara stopped him.

"Excuse me, sir," the first one said as the second unrolled a wide parchment.

Kalea skirted around the tables, keeping the knights between herself and the bouncer.

The knight continued, "Our establishment is missing a young student.

He's a mage in training. Has anyone with this likeness come in here?"

Though she hurried along, she glanced at their swords to make sure they didn't have one that stood out. They carried matching swords with short handles and slim crossguards—not at all like the one she was searching for.

The bouncer stretched his neck to watch Kalea until the knight mentioned "a handsome reward." Kalea scurried out the door into the soggy spring air. He might demand she give over some money for having slept so long in there, but Kalea hung onto her last copper.

The tall fleche of a sanctuary jabbed the sky behind rows of town rooftops. Evening was setting in, so she hurried toward it.

Along the way, she eyed every man in her path, checking to see if he carried a sword. She needed a shiny, molded one. Swords turned out to be a scarcity. Mostly farmers and workers of all sorts walked around here, no swordsmen. Another pair of Grey Knights strolled along one of the alleys, but they all carried the same typical, brass-hilted longswords with grey leather wrappings.

Gaulice's sanctuary could almost be a cathedral; it was bigger than her whole convent. She found her way to the back door after working her way through several darkening alleys. The orange sunset bathed light over the sanctuary's alley. Along each wall, several old, lame, and sick beggars had settled down, scooping scraps of mutton off broken trenchers. A handful of others ate pieces of trenchers.

Kalea knocked on the heavy oak door at the top of a few stone steps. After no answer, she knocked again. The door opened, and an elderly man stuck his nose out.

"Yes?"

"Hello, Father. I walked all the way here from the Hallowill convent, and I'm so hungry. I'm alone. Do you have any trenchers left?"

"Go away, girl, no prostitutes."

Prostitute?

"I'm not a prostitute, Father. I'm a vestal, and I need help. Can't you spare some leftovers?"

"You don't look like a vestal or a beggar to me. Go on now." The door slammed in her face.

Kalea looked down at herself. True, she hadn't brought her habit along, but in her normal laywoman's clothes, she didn't look *that* good. Dirt smudged her dress, and by the weight of her numb face, she must look haggard. She should've passed for a beggar.

She stepped away from the door. A thin-haired old lady on the ground licked mutton juice off her blackened fingers.

"You need it more than I do anyway," Kalea mumbled, and walked on.

She trudged along the street, collecting more mud on the hems of her skirts. Each step sent pins through her feet. Around a few corners, another pub opened. Its lamps were being lit and people filed in. She tucked her coin purse deep into her bodice so no one could pickpocket her last copper, and crammed in with the crowd.

Once inside, she sat in the corner. Elbows on her knees, she rested her head on her hand and watched the merrymakers, remembering to check out any sword to enter the room. None of them resembled the one in her dream, not in the least.

Plenty of busty ladies with plunging necklines moved about, sat with the men, and ate the food they bought. Those were prostitutes. Prostitutes didn't need to beg in the alley behind the sanctuary. She'd watched this exchange several times before as she hung around the pubs and taverns spying on men with swords. The ladies laughed and sipped ale, showering the men with compliments while petting their shoulders and twirling their hair around their fingers, and after a while they went up the stairs together in pairs. They worked this routine in all the places she'd visited.

Kalea scowled and leaned her head against the wall. She too had been offered food before by men like these. She had refused and walked out, retaining her pride and dignity—and her virginity.

Crossing her arms over her knees as if to protect the coin in her bodice from the pickpockets, she allowed herself to fall asleep.

Her arm tickled. A kid tugged at the shimmery handle of her washing bat. She swatted at him, and he ran out the door empty-handed.

"Find someone else to wash for you!" she yelled in her sleepy daze, although he had obviously wanted to steal it. After all, it gleamed like silver. It would be a tempting target.

The windows showed pale grey light, so it must be dawn. Half of the patrons from last night still moved about and occupied the tables in a calmer air than a few hours before.

The doorbell jingled as a new patron entered, heaving a huge pack on his back under a ratty grey cloak with one side thrown over the shoulder, hood drawn up. He looked like a turtle wearing that thing. He peered from side to side before rushing to a table to sit. He glanced around before throwing the hood off with a sigh. This man, who didn't wear the Grey Knights' livery, wore a sword. The tip of his scabbard peeked out the side of his cloak, a ratty, discolored scabbard with threads dangling off.

Kalea leaned far over to see more of the sword around the table. It didn't shine like the image Arius Medallus had shown her because it was bound in rags all over, including the hilt, which did slope like the sword she needed. No guarantee she'd found it, but she couldn't let this one go without a closer peek.

The newcomer appeared old enough to be her father. If only he were; ten years since seeing her dad might as well have been an eternity. She took off her kerchief and combed her fingers through her hair. Clearing her throat, she glided over to him, pausing until he finished murmuring to the barmaid, ordering "whatever they had" in a raspy voice.

She couldn't see much, especially after he moved his cloak over the sword like the wing of a protective mama-bird. Kalea released a breath through clenched teeth and cleared her throat again before swiping the spot on the bench next to him, close enough to touch shoulders. He jumped as soon as he noticed her.

"Hi," she said.

"What do you want?"

"Um…" She lowered her chin, dodging his eyes as they stabbed into hers. "Can I…can I see your sword?"

"Tch." He turned forward again. "I don't have time for a romp. Ask someone else."

"I'm not talking about a romp!"

He made a shooing motion with his hand. "Leave me alone. I've got serious business to think about."

Chewing her lip, she eased up off the bench. He kept his head low. She approached the bar and fumbled her coin purse out of her bodice. Slapping her last copper down, she ordered a pint of ale and placed it before the scruffy man.

"My treat," she said. He turned and eyeballed her with a lowered brow.

"I don't drink."

"Are you kidding me?"

"Sit down, girl." She obeyed. "And be quiet for a bit." He took a sip from the tankard. "Who are you?"

"My name is Kalea Thridmill. I'm a vestal from Hallowill."

His eyes dipped and returned to hers. "You're not wearing the costume."

"Costume? Oh, my habit. I'm actually an ex-vestal. I left. And now I'm looking for a shiny sword with a human figure on the—um—the flat part, you know?"

He frowned and eyed her again before inching away.

"Can I see it briefly?"

"No. Who sent you?"

"No one." She shifted her eyes. She shouldn't have mentioned the sword yet. The roads were so dangerous, people commonly traveled in groups, especially if any of them were skilled in combat. If she had used the I-need-an-escort angle, he might've been less suspicious. "I don't know if I can explain this to you, but I'll do my best if you'll listen."

"I suppose you've got as long as it takes me to drink this." He took a big swig.

"I was a vestal, but I fell in love and ran away from my convent. I planned to run away beforehand, but a terrible calamity happened and my lover got kidnapped. I'm looking for him." She peeked into his tankard to find the liquid halfway gone. "I need a swordsman to take me north."

"I'm not stupid," he said. "I haven't forgotten that you want to know what my sword looks like."

He opened his cloak and halfway unsheathed *a* sword. He possessed more than one, and showed her one with a short leather handle and brass hilt.

"That's not the one. But yes, all I said is true. If you have the right sword, I need you to escort me."

"I'm not exactly going north, madam. I'm going to Carridax." Carridax lay to the north-east by a few days' walk. "And I can't help you unless you explain to me why you need to *see* the sword."

"I'm a vestal. I experienced an ecstatic vision…from the Creator. He told me to find a man with a certain sword."

"Oh, for cryin' out loud." The scruffy man rubbed his eyes. "What can you pay me for my service?"

Pay him? Kalea had forgotten about the possibility of paying for an escort. She'd been so wrapped up in swords and her sighting of Arius Medallus that she'd failed to imagine the difficulty in persuading this man to let her follow him—that perhaps she'd have to strike up a real escort deal. He couldn't be the one if he headed toward Carridax. Kalea had assumed she'd be traveling due north.

"Hold on," she said. "I don't yet know if you're the man I'm looking for. You still haven't showed me your sword."

"I did."

"What about the other one you wear? I need a sword with a sloping guard and a naked figure sculpted on it."

He put his hands up. "Look, miss, I think you need an escort more than I need your money."

"I need you to be the *right* man."

He chugged the rest of his drink. "Don't they all say that?" He belched as he stood and headed for the door. "Thanks for the treat."

Her mouth dropped open. Before he reached the door, she grabbed his cloak. "Please don't go yet!"

He whirled around and drew a dagger in one quick motion. She gasped at the blade pointing toward her. He twirled it in his hand as fluidly as if he hadn't drunk a whole tankard a few minutes ago.

"Don't do that, miss."

"It took my last copper to buy you that treat. I'm done for. Please listen to me. I need help."

"So you expect an escort for free?"

"I have a close connection to the One Creator. I can pray for your sins. I can help you find the light or teach you to read or…"

He laughed in her face. "You're funny." He turned and went out the door with her clinging to his cloak.

"The box you wear looks heavy, so let me carry it. I can cook. I can sew. Even better, I can wash for you!"

He sighed and put his face in his hand.

A young man with his hair held back by a headband ran up to them. "Bow!" He grabbed the scruffy man's arm.

"What, Del?"

"The crazy man! He followed us here."

"What? Did he see you?"

The young man hesitated. "Yeah."

"Son of a bitch." The two of them took off.

"Wait!" Kalea called.

The young one turned back to eyeball her. "Who's the girl?"

"Our washerwoman, apparently. And our spiritual leader too."

The young man's nose wrinkled.

"You mean I can accompany you?" she asked.

He didn't answer, but would he have made that joke if he wasn't going to let her follow? Then again, she still couldn't tell if he carried the right sword. She'd follow until she found out, and make the next plan from there.

The young man—Del, the scruffy man had called him—sighed and grunted as he tossed some wood on the pile. "I thought we'd get to stay in a room tonight."

The scruffy man crouched by the woodpile, trying to ignite the kindling with flint and steel. Kalea hovered nearby, twiddling her fingers. She'd followed them all the way out to a meadow off the wooded road like a lost puppy. Del's eyes often flitted toward her with a frown, but then he'd shake it off and continue unpacking their food for supper.

He dropped down beside the scruffy man, stretched, and yawned. "So what's her story?" he finally said.

A crackling glow flared up, and the scruffy man poked the sticks under the new flame. He turned to regard Kalea and smiled before a laugh rattled out.

"I don't know," he said. "She wants to go north, and she paid me with a tankard of ale plus additional services: praying, washing, cooking, and whatnot." He fed a few more sticks into the little fire.

"You mean I can come with you?"

"I let you follow us all the way out here, girl!"

Del took a large smoking pipe off his pack, a thick and heavy-looking thing. He held it level, forearm muscles tensed, to stuff the bowl with tobacco. With a flaming twig borrowed from the fire, he lit it up.

"So what's the extent of your services?" Del asked.

She crossed her arms over her breasts. "I'm a vestal! My services involve cooking, washing, teaching, and praying."

"Not true," the scruffy man said, leaving the fire to grow the rest of the way on its own. "You told me you're an *ex*-vestal and you're looking for a lover."

Del asked, "Long term or short? Because I—"

Kalea threw up her hands. "Oh forget it! Eat your dumb questions! I no longer care!"

The scruffy man sprang up and grabbed Kalea's hand before she could walk into the forest. "He's joking, all right? He's joking. Best to ignore him; Del's a stupid kid. Now look, it's getting dark, and you don't want to go into the woods alone. Especially with a crazy man stalking around."

"Are my terms fair enough?"

"I saw your bracelet." He pointed at her wrist. "It gleamed like pearl. Considering the small size and softened edges of each segment, I'm guessing it's white abalone, exclusively found at Ravian Cove and arduously collected from the sand piece by piece."

She cupped her hand around her bracelet. "I can't."

"Then I can't help you, miss. I work for payment, not for prayers."

Her jaw trembled as she fingered the bracelet. Dorhen's sweet gift. He'd gone all the way to the crescent of Ravian Cove and picked up the little broken shells. He certainly had been all over the Lightlands. Finding him was most important to her.

She paused. "Let me see your sword."

His mouth formed a tight, straight smile, and he opened his cloak. "Here."

He wore two swords and at least one dagger as far as she could see. He pulled out the other sword, and its blade blazed with the sunset colors of the sky. The handle and guard were bound in a rag. He unwound the filthy cloth to expose more gleam. And yes, that sleeping nude figure lounged on the cross section exactly as she'd hoped. He flipped the sword over to show the word "HATHROHJILH."

"I figure this is the owner's name," he said.

"You're not the owner?"

"Not the original owner. My name's Bowaen. I'm a whitesmith. A piece like this would've been made for a king or a warlord."

"This is it. It's the sword I'm looking for." She slid the bracelet over her hand, its strung shells poking and snagging her skin the whole way. "Take it." She dropped the treasure in his hand. Dorhen had made it for her, and now it would help her find him. If this wasn't a part of the Creator's intricate workings, she'd never be able to see it.

Bowaen sheathed the sword. "C'mon, we've got jerky—and I'm not talking about my little friend, Del."

In retaliation, Del blew smoke at Bowaen's face as he knelt beside the box he'd been carrying on his back.

Del reached into a fine woven sack. "Oi!" He tossed a piece of dried meat to Kalea, and she fumbled it.

"Thank you." She knelt down and prayed to thank the Creator before biting into the sweet, smoky pork. It had been over twenty-four hours since she'd last eaten pine nuts gathered from the floor of a pub.

Bowaen unlocked the front of the box. Inside, many little drawers with little round knobs were arranged in rows. He opened one of the drawers and dropped her bracelet in before hastily closing it and locking the box.

"What's in there?" she asked before taking another savory bite.

"Orders."

"What's a whitesmith?"

"I shape precious metals like gold and silver. I work for the Wistara White Guild, but I also happen to be the best swordsman on the peninsula. As much as I'd like to, I can't keep my ass in the workshop. I'm the runner who delivers the orders to the noble houses across the Lightlands."

She pointed a limp finger at the box. "So you'll take my shells back to…"

"I'll keep 'em for myself and make new pieces to sell for my own gain. I'd like to open my own shop in Gaulice soon."

"Glad I could help." She averted her eyes away from the box. "So what does Del do?"

"Besides scuffin' his boots out behind the shop, smoking, and looking seedy? He's my apprentice. But he doesn't practice enough with metalworking. He might be the future official runner for *my* shop, when he's good enough."

"I get plenty of practice working metals," Del said, leaning forward to tap his ashes into the fire.

Bowaen raised a hand. "Not what I'm talking about, Del!"

"Talking about what?" Kalea darted her eyes between them.

Bowaen pinched the bridge of his nose. "The fact that he uses our sacred craft to forge skeleton keys and lock picks."

"I don't steal."

"Not from the guild, at least. Del's trying to go straight, and I do believe in him…but he's a work in progress."

"I see…" She turned to Del. "If you need, I can hear your confession."

Del's mouth dropped open in a partial smile and his eyebrow lifted. "Confession? Don't priests hear confession?"

"Yes, but I can too. I'm devoted to the Creator and confident I can be His medium. It'll help you a lot if you're trying to reform your life. It's like shedding an old skin and starting anew."

Del stood up. "No thanks. I've gotta shed some piss right now instead."

Bowaen shook his head and bit into his own piece of jerky as Del walked into the darkening forest. "I told you he's a work in progress."

"You have a lot of patience for him. Is he your son, or family of some kind?"

"Nah. He's a peasant kid I met when he was twelve. An orphan. He wandered in from one of the neighboring manors after many of the peasant houses burned to the ground. A horrible disaster. He staggered into my shop all covered in ash, begging for water. I gave him some, and he never quite left afterward." Bowaen shrugged. "He's been good company."

Kalea forced a smile. "I guess Dorhen is in Carridax."

"Dorhen?"

"He's the one. I'm looking for him."

"The name sounds elvish."

"Yes. He is an elf."

Bowaen bobbed his head. "And you think he's in Carridax because I'm going there?"

She shrugged. "He'd have to be. I was told to go north with a man carrying *that* sword."

"Told by the Creator?"

"Yeah." Her voice weakened. "It's not too far, I guess."

Bowaen made a kind smile for her benefit. "How far could he have gotten? And when did he…?"

"About a week ago, plus a few days."

"Who took him?"

She squinted into the dark forest surrounding their little meadow and huffed out a breath. "It was so dark. My convent was attacked."

Bowaen reared his head back and frowned.

"And then he burst in. He broke the door and tried to save us…to save me. I got out, and when I returned he was gone. They were all gone." She sniffled. "The chaos, it still jumbles my memory. But I remember men with jeweled gloves."

"Jeweled?"

"Yes, beautiful gloves. In red leather—maybe."

"Red."

"They were being rough with the novices. And with me." She shook her head and rubbed the back of it where it had cracked against the wall that awful night. The knot was gone, and the pain too. The memory brought it back, along with the feel of the man's erection against her hip and the cold wall at her back. Those memories easily blended with those of Kemp's attack.

"Doesn't sound good. None of it."

"It's too horrible to…" She stared into the fire, losing herself to its dance and her memories. "I also remember gold. Gold sticks and lightning. And a strange hum in the air."

"Sounds like they were casting spells."

"Spells?"

"Well. Have you ever seen…? There's been some bad people walking around lately."

"These were as bad as I can imagine."

He leaned forward to stir the fire. "Somethin' not right has been going on. My guild employed my help in training new guards in addition to Del. They're beefing up their security."

"Who are these people in red?"

Also staring into the flames, he shook his head. "I'm not sure."

Squinting his eyes, he returned to scanning the cold forest wall. "Del's taking an awfully long piss, ain't he? I'll make sure he didn't get lost." Bowaen stood. "Del! I've gotta talk to ya."

Kalea stood too as he went, the mysterious sword and his other one swaying behind him like two tails under his cloak.

She gazed into the forest…for Dorhen. The forest was his home, not any particular area of forest, but the forest as a whole, anywhere in the world. It was where he should be. It was where they both should be right now, instead of him being unaccounted for and her having to nag and bargain her way into the company of two strangers with filthy mouths. Not that she minded Bowaen. His kind heart lived somewhere under his mask of greed and nonchalance. But neither his filthy mouth nor his attitude mattered because he carried a sword she had expected to find. A sword shown to her by a fairy, proving her mental illness hadn't deceived her.

Someone waited crouched in the darkness, and it wasn't Del.

"Bowaen!" she yelled, and darted forward to catch his arm and pull him backward.

A small object whistled over their heads. A red-haired man in black leather lurched forward from his hiding place behind a tree and blew a dart, another one, and it bounced off of Bowaen's leather spaulder as he turned and unsheathed his brass-handled sword.

The man in the forest also drew a sword. Simultaneously, he threw a piece of glass down between them. It exploded into an expanding grey cloud so dense Kalea could only make out the glow of the fire to orient herself.

Swords clashed. She ran from the sound, toward the clear air. "Del!" she shouted into the forest. *Oh dear Creator, let him be alive!*

She found the tree line and called Del again after taking advantage of the fresh air. The clashing swords chimed in the cloud behind her, along with growls and grunts. Del never answered her. It must've been close to the new moon night for such a heavy darkness to cover the forest. She could trip over his dead body if she didn't take care.

"Del!" She closed her mouth in case the red-haired man wasn't working alone. She whispered Del's name instead.

A slight groan rumbled back.

"Del?" She continued with her arms stretched forward, listening for another groan while the swords clashed in the distance. At least those noises reassured her that Bowaen still lived.

Her hand found a tree and she traversed around it, calling Del's name softly. Her other hand grazed against fabric. She reached and patted her hand over the texture. A person. He was still warm, and putting off weak breaths along her arm.

"Oh, Del." Rough ropes were bound around his chest, binding him to the tree. She moved her hands to his face and found sticky wetness. She grazed her hands around the rope to the back of the tree to find the knots. Big, bulky, difficult knots. Untying them in the dark wouldn't happen easily, and she didn't have a knife—she'd never thought to steal one from the convent.

"K'lea," Del said, and let out a long groan.

"Yes, Del. What happened to you?"

His groan ended. "I've got a hell of a headache."

"I'm sure you do."

"He said he'd let me live until he got the sword. Like assurance or something."

"Do you mean *insurance*?"

He groaned.

"Why does he want the sword?" His head lolled as she cupped his chin. "Del?" She patted his face.

"Yeah."

"Did he say anything else? Is he alone?"

He didn't answer. She couldn't hope to inspect his head wound unless she could drag him close to the fire. He'd have to stay tied up for now. The best thing might be to help Bowaen if she could.

"Wait here," she whispered, patting his chest. No response.

She ran back toward the bright cloud behind rows of black tree trunks. The cloud was thinning and two figures appeared, clashing swords. Did the red-haired man aim to steal Bowaen's box of jewelry orders? Bowaen probably attracted more trouble than an average escort, though the attacker's vicious movements and angry growls were quite murderous for a mere jewelry thief. Then again, the Lightlands had come into hard days.

She stood watching, helpless, as their struggle went on. Bowaen panted hard, his movements becoming sluggish. His attacker couldn't have been much younger, but his energy endured. Getting any closer would prove dangerous. The clashing rang loud and rapid.

Kalea inched forward. Studying the scene, she must be standing about where the attacker had hidden when he shot his weapon at Bowaen. Straight across from her, a lone tree stood near their little camp. She walked around the circumference of the scentless, thinning smoke to the tree. A little red feather stuck out between the bark—the dart he had shot. Probably poisoned.

As she wiggled the dart free of the tree, a sharp *clank* sounded from behind. Bowaen's brass-hilted sword broke at its middle and he scrambled away, freeing the special sword from the sheath under his cloak. He used it to block the attacker's desperate swing at the last possible instant.

The attacker cursed and took the defense, chanting strange words while keeping his left hand free, tensing it into a cat-like claw. From his tensed fingers, he released wires of light, like lightning. Kalea's hair stood on end, and an eerie humming sound emerged with the wires.

Reflexively, Bowaen raised the sword in front of his face—and the blade ate the lightning. While the attacker stood and gawked, Kalea took the opportunity to sprint forward and stick the dart into the back of the man's neck. He whirled around, and Kalea winced. His eyes pierced her instead of his blade.

Bowaen sprang forward and tore his attention away. The attacker ducked, plucking the dart out, and ran, stumbling from side to side. Before leaving the camp, he slammed another glass ball to release more smoke. Bowaen jumped through the new smoke wall, but returned coughing a few moments later.

"You all right?" he asked.

"Yes, but Del isn't. He's tied to a tree!" She pointed.

"Watch my lockbox, will ya?" He took a flaming stick out of the fire and ran into the woods.

Kalea patted her chest to calm herself. They should be safe now, if that dart had been poisoned. She'd stabbed it deep into his neck. She had killed a man tonight. She'd have to go straight to the sanctuary in Carridax to confess this. A mighty penance would follow, but at least she was alive, and Bowaen, and hopefully Del.

On her way toward the fire and Bowaen's lockbox, a strong hand grabbed her arm with fingers long enough to wrap around her whole bicep, pressing tight enough to cut off her circulation.

"Not so fast."

The attacker had returned, though his eyelids drooped and his head bobbed. He fumbled through his belt pouch to retrieve another glass ball. He threw it a short distance, and a hole opened in the air, like the one the red-gloved men had made in her convent.

Before Kalea could scream, he hauled her through it with enough force to hurt her shoulder. On the other side of the hole, they emerged in the forest. Somewhere else in the forest, with a different camp set up.

He put himself in front of her and jabbed a finger toward her face. "You made me use an expensive spell glass, not to mention the wasted dart! That whole operation was an expensive effort, which you ruined."

He spat in her face; prickly bits of saliva sprayed over her skin. "Now listen. I need to get something from your friend back there. And since you so stupidly foiled me, I'll give you a choice. You can die, or you can help me get it."

Her throat trembled as she uttered, "What is it you need?"

"The sword."

Chapter 21
A Bargain for the Kingsorcerer

The Pointing Young Man, a constellation that had been on the rise when Daghahen and Orinleah exchanged their private vows, now pointed north. It represented Dorhen. It always seemed to align itself in special ways whenever Dorhen passed one of life's landmarks, such as a birthday or the time he had burned his hand in Orinleah's kiln and sent his mother into a frenzy for water and ointment—which was also the night he vanished.

Daghahen had followed the constellation ever since. Over the years, he'd gotten sidetracked for a while, sometimes opting to tuck his chin tight and ignore what the stars tried to show him.

In recent days, since he'd told some random vestal about his son, he'd decided to take on the task full force again. He had halted his duty in trying to woo the pixies because the lad was important too. He was the child Daghahen had made with Orinleah, the last remnant of the happiest portion of Daghahen's life. Dorhen's time on earth would be brief and dolorous, Daghahen had seen in his long-ago divinations, but he didn't know yet how or why. And in the past, he'd never dared mention such premonitions to Orinleah. Orinleah never even knew who or what her son was, something Daghahen personally wished to find out. She hadn't known who she'd married either. Sometimes Daghahen wondered if it would've been better had her clan's *saehgahn* murdered him on that fateful day.

In this area outside of his old hometown of Theddir, he could relax a bit and let his hood fall. Theddir, a moldy old town on wooden stilts, was the most elf-friendly place in the lower Lightlands. It was the closest human settlement to Norr's forest wall.

Not only had he and his brother spent their childhoods there, but many a new *saehgahn* made his way there as well, even in this age, to sleep in a bed and aid the needy. The women would doll themselves up extra nice and slink around the inns and streets when word announced a new *saehgahn*. They all hoped to get an elf's fabled gift of gold or magic, or whatever nonsense the folktales promised. However, some women truly needed help, and that's what *saehgahn* were for when they came out of their forest home. Other women abused their "helpless" status and fabricated atrocious stories to weep out to a *saehgahn*'s concerned face, to get him to murder their "abusive" husbands so they could inherit their money and attach themselves to younger, prettier men. Rubbish like that was the reason Daghahen had stopped helping villagers after a while. His hands stank enough by now.

Nobody in Theddir batted an eye at the mercyman, and after a nice rest in an inn, he strolled the fields as the constellation directed, drawing dangerously close to Norr, a place more hazardous for him than the human lands. Could Dorhen have found some way to thrive there?

On the other side of the farms dotting the land around Theddir, Daghahen tromped over the prairies and through small copses. As he crossed one stretch of land populated with thistle and thick barnyard grass, the eerie humming sensation began in his pocket again.

"What now?" Daghahen asked. "You wish to talk finally?" He opened his pocket and brought out Wik's holding sphere.

As soon as his hand made contact with the large glass ball, the voice began in his head. *Little elf, little elf, where are you going?* The voice sounded like the ocean inside an empty conch shell.

"Are you making fun of me?"

Is this what I've become? A bauble to horde and pet?

Daghahen smiled at the humming black glass balanced on his palm. "I rescued you from the witch you hate. Care to help me out?"

Are you going to release me?

"Are you going to answer my questions yet?"

My energy runs low, but I might try.

"Do you remember the Ilbith sorcerers, Wik?"

A hiss like running sand vibrated up Daghahen's arm, where it registered as sound in his head.

"Do you favor them?"

No.

"They tend to like you."

They have paid homage to me in ages past.

"And you don't favor them back so warmly."

Daghahen had to glean good answers fast before Wik grew tired. It wasn't a good thing to be trapped in a holding sphere, and the longer he spoke to the pixie, the faster it would exhaust. The sun sank fast behind the tall trees on the horizon, and the night should've made it easier for the pixie to carry on a conversation. Wik was known as the pixie of darkness, after all, but the confinement of the holding sphere canceled such luxury, and drained the pixie's energy during the time of day it should've flourished.

"So you won't mind helping me kill my brother, who is a member?" Daghahen asked, and was answered by the sand sound again. Hard to tell if Wik was laughing or not.

You already have the means to destroy your brother.

"What is it?"

Me. The sand sound escalated and fell.

"You'll do it? Do you hate the Ilbith faction too?"

I want to get out.

"How will you kill him if I let you out?"

How do you think?

Daghahen shook his head. "I want to kill Lambelhen. I don't need a Wikshen walking around."

What's more effective than releasing a fox into a hen house?

"Now you want me to release you in their midst? That would cause more harm than anything!"

You're a fool, little elf.

Daghahen took the sphere in both hands and shook it, though the motion never bothered the pixie inside. "Listen. I might consider releasing you if you tell me how to kill my brother. Tell me about the blessings from other spirits he wears."

Don't release me near the wrong person. I want a strong host. It's my demand if you wish my help.

"Answer the question!" His yell echoed far over the rolling field.

You want your brother dead, consider it done. Take me onward. Look at the stars. They'll tell you where to go. Look, they're speaking to you now.

Daghahen clenched his teeth and reacted by darting his eyes downward instead. He'd been so engaged in this conversation, he'd forgotten about the twinkling stars emerging one by one as the sky shifted into a clear black sphere above him, as if he were also trapped under glass and the stars were laughing at his misfortune. As much as he hated it, he'd have to look this time. If they offered a beneficial answer tonight, he shouldn't miss it.

Squeezing his eyes closed, he lifted his chin and opened them one at a time. He turned around to survey the whole picture, and acid oozed into his mouth.

"Oh, dear Creator. No!"

He dropped the sphere and gasped at his stupidity. Falling to hands and knees, he groped around to find it. The prickly thistle leaves scratched his hands and grabbed his hair. His trembling, sweaty hands fumbled the sphere off the thick grass upon which it landed. He checked the surface for damage anyway, not that he'd see any against the perfect black contents within.

The sand sound rushed louder than ever. *Better start walking.*

Before Norr became visible over the hill, another mile of fields and thickets dotted the landscape. The stars, mocking him after his revelation, pointed him deep into one of those skirting forests. A dense, cobweb-riddled area embraced him, a rotten place with moss-covered junk and ruins from an age before the Norrian war.

His feet sank deep into the rotten leaves hiding the soft, damp earth. So many webs stretched across his path. No matter which way he took, he couldn't traverse around them. He'd always encounter another. Using difficult paths like this might be the reason Dorhen had evaded him all these years.

Visible through the tree canopy, the stars winked at him as if gloating. Daghahen struggled on.

"Damn you, Wik!"

A moldy old mansion appeared along his path, dark and desolate from the outside. Surely Lambelhen wouldn't hide out in a place like this. Maybe Dorhen did.

Dorhen's shoulders were about to rip from their sockets as he hung from his wrists, exhausted after a whole night spent shackled in a cell. The burn mark on his side flared with each brush against his shirt. The wound ripped in his stretched position.

"No, no, no," Lamrhath said to the artist who sat on a stool, sketching Dorhen's face from the other side of the bars, "make him smile. He's happy and healthy, look at him! Dorhen, help the man out and smile."

Smiling was the last thing he could do.

"Come now."

He peeled his lips apart as best as he could to show his teeth. They trembled with the effort.

"Oh, kill me, his teeth are crooked. We could file that one down to make them look more symmetrical. Draw him smiling with his mouth closed."

Dorhen took Lamrhath's order as permission to abort the effort. The artist used a cloth to rub the smeared shapes on the vellum-covered panel, then returned to scratching a small lump of charcoal over the surface. He sat stiff-backed with that horrible elf leaning over his shoulder from his own stool. Lamrhath kept his arms crossed as he watched, often firing a scowl at Dorhen.

It would be nice to ask why his face was being drawn, but asking questions made things worse. Questions weren't worth the trouble anymore. Whenever he did as they ordered, his life improved. His questions weren't the reason he hung in chains, though. Yesterday, he had refused to hit a servant girl in training, one of Kalea's fellow convent novices, who had spilled his tea as he was made to sit beside Lamrhath and listen to a sorcerer talk, saying a lot of big words he didn't understand. He had not only refused to hit her, he reflexively threw his arms around her and took the hit on himself from a sorcerer. Lamrhath hadn't liked that.

The kingsorcerer slapped the back of the artist's head with a sparkling, ringed hand. The man stifled a grunt. "I thought you'd know already not to include his puffy left eye. Make it match the right eye, you idiot."

When the artist finished, the picture showed a happy, idealized image of Dorhen's face, so bizarre he hardly recognized himself when he stole a glance as the drawing changed hands. He'd never seen himself smiling like that in his reflection on the water's surface.

Lamrhath studied the vellum-covered panel hard. He'd begun nodding in approval when the door flung open and a white-robed sorcerer entered.

"My lord, we have an intruder."

"An intruder?" Lamrhath said, turning his attention away from the drawing. "Who found this place?"

The white robe swallowed. "A…well, a special intruder, my lord. You'll want to see him."

Lamrhath handed the drawing back to the artist and followed the white robe.

"Hey," Dorhen said to the artist. The man flashed him terrified, wide eyes and shook his head. "Listen."

"No!" He hurried to gather his tools, loading up his arms.

Dorhen persisted, "Please listen! Together, we should…"

The artist whipped out the door, almost closing it on his loose tabard, leaving Dorhen alone in its slamming echo.

"Drink it in, you fools," Daghahen yelled at the gawking sorcerers who'd dragged him into the mansion. Oh Creator, the stench: mold, sulfur, and various other oddities. Indeed, the sorcerers had established a hideout here in the old mansion. The dilapidated façade on the outside made for the perfect disguise. He'd left Ilbith far behind him when he had escaped all those years ago, but here he was again—this outpost might as well be the mighty tower itself. An old sense of loathing and dread flooded back even though he'd never actually been in this building. It was a new addition to the faction's grasping reach across the land.

This was why he hadn't kept the sword: not only to shake that crazed man's pursuit from his heels, but to wind up here amidst the swarm.

Though they'd hauled him inside after he knocked on the door, they didn't tie his hands. Instead, they had cast a slew of spells on the entrance since he came in. No matter for Daghahen; he knew his old faction's tricks. Now they all gawked at him.

"Who are you?" a bystanding white robe demanded.

Daghahen threw his hands out.

"You mean they never told you the story of the legendary Ibex?" He clicked his tongue and threw off his mercy hood.

"He's an elf!" someone shouted.

"He's not just any elf," an older one growled. "How did you find this place, old elf?"

"Because I'm one of you."

The white robes stood back, but some red robes ventured closer, sneering.

"Well?" Daghahen asked. "Is he here?"

The most prominent sorcerer crossed his arms. "Who?"

Daghahen snorted and threw up his hands. "Oh, for God's sake, I'll follow the smell of bodily fluids and find him on my own."

He strolled into a dark little corridor off the big fireplace room. The group followed, murmuring to each other the whole way. Daghahen smiled, listening to the fools.

In another dark alcove, the sounds of a servant girl moaning with a sorcerer's thrusts rang out, a common thing to run into at any Ilbith hideout.

"Stop that!" Daghahen shouted in their direction, though he didn't stop walking. "Don't you know the Creator is watching you?"

A shove rocked him from behind, and he stumbled. He'd finally annoyed them enough.

"We don't believe such nonsense," the dark-eyed sorcerer said as he grabbed Daghahen's lapel and jerked him closer.

"Not my problem." He ended with a brash smile.

"It's time you answered some questions, mercyman. Who are you?"

"I'll give you three guesses."

The man responded with a heavy, open-palmed slap to the center of Daghahen's face. He went down.

"Now, now," he said, staggering to his feet, "if you break my nose any more than it has been, you'll never guess who I am. Take a good look and guess. You've gotta look past the wrinkles, though."

"Dog's piss—he looks like the kingsorcerer." the youngest one said.

"Bullshit," another white robe replied. "He's way too old to look like the kingsorcerer."

"The kingsorcerer, you say?" Daghahen asked. "I always knew he'd get there, but not quite so fast."

The older, dark-eyed sorcerer crossed his arms again. "You must be the twin he's mentioned. You here to see him?"

"Oh no, don't disturb his fornications on account of *me* showing up."

A young white robe came running. "The kingsorcerer says to take him to the inner practice chamber." He stopped and panted as Daghahen was seized and dragged forward.

"Lambelhen," Daghahen said from his kneeling position on the floor, his face throbbing in several places after the initial beating. Deep breaths seared his ribs with pain. The white robes were shooed away as soon as they dragged Daghahen into this room, empty save for a wardrobe with a few candles dripping down its sides. He knelt upon old dried bloodstains; the fresh blood spatter was his. Three high-level red robes and one purple robe had entered with them.

"You don't listen! My name is Lamrhath now," he hissed, turning back around, steaming in the cold air.

"Lam-rhath," Daghahen said. "You mean our mother was kind enough to give you the name Lam-bel-hen—the one who 'stands strong and alone,' and you'd dash her gift in exchange for being the 'alone dreamer?'"

"You forgot the 'er,' you idiot—Lam-*er*-hath."

Daghahen nodded. "Oh yes, the word *saehgahn* aren't supposed to say."

"Your mother named me wrong."

"The dirtiest word in the Norrian language," Daghahen continued, "the one which implies desire. And I suppose you forgot: she gave birth to us both. She's your mother too."

"I want you to learn my real name so you can scream it on your dying breath."

Daghahen clicked his tongue. "Oh, I see what you did there. The 'er' word is smuggled in. You snuck it in there so that it exists, but people won't even realize they're saying it. Clever." He cleared his throat. "Well then, *Lonely Dirty Dreamer*, are you ready to talk?"

"No, there won't be any talking." Lamrhath opened his robe, revealing a scabbard on his belt from which he unsheathed an old iron fireplace poker, the same poker Daghahen had swapped with the sword twenty-two years ago. Lamrhath had saved it. "Your madness impedes any fruitful talk." He tapped the hooked end of the poker on Daghahen's shoulder and grazed the cold metal against his throat.

"Don't you want to know why I'm here?"

"No. But you've made my task easy. I've been looking for you for sixteen years."

"Well, I'm here now."

"How did you get through all the camouflage barriers?" Lamrhath played the tip of the poker under Daghahen's eye as if he would shove it into the socket.

Daghahen kept his back stiff. Lammy wouldn't allow him too much fidgeting; any wrong move could prompt another beating. "I know more sorcery tricks than you'd like to think."

Lamrhath reared back and stabbed the poker into his shoulder. Daghahen growled and curled over after the shockwave of pain ran down his arm. There would soon be a deep tissue bruise to cause pain at every movement, the first taste of what tonight would entail. Lamrhath might not even decide to kill him tonight. This could go on for weeks before the killing blow arrived at last.

"Feel better yet?" Daghahen asked.

"You really do want to die, don't you?"

"Of course I do!"

Lamrhath stepped back, lowered the poker, and smirked.

"You think I would've come here if I could come up with any more reasons to go on? Creator, all I need is a little assistance to help me go."

"You won't find death so easily here."

"I'm aware. Maybe I deserve some suffering."

"Now you're playing mind games with me."

"Am I?"

Lamrhath turned around. "Tch." He whipped the poker through the air like a sword. *Whooph!* "You're hiding something. What are you hiding, you conniving lizard?"

"Absolutely nothing."

"Are you sure?" He whirled around and swung the poker.

Daghahen twisted, and it connected with his back. "Ahh! Dear Creator!" What a long mark that would leave. His cheek was pressed to the floor now, his hands tied behind him. "No need for violence. I'll tell you everything."

"Is there something I'll want to know?"

He worked his way back to his knees. "I don't know."

"Or is it you're trying to annoy me so I'll kill you faster?"

"Well, I do need to die, of course."

"You won't have it. But you will get a lot of pain."

Daghahen grinned and chuckled until it shifted into a bloody cough. "I don't care anymore. Do what you want to me. My guilt for the few things I've done weighs far heavier than the many things you don't feel guilty about."

"I have no guilt because I don't do things that are wrong, I do things that are necessary."

"Like beat a tied-up *saehgahn* with a piece of iron?"

"Yes." He slammed it atop Daghahen's thigh.

Daghahen roared, falling to his side while the shockwave endured. He tried his leg. His femur was still intact. After he finished moaning, he groaned, "Would you like to make a trade?"

The yellow fire flared in Lamrhath's eyes, and his fingers fidgeted around the poker handle. "Are you trading for your life or for your death?"

Daghahen's muscles were weakening, the ache persisting in all the places he'd been hit. Bile flooded into his mouth and stomach convulsions began. Nonetheless, he worked his way back to sitting on his knees, spine straight, swallowing the bile.

"I want to see my wife!" He paused to swallow. "Let me see her! Is she alive? How has she fared? For the love of mercy, what have you done to her all these years? Where have you hidden her?" He stopped yelling before his trembling jaw caused his shouts to trail into inarticulate gibberish.

Lamrhath stood glaring. His fist tightened around the poker. His knuckles turned white. Daghahen sucked in a few controlled breaths to calm himself. Keeping calm was imperative.

"*Your* wife?" He stepped closer. "You want to see…*your* wife?" He raised the poker and laid it along Daghahen's cheekbone.

He whispered, "Did you kill her or not?"

"You'll find out when you meet her in hell." Lamrhath cocked the poker back, high above his head. He swung. The poker whistled toward Daghahen's cheekbone as aimed.

"I have Wik."

The poker stopped at a thumb's length from his head. Only the wind it created caressed cold across his hot skin.

"What did you say?"

He was still alive. Daghahen cocked his head and raised his eyes. "I…

have…Wik."

"What do you mean you *have* Wik?"

Daghahen eased his mind into a mask of peace. "Wik. One of the little pettygods you make offerings to. You wanna see him?"

Lamrhath lowered the poker. "Explain."

"What's to explain? I have Wik. I have him in my possession."

"How?"

"He's resting in a holding sphere. Would you like to have it?"

"How did you get it?"

"How do you think? I took it off a witch who had hoarded it for years."

Of course Lamrhath would be interested in this offer. His brother had tried and failed to contact Wik while Daghahen still participated in the faction. But old *dim* Dag wasn't as stupid as people liked to think. *He* had managed to find the witch who had kept it hidden for the-Creator-knew-how-many years! The pixie's entrapment prevented Lamrhath from making contact, and he never could have found out why unless he had bothered to do the work Daghahen had done.

"Where is it?"

"In a very good hiding place."

"And what? You're asking to trade it for your wife back?" Lamrhath asked.

"What an excellent trade, don't you think?"

"No."

"So let me look at her. I need to know if she's alive. Do you feed her well, at least? Even if she's dead, let me look at her bones. Let me kiss her forehead and tell her goodnight one last time."

Lamrhath shook his head. "Show me Wik, and we might talk."

"You'll have to untie my hands and give my belongings back."

Lamrhath crossed his arms. "You didn't have anything in your belongings more special than a flask of cat piss and that stupid old button you call magical."

"You know I'm not so stupid, Lammy. Crazy, yes. Stupid, not so much."

Lamrhath squinted before motioning a finger at one of his sorcerers, who grabbed Daghahen's bundle off the floor and dropped it before him. He sifted through each item, folding the garments and placing them aside before lifting and arranging the other items in a circular pattern. He picked up a rough leather drawstring bag and placed the flask beside himself. He brought out the wooden button between two fingers, placed it in his robe pocket, and patted the pocket down.

He continued to unload items—a comb, a smoking pipe, a head of cabbage, a small flute, a woman's hairpin—from storage bags and also arranged the bags into the pattern on the floor. Pausing to study the arrangement, he swapped two items and then two more. He took the cabbage and placed it in his robe's large side pocket.

"What the hell is wrong with you? Get on with it!" Lamrhath yelled.

Daghahen shushed him. "I need to concentrate."

"You're buying time."

"I'm not… I had a thimble. Where's my thimble?"

The purple-robed sorcerer responded, "You don't need a stupid thimble."

"I do! Hand it over, or I can't please the kingsorcerer."

The purple robe grunted. "Our seamstresses need supplies." He reached into his pocket, pulled out the little bronze object, and slapped it into Daghahen's open palm.

Leaning over the arrangement, he placed the thimble between the smoking pipe and a folded pair of elven *sa-garhik*. "There."

He raised his hands from the last piece with palms flat. He lifted the flask and uncorked it before swirling it under his nose. Sniffing the wildcat urine zapped him with a new, much needed, alertness. "Mmm. Want some, gentlemen?"

The sorcerers lurched away from his pungent bottle.

"Suit yourselves." He dumped the bottle's contents in the center of his arranged items. It spread into a wide, shiny puddle of stink.

"What are you doing?" a man yelled, as they all buried their noses in their sleeves.

"I only have a few seconds," Daghahen said, and plunged his arm into the liquid. His hand bypassed the stone floor through a portal that opened into an old box hidden deep in Goblin Country, overgrown with moss and hidden under a mess of twigs. Within the box, his fingers slid around a smooth, vibrating sphere. Wik's sphere.

Before the brief portal could close and sever his arm, he grasped the thing and yanked it back out. On this side of the portal, he threw his other hand around the sphere as well. One couldn't be too careful with this object.

Cradling the thing to his chest, he rose to his feet against a rage of trembling pain in his sore muscles.

Lamrhath stepped back farther and stared. It appeared Daghahen knew some elementary spells his dominant twin didn't. Lamrhath had skipped a lot of them in his obsession to master the high-level ones. He'd never bothered to use his brain and consider how useful and economical the low-level spells could be.

A wide grin spread across Daghahen's face. He lumbered closer to his brother, extending the object forward. "What's the matter?" he asked. "Didn't you want to see Wik? I told you I had him."

He opened his palms and let the orb rest atop them. A blackness swirled within the glass, and though it contained darkness, it emanated a soft purplish light.

"Come over here and touch it," Daghahen continued. He stared in a near-hypnotic state. "He's yours, big brother, take him."

The sharp glare vanished from Lamrhath's eyes and a new awe, similar to Daghahen's, replaced it. He stepped forward, reaching with both hands. Lamrhath shuddered at the connection and grasped the sphere firmly to keep from dropping it.

"Touching it takes getting used to."

"You didn't lie," he murmured. "This must be Wik."

"Can you hear his voice yet?"

"No. But I don't think he likes me."

"Are you surprised? He doesn't like me either. If you're pleased, let's discuss some mercy you could pay me, since I went to the trouble to bring you this treasure."

Lamrhath's eyes snapped from the mesmerizing object to Daghahen.

"Will you show me my Orinleah?"

Cradling the orb to his chest, Lamrhath opened the wardrobe and took out a spare red robe. "Not quite. Put this on," he said, tossing it to Daghahen.

Chapter 22
A Plan for the Damned

Lamrhath led Daghahen, wearing the red robe over his normal tan robes, to a room with a big fireplace and a gaudy throne. Anxiety turning to nausea, he glanced around for any sign of what Lamrhath would show him. Certainly not Orinleah. Nonetheless, Daghahen kept his eyes peeled for any sign of her he could spot, perhaps under one of the red hoods standing around the place.

"Wait here. Your surprise is coming," Lamrhath said, and he had no sooner finished the last word when the door slammed open with a boom of shouting men. A nimble figure slipped into the room before a pack of panting red robes.

"Dammit!" the newcomer snapped when he noticed what room he'd entered. He lurched to snatch a dagger out of one of the unsuspecting bystander's sheaths and brandished it as the red robes closed in around him.

"Dorhen," Daghahen whispered through a heavy breath. A sinking feeling hit Daghahen's being with a layer of sweat to his upper lip. Oh, Creator, he'd found him. He'd hoped all along Dorhen wouldn't be here. He'd gladly have given Wik's sphere over to Lamrhath in exchange for Orinleah. But this... The stars' counsel was becoming too real.

He stretched his neck to see over the crowd. No doubt about it. His son's big eyes shone exactly like Orinleah's, and his nose stuck out like Daghahen's. His hair hadn't shifted colors over the years; it showed the same rich brown from his childhood.

Dorhen was worse for wear at the moment, roughed up by the-Creator-knew-what they'd done to him. His open shirt revealed the pus-riddled, raw, and charred black scab of a brand the faction was searing onto its members these days. They'd instituted that tradition after Daghahen had left. A shame it now marred such an impressive specimen of Daghahen's own offspring. Even worse, of *Orinleah's* offspring! Daghahen ground his teeth, hating that he was being subjected to watch such treatment of his son.

"How long has he been here?" he asked Lamrhath.

"Not long, as you can see. He's a bad, bad *saeghar*."

"*Saehgahn*! Clearly, he is *saehgahn*, and you'd treat him as—"

"Shut up now, or we'll do worse to him."

One of the stronger men wrested the dagger away from Dorhen's hand, and the group beat him down to the floor until he sprawled helplessly. The group stepped back as a sorcerer began whipping him with a flog.

"You can stop now," Lamrhath ordered the flogger, and the room hushed.

Dorhen laid his head on the floor, gnashing his teeth, stifling his shouts of pain as Daghahen would've also done.

Lamrhath stood close, casting his shadow over Dorhen. "The doors are locked and warded. You can't escape, so don't try."

For an instant, Dorhen's eyes might've grazed over Daghahen, and he turned his face away to hide behind the red hood he wore.

"How did you escape, little *saeghar*?" Lamrhath asked Dorhen.

The lad groaned on the floor with glassy, squinting eyes.

"You shouldn't have been able to escape—not from both the locked shackles and the cell door."

One of the sorcerers who'd chased him in there cleared his throat. "He did something with magic, my lord."

Lamrhath's eyes brightened. "Is that so? When I asked you before if you knew magic, you denied it. Why would you lie to me?"

Dorhen raised his head to show wet, sincere eyes and shook his head as if unable to form any words yet.

"So, how did he escape?" Lamrhath asked the sorcerer.

"When we checked the cell, the shackles were…well…*melted* somehow."

Lamrhath's eyes narrowed to gleaming golden slivers. "Melted?"

The sorcerer bowed his head. "He ruined the cell door too."

"And yet you don't know magic?"

"No!" Dorhen cried.

"How many things have you melted before?" Lamrhath asked.

"None. I can't do magic. I didn't do it!"

"Oh, I think you did. I'll go see what they're talking about later, but I think you know something, or at least you know it subconsciously. And if it's what I think it is, it's very valuable, and I'm overjoyed to have you as my little heir. I'll help you make sense of whatever powers you're hiding as we go along. For the moment, I have a present for you."

Lamrhath held his hand out, but Dorhen didn't take it. With a scowl, he bunched Dorhen's hair in his fist and pulled to make him stand. Turning to Daghahen, Lamrhath waved him over.

Dear Creator, no. I can't let Dorhen see me here. Nonetheless, his feet moved because fear powered them forward inch by inch. Dorhen swayed and gawked until Daghahen ventured close enough to catch his eye.

"We have a special visitor tonight, Dorhen," Lamrhath said. "Do you recognize him?" He yanked Daghahen's hood off, making him feel as good as naked.

Dorhen's eyes fixed on him. He stuttered and blinked. There was nothing Daghahen could say to the lad, nothing he could do for him.

"F-f-father?" Dorhen said. He swallowed thickly and opened his mouth again.

Daghahen couldn't manage to dart his eyes away. Dorhen drew them in.

The lad's mouth worked, twitching and fighting against an uncontrollable quiver. "Father, where have you…?"

Daghahen shook his head, keeping his face as calm as possible.

A sob burst out of Dorhen's throat, and he fought it. "Father, please—" Tears ran down his cheeks. "Father, take me out of here! Help me!"

Daghahen shook his head more vigorously.

"Please!"

He took a step backward; Dorhen could've followed, but he remained planted.

"Please get me out of here!"

Daghahen shook his head again and tore his eyes away. He turned and retreated. A commotion erupted behind him. Apparently, the sorcerers were restraining Dorhen; maybe he had tried to pursue after all. Daghahen pulled his hood up and attempted to blend in with the other red robes.

"A heartwarming spectacle," Lamrhath said, taking the floor again. "But let's move on. A glorious thing has come into my possession, thanks to my brother, who perhaps does love me after all."

Lamrhath reached into a puffy velvet bag and brought out the holding sphere with Wik inside. He held it high. "Look what he's brought us."

The sorcerers' eyes flared wide, and some pulled their hoods down, revealing greasy heads and gawking, bearded faces.

"It's Wik," Lamrhath continued. "Do you know what happens when a pixie gets trapped in a holding sphere?" He paced around, flashing the swirling, humming object before the sorcerers' starving eyes. "They become usable. For many years, we've tried to contact Wik, one of our five gods of power, and found no response. That's because the whole time, Wik was trapped. In this."

The sorcerers stepped backward, creating a near-perfect circle within which Lamrhath could pace around.

"Have any of you ever seen anything like this in your lives?" Lamrhath asked. "Take a good look and watch carefully. What I hold in my hand is the fate of two societies, and the fate of Kaihals too."

Lamrhath stared into its black depths as dreamily as the awe-inspired crowd. "One could go mad trying to decide what to do with such an item of majesty. Since it is so alluring, one could look at it all day—or a lifetime. To think how the world won't be the same once I've broken this open. It'll change, yet return to the existence it knew ages ago."

He walked the orb around the circle once again, holding it out as if offering it to others as they stepped backward with defensive palms pointed at him.

Dorhen sat on his knees at the circle's edge. He'd been released, and now his hands held him up, trembling at the elbows. His blood-dampened hair curtained his face, hiding it from Daghahen's longing eyes.

Lamrhath stood at the center of the circle, giving himself plenty of space. "My era will unite the two most powerful societies in the Darklands!"

Lamrhath dropped the sphere before his own feet. It didn't hit the ground. Daghahen lunged forward, ignoring his pains, and pushed his brother aside to catch the orb.

"I think not!" He rolled it up his arm and behind his head to the other hand like he had done with crystal balls when he had entertained for food and shelter in his youth.

"Give it back!" Lamrhath roared. "Get that from him!"

Daghahen danced around, slipping past men coming from each side. He whipped off his outer red robe and flung it at a group of pursuers. Though he had shed one robe, his old tan robe's many dangling layers and folds prevented him from running around in such a packed room.

Several men managed to grab him at once, trapping him. He continued his old contact juggling tricks, confusing the men as the sphere changed hands and rolled away from them along his arms as if it had a mind of its own. Though their hands were in such close proximity to it, they grabbed for it shyly. If mishandled, it could fall on the floor, and whoever it shattered closest to would get the power. All meant to deliver it to Lamrhath. But how interesting would it be to see if any man present would betray the kingsorcerer and drop it on himself? It was almost worth finding out.

They all gasped and released Daghahen's robes to throw their hands in the air when he tossed the sphere high. He let them scramble for it, using the opportunity to slip away. Sighs of relief hissed out when it managed to fall into a pillow of many hands.

When one young sorcerer broke from the group, running toward Lamrhath, Daghahen shot forward and kicked his hand, bouncing the ball back into the air. The men shouted and moaned.

"You're dead!" Lamrhath screamed, and several similar threats echoed from other mouths. No one seized Daghahen, though, because they were all too interested in saving the sphere from shattering prematurely. Daghahen chuckled and stood by to watch their frenzy.

Dorhen remained on the floor, watching with interest, though defeated. If this were any other day, Daghahen would be tempted to use the distraction to run out of there together with his son. Getting outside the manor's walls with another person would be a struggle, but Daghahen could possibly do it, though getting out alone would be easier. Similar to the way Chandran and Rayna had warded the doors and windows of the inn with deadly spells, this manor was guarded with the keenest traps and wards the sorcerers could produce. Daghahen would need lots of time and energy to undo the wards. It would take careful planning and execution to escape any Ilbith outpost; he should know.

But he hadn't come here to save Dorhen. Daghahen planned to find Orinleah and kill Lamrhath, or at least set the gears in motion for that eventual outcome. Dorhen's will was already cracking under the layers of elaborate pressure the faction put on new recruits, so time was sensitive. This was why Wik had told him to watch the stars and hurry along. Wik knew things, as if pixies and the stars of the universe shared some unfathomable insight. The stars had been trying to tell him all along, each night tightening the formations of the constellations, shouting the answers over the top of Daghahen's head in his unwillingness to look upward.

This would end tonight.

Three men grasped the orb at once in all of their six hands and carried it to the kingsorcerer together. "My lord!" they said in unison and knelt, offering it to him. He lifted the orb off their hands, smirking, no doubt planning a slow murder for Daghahen after using it on himself.

"I don't know why you'd be so stupid, Dag," Lamrhath said.

He dropped the sphere.

It shattered in front of his feet, sending shards scattering. A loud sound popped with a billow of black smoke, and a zip of negative energy flashed across Lamrhath, Daghahen, and every other body in the room. Lamrhath stood with his palms open at his sides, sucking in long drags of air as the smoke spread and dissipated around him.

They all waited. His chest rose and fell for several long moments. Daghahen crossed his arms and shifted to one foot on the leg which hadn't been clobbered by an iron poker. Lamrhath opened his eyes and glared at him.

"Well?" Daghahen said. "How does it feel, my good deity?"

Lamrhath observed his own hands and frowned. "Nothing. There's no new sensation."

Daghahen fished through his robe pocket and pulled out the cabbage he had been saving. It had been his food supply before he changed course toward this house.

"Because I'm not the one stupid enough to give you the holding sphere."

He pulled off the strand of twine which helped to keep the cabbage's leaves together, and then peeled the leaves away to reveal the actual holding sphere containing Wik.

"You stupid, gullible filth-mongers!" he hissed. Many mouths dropped open, including Lamrhath's. "You're so hungry to collect trinkets and stack implements of power, you've lost the ability to tell a piece of glass with an amateur's smoke and negativity illusion from a sphere containing an actual pixie."

Daghahen flashed it around like Lamrhath had done with the fake. "I'm not playing anymore!"

"Daghahen," Lamrhath said, "give it to me." His expression had lost the knife-edge it usually showed. "Give it to me, Brother."

"You think you deserve to become a god?"

Sorcerers were inching closer as he spoke, showing off the sphere, far more magnificent with the glittering, liquid-like black smoke within. It put off a dark glow, as the being inside was a force of that element, making darkness a tangible thing, and not merely defined by an absence of light.

"We could decide better, gentleman. Now tell me: who wants to be a god?" He jumped forward, and even managed to spook the nearby sorcerers who were tempted to tackle him. He screamed it again. "Who wants to be a god?"

Me, Wik hissed again in Daghahen's head, reminding him who was the one with the ability to kill Lamrhath. But Wik wanted a favor in return: to get out. When Daghahen had looked to the stars, he'd discovered Wik had told half the truth. Pixies couldn't lie, but they could hold back. The stars knew of the one who could kill Lamrhath.

"Get that sphere!" Lamrhath yelled.

As the sorcerers dove at him again, Daghahen hurled the thing, the real sphere, and it arced across the room.

Clash! It smashed beside Dorhen. Daghahen's aim was true.

A gasp filled Lamrhath until he froze, golden eyes bulging, jaw trembling, as if the comforting demonic aura he'd bought with his years of sacrifice had suddenly left him standing alone after flying off into oblivion. Daghahen had never seen him so full of shock or fright. The room fell silent.

From the opened glass, an oil-like fog spilled and spread, engulfing Dorhen's hands as they held him up. He tried to pull them off the floor but couldn't. The oily smoke, black as a night underground, spiraled up his arms and smothered his face until he wore a mask of it over his mouth and nose. Then it passed away, freeing his face again after it seeped inside him.

Dorhen's eyes shifted around wildly. He batted at the rest of the smoke as it clung to his arms and moved to wrap around his chest, soon becoming a screaming, convulsing mess on the floor.

Daghahen's heart ached as he stood and gawked with the other fools. *What've I done?*

The rest of the black smoke disappeared, invading Dorhen's body until he appeared clean again. Tensing all his muscles, he growled and gnashed his teeth, trying to control one of his arms with the other. His fingers tensed like claws at the end of a stiff arm, grasping the wrist as if it were someone else's.

The tensed hand trembled before splitting open with an outpouring of blood. A small, sharp object shot out. A blade. It flew straight, slicing the throat of one of the sorcerers before dissipating into a light, glittery dust that floated to the floor before reaching the wall.

Dorhen cradled his mangled hand for a moment. His whole body lifted into the air—levitating, screaming.

The sorcerers launched into a frenzy, darting here and there, yelling and cursing, stepping over the dead man as if he were a rock or a twig.

"A fox in a henhouse," Daghahen recited.

Lamrhath stood gaping.

Dorhen flew as if thrown until he slammed against the wall. He dropped and crumpled, no longer able to thrash. He jerked and seized, out of control of his twitching limbs. Blood gushed out of his mouth as though he had bitten his tongue.

The fear made one man brazen enough to take Lamrhath by the shoulders. "What do we do, my lord?"

Lamrhath shook out of his trance and responded to the man, "We have to control him! Tie him up! Bind him tightly—his whole body—

hurry!"

The sorcerers forgot all about Daghahen. He couldn't watch anymore. And it appeared his chance to slip away before being killed in the impending rampage had arrived. With luck, Lamrhath would be dead by the morning. This whole place would be in shambles.

"I'm sorry, son."

Chapter 23
Her Monster

Daghahen lay in the tall grass, somewhere in a prairie outside Norr. The stars spun above him in a purple sky before the onset of dawn. He had vomited twice and couldn't find the strength to continue walking. All the places where he'd been beaten with the poker throbbed. Besides the spinning stars, the pulsing pain dominated his senses during the intervals when he spaced out. The grass waved over him in the breeze.

He'd released Wik. In the Lightlands. Wikshen would be walking around soon. Tremors worked up his throat until another sob escaped, and he curled over into the fetal position to bawl his anguish out.

He hadn't had the luxury of choice back there. If Orinleah still drew breath, some chance for her peace existed now, wherever Lamrhath had hidden her. Though he'd just succeeded in killing Lamrhath and crippling a prominent sorcery outpost, the war against Ilbith would go on. Although they'd choose a new kingsorcerer, Daghahen might be able to rescue her now.

And Dorhen.

His sobs escalated to uncontrollable dry heaves.

Dorhen had made a great sacrifice tonight. Though he didn't know it, he'd done a great service to his mother. Such was the duty of the *saehgahn*. Many of them died young. Many Norrian families lost sons and continued on without regret because they kept in their hearts the deep honor the dead did their lineage.

None of those rubbish thoughts comforted Daghahen this morning. Dorhen was dead. Just as Daghahen had known would happen. It had happened sooner than expected.

"Orinleah won't like it one bit," he whispered. She was more Norrian than Daghahen, as a matter of fact. She would eventually accept it after he told her how her son had died for her.

Shakily, he worked his way to his feet. He wasn't finished yet.

Kalea pushed away from the man who dragged her through the portal and darted. She stopped short with her head jerked backward and fell flat on her back. He'd grabbed her hair. In attempt to get to her feet again, she rolled to her hands and knees.

The man twisted her hair around his fist and yanked her upward. She wriggled, caught like an animal, and batted at his face. Anything to make him let go. A hard hand came down along her face, delivering an earthshaking swipe. She screamed.

"Shut up!" he yelled.

The sound of leather squeaking preceded a cold metal blade against her throat. She stopped struggling. It grazed her skin toward her artery and pressed down. Even her weeping stopped, although the tears continued. Sweating from the struggle, she strained her exhausted eyes to see him.

"Did you hear me?" he asked. "I said, I want the sword. If you care to live, you'll cooperate."

Perhaps this was meant to be. This man wanted the sword. If he wanted her too… If he was meant to obtain the sword, she could follow him—as much as she disdained this alternative escort. As long as Dorhen was somewhere along the path.

He sat on the grass, dragging her down with him, and held her close with the dagger pressed to her jugular vein. He sighed and rubbed his face, most likely feeling the effect of the poisoned dart she had stabbed him with, and returned the knife to her neck.

She opened her mouth and found her throat dry and croaky. "You said you want the sword. I'm following the sword too," she managed to say.

He stopped rubbing his face and sniffed. "Why do you want it?"

"It's not that I want it. I *need* to be with the man who carries it. Which could be him…or you. I'll do anything to keep following it if… if you let me live."

He used her hair to turn her head, squinting as he studied her face. He loosened the knife's press.

"It's a deal, love. But right now you're on probation. I'll be putting you through a *program*. When you pass the program, you'll earn yourself the right to walk freely and serve me. One bad move, and I'll kill you. I'll do it slow if you annoy me enough. Your death'll summon at least four or five—ah, forget it. If you do as I say, we might establish a relationship."

Kalea closed her eyes to swallow, working out the tightness in her throat.

He removed the dagger, leaving a sharp irritation line across her skin. "My name's Chandran, but you'll call me 'master.' In my faction, we can take personal thralls, and that's you. You'll learn what it means in good time."

He opened his mouth wide and pushed his tongue out far to slide against her cheek, leaving a long, moist slug trail behind. A freezing chill pierced the back of her neck. He fetched a rope to bind her wrists.

After lighting a lantern waiting amongst his stash of belongings, he tied her rope to a tree and murmured while touching his index finger to the knot. A lavender glow within the rope's fibers flared and died. He repeated the process with the knot at her wrists. The glow flared again—she hadn't been seeing things due to her delirious exhaustion and hunger.

He stumbled and sat down with a sigh, rubbing his temples, and pulled a mushroom from his pack.

"Enjoy your supper," he said, tossing it to her. "In the more convenient future, you'll be cooking *my* supper. Tonight you'll eat like me."

Kalea scarfed the skunky, dirt-sprinkled mushroom. He didn't toss her a second one, and she abstained from asking even though her stomach ached. She'd only eaten that one piece of jerky at Bowaen's camp prior to this. She hugged herself and shivered as Chandran proceeded to eat the rest of the bunch in front of her. The air felt warmer tonight, as spring had set in, but she shivered for a different reason. The trees, mostly poplar, appeared similar to the ones around Bowaen's camp. How far could they have come from there? Had Bowaen seen her get abducted through the magic hole in the air? Would he find and rescue her?

She put the thoughts away as Chandran's hateful eyes met hers. She would have to pretend to be loyal to him, or else he might kill her.

His hair was more of a dark auburn than red, and his eyes were outlined with black paint or soot. He sported a ratty bandana tied around his neck with a white, blood-stained cloth peeking out from underneath it. The fingerless gloves he wore were black, not red with jewels, but he had indeed created a hole in the air. If he wasn't in league with the raiders of the novice dorm, he still knew their magic.

After eating the last mushroom, he trudged into the dark forest, his movements sloppy under the effect of the poison she'd stuck him with. He took the lantern with him. His footsteps trod the leaves for a long way until the sound faded. Whatever he had done to the ropes, he must've trusted they'd hold her.

She worked her wrists to try and loosen the knot. As she did so, a vibration ran along the rope with another lavender flicker and went straight into her ears as a stabbing whistle. She flailed over, falling on her side. It only lasted a second or two, but long enough. She stayed on the ground for a few moments. He had cast a spell on the rope!

She tried the knot on the tree. She could've easily untied this one with her bound hands if not for the spell. When that pretty little glow started traveling across the rope again, she choked on a scream and tried to run away, forgetting the rope would yank her to a sudden stop. The whistle lasted a few seconds longer than the last one. Apparently, its duration increased with each escape attempt.

Hold on! Kalea tested a scream. A different pulsing vibration moved down the rope, and when it connected with her wrists, her throat tightened up and squeezed off her oxygen.

She couldn't scream. She couldn't call for help. And for a moment, she couldn't breathe. For this round, her throat closed longer than before. By that logic, if she tried to scream enough times, she'd die of suffocation.

Kalea shuddered. What kind of bastard was that man? Sword or no sword, she was stuck with him.

"The cellar, it's… Please, my lord, see it for yourself."

Lamrhath followed the pale-faced man through the manor outpost all the way to the deepest cellar. They had lost track of Daghahen last night after the old lizard caused a huge stir, wasting the most valuable relic on the continent, and then escaping somehow. He'd left Lamrhath and the pitiful handful of sorcerers who manned the outpost to deal with the damage.

"Calm down!" Lamrhath said after a string of incoherent stammering from Harn's mouth. The man held a lantern with a fatty candle inside, its flame beaming through magnifying pieces of faceted glass. Its trembling light gave away his stirred nerves. "Tell me what you saw in there."

"Well, nothing, in fact. But it's changed. The whole room. I don't think the boy-o is in there anymore. But something's in there."

Lamrhath should be back in the Ilbith tower by now with his new heir. It looked like he'd be delayed for a while, picking up his nephew's limbs from the cellar floor.

Lovely. He grunted. "How far into the cellar did you go?"

"Not far, my lord. I didn't dare. The shakes overcame me. I've never seen such a…a dark stain on a room before. On the walls. Clotting the air."

Other, lower-level sorcerers joined their group along the way. They squeezed into a tight corridor packed with sorcerers, each peering over the shoulder of the man in front. A chorus of whispers echoed in the small space. At the end of the narrow, sloping passage, two men at the door took turns with the peephole. They all pressed hard against the wall to make way for the kingsorcerer's passage. Curious servants packed themselves in too, looking for a turn to peek at the alleged monster.

"Cuanth, Kaskill, accompany me," Lamrhath said to two young rising red robes. "And Harn, bring your lantern."

The crowd shifted to let them into the center flow. An elderly sorcerer stood by the door, holding a ring of keys. The peephole showed a stone floor at the bottom of the stairs, faintly aglow with light from one of the small windows. Harn hadn't exaggerated about the strange shadow; the cellar should've been flooded by more morning light than it was.

At Lamrhath's signal, the old man worked the lock, the keys jingling in his shaking hands. All the whispering stopped. The door's groaning hinges became the only sound in the whole wing. The old man flattened against the wall and edged away. Lamrhath entered first, followed by Harn, Cuanth, and Kaskill. The rest clogged the doorway.

The air hung thick, like a gelatinous smoke. It pressed on his shoulders. Whatever dwelled down here had confiscated the space. Leading the way, Lamrhath edged down the stairs, often checking to make sure his companions didn't lose their nerve and retreat. One step at a time, he pushed himself through the darkness.

They approached the back of the room. Lamrhath waved his hand for the lantern, but there was no telling if Harn even saw his hand beyond the lantern's glow. The warm, flickering orb of light fell over him as Harn approached. Lamrhath took his wrist and lowered the glow closer to the floor.

A pair of pale feet placed together peeked from the shadow. They didn't move or bother to twitch in the light's nearness. The dark, mist-like air beyond the light drifted like fog on a damp morning.

"What do you suppose happened to him?" Kaskill whispered at his other shoulder.

Lamrhath shushed him.

Harn responded in a quieter whisper, "We should have watched 'im throughout the night."

Lamrhath inched forward, eager to see what corruption of nature had replaced his nephew. The faint candle glow glided up the shins attached to the feet, covered over with a heavy black drapery, above which was a pale chest with wide shoulders and corded muscles. The light couldn't manage to break the shadow veiling the creature's head.

"That's not the boy-o," Harn whispered, the lantern in his hand trembling harder than before. "What is it, my lord?"

Lamrhath's stare turned into squinting. "A real pixtagen, I suppose," he said. "A rare mutation, the result of a pixie's possession over the body of a mortal person. But this one is greater than most… It might've been me if things had gone different. If the sphere really did house Wik as Daghahen said, we're in for an experience."

"Will he harm us?" Cuanth asked.

"We'll have to befriend this creature fast or try to restrain him." He squinted his eyes to see into the supernatural shade. The creature stayed motionless and quiet.

"His...hair," Cuanth said, leaning forward as if to see better without taking any steps.

Lamrhath nudged Harn's begrudging lantern hand closer. The shadow over the creature's face didn't move or weaken, but a glint of colored reflection caught the light. Damp strands of long hair flowed over the creature's chest, highlighting blue locks, deep blue like lapis lazuli.

"It changed color... That is, if this is what's left of Dorhen," Lamrhath said.

The hair hung longer too. The creature was larger with longer limbs. This wasn't Dorhen, whoever it was. The figure in the shadow stirred and turned its head.

"What is he wearing?"

Harn's face had paled and wore a sheen of sweat. "He didn't get that from us, my lord." The long black sheet wrapped around its waist and pooled on the floor around it.

"Look," Kaskill whispered. He rejoined the light after a brief step to the side, holding Dorhen's clothes, ripped to rags and discarded, shreds of white shirt as well as his mismatched leggings. Yet there were no pieces of the lad's body to accompany the rags.

Lamrhath turned back to the new creature. "Speak," he commanded. It didn't respond. "Tell me, where did you come from and what became of Dorhen? Explain in great detail."

The figure's head shifted again, and its eyes caught the light and glowed like hot, bright turquoise. It made odd, sporadic head movements like an owl; otherwise, it kept motionless.

"Should we bring a torch?" Cuanth whispered, leaning in close to Lamrhath.

"Not yet. He might not like the light." He turned to the sorcerer on his other side. "Kaskill, greet him. Offer him your hand."

Kaskill's eyes bulged, and he pointed to his chest.

"Don't be afraid."

Embracing its knees, the creature slowly turned its head in Kaskill's direction to watch him approach. The young sorcerer reached his hand toward the creature. "G-greetings." His hand breached the densest shade behind which the creature hid.

In the same moment, Kaskill screamed and lurched backward with the creature's teeth locked around his fingers. He pulled and wriggled like an animal caught in a trap. The creature didn't let go. As he worked his way backward, his screams ringing like a huge bell against the stone walls, the creature grabbed his arm to prevent his escape and pulled him into the shadow again.

"Bring light!" Lamrhath shouted, and more lanterns were passed into the cellar, revealing Kaskill's struggle.

Blood ran down the creature's chin. Calmly, it ground its teeth. As Kaskill used his entire body weight to pull away, he finally broke free and tumbled backward. Blood spurted from the remaining half of his finger.

He scrambled away, and the creature didn't pursue. The new light showed his strange hair in greater detail. Kaskill rejoined the group, hands shaking as he tried to squeeze off the blood flow.

Lamrhath turned to him. "What were his teeth like?"

Kaskill took several short, sobbing breaths before attempting to answer. "N-n-n-normal! Like m-m-mine." Pulsing blood wet his hands.

"You did well," Lamrhath said. "Remember to use this experience in your meditation. Sometimes you'll need to cast spells during excruciating pain."

He nodded rapidly. "Y-y-yes, my lord."

The creature spat the other half of Kaskill's index finger across the room. It bounced off the adjacent wall before hitting the floor. A loud, unnerving laugh, lacking both harmony and pleasure, echoed out of the creature and merged into convulsive sobs.

"What's the matter with you?" Lamrhath asked it. "Do you need something?"

It didn't respond, but petted its own hair with one hand. The other hand searched the rough stone wall as if of its own will. Both hands were intact, unlike Dorhen's, which had been mutilated last night.

The searching hand found its way to the floor, where the creature sat next to scattered shards of mirror. The increased lighting showed how the place rested in shambles. Crates lay overturned and smashed. Flour spills covered most of the floor, and the creature's large footprints dotted the area in erratic patterns.

The hand stroking its hair found its face and patted its cheek. The searching hand grabbed a shard of mirror without any discretion and clutched it tight enough to draw blood. When it opened its hand again, silver dust fell to the floor from its palm, glittering in the faint light, followed by a few drops of blood.

"He knows transitional magic," Lamrhath said. "I told you all, didn't

I?"

He turned back to his new subject. "Welcome. I'm Lamrhath, Kingsorcerer over the Darklands. I assume you want to be called Wikshen now. What can we get for you? Your desires will be provided for."

He turned and scanned the terrified faces in the doorframe. One of the tubbiest sorcerers in the outpost held a greasy, half-eaten goose leg. He must not have bothered to let it go when he had hurried straight from the dining table and rushed down here when the news spread.

Lamrhath pointed to him as he nibbled vacantly. "You." The fat man's eyes widened. "Give that to Cuanth." He sighed and did so. Cuanth, however, stiffened up, frowning as he took the food.

Lamrhath turned to the creature. "Are you hungry? There is much more if you want."

Cuanth trembled, his mouth hanging open as he stared at the shadowed creature. Lamrhath prodded him. "Offer it to our guest."

Cuanth approached, shaking like Kaskill had, and the creature stood, rising to a towering height. The lantern illuminated its pale face, like a *saehgahn*'s but not quite recognizable as Dorhen's. The face's slim bone structure displayed a prominent nose and strong angles at the jaw and cheekbones, a face more mature than Dorhen's.

With its movement, the dense shadow around it grew larger. It paced side to side, staying within the small, shadowy space. Dorhen had been at least a foot shorter when they had dragged his bound, convulsing body down here. The creature's kilt-like garment dragged behind it. Its stringy hair covered half its face like a slimy curtain and hung in dark trails over its pale chest.

Cuanth opened his fist, exposing the food on his open palm as he would offer it to a horse. He held it out, keeping as much distance as possible.

The creature paused to regard the food in the man's quaking hand and lifted it off with two fingers. After a whiff of its smoky fragrance, it licked the greasy meat. Its reflective turquoise eyes locked on Lamrhath as it took a small bite.

Lamrhath whirled around. "Bring more food."

Two sorcerers shoved back through the doorway. The creature dropped the meat on the floor, still unfinished. Its attention returned to Cuanth, who lingered, shifting his eyes anywhere to avoid eye contact with the monster.

The creature extended its arm toward him, fingers pointing up. The shallow surface of its palm filled with liquid mercury, which hardened and reflected like a mirror. Cuanth caught a glimpse of his own ashen face in the silvery sheet glazing the skin.

"See how he recreates the mirror?" Lamrhath whispered to the sorcerers standing close behind him. "He's bringing it back. Where was it?"

As Cuanth's shoulders relaxed, the creature stepped forward and slapped the mirror-hand over the sorcerer's forehead, shattering the glass and removing it from its body. Cuanth stumbled backward, holding his bloodied face. The creature walked along the wall until the darkness trailing behind it smothered what little light gleamed through the window. The shadow thickened and smothered the lantern light.

Several sorcerers cast spells of hovering light globes, which glowed like cool-flamed candles. Cuanth huddled beside Kaskill, wiping blood off his face and plugging the gash on his forehead with his robe sleeve.

The additional food hadn't arrived yet. Instead, a woman's voice murmured in the doorway above, inquiring about the commotion.

"Bring her in," Lamrhath said to the men clogging the doorway.

She let out a scream as they grabbed and pushed her forward. The noise level elevated higher than he'd prefer around this unpredictable creature. They ripped off her corset and tore at her gown until it hung on one shoulder by threads, exposing a lot of her flesh. Lamrhath didn't care what condition she arrived in.

"Remember Selka?" Lamrhath asked, taking her bare arm and pulling her forward as the creature stood proud and silent. She didn't fight as much as before and she stoppered up her protests. "You enjoyed her a day ago. You can do so again. Whatever you want, I will provide," Lamrhath said. "In my house, you can sate every pleasure within your creed."

He shoved Selka forward. She froze when the creature didn't move at first.

It paced around her in study as she trembled and whimpered. It grabbed a lock of her hair and leaned in to smell it. Its fingertips slid from her bare shoulder down the length of her arm. Wrapping its fingers around her wrist, it lifted her hand to smell her skin.

It sank its teeth in. She screamed and writhed as if her hand were mortared into a tall brick wall. Her blood added to the existing stain on the creature's chin.

Many sorcerers drew up their red hoods, as they customarily did for sacrifice and torture. With their hoods up, they became one amorphous body of red, standing emotionless and detached from the frantic scene before them.

She fell to the floor with a slap across the stones when its jaw unlocked. Forgetting about her bleeding hand, she winced and shielded her head.

Instead of falling atop her, as Lamrhath and everyone else expected, the creature stepped over her and sprang toward the sorcerers. It snagged the back of Cuanth's hair and slammed his forehead into the stone wall. He left a dark trail down the rocky surface as he slid peacefully to the floor.

The rest of the sorcerers scattered in the creature's path. They packed into the corridor until they became wedged in. The creature stalked up the steps and yanked a few into the room with him as others willingly jumped off the stairs to get away.

Harn got to work ordering men out of the kingsorcerer's path. The creature chased the scrambling sorcerers, snagged one, lifted him high, and threw him at the wall. His neck broke on impact; the next few weren't so lucky. Some sorcerers kept the creature distracted so Lamrhath could climb the stairs and exit the area. Bodies flew and crumpled; the creature ripped hair and clawed eyes along its way toward Lamrhath, who walked the up-sloping corridor.

When it found a clear path, the creature broke into a sprint. Wind caught its blue hair. Lamrhath turned at the sound of the rapidly padding feet and extended his palm, from which blossomed a "fire flower," dancing and blazing with intense heat.

The creature stumbled to a stop, beads of moisture quickly forming on its chest and upper lip. It walked backward. Lamrhath advanced, pushing the small inferno at it.

"Oh, now I remember. You don't like fire," he said over the roar of the flames. "Well, you'll learn to respect me because I know *all* the fire spells through each advanced level, and I'll incinerate your ashes into diamonds if you want to try and fight me. I told you I am kingsorcerer. I'll also tell you I have no sense of humor, so don't *think* of disobeying me, you putrid maggot."

He pushed the fiend all the way back into the cellar, where it fell off the stairs, landing on its feet with a surprising show of grace. When Lamrhath eased his fire flower down to a puff of smoke, a sorcerer standing by closed and locked the door. Caging the creature was more important than freeing the last remaining injured sorcerer, who begged them to open the door, or Selka, who had fainted.

Lamrhath walked away as the last two sorcerers standing outside the door listened to their companion sob and beg to be let out. His voice ended in a wet gurgle, followed by a heavy thud.

"Ssss-i-lencccccce," rasped an inhuman vibration through the wood grains when the screaming ended.

The next morning, Lamrhath and his associates rushed down to the basement. The metallic smell of blood wafted out when the door opened. The same airy, black substance filled the room, like yesterday but thicker.

Lamrhath motioned to his four lantern bearers. They also brought every chain accessible in the manor. The lantern bearers descended first, followed by one sorcerer prepared to cast a large fire flower to clear the room of the living darkness, and then Lamrhath.

The leading lantern bearer stumbled over one of the bodies from yesterday, sprawled at the foot of the steps. Holding the lanterns high, they began waving the lights around when it became apparent how the darkness parted around them like a dense school of frightened fish. Their hands trembled. The silence hung as heavy as the cloud. No sign of the creature yet.

One of the lantern bearers stuttered, "Hurry and cast it already."

At Lamrhath's nod, the one with the spell pre-charged in his glove stepped forward. They should've reached the center of the room at this point. Everyone lowered their eyes for what would occur.

A bright flash filled the room, chasing the majority of the shadow away. Afterward, they could see all the way to the back wall.

The creature had been stalking around soundlessly, but it jolted and fell in the sudden extreme light. The caster's fire flower blazed for a few seconds and extinguished slowly, leaving them with lantern light and the windows to light the room. The creature's face showed shock and oblivion, his eyes never quite settling on any of them.

A woman groaned. Selka. She was still alive.

The lantern bearers stood to protect Lamrhath, holding their lights forward as he moved behind them toward the woman huddling in the corner opposite the creature. He took her hand and squeezed it. She didn't respond, so he patted her face, applying more pressure when she remained lethargic. Her face wore a large smudge of dirt and she smelled like urine.

"Selka," Lamrhath whispered.

"My lord?"

"Yes."

She rubbed her eyes. Her other hand showed black and blue splotches around a swollen, scabby bite mark running across half her hand. Selka was tiny compared to the monster; he could've bitten the whole appendage off at the wrist. When she noticed the creature cowering under the lanterns, her eyes teared up and she gnawed her sleeve. Her clothes were in horrible condition, though not much different from what Lamrhath remembered.

Lamrhath took her good hand again. "Tell me what happened to you."

"Well, I—I fainted, I think."

"Were you awake at any point last night?"

"I think so."

"So what did he do?"

"Um." She looked again at the creature. Whatever was happening to him, he had become a stupid, mumbling oaf, petting his own blue hair and stroking the wall with his other hand.

"Don't be afraid, we're here now," Lamrhath said. When her eyes returned to his, they were large and watery. "Did he rape you?"

She looked down at herself, still groggy, and cupped her exposed breast, her fingers pressing into the soft flesh. It had been showing since yesterday when the sorcerers had torn her clothes. The sight of its pink, pointing nipple distracted Lamrhath. He'd tasted that part of her several times since this outpost's establishment, and the memories ushered in his relentless ailment again. It had been a few hours beyond what he usually managed with his ailment. He'd spent the entire night scouring the library with his associates for information on Wikshen, rather than what he usually did.

He squeezed her hand for his answer.

"No, I don't think so. At least not while I was awake."

"Did he attack you?"

"No."

"What did he do?"

"Nothing. It was too dark. But he never bothered me. He didn't even acknowledge me."

Lamrhath pointed behind him. "That's the young elf you pleasured the other day. Are you aware?"

Selka squinted, and then covered her mouth as a spark of recognition hit her. "What happened to him?"

"A disaster."

He helped her to stand. Her legs shook, and she leaned on him for support. He leaned away to stave off his growing erection, and she wobbled on her own feet before fixing her equilibrium.

He pushed her toward the door, and she stumbled on her own. "Go on. Before something else happens."

Picking her way around the dead bodies and sticky blood pools, she made it to the steps and climbed them with both hands and feet. By now, Lamrhath's heart was pounding with sexual thrill, and he averted his gaze from the impression of her rear showing through her thin, ragged skirt.

Lamrhath rubbed his face and returned to the creature being bound in chains. Dire trouble could be facing his faction, but his ailment never cared about order of importance.

"This isn't working, my lord," one of the sorcerers said.

"What isn't?"

"These chains. Every time we put a shackle around his wrist, his skin swallows the iron."

Three days later...

They'd made good progress with the creature. After the second day, he spoke his first sensible words and confirmed his name was Wikshen. Daghahen hadn't lied. But Wikshen refused to comply, and they couldn't simply set him free, not when he offered such delicious possibilities to progress Ilbith's agendas. Alternately, if they set him free, he might try to conquer Ilbith and advance his own cult's status instead—or so they had read in the one book found in the manor's library which happened to share tales about Wikshen.

Wikshen himself was a legendary conqueror who came with his own following of worshippers. Lamrhath had to leash him up. Ideally, he would absorb the Wikshonites into Ilbith, uniting the two societies to create a new one more powerful than history had ever seen.

Holding a Wikshen required special procedures. They couldn't use iron or any other metal to bind him because he could absorb any mineral into his skin for an easy escape. After discovering how the light helped subdue him, they moved Wikshen to the highest turret in the manor.

Lamrhath ventured up there often to see his progress. No sounds came through the door as Lamrhath turned the key, which was normal. Wikshen had made it known he was a reserved type of monster, waiting for the right moment to strike.

Inside the round room, every mirror in the outpost had been dusted off and set around a large, wooden armchair bearing Wikshen tied down with rawhides and ropes. The mirrors reflected sunlight through the windows, the beams fed through lenses they'd scrapped from spyglasses and various instruments, guiding the sunlight directly onto Wikshen to render him as helpless as a feeble old man. Wik, being a spirit of darkness, dwindled in sunlight, which voided his magic abilities and a lot of his bodily strength too.

They couldn't feed too much sunlight to him, however. Occasionally, an attendant turned mirrors or put a screen over a window to prevent the sun from killing him. They had assessed the sun's effects when a sharp ray made a spot on his skin sizzle and blister. He wore a few blisters already. They couldn't let him catch fire and die. If they did, the pixie would escape. It was more valuable to them now, trapped within this body.

"Good morning," Lamrhath said to Wikshen. "Are you still alive?"

He said nothing and his breaths came shallow, head flopped against the back of the hard chair, eyes closed. His whole form sat limp, as if he were melting.

"Are you ready to talk and explain all of your secrets?"

When Lamrhath moved to see his face better, he turned it away, keeping his eyes closed. "Come on now, look at me." Apparently, Wikshen preferred looking toward the bright sunbeam on his other side.

"I want to be your friend. I want to make you comfortable. We found some reading material about you. You like pleasure—so do we. You particularly like good, flavorful food. Well, we have a good kitchen and lots of resources. We'll prepare anything you like."

Wikshen's throat rasped, his chest rising and falling deeply.

"All right, here." Lamrhath moved to the window on that side and dragged a folded room divider in front of it to block out one of the stronger sunbeams. Wikshen finally opened his eyes and sighed in the dimmed lighting. He lifted his head.

"And if you speak to me, I'll order them to light one less candle to plague you tonight." They'd brought most of their candle stock up here too, using the same lenses and crystal balls to magnify their glow.

He pulled up a chair beside Wikshen and sat. The rawhide had been wound over and over around his forearms and looped under the arms of the chair. His torso was bound to the back of the chair, weaving the strands through the intricately carved holes. All the knots were tied at the back of the chair so Wikshen couldn't reach them. No chains or buckles were used to bind him, or else he might absorb the metal into his skin the way Dorhen had escaped his cell the other day.

Dorhen had known transitional magic, though he might not have realized it. All of Wikshen's previous incarnations had known it too. Dorhen and Wikshen shared this in common—an extraordinary coincidence.

"I have great things planned for you, my friend," Lamrhath went on. "Your presence with us was unexpected, but since you're here, we're going to make the most of it. I said it to Dorhen and I'll say it to you: the more you comply, the better life will be. We have comforts and pleasures we mean to share with you as our brother, and in return we want you to share your talents with us."

Wikshen frowned and narrowed his brow, glaring forward.

Lamrhath continued, "There is a man out in the Lightlands named Chandran who is doing important work, trying to find a sword I need. Chandran holds a high office in our faction. If and when he dies, I'll install you in his place." Though he waited, Wikshen showed no reaction. "You're probably the greatest ally Ilbith could ever acquire. If anyone can get the sword back, you can."

Wikshen's voice finally rasped out, "What will you give me?"

"Oh? He hasn't lost his voice to the sun. What do you want, my friend?"

"Freedom."

"You'll have it. We have to go back to the Ilbith tower soon, though we're low on gold now, so you and a handful of others will travel on foot. You can walk freely. You can walk freely with entitlement, but I do need your support. I mostly do my work from the tower, but you'll be my hand on the earth, won't you?" He waited a few seconds for a rare response from Wikshen. "You're free to grow your cult if you wish. But you have to agree that your cult, the Wikshonites, are now a branch of Ilbith. How about it?"

"Open the window," Wikshen said.

"You don't agree? I see… I won't open the window. And I'll take a candle away for tonight because I'm confident about you. You'll have your freedom, but in the kingdom of Ilbith, freedom comes with a tax. Your tax will consist of a few oddball errands here and there. When I say bring me a sword, you'll bring it. I'm thinking you're the only one who can. Order your Wikshonites to carry out my silly requests and see if I care. What do you say?"

"Open the window and let me die."

Lamrhath snapped his head downward. "See that brand on your side?"

"The one which still burns like *fire*?"

"Yes. It'll produce a real fire if you don't comply. We've been reading about Wikshen and his aversion to heat. But we won't kill you with it. We'll just set you on fire and put you out again and again."

Eyes locked forward, Wikshen sneered.

"If you can't be bothered to put in a little work for the governing faction, we'll have some fun instead. And fire isn't the only spell the brand can channel. If you do happen to incinerate, we'll trap you in another holding sphere and store it in a pot of boiling water."

At Wikshen's continued silence, Lamrhath moved toward the door. "You'll change your mind. You'll be out in the cold night air soon. If you like dark settings, you'll think about your duty to Ilbith."

Chapter 24
Her Broken Stone

With pain stabbing her feet and back, Kalea trudged along the dirt road through the woods to the creek behind the convent. A typical day. She daydreamed of Dorhen as her chores stretched on.

Her arm ached as if it would soon fall off from hauling the basket with its broken wicker twigs scratching her skin. What a terrible cloudy day, grey like her dowdy vestal tabard. She groaned at the basket full of dirty clothes. Pointless. By the size of the incoming black rain cloud, the laundry would never dry. She went through the motions, the rhythm of her life. Washing clothes to keep the never-ending cycle turning.

She arrived at the stream, its bank already littered with old vestals wailing out tears, more like giant black birds than women. Nothing out of the ordinary. Kalea put some clothes into the water and went to work. One garment down. Without the need to look, she went to the next.

The wind picked up. She sighed and continued to the next garment, scrubbing it against a rock. It never took long for her hands to grow sore. A huge gust of wind blew over her, taking her veils away. She grunted and grabbed a lock of hair from her face, not noticing the blood trail her fingers smeared across her cheek.

Getting back to work, she gasped at the blood billowing under the water like the clouds in the sky. An odd shirt mingled with her laundry. Her heart rate increased when she lifted it out of the water by its shoulders. It was a man's white undershirt, sopping wet and drenched in blood. Dorhen's shirt.

Blood blossomed at the side and dripped like thick milk.

The old women's wails grew louder and more grievous as Kalea added her own to the mix, screaming and wrenching the shirt in her two fists.

And then she woke up.

Twice, she had experienced similar dreams featuring a bloody shirt, and after the latest one, she awoke to the nightmare of living under Chandran's command. In the morning, he untied her rope and used it to haul her down a couple of steep banks to a creek.

"Strip," he said. "And hurry with your bathing. I don't have all morning."

He strode over and untied the rope from her wrists. "Don't try to run," he added as her eyes darted for possible escape paths. "If you try, I'll beat you."

He smiled, and his eyes brightened. "I'll give you the choice: magical punishment or physical." What could be worse than using magic ropes to suffocate her?

When the ropes were off, he stepped back. "Hurry up now. You stink."

She untied the knot at the top of her bodice and paused. "Are you going to watch me?"

He crossed his arms. "Of course. Can't have you escape, now can I? Besides, if you're my thrall, you'll learn to…do things while I'm around. We don't have time for modesty."

She continued with the laces and refrained from asking if he planned to molest her eventually. It was easy to assume he would someday. Would that be the price of finding Dorhen and the novices?

She shivered in the cold air as her kirtle dropped into a pool around her feet. Her thin chemise dropped next, and Chandran's eyes darted straight to Dorhen's moonstone hanging between her breasts. He stepped closer and reached for it. She reflexively slapped his hand.

"Sorry!" she said, and shielded her face.

He was glaring when she lowered her hands, his fist balled. He lurched forward and grabbed her hair, steering her to the ground and pinning her as she whimpered and whined.

"Please! Don't."

He choked her with one hand and lifted her moonstone to inspect it. When he released her throat, she sucked in a desperate gulp of air but immediately grabbed for the stone in his hands.

"You want to die, don't you? Or maybe you want something else, since you got us this far."

Tears welled in her eyes. "That's mine," she said.

"Who ever said my thrall could have personal items? What does this do, pretty?"

She coughed. "Nothing. Well, it glows, that's all. It's sentimental. Please."

"It glows, huh?" He shifted his narrowed gaze to her. "You're an interesting girl, aren't you? Tell me, what do you know about magic stones?"

"Nothing. I'm a simple vestal. Someone gave it to me. All I know is it glows."

He forced it over her head as she screamed and thrashed. "Relax!"

He wrestled her arms down and lowered his face so close his sour breath wafted up her nose. "I'll keep it for a few days to give you a little incentive to earn it back. You act like it's important to you."

A smile curled at the edges of his mouth. "You said you were a vestal?" She swallowed and nodded. "Real cute. If it's true…bet you never sucked a cock before, huh?"

She didn't want to show any reaction, but her eyes widened and her lungs stopped anyway.

"Relax. For now, you're working for this stone. Glowing isn't the most impressive thing I've seen a stone do, so I don't mind you keeping it. But you're still on the program, and after you pass you can have it back. Deal?"

She nodded again. At this point, she'd have to find a way to escape without the stone, a necessary pain. She'd already given her shell bracelet away to Bowaen, and now this man had taken her last memento of the elf who loved her. Her virginity was more valuable than jewelry, and she intended to give it freely to Dorhen.

Unable to control her pout, she began bathing as he'd ordered, choosing to sit on a rock and splash the freezing water on herself rather than immerse in it. Her lip quivered with grief and her teeth chattered in the cold. In her peripheral vision, a fresh green plant swayed on the other side of the river.

Del! It was Del, he'd found her! He and Bowaen must've cared enough to look for her. His dark form showed through the patches of green, and Kalea caught a glimpse of his eyes. Then she realized she was naked. And he was looking at her. She covered her breasts with her bare arm.

"What're you on about?" Chandran roared, and stormed toward her. "Sorry, I—"

"Hold on." Chandran sniffed the air. Del always stank like his pipe smoke. Across the river, the bushes rustled as he crawled away.

Kalea threw her arms around Chandran's neck. "Oh, please!" she cried. "There's a fox over there! Don't let it bite me. Help me, Chandran!"

He reared his hand back and slapped her across the face. With an echoing sound, the shock jounced her into the shallow water, and the freezing current rushed over her naked flesh. She was too rattled to rise yet, and the pain blossomed and spread across her skull. It took several long seconds to notice her disgraceful position, legs wide open, sprawled on the muddy river bottom. Chandran loomed, staring down at her. She closed her legs.

"Don't be stupid!" he yelled. "And remember to address me as 'master.'"

He turned and went back to his toil with his herbs and pouches spread out on a tree stump. Kalea remained sitting in the water, forgetting about the cold as she cradled her aching head. At least she'd prevented him from detecting Del.

After that incident, Kalea tolerated Chandran's routine. Bowaen and Del knew what had become of her, she kept reminding herself. They'd come for her soon. For now, her virginity remained intact, but as the days went on, the tension of if or *when* he'd decide to molest her tightened around her mind. He kept busy with his herbs, weapons, and meditation. He tied her hands less often, though his eyes remained constantly on her, and he flashed the stone around his neck as a reminder to behave.

He spent a few hours one night trying to make it glow. "Someone swindled you," he said. "It won't glow. How do you make it work?"

She lay on her side with the warded rope tied to one wrist, cradling her head on her arm. "I don't know. I've never been able to make it glow."

Chandran laughed. "It must be cracked or something." Squinting, he brought it closer to his eyes in the lantern light. He might've been correct, considering Dorhen had dropped it during the raid.

Her imagination flaunted horrible images of Dorhen fighting those men and what must've happened after she left him. The chaos in the convent must've gotten pretty rough. She forced the fabricated images out of her head before emotion overcame her. Another possibility was the stone could've broken the moment she batted it out of Dorhen's hand. Or...

Chandran continued, "Or you got swindled."

The next morning, Chandran roused her at the earliest hint of sunrise. "I've got a lead," he said. "Want to earn a visit with your broken stone?"

She yawned and pushed herself up off the uneven, rocky ground. At least he had given her a blanket last night. "Yes, master."

She'd taken up the habit of doing little things like obliging to call him that, which pleased him enough to slacken her ropes or gain an extra portion of food. She had decided to be okay with his rules for as long as it took Bowaen and Del to rescue her.

He opened his pack, pulled out a purple dress, and tossed it to her. "Put this on."

It consisted of two garments, a bodice and a skirt. The bodice's sleeves were short and a slit divided the skirt at the side to show her leg. Long rows of beaded fringe were sewn in tiers to the hips. What humiliating thing was he about to make her do?

Chandran held the end of a thin stick in the lantern's flame. He scraped a knife blade along the charred edge and returned it to the flame for a few seconds. Approaching her with it, he seized her chin in his strong hand.

"Sit," he said, taking his own seat on a stump. Kalea lowered to the ground in front of him. "The best way to lose an eye is to struggle." He tended to spout a lot of similar lines.

Is that how you apply your own whore make-up? Oh, how she wanted to ask it aloud. She'd watched him smudge ash on his eyes a few times already. He went all around her eyelids with the smelly, scratchy stick, and followed up with his callused, unkind thumb. Forget about black, her eyes should be red by now.

When he finished, he leaned back and observed his work, squinting. "Eh. You look fine, I guess. My standards exceed you, but I'd pork you in a pinch."

"Is that what you're going to do?"

She winced as he cocked his hand high. It didn't spring. His gesture shifted to a pointing finger. "No. Now pay attention." He bent over his things, put away the charcoal stick, and uncovered a large, gourd-shaped instrument with a long shaft and four strings from its canvas covering. "What do you know about dancing?"

"It's moving your body to music."

"I mean, what's your experience?"

"Vestals don't dance. We're not allowed to."

He rolled his eyes. "Follow my instruction. Push your hips to the right and hold it."

She obeyed, jutting her right hip out.

"No, now you're standing on one foot. Flatten your feet. Good. When I pluck this pipa string, swing your hips to the left—without raising your feet." He plucked the same string repeatedly, and Kalea did as he ordered. "Roll your pelvis to the front. Good," he said, "faster." After a while, she got used to the rhythm. "Now roll to the back." The change of direction jarred her, and he growled, but she picked up the slack and found the rhythm.

Chandran stopped playing. "Now raise your arms and use them." He bent one elbow at a time, covering his face with the back of his hand, and shifted to the other hand with a smooth, swooping motion.

Kalea mimicked him, trying to get it right. He started playing again, and she worked to keep both movements going at once. "Tighten it up. Form! Think of your form." Sweat beaded on her forehead.

"Good. Here's another move." Putting the pipa down, he stood and put his hands on his hips. "Flick your ass muscles, one cheek at a time."

He demonstrated, and his hip did a sharp snap to the side. He alternated to the other side and back. He sat again. "Think of your muscle and snap it. Tighten and release as fast as you can."

She tried it. Her hip snapped successfully and managed to jiggle the rest of her too.

"Concentrate it. Just your hip. One hip at a time." She tried again and must've made progress, because a smile spread across his face. He started playing. "Listen to this note." He played a high one and repeated it. "Snap your ass muscle whenever you hear this note." She did. Keeping the rhythm proved harder with this move. "I'll be inserting this note into the song, and you'll snap whenever you hear it."

After a few more hip snaps, she dropped her arms. "This is the most disgusting thing I've ever tried to do."

Chandran's frown returned. "The men in the tavern won't think so."

"Men in the tavern?" Kalea's mouth went dry, and not because of all the exercise.

"Yes, particularly Bowaen."

"Bowaen?"

He balled a fist over his instrument. If not for the pipa, she might've gotten socked for asking so many questions.

"Your friend. The one with the sword I need—Bowaen! I project he'll stop at the big tavern in Jumaire. If not, he'll stop somewhere eventually, which's what people do when on the road. You're not only my thrall, you're my partner. This is the kind of thing we'll do according to our kingsorcerer's divine requests. You're going to dance, and he'll see you, and you're going to get him so randy and mesmerized, I'll be able to do my work more easily. With the help of a few spells, your distraction should do fine. But first, we have to choreograph a dance."

"What if I don't want to dance in front of a bunch of men?"

He paused to stare. Another smile curled. His eyes perused her body. "I think I can find a way to punish you."

"If I'm your partner, how am I supposed to function the way you want when you keep threatening me?"

"You haven't passed the program yet. You think I'm stupid enough to trust you after three or so days?"

She crossed her arms over her exposed stomach. "I told you, I have to follow the sword. I want to be with you as long as you get it. It's my will."

"Sure it is, pretty. As long as you cooperate, we'll get it. Now pay attention."

Certain of Bowaen and Del's intended path, Chandran shoved a white-haired wig in the style of the Sharzian ethnicity on Kalea's head, threw a cloak over her, and took her into the tavern in Jumaire, the town north of Gaulice.

The upstairs loft looked packed to the point of bursting so that all the folk up there might pour down at any moment. Kalea stared at the packed crowd until Chandran grabbed her arm and jerked her to attention.

"Wait!" she said. "I can't dance in front of all these people. I've not practiced enough."

"Be silent and do as I say. Besides, this tavern gets a lot of greenhorns. These men will be more interested in your willowy body anyway."

He pushed down on her shoulders to make her sit on the stairs leading to the loft. "On my first note, you'll slide out of the cloak and begin your dance."

Sitting beside her, he unslung the pipa and waited, watching the door. Kalea's eyes roved over the crowd again. She would have to shake her hips in front of all these men. Hopefully, Bowaen had a plan.

Elbowing her arm, Chandran pointed to the open door. "It's happening. Get ready." He stalled, hands poised on the pipa strings, and stared from under his hood like a snake under a rock.

Bowaen was unmistakable with the turtle-like box on his back, hidden under his cloak. He and Del pushed against the thick crowd to snatch a table as soon as its drunkards left. Bowaen's eyes shifted as he spoke to his apprentice. The younger man's long, heavy smoking pipe dangled against his back by a leather strap, which he removed to load with tobacco.

Chandran allowed them a moment to talk to a barmaid before readjusting his hands on the instrument. "Begin," he whispered, and struck a note followed by a chain of up and down strumming.

The crowd hushed, eyes gravitating toward her and Chandran. Lightheaded and heart throbbing, Kalea rose up, her arms emerging from the cloak before the rest of her body. Her stomach lurched. Unless she could mentally block out the reality of the crowd's many eyes, she might end this performance with a vomit. Would Bowaen even recognize her wearing the wig?

As she swayed and sauntered around the room, doing the variety of moves Chandran had taught her, the men cleared a path. She might've forgotten some of the routine, so she filled it in as best she could, trying not to freeze up at the individuals who eyeballed her body without reserve. Chandran had played for her a specific note and made her memorize its sound. The note told her to go five paces more. Because they couldn't predict where Bowaen would sit or stand, Chandran would have to figure out as she danced where she should linger and hold the audience's attention.

Chandran struck his special note, telling her to go farther. His song flourished, plucking single strings and swiping all four. The special note rang again and she increased her distance, going to the far side of the room where a slim patron with a white cloak sat by himself. A large, silver bird with a red tail and a black, hooked bill perched on his shoulder.

She swung close enough to spy youthful blue eyes under his white hood. He placed his hand on her naked waist when she twirled past him. His hand made a full rotation around her middle. She couldn't bother to be mad in her concentration.

She remained swaying and shimmying her hips next to this patron because the special note remained absent. In fact, Chandran struck the hip-snapping note rapidly. *Twang, twang, twang-twang-twang.* The note increased in speed. Sweat dripped down her face. Some patrons' mouths dropped open.

Twang-twang-twang-twang. She'd collapse soon, or at least lose the rhythm and look sloppy. Her buttocks jiggled, her chest jiggled, her belly dripped sweat, and nearly a hundred faces gawked at her. Hardly a week ago, she had taken her vows to become a vestal, covered head to toe in linens and silks.

Kee-erp! Kee-erp! The silver bird screamed and took off from the white-cloaked man's shoulder. The bird's owner gasped.

Chandran stood poised with a long pipe to his lips, ready to blow a poisoned dart into Bowaen's neck. His weapon was painted to look like a flute. Dangling by his side from its woven strap, the pipa continued the hip-snapping note on its own by some enchantment so he could aim the shot.

Rising from his seat and flinging his arms forward, the white-cloaked man shouted, "*Keelinga!*"

A wire of lightning shot out of his ring and arced across the large room to zap Chandran. The flash stunned the crowd, and they dove out of the way in all directions. The lightning knocked Chandran to the floor.

"Sorcerer! Get out of here, everyone!" the white-cloaked patron yelled in a soprano voice, and the majority of the crowd took his advice and flooded through every exit in the tavern.

Amidst the tumbling confusion, Bowaen climbed to his feet, freeing the mysterious sword once again because his normal one had broken a few nights ago.

Chandran rolled away from his strike and threw a glowing glass object at the wall. After the crack of glass, a heavy steam spilled, out of which rose a glowing wisp with a skeletal face.

The white-cloaked man gasped and grabbed Kalea's arm to push her toward the door. "Get out of here!"

The door gaped, unobstructed, after all the establishment's patrons evacuated. She ran a few paces but couldn't abandon Bowaen.

The white wraith from Chandran's glass ball set its empty eye sockets on Bowaen and hissed. It sucked a strong pull of air into its howling mouth, which generated enough wind to make Kalea's hair fly.

The wind blew off the stranger's hood, revealing the white hair native to Sharr, the island south of the Lightlands. Under his cloak, he wore a uniform tabard similar to the Wistaran Grey Knights, but he didn't carry a sword. His bird perched on the second floor banister after a few passes around the room.

"Kalea!" Chandran called as she gawked at the white-haired stranger. "Stop him! Distract him!" He pointed to Del, who, being closest to the wraith, had ducked under a table to escape the sucking wind and now emerged with his heavy smoking pipe gripped in one hand.

"Get down!" the white-haired stranger yelled as the wraith spun, sending a reverse wind this time.

She ducked under a table, mimicking Del. *Tap, tap, tap-tap!* When the sound stopped hitting the tabletop, she chanced a peek. Pale, glassy quills were lodged into the wood. They vanished within seconds, leaving splintery notches in the table. Those things would've turned Kalea's flesh into chewed meat if she hadn't listened to the stranger. He ordered her to stay low. She stood anyway to check on Bowaen, who fended off Chandran's aggressive strikes. She darted to the next table, making her way closer to Chandran.

The white-haired man snatched the pipe out of Del's hand when he rose from his hiding place. "That's mine!" Del grabbed for his pipe, and the young man held it away.

"Get down and stay down!" he responded in his soft, yet commanding voice.

The wraith began to suck the air again, and Kalea's hair stirred stronger than before. Her feet slid along the floor—she'd ventured too close to the spirit.

As soon as the wind died, she was tackled. She screamed, but let herself fall below the table. The white-haired man had grabbed her. He pulled her under with him, Del's smoking pipe in his other hand. The sound of clashing blades rang on.

"Are you a Grey Knight?" she asked.

"I'm a Grey *Mage*."

She'd never seen a Grey Mage patrolling around before.

Thok, thok, thok-thok! The hammering sound of larger quills muffled her reply.

"You have to sprint for the door," he said, "before the sprott's quills grow large enough to obliterate these tables."

"Sprott?"

"Yes, the spirit. Go now!" They both stood, and he pushed her again, though she refused to leave.

"Kalea!" Chandran called again.

She ran toward him, lifted a stool which used to stand by the fire but had been sucked across the floor, and threw it at Chandran. It banged his shoulder and he roared, his eyes blazing in anger.

Bowaen took the offense, and Chandran dodged and parried his swings.

The sprott sucked again, and Kalea squealed as she fell and slid toward it. She crawled to another table at the next opportunity.

Slam, slam-slam, slam! The wood splintered above her head. The tip of a glass quill glinted through. The tables wouldn't stand against the next wave of quills.

The Grey Mage righted one of the tables close to where the sprott hovered, climbed onto it, took a long drag of Del's pipe, and blew a large puff of smoke at the creature. The tobacco smoke made it fade and separate into wisps which drifted back together within a moment.

It sucked in again, but so did the Grey Mage. He also raised his hand, decorated with a few stone rings. The mage blew the smoke before the sprott finished its pull. With the introduction of tobacco smoke into its being, it lurched and put off red sparks as it disappeared for a few moments.

The mage took the moment to release another charge of lightning toward Chandran. "*Keelinga!*" The bolt arced across the room and hit him again, but this time branched and touched Bowaen's extended hand as well. The two collapsed.

Kalea sprinted that way, hurdling over disarrayed tables and benches. Bowaen groaned, on his back, the sword out of his hand. Chandran sprawled in about the same condition. She crouched over Chandran.

Another pull of air stirred. "Damn it, I need more tobacco!" the mage yelled behind her.

Del yelled to her, "Kill him! Kalea, kill him!"

The wind picked up hard. She grabbed Chandran's clothes to steady herself. There weren't any blades within easy reach she could use to slit his throat, but she had no intention of killing anyone anyway. She ripped open the button at the top of his vest and found Dorhen's moonstone.

The wind sucked stronger. The mage cursed. "Where's another pipe?"

Chandran's eyes opened and focused on her. The pendant's thong was caught under his straps and garments.

"You have to get out!" the mage screamed. "All of you!"

The next wave of quills wouldn't be kind. Kalea gave up on the pendant and dragged Bowaen toward the hearth, now cold because the fire had long been sucked away. He came to enough to finish dragging himself. She huddled beside its stonework. Bowaen couldn't quite fit beside it with her, so he crouched, using his strongbox as a shield.

Clink, clink, clink-clink! The hearth stones sprayed chips as the quills ricocheted off of them. Afterward, Bowaen's box showed scars under his shredded cloak. Its surface had remained intact because of the iron reinforcements.

Chandran must've prepared himself for summoning such a dangerous creature, because no quills stuck out of his body. He slowly came to with fluttering eyelids and grunts. He turned over and crawled toward the sword on the floor.

Kalea lunged and beat him to it, swung the blade in an arc, and stopped it short over his head. "Lie flat, Chandran!"

He scowled at her from the floor, balling his fists as the blade pointed at his face. "I should've known…"

"You should've! Give me my stone now."

"Kalea!" Bowaen called.

The wind stirred again.

Chandran fumbled the stone out from under his shirt. "There!" He threw it, and she chased after it.

The mage found someone's abandoned tobacco pipe and hurried to suck its smoke into his lungs and hastily expel it into the sprott's ingoing air.

Del, in possession of his own pipe again, slammed it atop Chandran's head before he could rise to his feet and engage Bowaen hand-to-hand.

The pendant bounced off the wall and Kalea tracked its path, diving for it as the vortex of wind died. Another burst of quills would happen in a moment. The moonstone didn't break when it hit.

"Kalea, take cover!" Bowaen called.

No table stood nearby, and most of them were full of holes anyway. The wind blew. She couldn't run up the stairs; they were too far away. She crouched and covered herself. She put the sword over her head, hoping its wide blade could stop a few quills.

The wind roared. Stinging grains of sand brushed Kalea's hands and arms like sleet. Red sparks fired off, crackling and popping and intensifying until the sprott vanished in a loud inward zip.

Kalea lowered the sword from over her head.

"Is everyone all right?" the mage asked.

Chandran had fled.

"Been better," Bowaen answered.

"I'm alive," Kalea mumbled. She inspected her naked torso and arms. The little grains in the wind had made tiny red streaks on her skin, but that was the extent of the damage. She smiled and put the stone around her neck where it belonged.

The mage whistled, and his parrot glided down from the upstairs on wide silver wings. Kalea made her way over to thank the young man and ask his name.

"You didn't see me. Tell no one," he said.

She stopped and frowned as he put his hood back on, now full of holes, and rushed out the door with his bird's wings flapping to keep balance. After gawking at his behavior, she held out the sword to Bowaen.

"Here. This is meant to be with you."

Bowaen cocked his head and hesitantly reached out to receive it. "I don't think I want it anymore." Nonetheless, he sheathed it and motioned to Kalea. "Did he hurt you?"

She shrugged. "It's over now."

He took a moment to study her face, which she kept as level as she could. "Well, here we are again. We found you with him two days ago. We were trying to figure how and when to make a move, but at the same time we had to play dumb. We kept traveling to make him think he was following us instead of the other way around. I guess I'm…well, sorry we couldn't free you sooner."

"Don't worry about it," she said. "It was a difficult situation, but we made it in the end, didn't we?"

After a sharp nod, he turned and called Del's name. "Let's go!"

Outside the tavern, a huge silver bird rose into the copper sky. A man, tiny in the distance, rode on its back with a white cloak flying behind him.

Chandran sat in a dark alley, listening to the whisper stone the kingsorcerer had granted him. The groaning voice echoed inhumanly off the shining facets.

You've wasted too many valuable spells, Chandran. I'll give you one more chance. Say your chants and your prayers to Naerezek. Abort the process if you manage to get the sword.

Chandran clapped his fist around the stone as its vibrations faded.

Chapter 25
A Use for the Monster

Wikshen serves no one, you fool! Wikshen serves no one, you fool! Wikshen serves no one, you fool!

"Are you listening?"

A tremor rushed through Wikshen's body and lingered across his back. They had hit him? The blur coiling around in his vision separated and settled into discernible shapes. He closed his eyes.

"He's not even as useful as the dunces, eh, my lord?" Harn said, standing beside the tall oaf with blue hair who stared into oblivion. He hadn't even reacted when Harn hit him with the cat o'nine tails.

Lamrhath rubbed his face with both hands. "I'm going to kill Daghahen when I catch him again. Not a word will be shared. The moment I see him, or anyone like him, their head will come off."

He lowered his hands and glowered again at the lumbering, incoherent monster his nephew had become. Dorhen was the wrong candidate. After the last few days spent reading the only book at the outpost to mention Wikshen, hardly pausing to eat or even alleviate his sexual malady, and holding a few long communications with his followers at the tower through the whisper stone, Lamrhath had learned much.

First of all, Dorhen was an uneducated idiot, yet only one past Wikshen was said to be particularly intelligent, so that couldn't be the issue. And Dorhen had possessed a potent ability in transitional magic—a phenomenal coincidence which should've been an enormous help. But after poring through a list of traits, histories, facts, and myths, Lamrhath settled on one important trait Dorhen didn't seem to have: aggression.

The very first Wikshen—recounted several hundred years after the fact in history books because the historians had gone around listening to word-of-mouth tales retold in the Darklands—had been a vile brute, full of anger and piss, who led a misfit army around the grasslands raiding for fortune and women. The man Wik had freely chosen was neither magically talented nor smart. He was aggressive, and so were the following five Wikshen-candidates. That trait was the one Dorhen seemed to lack. Although he had tried to escape and killed sorcerers here in the outpost as well as in the convent on the night of the collection, he had still lacked a certain level of grit typical to other Wikshen-candidates. Another remarkable thing was his docility, considering the fact that *saehgahn* were typically more aggressive than men in their natural instincts—they were just more apt to control their instincts than men were.

The problem Lamrhath faced was that there was no good fix for their dilemma. If they destroyed this Wikshen, Wik might be too weak to perform any more feats for another few centuries. According to the books, it took a lot of a pixie's energy to perform pixtah, even though breaking the sphere had forced him to do it. The pixie naturally drifted around, collecting energy from its environment. As Wikshen, he would use transitional spells to absorb minerals and a much larger cache of energy from the earth.

Sadly, Wik had spent the past six hundred years or more cooped up in a glass ball, unable to collect any energy. If they released Wik from its current host now, the pixie might devolve to a minor fairy form. The better choice would be to let him live as he was and see if they could use his special Wikshen talents to suit their faction.

It was time to go home. They had a larger library in the Ilbith towers from which to glean more information. Who knew what secrets waited to be uncovered?

Lamrhath approached the blue-haired oaf. Numerous red streaks wound around Wikshen's naked torso. Some of the older ones from this morning had sealed up and faded already; the books had said Wikshen healed fast.

He still wore the long, black sheet they'd found him in the day after the incident. They couldn't remove it from him. They had tried to so he could wear their faction's uniform, but the sheet would not budge. A thick cord, made from a material they couldn't place, was strung through it, trailing from the side of his hip diagonally to the front, where it ended at the open slit above his knee. The knot at the end of the cord wouldn't come undone, and they couldn't cut it or the fabric. In their persistent fight with the fabric, it even began to move, avoiding their hands as if it were...alive.

So there Wikshen stood, wearing a black shift draped around his waist, with no shirt or leggings or shoes. Every once in a while, they found him wearing black fingerless gloves and matching toeless socks, but those garments came and went mysteriously.

He'd gained enough height to surpass Lamrhath's proud stature, but Lamrhath wouldn't be intimidated by anything. He grabbed a lock of Wikshen's greasy blue hair in his gloved hand and yanked it downward.

"Bow your head when your kingsorcerer approaches."

Making him do it proved harder than estimated. Wikshen was solid, even though his form appeared more nimble than heavy, and he swayed like a drunkard. Lamrhath put in enough muscle to get results, however.

Bent over awkwardly with his hair caught in Lamrhath's grip, Wikshen's dull greenish eyes ventured to meet his.

"Lower your eyes too," Lamrhath growled. To emphasize the point, he applied a small electric shock from the stone in the palm of his glove.

Wikshen jolted and fell.

"That's better."

On the floor, Wikshen continued to sway, his eyes drifting as if the world spun. His face wore a lasting grimace from the unpleasantness of the shock. He still insisted on making eye contact with the kingsorcerer.

"Listen now," Lamrhath said. "We are about to depart for home, and we're taking different paths to get there. When you arrive in our kingdom, I expect to hear good news about your behavior. Your traveling company will make a few stops for supplies. Take any chance you get to please me. Rewards await you in Ilbith."

Wikshen sneered.

"Wait!" Gaije ran up the path marked between the rows of many tents shared by the new recruits. The tents were being dismantled as he sprinted. He'd barely had enough time to let the ink dry on his letter before he hastily wound twine around it and took off. The *saehgahn* who shared his tent had graciously agreed to break it down so he could finish his letter and run to catch the courier.

The sound of the donkey braying announced he wasn't too late. The courier was still riding down the line, collecting other young recruits' letters. It wasn't Togha. Gaije wasn't sure if he should be relieved or sad about that. Regardless of how bitterly the two had fought in their youth, Togha was a familiar face, a distant cousin even. If he had been the courier, it would have meant Gaije wasn't all that far from home. But it wasn't Togha; his letter would change satchels a few times before being passed into Mhina's eager hands, courtesy of Togha. Gaije caught the courier right at the edge of camp as he collected the last few letters.

He'd made it through an intense training period, and now all the new recruits headed to the next outpost to be sorted into the Norrian army's various divisions. His road would take him all the way to the northwest side of Norr, to the royal palace where he would continue training for the queen's guard.

Along with everyone else, he scrambled to dress, collect his things, and fall into line. In three long rows, the young *saehgahn* ran in formation. The *saehgahn* were allowed one pack to wear on their backs with a bedroll attached, a secondary pouch and waterskin on their belts, a cloak, a knife, and a sword or bow and quiver. While they ran, the archers were made to carry their bows in hand, strung and ready to use if need be. During training, they practiced running long distances while carrying bags of sand draped around their necks, strapped to their backs, or carried in hand. This practice was common at home, but army training was enhanced; the *saehgahn* were pushed to their limits in the few weeks they spent in the initial phase of recruitment. Though the swordsmen were destined to wear heavier armor than the archers, they were all put through the same trials. Gaije could already tell a difference as he jogged on in the tight formation of archers. He could run for longer than before, and he had added at least twenty extra pounds to his limit.

Lately, his belt pulled tighter around his middle than it used to and his *sa-garhik,* his leggings, stretched tighter around his thighs. He had realized it the other day when he pulled them on after a cold bath in the river. He had paused to consider a forbidden thought. At the next outpost where *faerhain* lived and worked, he could tuck his tunic tails up around his belt during his free time around town. He'd seen other *saehgahn* do that at home. They were shunned by the Desteer and laughed at by other males for doing so, but they did it anyway. Many *saehgahn* showed their bodies off at any opportunity and to as extreme a degree as possible. The eyes of the *faerhain* were always wandering, always peering downward. They liked to see the shape of a male's legs in his *sa-garhik* and the bulge in his braies.

If Gaije was lucky, if he could catch one's attention and get married before his initiation into the queen's guard, he'd be free. He might not be able to marry Anonhet, but he'd be married nonetheless. A life he preferred.

He whipped his cloak off as soon as he was set free at the outpost town. Ildahar was one of Norr's larger towns, founded long ago by one of the oldest clans. Its ancient heritage showed in its permanent citizens with their hair black enough to challenge Lehomis's. With his grandfather as living proof, it was common belief that Norr's original bloodline produced black hair until elves from other places had moved in and joined them. In this age, the idea of breeding with foreign elves was considered blasphemy against the Bright One.

As soon as Gaije stepped out of the barracks to join the town in prayer within their grove, he pegged himself lucky. *Saehgahn* always whispered about how *faerhain* were looking for variation—someone "exotic." So far, his red hair was the most exotic thing he'd seen. He was the only redhead in his company of recruits, and among the town's bustle of citizens, medium brown was as exotic as hair color ranged.

The Bright One's sacred grove spanned ten times wider than the one belonging to Clan Lockheirhen to accommodate such a large number of citizens and army affiliates. The worship ceremony was a different experience too. The Desteer members, with their long black hair and spooky painted faces, had a tighter grip on their telepathic abilities than those of Clan Lockheirhen, and they utilized it to stretch their message in three directions. Three maidens moved through three sections of the massive circle of elves seated on the grass. They spoke the exact same words at the same time and with the same length of pauses, thus stretching the same voice to three different crowds.

"The Bright One sees all!" The head maiden's voice rose and fell in a special rhythm like his clan's Desteer. This one's voice boomed, unlike Alhannah, the head of the Desteer at home, whose voice pierced. Each maiden speaking was accompanied by two other maidens to echo her in perfect unison.

"Even at night, the Bright One uses the moon and the stars to look upon us, and when those aren't in view, He uses the glowing eyes of owls and cats and all living things to watch over us. It doesn't matter how dark the night grows! As dark as our forest can become, the Bright One can always see us!"

She and the others paused for a breath. "Be glad you are alive. Be glad you walk under the Bright One's reach. For there is no shadow darker and deeper than the void you'll find when He rejects you. Stay sharp, *saehgahn* and *faerhain*. He sees your actions!"

"He sees your toils," the secondary maidens added.

The maiden handling Gaije's section of the audience stood over him. His coppery hair made him stand out—not such a welcome occurrence at an event like this.

The speaker's arm extended, her finger pointing, and she singled out a young *faerhain* to Gaije's left. "He sees your tears!" The *faerhain* wasn't crying at the moment, but Desteer maidens had ways of knowing things, and they all seemed to take a certain sick level of delight in hinting at their knowledge of someone's secrets. She pointed to Gaije. "He *knows* your thoughts!"

Gaije dipped his head and hugged his knees. *Saehgahn* weren't supposed to sit in certain shameful poses, but her words stung. He had been thinking a lot about *faerhain* lately. *Saehgahn* were supposed to think about death, work, fighting, and their families. Tightening his jaw, he kept a low profile until she moved on. Perhaps he should've worn his cloak and hood.

With the starch gone from his back, he reentered the hub of Ildahar with the huge crowd of *saehgahn* who walked about as confidently as he did after the religious experience. The buildings were sculpted out of earth like his home, but crammed in more tightly. Most of the trees in the area were left standing, some growing through the center of household courtyards and others lending support for the buildings.

Gaije moseyed through the central plaza, a large hub at the center of town kept clear for social gatherings, important town assemblies, and trading with neighboring clans. The ground of this one was loosely tiled with clay stones; little patches of grass grew between them. The Desteer hall loomed over the area, like at home, with its domed ceiling supported by stacked stone brought in from Norr's quarry in the southwest. Such large building stones were brought in for the most important structures, like Desteer halls and sometimes the elders' houses. The elder usually boasted the biggest family, though that wasn't the case for Clan Lockheirhen. Lehomis's immediate family had dwindled over the centuries down to Gaije's brood through Gaije's father. Poor old Lehomis had survived past all those generations, and he would surpass Gaije's lifetime too.

In the central plaza, *saehgahn* ran back and forth as they set up for supper to feed the new army recruits. Tomorrow they'd all be dispersed, but tonight Gaije could enjoy some free time—probably his only free day for a long time.

Surveying the area, he counted the *faerhain* out and about today, and found about twenty that he could see at the moment. Twenty *faerhain* among one hundred or so *saehgahn* just in the plaza. This was why *saehgahn* were told not to think about marriage or private relations. If all twenty of the *faerhain* were unmarried, a mere twenty of the *saehgahn* moving about would be chosen. Gaije put today's stern sermon behind him and hurried to tuck his tunic tails around his belt, at least while he was out tonight.

Of course, all twenty-something of the *faerhain* in the plaza weren't single. Some of them wore darker colors to signify their marriages. They were local wives who'd come out of their houses to help host the new recruits. The single *faerhain* wore brighter, spring-like colors, which made up about half of the *faerhain* present.

"*Saehgahn*, hear me!" a loud, feminine voice shouted from across the plaza. Most of the company paused to look up. "All are welcome to the elder's estate tonight for a retelling of Lehomis's adventures!"

It was the elder's wife, the clan matron, who shouted. She strolled tall with her shoulders back, cutting the crowd apart, dressed pristinely in her traditional *hanbohik* which displayed a large symbol of Clan Kanarihen, a moth perched on a scroll, on the front of the skirt. Two of her daughters walked at her sides, their hands clasped neatly together as they walked, as crisp and graceful as their mother.

"Tonight, after supper," she continued, "the retellings will be accompanied by shadow play, performed by my own daughters! Please come! There will be tea and cakes! All are welcome! *Saehgahn,* hear me!"

Gaije stood cold and stiff as they passed, her voice growing louder before receding to the back of the crowd again. For an instant, one of her daughters glanced at him, thanks to his red hair. She didn't smile or let her eyes linger, as was proper. Her eyes might've lingered if she wasn't in a place of concentrated attention. Tonight was special, the perfect opportunity to show himself.

Gaije headed straight to the elder's manor the minute he finished eating. The clan matron stood at the entrance to the house's large courtyard, greeting all the new faces as they filed in. The head Desteer maiden had come to protest the event. The stories of Lehomis's exploits were a controversial subject, their acceptance varying from clan to clan. Gaije's clan, being the one Lehomis had personally founded, celebrated his legend, and their local Desteer were forced to accept that fact.

The Desteer maiden, standing opposite the matron by the ingoing crowd, kept her stiff finger extended and her reprimands flowing. As Gaije approached the threshold leading into the house's courtyard, some of those scoldings were directed at him.

"That goes for wild redheads too. Go back to the barracks, *saehgahn!*" she said.

The matron laughed. "Do you know who this is, Gildayha? He's from Clan Lockheirhen. Pass through, *saehgahn.* You are welcome here."

Gaije obeyed. Anyone would've known where he came from by his mantle. All *saehgahn* wore mantles over their shoulders displaying their clans' symbols on their backs. Lockheirhen's symbol was a horse's head biting an arrow.

"Thank you, *faerhain,*" he said to her and proceeded through, leaving the matron beaming and the Desteer maiden scowling behind him.

The courtyard had been converted into a theater for the night, with ambient purple, red, and yellow lanterns hanging from tree limbs and the house's awnings. The fragrance of herbal tea enhanced with dried fruit drifted through the air. Gaije was able to find a good spot on the ground, which was covered with many colorful rugs for the occasion.

The proud elder and his wife had a good number of daughters and plenty of sons of all ages. Gaije couldn't hold his blush when one of the daughters came through with a tray of tiny teacups, smiling at him when he received his.

The courtyard filled up fast; additional *saehgahn* climbed the wall and perched atop it while others piled in at the gate to peer through. The shadow play was better than Gaije expected. Two of the house matron's daughters hid behind a wooden wall with a cutout window fitted with a silk-paper screen. They could easily afford to build such an oddity here because Ildahar was where all of Norr's paper came from. That fact had dawned on Gaije when night fell and a number of white moths had landed on him as he made his way through town.

Behind the satiny white screen, a few candles glowed to emphasize the little paper shadow puppets the *faerhain* manipulated with thin rods. Nothing like this had ever been organized in Gaije's clan. One of the elder's sons sat beside the screen, reading off a script to add voices and narration to the story, and two of his young brothers sat on the other side, playing little pipes and percussion instruments for magical effect.

For a moment, Gaije was taken away to an era long ago, to the Darklands, where his grandfather galloped across the grasslands, running for his life with a gang of angry bandits in pursuit. Gaije had heard the stories verbally from Lehomis's own mouth. As good a storyteller as he was, it couldn't quite compare to the beautiful images within the little screen these *faerhain* created for his eyes.

They even included in their story a little flirtation between Lehomis and the *faerhain* he found in the Darklands, Kristhanhea—the *faerhain* who would someday become his wife and the matron of Clan Lockheirhen. The storytellers kept that part brief and minimal however, or else they'd face an enormous amount of trouble with the Desteer. The story focused heavily on Lehomis's battle experiences instead. Gaije laughed out loud a few times at the antics. It wasn't told exactly the way he understood the story, but that didn't matter.

The entire production was hosted by the elder's wife and her children. The elder himself kept quiet, sitting to the side with his own little teacup, enjoying his children's skillful performance.

At the end of the show, when Lehomis succeeded in rescuing Kristhanhea from the evil bandits, the many *saehgahn* in the audience roared with applause, and the house matron stepped in front of the screen with her arms raised, grinning ear to ear. She thanked them all for coming, welcomed the new recruits to their town, as short as their stay would be, and led them all in a prayer to the Bright One asking Him for protection for the *faerhain*, guidance for the *saehgahn*, and fertility for their people.

Then she made an announcement for one of her daughters who had worked the shadow puppets. "My daughter has recently become *faerhain*! She chose the home!"

The *saehgahn* cheered louder than they had at the end of the show. "So stand tall. She'll be looking at you." Her comment was met with a mixture of cheer and chuckles.

"Please stay a while. There's more tea left. You're free to mingle and discuss our production. These young ones worked on it for the last year."

Gaije stood up, as many others did. His heart pounded. This might be a good opportunity. He came from Clan Lockheirhen, and anyone could see that. He had insight few others could hope for. In fact, he was directly descended from Lehomis and knew all the stories by heart. He'd heard them again and again from the source. He could talk to *faerhain*—more of them than the elder's daughters were in attendance. After such an extraordinary experience, the *faerhain* in the audience might be deeply amused by the idea of Clan Lockheirhen and its exalted hero. And Gaije was his grandson.

Gaije tightened his tunic tails in his belt and moseyed toward the *faerhain* who poured the tea, clearing his throat and working his tongue around the careful words he'd use to ask for a refill.

"Lockheirhen." A hand landed on his shoulder, startling him out of his concentration. It was Gaije's captain, Malmirhen, his piercing eyes boring into Gaije. "Back to the barracks, *saehgahn*. Tonight, we're passing out the new mantles. We depart at dawn. Tell anyone you see on the way back."

Gaije's shoulders slumped. So much for talking to *faerhain*. He couldn't have won anyone's favor in one night anyway. *Faerhain* observed older *saehgahn* for years and made calculated decisions when they were ready. Gaije had no chance of being picked. He was too young, he had no merits, and he wouldn't be in town long. How could he win a wife on features as tawdry as his hair color and his tight *sa-garhik*? Gaije pulled his tunic tails out of his belt and let them hang naturally as he trudged back to his temporary bed.

In the barracks, all the new recruits lined up and formally received crisp new mantles to wear around their shoulders. This mantle displayed the royal insignia, a white ox with wings, on the back of the left shoulder and each *saehgahn's* home clan symbol on the right. As each *saehgahn* was handed his mantle, his destination was declared aloud.

"Gaije Lockheirhen," Captain Malmirhen said, "graciously receive your mantle. You are hereby inducted into the army of Norr. Your destination lies at the palace, where you'll train for the queen's guard."

He unfurled the small garment to show the skillful needlework displaying the winged ox beside the horse biting an arrow, and placed it around Gaije's shoulders. The captain stood back, and Gaije gave the formal bow.

Back on the path winding through the towering white trees, Gaije's company ran in three long rows, carrying all their belongings on their backs. His original company had split into three back in Ildahar. Gaije's current, shortened company was still the largest, destined for the royal palace in the territory of Clan Tinharri. The other two parts of his company had dispersed to stations in other parts of Norr.

They had been running without pause for the last four hours, and Gaije was becoming winded. He wasn't alone. A rest would be in order soon. The morning air warmed as noon approached. He ran with his mouth hanging open like a panting dog, when a crack of thunder startled the company.

A sharp stab of light plowed through the *saehgahn* up front. Afterward, a tremor rattled the rest of them, striking Gaije's body like a mallet. The air in his lungs whooshed out of him. He fell.

Chapter 26
A Letter for the Farhah

"Go back home, Lehomis Lockheirhen," Alhannah said with her little lackeys nodding behind her.

"So then…you've heard nothing from them?"

"We have more important things to worry about than whether some *saehgahn* will fail to marry in this generation."

"Well, it'll matter to *them*, lass. What could be more important?"

"Nothing that concerns you right now. Go home and sharpen your arrows and watch over the clan like you're supposed to do."

Lehomis rubbed the bridge of his nose between his eyes. "It's been weeks since my grandson left for the army, and my *saehgahn* have been asking me about the look on my face. They can smell the looming trouble, but I've kept my jaw locked up tight. What am I supposed to tell them?"

Alhannah rose as the other Desteer maidens kept their seats on the floor. "Absolutely nothing. We don't need another civil war, wouldn't you agree?"

He huffed and averted his eyes. "Yeah." He stood too. "Okay, look." He sharpened his eyes and pointed them right at hers. "I don't know how old you are, but I'm fairly confident I've got you beat. Now, it's not you alone who guides this clan, and not me either. It's both of us. You tell the females what to do, and I tell the males. If you'd like to prevent elves from spilling the blood of their own, you'll listen to me. You have to handle the royals, or they'll get cockier than they already are. Matter of fact, we might have to fight 'em—and hurt 'em a little—to make it clear they're not the only family in Norr with the right to reproduce."

She stepped forward and jabbed her finger close to his nose. "We won't fight the Tinharri Clan. Go home and tell your *saehgahn* nothing. If it comes to it, you can arrange a campaign with the unmarried to sweep the Darklands for stray *faerhain*."

He put his hands up and drew his mouth tight. "Fine. We will. But you'll be left with a meager company of *saehgahn* to protect you after we leave."

Alhannah frowned while he spoke.

"It ain't that easy, lass. We have to be firm with the royals, or we'll wind up like the humans, begging and scraping under a full-blown monarchy."

"It can't be so bad," she said. "Trisdahen is home now, and Tirnah will be pregnant again soon."

He balled his hands into fists and turned around with a growl. He went halfway to the large double doors before stopping. He pointed his finger across all the seated females and counted their painted faces.

"Fifteen, not counting the head maiden! Excessive, don't you think? Fifteen of you, across a mere three generations, chose the hall over the home." He shook his head. Most of the fifteen were in their younger years, proving an increase in the last two generations. "And all of you except the head maiden were born in this clan."

Alhannah threw her arms out to the sides, extending her wide sleeves like walls to protect her sisters. "I know where you're going with this, Elder. Stop it!"

"Why did so many of you choose the hall?" He yelled it.

The younger *faerhain* eyed each other and mumbled; a slight hint of guilt touched the faces of the youngest few.

Alhannah pursed her lips. "Fifteen is not excessive."

"It's more than this clan has ever seen at one time. Do we need so many of your rank bossing around the *faerhain*? Hell, if we keep going like this, you'll outnumber the *faerhain*. Who will you have to boss around then?"

"When you use foul common-tongue language, you're no longer welcome in this hall."

"Bah!"

"That also… You're getting too tense. Go home. You're excused."

He crossed his arms. "Well, I'll be back in a week to ask again how you're handling the royals."

"The *Tinharri* Clan knows what's best."

He forced his mouth into a smile. "Keep sayin' that. And keep encouraging young *farhah* to choose the hall. We'll be dispersing into other clans if we can't get some *saehgahn* mated. Oh, but I guess you Desteer don't care 'cause you're used to getting passed from clan to clan."

Alhannah shook her head as he turned and left.

The lock slammed on the door behind Lehomis. "Tch." He tried to smooth his expression. Another day, another argument with the Desteer: the life of the elder.

He gathered up his hair and draped it over one arm like a sash. It hadn't been braided since he last washed it; Mhina was too busy being charmed by her father. He didn't want to bother Anonhet for the sake of his hair either. Now that she was eligible, he did his own housework so she could go to the practice yards more often to watch the *saehgahn* practice. It was an old tradition practiced widely among Norrian clans, but the Desteer had banned it recently for being "vulgar" somehow, so now the *faerhain* spied on them in secret. Lehomis would escort her there himself if need be. He had also shown her the new private location where the Desteer had ordered the *saehgahn* to bathe in the river so she could watch. A few other *faerhain* had already planted themselves behind the rocks and bushes, chatting to each other in whispers, when they arrived. The main thing Lehomis lamented about it was Gaije's absence during Anonhet's critical time. Nonetheless, along with his duties, training, and relocation, he'd be in the eye of other *faerhain* from other clans. All the better if he could bring one into this clan, but he'd have to accomplish the task before his initiation into the royal cult for a blessed discharge from the program. As Trisdahen had informed them, the queen didn't want married *saehgahn* in her entourage.

Lehomis's mood lightened when he arrived at Tirnah's house and was graced by the smiling face of his little granddaughter, Mhina, as she ran across the field from her mother's kitchen. She was the future. She, of all females, would choose the home. The clan was in her hands—and Anonhet's, of course. A few other unmarried *faerhain* in their clan were still trying to decide on a husband, and a handful of young *farhah* would come of age soon. But day by day, the Desteer were imposing more rules on the *saehgahn* to prevent them from flaunting themselves before the females. Now they couldn't even watch the *saehgahn* bathe or practice. Ridiculous. One wondered if the Desteer privately groomed the young *farhah* to choose the hall.

Mhina ran up and hugged his leg. "Good morning, Grandfather!"

"Good mornin'!" He knelt and hugged her.

"What brings you to my house today?"

"I'm here to see *you*, of course. Look what I made." He reached into one of his long tunic's pockets under his poncho and presented a small wooden horse he'd been carving for her. Her eyes lit up. "This is Miktik," he said.

"Your best horse friend!"

It was lacquered in a deep, glossy black, like the real horse he had ridden centuries ago. Some additional gold leaf highlighted its hooves and closed eyes. The horse's legs were curled underneath him as if he were resting.

"Oh, Grandfather." She threw her arms around his neck. "I'll treasure it always."

A donkey brayed in the distance. Mhina gasped with a smile, and her hands shot to the satchel she'd been toting lunches around in. "Togha! I'm going to show him Miktik."

Lehomis sighed as she took off toward the beaten road. Gaije, the sharp lad, had been right about Togha being a horrible marriage candidate. She wouldn't be marrying him; he could easily cause enough trouble to receive the *sarakren* brand before long, labeling him unmarriageable forever. At least for now, he'd sparked her interest in marriage. She'd grow up to choose the home.

Mhina stopped and gawked when a different courier rode around the bend. "Where's Togha?" she asked the dark-haired stranger on a pale, spotted donkey. He opened the flap on his shoulder bag.

Lehomis moved closer, straining his ears.

"I don't know, *farhah*," the new courier said. "I received his route, but was not told why."

"Is he okay?" she whined.

The stranger handed her an envelope. "With apologies, *farhah*, I don't know."

Mhina's mouth hung open when she turned back to Lehomis and the courier moved on.

"Oh, dear. I heard what he said, lass. So sorry."

"What'll I do without him, Grandfather?"

"What did the new courier give you?"

Mhina inspected the letter, and her smile returned. "It's from Gaije!"

Lehomis dropped to a squat and crossed his arms over his knees. "Well, let's hear it."

After untying the twine, she unfolded it. A tiny stick fell out. "Look what he sent me!" She picked up the twig and smelled it. Lehomis detected the cinnamon-like scent before she opened the letter.

"A twig from a Norrian spice tree. He must've traveled all the way to the west coast to find it for you. Put it in yer teacup, and it should last you at least a week."

"Oh, that brother of mine!" She took a long whiff with her eyes closed before opening them to check the letter. Her eyes ran across the many words to the one at the top. "Dear Mother, Mhina, Father, and Grandfather...'"

The lass struggled through a short story about how Gaije had met new friends, camped on a tall bluff looking across an endless black ocean with the moon glowing behind heavy clouds, and earned a copper hair cuff for his braids. His superior had joked that he'd lose it in his copper-colored locks. Gaije finished the letter with the usual Norrian formalities.

"'I am honored to have…r-received this path, but…wish to return to protect the females I love. I pray I'll see you again…someday. Please tell Anonhet I said…hello. From Gaije.'" When she looked up again, her eyes were glassy. "I miss him, Grandfather."

"Aw, ha ha, come here, lass. He'll be fine, and you'll see him again soon. Let's go have a cup of tea and use that spicy twig, what do ya say?"

Gaije collapsed, smoke swirling off his singed clothes. A sudden roaring spark of lightning had engulfed the *saehgahn* walking next to him, narrowly missing him. A larger, stinking pit of charred death was left up ahead where the brunt of the lightning had hit. He'd be dead, too, if he'd been in the slightest contact with the *saehgahn* next to him.

Where had the lightning come from? There were no clouds today. A storm might happen later, but today was as bright and cheerful as a spring morning could be.

Another angry roar of light jumped across the company. It came from the forest.

Gaije lurched backward before it could connect to him, falling into those who stood behind him. They tumbled into a pile and struggled to rise from the confused tangle while all around them their friends fried in raging circles of light. The victims continued standing until the crackling wires dissipated and released their charred bodies to fall into their own burn-scented pile of smoking corpses.

An arrow thudded into the *saehgahn* who struggled beside Gaije. The injured *saehgahn* wheezed, his lungs filling with blood, and he quickly became a limp weight atop the other poor soul beneath him. Gaije dragged the dead comrade off the live one and helped him to rise. Due to his vulnerability, he had to trust the rest of them to pick themselves up.

He collected his bow from the ground and nocked an arrow, pausing to survey the wooded road. Some trees had caught the lightning bolts and were badly charred, if not on fire.

Humans wearing dark colors, no uniforms or banners, crept about, raining fiery arrows into Norr. Others were chanting and rubbing stones between their hands to summon more lightning.

"Scatter!" Captain Malmirhen yelled. "Scatter to stop the lightning!"

Many of the humans brandished swords and bows, but the group obviously prided themselves on their vicious magic. Gaije ran to a wider area and stopped to aim his bow at any human rubbing his hands together. He pulled back on the bowstring and breathed as Lehomis had made him practice since he was four. The rock-like surface of his three fingers knew the string well.

He paused and let the bow rest. His cloak became a nuisance, so he untied it and flung it aside. It happened to land over a charging human warrior's head before he could slam Gaije with a mace.

Gaije reflexively drew and released, his arrow pinning the cloak to the man's throat. He exhaled. His large jumble of emotions rolled around inside, but any welling pride withered at the sound of Grandfather's voice in his memory calling him a knockhead.

Stop thinking and shoot, knockhead!

So he did. He nocked another arrow and released. Nocked and released. In training, Gaije had learned to hit the bull's eye as well as the mark with friendly figures standing beside it. His training had graduated through the years to mock battles with real *saehgahn* sparring each other on the field as the archers stood on the hill and practiced hitting thin wooden target posts among them. The mock battles had graduated again with brother *saehgahn* playing as assassins and sneaking up on the archers. He'd had to stop all mock attempts on his life and continue his duty to thin the enemy on the battlefield.

In real battle, his wits and stamina drained fast. He missed a spell caster and then watched another eruption of lightning murder his comrades. A cold sweat beaded on his brow and stung his eyes as it dripped. He focused, ignoring the carnage, and concentrated on hitting the proper marks. The humans wore scrappy leather armor with openings easy for him and the other archers to target, but many were quick to raise some sort of glowing shield to deflect the elves' arrows. The shields lasted a few moments before the enemies had to recast them, giving Gaije opportune shots between magic shields.

His arrows were dwindling, and soon he'd have to perform the skillful task of entering the battlefield to scavenge more. He had practiced that in training too, but they hadn't used head-frying electrical magic in the practice yard. Thank the Bright One for his father's honorable discharge and the fact that his grandfather lived near his mother and sister. If Gaije died, he would be one less *saehgahn* to protect them.

He drew back and released. A kick to the back of his knee brought him down, and his last arrow flew wildly. The human he'd shot in the throat wasn't dead. He tackled Gaije, grinning eerily. His throat gash didn't bleed—the arrow must've pierced only skin.

Pinning Gaije to the ground, the man reared back with a dagger pointed at Gaije's eye.

Chapter 27
Her Religion

"Well, here we are," Bowaen said, putting his arms out. Del sighed and stretched as if they could stop and rest already, though they'd merely crossed through the portcullis.

"Carridax?" Kalea said, looking around at the vaguely familiar scenery. Father Liam had brought the vestals and novices here on pilgrimage when she was fourteen. Back then, the portcullis had marked the doorway to Kalea's future—the moment she had decided to live for the Creator alone. She'd forgotten her long-running homesickness and bonded to Father Liam and her convent sisters on that trip.

The portcullis seemed smaller now; it spanned wide enough to squeeze one wagon through at a time. The road behind it serpentined between the buildings and disappeared around a distant curve. The fabulous cathedral spires poked the sky from behind the houses.

"Of course, Carridax," Bowaen said. "I told you I was going there. Here we are. You can look for your elf lover."

She stared down the road. "You're right. I followed the sword, and it led me here. Dorhen must be here. My sisters could be here too."

"So, uh…" Bowaen sniffed, avoiding direct eye contact. "Take care. Hope you find him."

Kalea smiled. "Thanks. And thank you for indulging my madness. I'm sure you don't think I'm all there, but you did a great thing."

Bowaen chuckled. "I believed ya then, and I still do."

Kalea turned to Del. "Work hard. And stop smoking."

He shook his heavy pipe at her as it hung off his arm. "My smoking saved your life the other day."

She giggled. "Someone else's smoking saved our lives."

"Yeah, yeah, yeah." He waved his hand and turned his attention to the city.

As they walked away, Bowaen whirled back around. "I'll be visiting the Dax Manor for a day…just in case you need help or something. You get me?"

A shaky laugh burst from her throat. "Thank you, Bowaen, that's kind of you."

He bowed his head. "And if you and your elf need an escort anywhere on the way to Wistara, I saw you have a valuable stone worth bargaining for."

She put a hand over the lump under her bodice. "I won't need another service, thank you."

"All right." He turned and walked up the road with Del stalking behind him, their cloaks waving in the afternoon breeze until they turned down an alley.

They'd been walking for a day since the incident with Chandran at the tavern. Bowaen and Del had kept her things safe during her time with the sorcerer. She had abandoned the gaudy dancer's outfit and changed back into her comfortable old kirtle and cloak after finding them at the place she and Chandran had stashed them before entering the tavern.

She hoisted her old laundry basket and took the road weaving in the direction of the cathedral's fleches, opposite the road Bowaen and Del took.

The soothing, meditative sound of chanting and murmured prayers blended with the smell of sage smoke which greeted her inside the cathedral. Kalea sucked in a long whiff and sighed at the pleasure of its familiar ambience. Though she'd seen it before, she paused to gawk again at the magnificent soaring ceilings and frescoes and stained glass windows adorning the huge nave. Five vestals from some other convent knelt at the altar, heads bowed. Their habits were close enough to the one she left behind. She glanced at the old clothes she wore, a laywoman's clothes. She'd also left her old novice tabard at the Hallowill convent along with any other item that might remind her, or Dorhen, that she would've once chosen the convent life. When she found him, she'd prefer he not be reminded of the life she had boasted about being more important than his love and patience.

Small sections of pews were roped off for the rich's use. The poor laypeople were kneeling on the marble floor, and Kalea joined them. She'd prayed this way six years ago too. Without missing a beat, her mind's voice went into a Sovereign Creator and all the rest of the practiced prayers she'd memorized.

She hadn't seen Dorhen or any hint of him since she had entered town, not that she knew what hints to look for after he had been snatched up in the night by sorcerers. Their red-jeweled gloves were her solitary clue. Now that she'd made it here, she could take as long to find him as needed. Until then, she'd pray for him, for his well-being, and also plead for help in finding him. She'd also ask for lodging in the cathedral in exchange for work. Between whatever duties they assigned her, she'd go out and look for Dorhen in town.

"Newcomers, please kneel for your daily blessing," the priest said, and all the laypeople around her stood and filed toward the rail before the altar. She did the same. The daily blessing was a sip of sacred wine and a small prayer the priest said over their heads.

They all filed in at the altar's base with their knees upon a long, straw cushion, worn and flattened from years of regular use. The priest's murmuring voice echoed from the front of the line; Kalea filed in at the end, giving her longer to bow her head and continue her personal prayers for Dorhen and her sisters' well-being.

...but, my Creator, I must say there's an issue I haven't spoken to You about. I took my vows to be a vestal, and then immediately changed my mind and ran away from the convent. I hope someday I can redeem myself. I hope You can understand why I did it... Maybe You understand better than I do...

She sighed, and her mind's voice went silent. So much had happened, and she couldn't find the time to process it. Many tears waited to be shed. This past day, she'd walked numbly behind Bowaen and his apprentice. In order to get through each harrowing day, she had stuffed it all into a mental wardrobe in order to push on. Is that what life had been like for Dorhen after his house burned down?

The murmuring grew louder. A few people away, the priest slid a stone bowl across the polished wooden blessing rail. The bowl put off a dense stink. The people weren't drinking from it. In fact, it didn't have wine in it; each person placed their fingers in the bowl and drew them out covered in syrupy red gunk. Blood. While their fingers rested immersed, the priest touched their heads with his open palm. He wore a red glove. A stone embedded on the palm side of it twinkled when he took his hand away.

A red glove with jewels. He only wore one of them. She'd never heard of a custom of dipping fingers in a bowl of blood!

When he reached the person on her left with the noxious bowl, the man obediently dipped his fingers in as the priest slurred through the blessing which was supposed to accompany a sip of wine. The blood flared with a soft light and went dark again.

The priest leaned in. "Child of the Creator, you are special, I see. Please accompany Brother Josset to the prayer room for a blessed conference." The man did as he was asked, following another priest through a door leading to the back rooms.

The priest with the bowl smiled at Kalea. She rose to hurry away, but he snatched her hand, leaning over the rail.

"Where are you going, child?" he asked, and she didn't answer. She hesitated, looking back at him. "Don't be afraid. Please kneel and receive your blessing. This bowl is filled with the Creator's sacred wine."

That's not wine! She wanted to say it out loud, but her mouth had dried up.

Another attending priest approached from behind, his body heat radiating against her back. With the other priest's arrival, the commanding priest released her hand.

"Don't make a scene now, child. The One Creator implores you to partake in his sacred ritual."

Kalea swallowed air for lack of saliva. Still standing, she reached one hand toward the bowl. The smell it emitted made her nauseous. Her hand shook, and she couldn't make it move any faster than a hovering cloud in the sky.

"Come on now." The priest smiled at her, but an air of impatience appeared in his eyes. His crow's feet deepened. "Hurry, please."

Kalea's hand passed under the bowl's rim, toward the blood. The dark red surface rippled. The rippling intensified the farther she reached.

The priest squinted deeper, his smile relaxed. The blood's surface waved softly in all directions—away from her touch.

"Why's it doing that?" she asked, but he didn't answer.

The bottom of the bowl became visible as the blood climbed its sides, a little spilling out onto the rail to escape her touch. What was this strange liquid?

When Kalea's middle finger landed on the bowl's surface, no blood remained to soil it. She looked up for some kind of explanation, even in the form of a facial expression, only to find the priest's face utterly astonished. What did it mean? Why didn't it glow like the last person who put their hand in? Why was it doing *anything* when she dipped her hand?

The blood flowed up the sides in soft ripples away from her hand, which began to tremble. She shook her head and yanked her hand away. The liquid relaxed, falling back into a natural pool in the bowl's cavity. She pulled her hand to her bosom and rubbed it with the other.

The priest stared hard at her and the soft-hearted, priestly nature left his voice. "I think you should come with me, miss."

She shook her head. "Sorry, I have to go."

When she attempted to sidestep away from the crowding priest behind her, he grabbed both of her arms.

"No!" She kicked her feet and lifted both of them off the ground in his strong hold. She put her feet back on the floor, and he dragged her toward the door the other man had disappeared through after he made the blood glow.

"Please don't worry about her," the priest said to the small collection of people kneeling on the floor to pray. "The Creator knows what's best for her, and she will soon see for herself. Carry on."

He closed the door behind them when the second priest dragged her through the door, now hugging his thick arms around her.

"What are you doing?"

He didn't answer. She let out a scream.

He carried her past a section lined with ordinary-looking offices and into a descending corridor. A steep set of stairs took them into the bowels of the cathedral.

"Let me go!"

Her screaming was finally answered by other people's screams, and she stopped to listen in shock. A collection of disgusting smells mingled in the atmosphere. The ceiling hung low over a large area sectioned off by pillars with tarps strung between them. He dragged her past corners where men in red hoods lounged, some smoking, some sleeping. Others walked around dressed as priests, doing menial chores like stoking a fire under a huge boiling cauldron. Someone else was throwing large objects into the steaming pot.

Stretching her neck to see around a tarp, she saw through a crevice a large pile of bloody objects. She squinted, unable to guess what she was looking at. Whatever it was, the smell was horrendous, like something dead.

The dark ambience of the underground world was combated by various fires, an effect that teased her eyes with irregular bouts of deep shadows and bright lights. A raging fireplace highlighted a table full of glass bottles and herbs among some supplementary candles. A priest moved about the table after removing a big iron kettle from the fire. He wore another red hood and removed it to wipe his glistening head, briefly noticing as Kalea was pulled through.

The priest who had brought her here now held both of her wrists in one huge hand, dragging her behind him. She leaned back in an attempt to counter his pull, but it was useless.

Through an archway, a dark, narrow corridor wound around like a big circle. Once in a while, an occupied room with a candle or two came around the bend, showing more priests or red-hooded sorcerers at work with instruments, bottles, fires, or heavy books.

A particular room was put on display when her priest paused to let another enter its locked door. The other priest was leading a shirtless man into the room to join a large collection of other grimy shirtless people, men and women, all wearing ropes around their necks like the first.

"Hey, dunces!" the other priest yelled. "Here's another dunce to join your dunce party. Go easy on 'im, won't ya?"

He barked a laugh and pushed the new one into the crowd. They all continued standing, making no reaction. They did nothing beyond stand. They didn't sit, talk, scream, or struggle. They stood as a crowd, staring into oblivion, their eyes dull and unblinking. The additional shirtless man joined them without a struggle; his rope leash dangled down by his belly like the others'.

At this point, Kalea's priest was pulling her onward through the corridor. When she stretched her neck to see more, one of the other shirtless males made her shriek and jerk free.

"Dorhen! Oh, my Creator—Dorhen!"

She ran, arms out toward the one to the side, facing away from the door. He had cropped, shoulder-length hair like Dorhen's, and his height was right.

"Dorhen!" His name came out half a sob. She grabbed his arm and turned him around. He responded easily to her guidance. A scruffy face with a short, stubby nose and dead eyes greeted her. Though he was young and handsome like Dorhen, it wasn't him. It wasn't an elf either.

After a shocked hesitation, Kalea closed her mouth. A new kind of sob escaped her mouth, and a set of tears came too. It wasn't him. The lifeless man offered nothing to her: no words, no expression, not even a blink. Perhaps it was better not to find Dorhen in this state. Who could say what was wrong with these people and how to help them? Finding Dorhen in this situation would be painful.

Her priest approached with a chuckle. "Found yourself a dunce ya like, girly? Too bad, they're not for sale."

He yanked her back toward the door. Just in case, she looked over the rest of them to make sure none of the others were Dorhen either. The door slammed and the lock click echoed behind her.

"What do you want with me?" she asked once they were in the dark again, a good way away from the *dunces'* room.

He stopped, unlocked another door, and pushed her inside. No lifeless people stood in here. A table with a candle was at its center. A tiny window gaped high on the wall to provide more light. A red-hooded man sat at the table, scratching a quill along a sheet of paper. The smell of ink hung potent in this room's atmosphere.

"Another one?" the man said after looking up from his papers. "Two in one day?"

Kalea's priest began, "Yes, but…" He allowed her to stand on her own and closed the door. "This one is different."

The man at the desk laced his fingers together. "Different how?"

"The blood… It separated at her touch."

The other man's eyes lit up. "Really?"

"I'll leave you to it," Kalea's priest said, and made a hasty exit, leaving her standing before the red-hooded man's quizzical expression. He pushed his hood back and dabbed his receding hairline with a handkerchief.

"So," he said, returning his gaze to her. "The Creator's wine *separated*."

"That wasn't wine. What are you people—?"

"Shut up," he snapped. "I do the questioning. You answer to the utmost the truth as you know it. Every detail, you'll tell me."

Kalea darted her eyes around, her hands fidgeting by her skirt until one of her fingers grazed her washing bat. She'd left her basket in the nave upstairs, but she'd forgotten about the bat tied to her belt. He must've seen it, but showed no sign of concern.

"Who are you?" he asked.

"Leah. I'm a washerwoman, sir."

"I can tell." His eyes dropped down her body and slid up it again.

She resisted touching the bat's wood grains. She jumped when he stood up. As she reflexively turned around to regard the door, he lurched forward and grabbed her upper arm, pressing his fingers in deep.

"Don't think about leaving. We've got a lot to talk about."

"What do you want with me?"

"Sit over there," he said, and pointed to a stool in the corner. He pulled her over and slid the stool out. "Sit down."

He strolled back to the door to lock it with a key from his belt. Returning to the desk, he lifted a large book off the pile on the floor and dropped it on the desk with a dusty slam.

"Separating liquid," he mumbled as he thumbed through the pages. Lifting his head momentarily, he said to her, "Obviously, you won't be able to explain what you did to the wine, but…" He sighed. "Well. In your life, has anything"—he twirled his hand around as his eyes rolled upward—"extraordinary ever happened to you?"

"No," she said.

"Are you sure? Your quick answer and high tone implies lying."

"When can I leave?"

He cleared his throat loudly. "Has anything special ever happened to you?"

What could she possibly say? A few agonizing moments passed before she could think of anything. "I'm told I'm mentally ill."

He regarded her again, this time with an eyebrow quirked. "Elaborate."

He continued to peruse the pages as he waited for an answer.

"Um." Her voice shook; she could hardly hear it anymore when she decided to begin loosening the string on her washing bat. Being so engrossed in the book left him vulnerable. Maybe with good aim and the right amount of force, she could knock him out. But if she stopped talking, he'd look at her again. He drummed his fingers on the table as he waited.

Her answer popped out. "I tend to talk to myself."

"What do you mean?" He lifted his chin, but his eyes remained on the pages. Kalea almost abandoned the slow untying process.

"I don't know."

Say something to keep him satisfied! He couldn't get too interested or too bored, or he might stop staring at the book. "I talked to myself a lot, and it annoyed my parents and they complained about my sanity."

He sighed. "Do you hear a voice talking back?"

"Sure. I talk back to myself."

He flipped the pages more rapidly. "So is it your voice or a different voice talking back?" His eyes shifted across the script as if he were looking for something specific.

"It's a—a different voice. And also...also sometimes I have trouble tying my own kirtle. My hand coordination isn't so good." An image of Rose's sweet smile flashed in her mind.

"But you said you were a washerwoman."

Kalea coughed, wishing she could sock herself in the face. She needed a good lie, and Rose's poor coordination had come to mind. Come to think of it, she hadn't seen any of her novice sisters in these underground corridors. Even though she had thought she'd seen Dorhen, he wasn't here either.

"I'm a lot of trouble," she went on. A loop came undone on her washing bat's cord. A few more steps would free it, but she couldn't let it fall and make noise. "And I was once caught looking at a dirty book. I enjoy looking at that sort of thing."

She snapped her hand away from the knot when he twisted around with a sneer. "I don't care about your perversions—I want to know what extraordinary things you've seen or heard or done!"

"Sorry!" She dipped her head and cleared her throat.

He turned back around and flipped a few more pages. "Any special dreams ever come to you?"

Kalea's throat went dry, and she croaked, "Dreams?"

"Yes, girl! Have you?"

"Um...sure."

"What kind of dreams?"

"Um… Sex…dreams?"

He hissed and looked at the ceiling. "You're lying, and I'm sick of it."

Lying? That one wasn't a lie.

"All you're doing is agreeing to everything I say and giving me random responses!" He approached her. "Now look at this." He raised his palm before her face to flash a yellow gem within his red leather glove. "I don't have time for this nonsense, so I'll give you a little treatment and deal with you later after you've had a nap. Look at the stone."

Its bright, sudden flash blinded her for an instant. She pulled her face away and closed her eyes, releasing the bat from her belt. She swung blindly, refusing to look at the stone.

His scream filled the darkness. She opened her eyes again to find she'd aimed well. Her bat had hit the stone in his glove, and a small, tubular surge of wind rushed around his hand. As he stumbled close to the desk, the little tornado around his glove stirred papers into the air. Colored sparks flickered in the vortex.

He fumbled the glove off his hand, providing her the chance to smash him in the head. He stumbled backward, his gloved hand still humming and sparking. She swung again and got him in the face. Blood rushed over his mouth from his nostrils. She hit again, using the bat's narrower edge to land a sharper hit. With one more whack, he was out, lying flat on the floor.

Kalea backed away from his active glove. Who knew what it could do in its disordered state? She pushed the desk against the wall with the window and used her bat to break the glass. More light flooded the room with the removal of the dirty pane. In a jittery panic, she knocked out the remaining shards to avoid any cuts. The possibility of someone walking in made her want to crawl through without regard for her skin.

She didn't look back to wonder or worry if the man would wake up and grab her. It was a tight squeeze. She quaked all over in her struggle through, weak, thirsty, and exhausted. Putting the washing bat through first, she grasped the grass growing on the outside as if it could help drag her out. She kicked her feet, but they dangled with nothing to kick against. All depended on her scrawny, numb arms.

After squeezing her rib cage through the little basement window, she was, for once in her life, thankful for having such a stringy figure and lack of a fanny. Next came her legs, along with the bulk of her dress. She pulled herself free.

Grabbing her bat, she sprinted to the nearest shadow along the cathedral wall and collapsed for a rest. She couldn't rest long, however. If anyone found the unconscious man, or if he woke up, they'd easily track her to this hiding spot. As much as she wished to get far away from the cathedral, she'd be desolate without her travel supplies.

The sun waned, and the shadows grew within the cathedral walls as she made her way back in. She waited until a certain bell when the sanctuary welcomed a new wave of people coming in for the evening blessing. Blending in with them, she slunk in past the cathedral's towering pillars and attending priests as they moved through the throng with baskets to collect the people's money offerings.

Her basket was still abandoned on the floor where she had knelt earlier. Clinging to it with both arms, she hurried back into the shadows, avoiding the waning light through the windows and the glow of the votive candles lining certain walls. She rushed out the door, frequently glancing over her shoulder.

This place had been taken over by sorcerers like Chandran and the red-gloved convent raiders. The cathedral she'd earlier loved and thought about was now a sham—a place to corrupt the innocent citizens. How many other sanctuaries did the sorcerers control? Would her convent soon become the same way?

Bowaen. I have to find him.

Bowaen was her only friend here. Where had he said he'd be?

Out on the street again, she rushed to the easiest avenue she could access, anywhere to get away from the cathedral.

What was the name of the place Bowaen talked about? "Ax," she tried aloud. "No… Max? The Max Manor?"

She growled and tugged on her ragged hair. It smelled. She stank. She could smell the cathedral's dank stench all over her. In her clothes too. She stifled a whine. Crying would be a relief, but she refused to give in.

She reached out to the next person to pass along the road. "Excuse me."

The man stopped and gave her an impatient glare. Reflexively, she checked his hand for a glove. He had none on his visible hand, but the other hand was kept shoved into a pocket.

"Where can I find a manor called the—the Ax?"

"You mean the *Dax* Manor?"

"Yes, that's it." She clasped her hands together.

The man looked her over and grimaced. "You think Lord Dax'll want to talk to you? That fat, greedy ol' fart's too busy for us poor folk. Try the Carri Manor if you're hungry."

"No, please, I need the Dax Manor."

With a smirk, he turned and pointed down the road toward the sunset.

"Thank you." She ran in that direction. If the Creator really cared about her, Bowaen would still be there.

Chapter 28
Her Friend Rem

Wild, pale eyes blazed down at him. A stench like no other polluted Gaije's air. His last breath would be filled with it. No blood leaked through the hole gaping open on his attacker's neck. A bit of embedded wood showed where he had broken off Gaije's arrow shaft.

No blood…

Gaije wriggled to the side and pushed against the man's head with his free hand as the dagger stabbed the earth beside his ear. It caught some of his hair, which ripped when he moved.

Kneeing the man's ribs, Gaije rolled over, took the dagger out of the earth, and stabbed him under his collarbone. He pulled it out and stabbed again. This human wore a helmet, but his vest, made of small leather plates, hung open, torn at one shoulder. The vest was meant to be worn under heavier layers anyway. When Gaije stood up, the man still lived, though he writhed uselessly on the ground.

A horn blasted.

"Archers to the east!" his captain yelled and repeated.

Putting distance between himself and the sloppy warrior, Gaije stole a glance at the field. Most of his company lay dead. The electrocuted ones lay fallen in heaps. The remainder of his fellow archers were answering the call. Gaije shook his head.

Many boots stirred the leaves behind him, along with the sound of shoddy clanking armor and murmuring voices in some other language. Gaije bolted the other way, out of the approaching company's path and the opposite way from which his captain called. He ran into the forest, leaving the horrific sounds behind.

Unable to control her quivering lip, Kalea pounded on the heavy wood with her fist. The shoulder supporting her laundry basket ached. Who knew if her knocking was heard on the other side of the door?

She tapped her washing bat against the smooth surface next. Quite an expensive wood had been used to make the door. The Dax family really was rich, perhaps greedy like the townsman had said. In an effort to stop her tears, she ran her stare along the wooden surface as she waited, looking for seams. There weren't any. The door had been made from a solid tree.

She knocked again with her bat, unable to remember if the polite amount of time had gone by since her last knock. A tear leaked out of her eye, but she hardly noticed it. The next one registered better. Her shoulders began to quake with the oncoming sobs. She leaned against the door, smashing her cheek on the wood, and cried.

Dorhen.

A nightmare was all it was. When she woke up, what part of her life would she return to? The part where they were planning to live together? Or the part before Dorhen's arrival when she had lived peacefully with her sisters at the convent?

She slid down along the door to the step and huddled there. Burying her face in her hands, she let the sobs come. She wanted the "Dorhen" part of her life to be real. She wanted to wake up to his smiling face, to his voice.

The door opened, and she fell over. She jolted awake after what must've been a light snooze.

"Oh, dear," an old man said from above.

Kalea rubbed her eyes and looked up.

The old man's face looked long. "Lord Rem was right. Girl, why didn't you ring the bell? I would have heard it better."

"Oh." She finally noticed a bell chain dangling by the door. She must be so exhausted, her brain wasn't working properly.

"I'm sorry," she said to the old man. "I need help. I'm looking for someone."

"Say no more." He bent over to help her up even though he grunted and trembled himself. As they both stood up, she continued clinging to his fine tabard, unsure she could stand on her own anymore. "Can you walk up any stairs?"

"I don't know," she said. "I can try."

Her head swam as she stepped over the threshold and into the darker atmosphere with candle-smoke-filled air. Nothing too creepy struck her about this place. The inside of the house was lovely. A maid shuffled past the opening of the foyer with a candle.

"You can put your things down here, madam," the old man said. "We'll take good care of your belongings while you're in there."

"In where?"

Every manner of inner voice and guardian instinct within her screamed *no*. She didn't know this man or this place; she shouldn't trust anyone or anything, or this town. But she'd reached the end of her energy. She'd pass out if she had to take another step. Yet she kept going, clinging to the stranger's arm.

"The oddest thing is unfolding right now," the old man said. "My lord has a guest who told me of your arrival. He said so before the maid informed me of your rap at the door. He said to hurry because you would be worse for wear. When I opened the door, there you were: collapsed."

"How did he know?"

"I don't know. I know nothing of this guest, besides his elfishness."

"Elfishness?"

"You'll see. Please come along. He was urgent about your arrival."

It seemed a crime how Kalea's filthy feet trod across the gorgeously woven green carpet in the lounge they passed through after stepping under two symmetrically arching staircases in the hall. This was the cleanest atmosphere she'd seen since the convent. At the back of the lounge, the old man led her under a tapestry Kalea never would have guessed hid a small door.

Behind the door waited a library with a low-hanging ceiling. Many shelves were built along the walls, and freestanding ones partitioned the space into sections. The library was also incredibly tidy, though no one lurked around at the moment. From this room, a spiral staircase led into a wide turret. There wasn't even a cobweb showing under the steps she climbed.

No sign of Bowaen so far.

"Isn't this the Dax Manor?" she asked. She couldn't recall any actual indication from the outside that she'd found the right house. It was the first manor along the road the man had pointed down.

"Of course, madam," the old man said. "The only other manor in town is the Carri Manor, and it's on the opposite side."

"Who are you?"

"I'm the butler. Now, I don't want you to worry. Lord Dax and his guests will greet you in here, and I'll get right to preparing your room for tonight."

"My room?" Kalea teetered, and his arm tensed around her. She braced her hand on the wall in effort to keep from falling. If she fell, she'd surely take the old fellow with her; he was thin and elderly, after all.

"Oh please, madam, be careful," the butler said. "I'd be heartbroken if you hurt yourself. Lord Rem would be too. You should've seen his eyes as he pleaded with me to go and receive you. Such a genuine nature he has. I went in there to deliver more cream to the tea table when he sent me right back out to open the door for you."

"Yes, thank you, I'll be careful. But I have no idea what all the fuss is about, and I'm very suspicious as to why."

"I understand, madam, and so does he. Someone as simple as me could never explain what's going on, so you'll have to bear with me and see what he has to say." His voice struggled through his panting as he spoke.

"Here we are," he said as they finally reached the top landing with a narrow, rounded door. "Go on in, madam. Don't be shy."

What had she done? So easily, she had let this old man, as kindly as he appeared, bring her into the house, take away her things, and lead her deep into this place. Would she even be able to find her way back in a last minute bolt? There was no guessing who she'd find on the other side of the door—probably sneering, red-gloved sorcerers! But in her dizzy exhaustion, here she was, about to walk in on the-Creator-knew-what.

At least she'd lived a good life. She had come as far as she could and used up her energy. She'd known the love of a magnificent and sweet *saehgahn*. Even if their relationship had remained chaste in the waking world, the world in her dreams had been the frolic in passion she'd wished for. Maybe she'd see Dorhen again in the Creator's palace if she died here. As long as it could be quick, she'd be willing to concede, to accept her death.

The butler tapped three times, and swung the door open.

Two men sat hunched over a table, conversing softly. A dirty young man stood behind one of them—Del! He waited beside Bowaen's lockbox on the floor. Bowaen sat at the table opposite a man in green velvets. His face showed surprise. And…

"Ah, here she is," a pale-haired man said. He'd been stooped beside an ornate bench with the seat flipped up. From inside the storage compartment, he unfolded a light blanket. Rushing to Kalea's side, he threw it around her shoulders. "My dear sweet lady, come sit down."

This huge, round room at the top of the turret was a simple, elegant space, designed with pointed arch windows standing all around. A fine woven rug in the center of the floor brought together the three main elements: the desk, a little tea table, and a large bookshelf with its companion bench against the wall.

"Lord Rem," the man in velvets said in the background.

The pale-haired one ignored him. "Kalea, that's your name, come on, I have a cup set for you. I'm glad you made it. I only regret I could help you in no other way and didn't hear much of you *before* you reached our doorstep."

"Do I know you?" Kalea asked.

His arm squeezed around her the whole time as he guided her to a chair at the little table. "Here, sit by your friend."

He pulled out the chair between Bowaen and the man in velvets, and when she sat, he dropped to a knee and began untying her shoes. He was an elf, just like the butler had implied. Another elf, here in Carridax, and in a lord's manor.

"Erol," he said to the butler who stood by, "bring the bucket, please."

His eyes met hers for a brief moment, flashing the prettiest cornflower-blue she'd ever seen. Who knew eyes could shine like that? Dorhen's were similar. All elven eyes must be brilliant like theirs. His hair hung long like pale yellow silk. Everything about him glowed, crisp and pristine, unlike Dorhen, who had lived out in the wilds. This elf wore fine silken robes, his features delicate and gentle, like the hands which roved over her filthy feet with a damp rag from the bucket the butler had set beside him. The cool water soothed her aching feet. She could have fallen asleep, but Bowaen cleared his throat behind her.

"Hey, Kalea," he said.

"Bowaen," she responded, twisting around to see him. At least she had found him before he finished his business here. Her face suddenly went hot when she noticed everyone else in the room staring at her. "I came to find you," she said to Bowaen. "I've escaped such a—"

"Terrible calamity," the elf at her feet finished for her. "Oh, forgive me." He dropped the rag into the bucket and put it back against the wall by the bench before drifting over to the table to pour tea into Kalea's cup.

"You'll stay here tonight," he said before pausing, his eyes lingering long on hers, his handsome mouth hanging open. One of his eyebrows twitched. "And there I've forgotten to introduce myself again. Dear, so sorry. My name is Remenaxice, often referred to as Rem." He motioned toward the man in green velvets. "And this is Lord Dax, our host."

"Is this why you insisted on setting an extra cup, Rem? You know this girl?" the man in dark velvets asked.

Remenaxice smiled. "Of course," the elf said in a soft drawl.

He turned to Kalea as she attempted to sip the hot, spicy liquid. "Don't be frightened. You're safe now." He slid a tray of powdery biscuits to her; his hand was decorated with many gold and silver rings sparkling with colored stones. "The Creator knew you could get yourself out of that horrible cathedral basement."

She choked on her sip of tea and covered her mouth to keep from spewing it out.

"He alerted me, and then I alerted the butler. And I'm glad you're here now."

"What are you talking about? The Creator?"

Rem motioned toward the biscuits. "Yes. Now be at ease. Lord Dax and this gentleman were talking. He's our host."

Lord Dax, the man in velvets, cleared his throat. "I *am* the host, but sometimes Lord Rem forgets it. He also forgets he's a guest and doesn't need to tidy and dust this room."

"Helps me concentrate," Rem said, taking a seat opposite Kalea and smiling at her again.

"So"—Lord Dax turned to Bowaen—"you're the famous runner for the Wistara White Guild."

"I am, my lord," Bowaen said. "I've brought your order."

"I'll see it now."

Del went straight to unlocking the box. He opened one of the many little drawers and handed a folded piece of velvet to Bowaen, who unfolded the corners and displayed atop his outstretched hands a pendant. The piece was sculpted with intricate, weaving vines wreathing the jeweled Dax family crest.

Lord Dax took the whole bundle and used a small magnifying glass dangling from a chain around his neck to inspect it further. "Tiniest engravings I've ever seen," he said after a moment.

Kalea caught Lord Rem smiling at her again. She cleared her throat. "May I ask what's so amusing, Lord Rem?"

"Oh, forgive me," he said, and shifted his gaze to the pendant instead. "Has he delivered the correct piece?"

Dax folded the cloth back over, more slowly than Bowaen had revealed it. "Yes."

"Excellent."

Noticing Kalea, Rem's smile dropped. His stare trailed to the platter of biscuits she hadn't touched. He nudged the platter closer. "You haven't tried one?"

"I'm not hungry," she said. In truth, her stomach churned like a stormy sea.

"Oh, dear. Please do not be uncomfortable, my lady. You are my guest and mine alone, and I aim to make sure you leave in a better state than you came. Let me ease your mind. You've been through a lot, you're very hungry, and part of the remedy of easing one's mind can be accomplished by eating, don't you think?"

While Kalea stuttered for a response, Dax tucked the bundled pendant into his vest pocket. "Bowaen," he said, "your reputation as a runner and a swordsman precedes you."

"None other." He shrugged, but his face gave off a slight smirk.

Dax leaned forward. "Are you interested in making quite a bit more money?"

Bowaen leaned forward also, laying his arms on the table. "Depends."

"On what?"

"The money."

"What about time? And danger?"

Bowaen leaned back and smirked. "Why don't you come out and tell me what you want, Lord Dax?"

"A missing person."

Bowaen's eyes shifted to Kalea and back. "Who?"

"His name is Damos. Soon after entering the Wistaran College for Grey Mages, he ran away from it."

Bowaen reached out and grabbed one of the powdered biscuits Kalea still hadn't touched. "You want me to catch a brat? I can do that," he said with his full mouth sending out puffs of powdered sugar.

His chewing slowed. "Hold on." He swallowed. "A Grey Mage? Are we talking about a kid with white hair and a pet bird?"

"Exactly that person. So you've seen the posters?"

"Yeah." Bowaen's face soured more than ever. "I saw more than posters. He electrocuted me and then flew away on a bigger bird."

Kalea put her finger up. "It was a ravian." She shriveled under everyone's redirected attention. "Sorry."

"She's right," Dax said. "He has a parrot that can shift into a ravian, and he knows state magic. Technically, he's dangerous, but don't be afraid of him. He's a good person, though a little rash—he's only seventeen."

"But how am I supposed to make him come home?"

Dax tapped his finger on the table. "I don't know. Reason with him if you can, but you *must* bring him home alive. Hog tie him if it comes to that. But listen."

Bowaen leaned forward.

"The Sanctified and the Grey Knights are looking for him. If you capture him, do not hand him over to either of those groups."

"Why not?"

Dax cleared his throat loudly. "Deliver him to my people who bear my crest, no one else. And there's something else which could make your job easier."

Lord Dax reached into one of his buttoned pockets and produced a ring box. Sliding it across the table, he said, "At the least, give this to him and make sure he wears it. If you can't make him come home, our mages can follow its ethereal trail to find him."

Bowaen turned the little gold ring between two fingers in the candlelight, his frown deep and eyebrows furrowed. It appeared to be a simple man's ring with large emeralds across the band.

"That was mine, one of my usual rings," Dax said.

Rem took over his statement, "But it took a lot of my energy to enchant it with the signature spell. It'll work, no doubt."

Bowaen shook his head and spread his hands on the table. "Is Damos your son?"

"No. But he's just as valuable to me."

"What's so special about this kid?"

"I can't tell you. Better to do as you've been asked."

"Well, why should I care?" Bowaen's voice rose. He had mostly kept his raspy voice low for as long as Kalea had been around him.

Rem's eyes moved to Kalea, and she saw that their color had deepened, unless her imagination played tricks.

"Mr. Exaliss," Dax said over crossed arms, "have you noticed an increase in the color red moving around the cities?"

Rem held Kalea's stare as they listened. Kalea had noticed it. Rem knew.

"Maybe," Bowaen said.

"Bowaen," Kalea whispered, turning to him. He glanced at her for a brief second.

"Listen carefully," Dax said. "There's been an infiltration into the Lightlands."

"An infiltration of what?"

"Sorcerers, Bowaen. Red is their faction color."

Kalea reached out and grazed his arm. "Like Chandran," she said. "Like the men who attacked my convent."

Dax took everyone's attention back. "They've charmed many bishops in high offices in the last decade or more. They've been given offices within the Sanctity of Creation, the religion we once revered. They have also befriended rich land owners—lords who hold offices for the king. And they've even wriggled their way into Wistara, the control center for the legions of knights and mages who are supposed to protect us."

Bowaen's face went grey. A clammy sweat formed under Kalea's chemise. She'd known about Chandran and his schemes and she'd escaped her own convent raid, but hearing of the wider range of sorcerous activity was too much. Their homeland might never be the same.

Bowaen attempted another smirk, which showed up weakly. "You're crazy." He looked around before returning to Dax. "That's why we have the big gate."

"You mean Hanhelin's Gate?" Dax glared at Bowaen over laced

fingers. "They've found a way through. Even Rem is still trying to figure it out."

"And so, you want me to find a kid—"

"Yes," Lord Dax cut him off. "Damos. We need Damos alive."

"I don't know." Bowaen crossed his arms over his broad chest. "The shock he gave me hurt like I never felt before. Might as well have been struck by lightning in a storm."

"Learn to use my brother, the sword, and you won't get shocked again," Rem said suddenly.

Bowaen squinted and smirked at him. "Is he all right?" He jerked his head in Rem's direction.

Dax tapped his flat palm on the table. It could've been louder, but he was clearly trying to keep his temper. "Bowaen, the task."

"Lord Dax, I don't think—" He stopped talking when Dax slid a fat coin purse across the table. Bowaen stared at it.

Rem winked at Kalea when her eyes drifted back to him.

"It's all gold," Dax said. "The Sanctified and the Grey Knights are offering six thousand silvers for his return. I'm offering more. This gold is in chip form so you can blend in to the Darklands better, should you need to."

"The Darklands!" Bowaen half-stood up, scooting his chair out.

Dax raised his hand. "I said, *should you need*. Damos is traveling in a northerly direction, is he not?"

"He was," Kalea said, "when we saw him fly away."

Bowaen's eyes pierced her.

"He's serious about running away," Dax said. "The best way to accomplish it would be to slip into the Darklands, if he can find a way." Lord Dax leaned forward and rubbed his face. "Rem informed me of a weakness in the barrier. Somewhere, there must be an opening."

All eyes shot to Rem, whose face had gone long and wan. "This is a matter of terrible urgency," Rem said. "The Creator watches closely."

"Why do you keep mentioning the Creator?" Kalea asked him, and his eyes fixed warmly on her.

"I've met Him, my dear."

Kalea's mouth dropped open.

Before she could say anything else, Dax reclaimed the attention again. "This is why we're asking *you*, the greatest swordsman in the Lightlands."

Bowaen made a fist with the ring settled around his fingertip. "Are you sure I'm the greatest?"

Rem stood and recited, "Bowaen Exaliss, former student of Wistara, kicked out for fighting in the dining room. Continued his training under

Master Eingeld while also melting metals in Eingeld's forge, developing a fascination with gold and silver. Served as a bouncer at the Dropped Hat for a while before his recruitment into the guard of Lord Elkin of Logardvy and fought a lot of bandits during his time guarding those gold mines, creating his dangerous reputation. Made quite a name for himself before deciding to retire and join the Wistara White Guild. Now the guild boasts having quite a dangerous runner to deliver their products. Too bad his real love lies in crafting the glittering baubles, not quite so much for dismantling a man's face."

Bowaen sat down slowly, gawking at Rem before sliding his eyes to the coin purse. "He reads a lot of records, doesn't he?"

Rem grinned widely and sat after him. "Remember when you ran into Lord Elkin's young wife behind the stables that one day?" Bowaen's wide eyes glared at him this time as Rem sighed. "What a lovely day for a love story. She misses you, you might like to know. But don't worry, the lord doesn't know. And congratulations, Lord Elkin's daughter is actually yours—"

"Fine! That's enough, I'll do it."

"I didn't know you had a daughter, Bowaen," Kalea said.

"Neither did I," he mumbled to his hands in his lap.

"Your secret is safe with us," Rem murmured, and nudged the tray of biscuits toward Kalea again.

"You said you'd do it," Dax said. "I knew Rem would convince you, I just didn't expect him to do it so quickly. You'll also be supplied with plenty of silver and copper chips to use as needed while you're out. We'll supply you well. When you bring Damos home, we'll award you a greater amount—in gold." Lord Dax took out a handkerchief and dabbed his forehead. "Be wary of the sorcerers."

Kalea's stomach bunched and her lips tightened at that word.

"The sorcerers," Dax said, "are offering silver because they need gold for much of their spell casting. I'm offering you gold because to me it's only money. I'm happy to part with it. Damos is worth more than gold. When you find him, don't be tempted to give him over to anyone but my people."

Bowaen grunted and reached for the coin purse. "He's a reasonable kid, right?"

"Absolutely."

Rem stood up again. "Take Kalea with you, if you don't mind."

Bowaen dropped the purse on the table. "Why her?"

"She's a valuable asset."

Rem reseated himself and held his hands out to her across the table.

Instinct alone made her return his reach. He squeezed her hands in both of his and bounced them as if they were best friends. She hadn't even been properly introduced. Why was he acting like this?

"Well," Bowaen said, "she wanted to go north. I guess she would've been asking to go with me anyway."

"It's more than that," Kalea said. When she turned to Rem again, she stuttered, and he waited for her words to align. "I don't understand," she finally got out.

"There's too much to try to understand, my dear."

All the confusing words and emotions choked her.

"You'll have to excuse him," Dax said. "It's my great honor to be hosting Lord Rem. He's a pivotal figure in our fight for the Lightlands. His vast...expertise is something we struggle to decode, though we've become used to it."

Rem's everlasting smile now appeared doll-like in its eerie blankness.

"Wait a minute," Kalea said, getting a bit breathy. "What was that you said about meeting the One Creator?"

"I did meet him." Rem bowed his head. "The Creator gave me a great gift." He squeezed her hands. "He gave you one too."

"Wh-what?"

"The Creator ordained much of this. In fact, He sent a spirit named Arius Medallus to tell you to follow Hathrohjilh, didn't he?" He pronounced the long, strange name with the eloquence of a native Norrian speaker.

She nodded with her mouth hanging open and stood up. "So then—"

"My brother will lead you."

When he motioned for her to sit, his sleeve fell past a gold bracelet around his forearm. Small spikes had been grafted to the insides of the bands, sticking into his skin and creating bruised spots in different shades of red and purple.

The painful sight closed her throat and stopped her voice. She eased back into her chair. When he reached for her hands again, she hesitated to relinquish them.

Rem continued, "I can't help but sympathize with you. Go with Bowaen, and if you cross into the Darklands, look for my other brother, Ray."

"Ray?" Kalea said.

"Yes. His full name is Adrayeth. He can help you better than I can. My head is swimming all the time; I can barely tolerate the Creator's gift. But Ray understands things better than I. In truth, the gift the Creator gave me is also a divine curse. I'm trapped in this office and can't send more than my sympathy with you, for I have been in love too, though it ended in sorrow.

"On the other hand, my brother, Adrayeth, is trapped on the other side of Hanhelin's Gate. We can no longer contact each other, save for on special days. But you've found me, and if you can find him, you'll also find your way. He can teach you much, and tell you where to go from there."

"Oh." So much was involved in his speech, she couldn't decide which part to respond to. "Lord Rem." She cleared her throat. "I'm looking for a *saehgahn* named Dorhen."

Rem's smile dropped. "Oh, no, no, no. Don't go looking for any *saehgahn*. They're nothing but trouble. Please, just look for my brother. He'll know more than I."

"Why can't I go looking for him? What's wrong?"

"An end, that's what you'll find. There's nothing out there. Only the emptiness." Rem closed his eyes and nodded his head repeatedly. "Follow the sword, yes, but look for my brother. It's all you must do for now."

Kalea's heart hammered in her chest. He let go of her hands, and she finally opted to eat a biscuit in attempt to settle her stomach. A lemony flavor mingled with the sweet bread. A new smile formed on Rem's lips and brightened to something more genuine than before as he watched her eat.

She swallowed the bite and cleared her throat. "Lord Rem, can't you tell me if Dorhen is all right, though?"

He blinked. "Dorhen? Who is he?"

Kalea aborted her next bite. "He's the one—"

"By the way, a bird landed on the windowsill this morning and told me the lilies have dispersed. Some of them were crushed underfoot, while others are waiting to be picked. Don't you love the fragrance of lilies?"

"Um…"

"Lord Rem, my friends," Dax said, standing up. "He has excellent ideas which he forgets a moment later; he knows one person's name but not the other's. And sometimes he goes on fabulous tangents we've taken to transcribing so we can decode them later."

"Like the ecstasies of the saints," Kalea said. "I've read lots of those."

"Yes," Dax said, snapping his fingers. "Exactly like those. Except Remenaxice never comes out of his ecstasy. It's puzzling he has such an interest in you, though don't be alarmed that he said anything somber. We've found he can be quite cryptic sometimes, and it's common for him to lose his thought or get distracted."

"Well, thank you, Lord Rem," she said as he smiled over his folded hands.

"Don't thank me." With his elbows on the table, his sleeves had fallen to show his mangled skin under the bracelets again. She bit back her question as to why he wore those wicked bracelets.

Bowaen rose from his seat after pocketing Lord Dax's ring and the fat coin purse from the table. Kalea and Rem stood too, and he reached for her hand again. "You have great ability, Kalea."

"Thank you." She turned her blushing face away.

"Norr," Rem said. "Go to my homeland. Norr."

Dax pointed to Bowaen after Rem's words.

"We will," Bowaen said.

Ever since that horrific episode, the dark had moved over Dorhen's being like hundreds of snakes. He was lost in a bog-like place of thick mud. There wasn't any air to breathe. Only darkness slithered down his windpipe, into his lungs, and all over the outside of his naked body. It, at least, seemed like his clothes weren't there, and he had no way of telling. Clothes were the last thing that mattered. He couldn't possibly tell where he was, where he'd been, how long he'd been here, or how to get out. He could see nothing. Nothing. It was a vast—or enclosed—nothingness. Maybe he was dead and buried, and the snakes were actually worms. They were still there, grazing across him, though he couldn't see them.

Having these thoughts and observations was a good sign, though. A mental awareness strengthened the notion of his existence. He had even experienced brief snaps of wakefulness on occasion, quick blips of light now and again. The light was so bright, it hurt. Like fire. Sometimes he'd see the fiery eyes of Lamrhath in those flashes.

The snakes tickled, sometimes playfully. Wet and energetic like Selka's mouth. Sometimes an aching arousal wracked him, and sometimes a deathly exhaustion oppressed him. The light streaks came and went, and he'd fall asleep, or dead, again.

And now here he was. That voice might return. The grating, hateful voice, the only companion he'd known for the last eternity. Or he might see another flash of light. Maybe Lamrhath's eyes. No sexual bliss right now, though; those usually put him to sleep. If he resisted the seduction, he could possibly wake up. Next time. Next time, it would be different. He'd let no one touch him, neither women nor snakes. He'd fight.

He attempted to move his arms, to lift his head. The darkness weighed heavily on every part of him, similar to a layer of thick, heavy mud. At first, nothing happened. He couldn't move. But he'd keep trying.

Chapter 29
Her Hands

L ord Dax ushered the visitors out of the high, round room.

"Lord Rem," Kalea said over her shoulder before she reached the door leading into the narrow spiral stairwell, "are you coming to dinner?"

Standing beside the tea table, Lord Remenaxice spread his open hands. "I can't," he said.

"Don't worry about him," Dax said. "He doesn't even eat. Anyway, he has work to do up here. Come to dinner, and tomorrow we'll get you well-stocked for the journey."

After a hot bath and a filling meal fit for a lord, Kalea and her friends were guided by candlelight through the manor's dark, wood-paneled corridors to some private chambers, three in a row.

The butler, Erol, lingered with Kalea after Bowaen and Del said goodnight and retreated into their rooms. He patted her shoulder. "You've got warm milk by your bed, ready to be enjoyed. The garderobe is at the end of the hall, should you need it, and you're welcome to browse the library if reading will help you sleep."

She bowed her head. "Thank you."

The butler moved on with his candle, leaving her in the light shining through the open door beside her.

Kalea inhaled deeply and went into her own room, closing the door behind her. Her first moment of solitude in a week. She tried not to think about Dorhen or the things Rem had said earlier. She'd leave with Bowaen again and continue her search as Arius Medallus had instructed. Pushing her elven sweetheart out of her head was impossible, though. Her mind had coiled so tight, she might never fall asleep. On the other hand, her body ached and sent tension running up the back of her neck and into her head.

The bed was built into a cozy wooden box against the wall, decorated with gilded flowers running along the edges. A brocade curtain draped over the opening, tied back, promising a toasty sleeping experience. She sat on the bedside, resting her feet on the step to the box's opening, and drank her milk.

Silence hung heavy in the chamber.

Are you saying you'd like to be married instead? She had once asked Vivene that question. She had hardly given it a thought before their conversation. Assuming she'd have a house, being married must be like this: having a private room with a bed shared with another person. Except it wouldn't be so silent. She'd have someone to talk to before falling asleep, and to laugh with. She could wake her husband up if she felt scared. If she awoke from a nightmare, she'd feel him next to her and then be relieved to find herself not alone.

Her hand shook as she brought the cup to her trembling lips again. Another sip might stop the oncoming sadness. It was still warm. Erol must've set it there as she climbed the stairs with Bowaen and Del. The thick, heated milk running down her throat warmed up her core, but didn't soothe her as much as she'd hoped.

Another thing would come with sharing a room with a husband: intimacy. Gossiping townswomen she'd passed on her way to the hospital or the market would make comments about "what husbands demanded," or for some reason said that pleasing a husband was some kind of marital obligation a woman suffered. Though Kalea had never done that in real life, in her strange dreams of Dorhen, the feeling was quite mutual. Those women's claims were off somehow. They were fools who didn't realize what they had.

A sob crept up Kalea's throat, and she covered her mouth. The bed behind her was quite dark within its wooden box frame. Too dark. Her candle still stood tall. Reading might be the best thing for now.

Whipping the lid open, she dug her hand into her basket, past the quilt she'd taken from the convent to find her *Lehomis* book. She watched the light dance across the slim lines of the gilded arrow on the spine.

"I wonder if Lord Dax has the other installments in his library," she muttered.

Through the hall, she tiptoed with the candle from her bedside. The house wasn't as complex as she would've thought. Down the stairs at the end of the hall, she turned the corner into the lounge, where many plump cushions were arranged around a recess in the floor. In the middle of the recessed area stretched another fine rug. The tapestry hanging on the back wall was woven in many shades of green with tree shapes, spiny pine trees like the forest in which she had grown up. Kalea hadn't noticed all this on her first trip through.

The door to the basement was concealed at the back corner of the room; she remembered that part. The basement was colder than the rest of the manor, and the stones chilled her hand as she grazed it along the wall down the steps. At the bottom, darkness enshrouded the library.

She moved to the first available bookshelf that came into her candlelight to browse for more gilded arrow books, but stopped short. Banging sounds thumped overhead. And muffled voices. Was Lord Rem still up there? Did he sleep up there?

At first, she took one step closer to the bookshelf. Why should she bother anyone tonight? A sad wail stopped her again. Her mouth dropped open. Was someone hurt? She could offer help. She moved toward the spiral stairs she and the butler had climbed earlier.

The voices grew louder. "Lord Rem, please—"

He *was* still up there. Lord Dax must be the voice she heard. Footsteps stomped across the round span of ceiling above.

"N-no! I just… It's not—No!"

"Please. Try to be calm!"

A loud *thunk* hit the ceiling. Kalea jumped and paused midway up the stairs. Nosiness was one of those minor faults her convent superiors used to preach about, and there must've been good reason for it.

Another somber cry startled her again. It had to be Lord Rem. He had been so kind to her earlier, maybe she could help him in return.

"Rem, is it about Damos?"

"Trees! And, and…"

"And what?"

"Idiots!"

"Who's an idiot? Lord Rem, try to sort out your thoughts. Rein them in. Breathe deep."

"They're dead!"

"Who?"

"You fool!"

"Me?"

"No, Lord Dax, not you!"

A long growl rattled in a masculine throat.

"Erol, go get some sage—and lavender. Bring anything you think might be soothing."

The door slammed open. Kalea pressed against the wall. There was no hiding here.

"Thomas, are you writing all this?"

"Yes, my lord!"

The door slammed closed behind Erol, and he descended the steps as fast as his old bones could handle.

"Kalea, is that you?"

"Yes, sir," she said as Erol reached her step.

He put his free hand on her arm; the other held his own candle.

"Don't be frightened. You can go up if you wish. My lord told me to bring anything to soothe Lord Rem. You might help. He seemed to like you dearly. Go on up, no one will mind."

Her eyes trailed up the winding steps as Erol plodded down past her. Against all of her fear and hesitation, she ascended the stairs and reached toward the door handle.

The scene beyond the door glowed with many candles. A young man sat at the table where they had drunk tea earlier, scribbling sloppy words onto paper with a drippy quill. Lord Dax stood over Rem. The otherworldly elf was crouched on the floor, scrubbing the boards with a wet rag. A soapy bucket stood beside him. His teeth were gritted and his eyes glassy and hurt.

The scene looked oddly like a mother punishing a child with housework. But that wasn't the case. Lord Dax wasn't making Rem do anything. It took a long time for any of them to notice Kalea. Rem saw her last.

"Look," Dax said, "your friend, Kalea, is here! Tell her. Tell her what you saw."

Rem shook his head and scrubbed the floor more furiously than before.

"No. Her least of all." Lord Rem stopped talking. His body trembled, and he fell over into a full crouch. The wet rag slapped against the floor. "No." His voice croaked, more sad than frantic. "My mother."

"What about your mother?" Dax pressed.

Rem sobbed with his face buried between his arms on the floor. "She'll be so sad."

Dax's eyebrows narrowed, and he regarded Kalea. Her arms hung by her sides, and she felt more useless than at any other moment in her life. Dax looked at the young man at the table, who'd paused to observe the scene also.

"Rem," Dax said, "that doesn't make sense. If my Norrian history is right, your mother has been dead for almost fourteen hundred years."

"Don't remind me." Without raising his head, Rem reached out to grab the rag and continued wiping the floor, this time limply and absentmindedly.

"Lord Rem," Kalea said as politely as she could over his sobbing. "Why will your mother be sad?"

Dax's eyes returned to her, burning with intensity. Had he not thought to ask such a thing?

She ventured over and knelt beside Rem, keeping a distance between them.

Dax twisted around and whispered, "Thomas." He waved his arm as if writing in the air. Thomas poised himself with the quill.

Rem's shoulders shook violently. "Because"—he worked the words in between sobs—"how can they do this to her homeland? Her people?" The last word he whispered.

"What did they do, Rem?"

"They're doing it right now." His hands balled into fists. His tensed arms caused his spiky bracelets to dig into his flesh, and blood flowed from some spots. "I wanted to be a good son." His voice twisted into a growl. "It was Hathrohjilh's fault."

Kalea reared back as he resumed his vigorous cleaning. "Hathrohjilh...?" The name's breathy syllables were easy to whisper.

Kalea joined Dax's side. "What's going on?" she asked him.

He jerked both hands in Rem's direction. Some of Rem's next words were gibberish. Some of it sounded Norrian. "It's another ecstasy," Dax said.

"This can't be an ecstasy. He's suffering."

"We know, woman!" It was hard for them both not to stare at the spectacle on the floor. Rem's robes were half soaked and his hair hung in soapy clumps. "This is new. He's never panicked like this before."

"Well, if there's a problem somewhere, can't we remedy his suffering by...doing something?"

Dax's next shrug was emphasized with tense hands. "It's impossible! Sounds like something is happening in Norr. Whatever is happening and wherever it's happening, we can't hope to remedy it without more information. And even if he could tell us more, I'm sure we don't have the resources to help with Norr's problems."

She waved her hands. "All right, sorry. We don't need to add to the stress."

Lord Rem shot upward, arching his back and hugging his stomach as he gasped at the ceiling. Every muscle in his neck tensed. He fumbled words as they forced themselves out of his mouth. Out of the mess, a statement became clear. "Then I can show you the life of a god!"

Kalea and Dax turned to each other.

"You heard it too, huh?" Dax mumbled. "Thomas!"

"Got it, my lord."

Rem's convulsing intensified.

"I can't watch this anymore," Kalea said, and ran to the basin beside the tea table.

"What are you doing?"

She ignored Dax and filled the basin halfway. Dropping to her knees as fast as she could without spilling it, she set it on the floor beside Rem. "Rem, it's me, Kalea."

He didn't respond but continued to shake and convulse.

"Look at me." She dipped her hands in the fresh water and took his head between them. He stopped crying and mumbling. "Shh-shh-shh-shh." She made the sound in the rhythm her father had used when she'd cried as a small child. Rem's eyes focused on hers, staring blank and empty. Her voice softened. "That's right."

She dipped her hands again and caressed the cool water along his hot, red face. She laid her palm along his forehead. His eyelids relaxed and he bowed his head.

"You can lie on me," she said, and pulled his head into her arm. He relinquished control to her and laid there as she bid, keeping quiet and allowing her to caress his forehead and hair. His hair strands were softer than any human's she'd ever seen. Softer than Dorhen's too. "What's wrong now? Why so upset, Rem?"

He groaned.

"Something big seems to be bothering you. Please tell me. We're friends, right?"

"Yes." A small sob escaped as he trembled in her arms. His entire form was clammy. He added another odd statement, "And then he saw darkness…"

Kalea waited a few moments for him to continue. "Who?"

"All of them."

The hair stood up on the back of her neck. "Rem. Please explain what's the matter."

A string of incoherent mutterings followed her question, some sounding Norrian. "Idiots and—and—I don't know."

"Rem," she whispered, "if you can sum it up in one word, what word would it be?"

His trembling continued for a moment before his breaths worked into an answer. "Wikshen."

Then he fell asleep.

Chapter 30
Her Departure

"This is the first time I've ever seen him sleep," Lord Dax said, squatting beside Kalea as she supported Rem's head.

She gave him a quizzical expression. "How long has he been staying at your house?"

"For the last year. Come on, let's put him on the bench."

Rem didn't weigh much. Lord Dax scooped him up and placed him on the large reading bench with several plump, velvety cushions.

"What brings you up here anyway, girl?" Dax asked, stepping back beside her to observe Rem's pitiful pose as he leaned into the bench's corner, his hands crossed limply over his middle.

"I went to the library. Erol said I could read the books," she said. "I heard the commotion... Well, I must admit I've been curious about Rem ever since we parted."

Dax put his hands on his hips. "He's a curious creature."

"Why is he here?"

"He's here to help us sort out the sorcery infiltration. Sometimes he can tell us which dignitaries have been seduced by the sorcerers, or which ones have adopted the practice. A lot of what we get, though, is puzzles." He motioned to the limp elf.

The sight hurt her for some reason. He'd been so sweet to her earlier today. "You don't mind having an elf in your house?"

He eyed her. "Why would I, when the sorcerers are thumping at my door? I can't even attend sanctuary anymore. In these days, I'll take whoever is willing to make themselves useful."

"Sorry," she said. "They arrest and throw rocks at elves where I grew up. I was surprised at your hospitality for one."

"Speaking of which, it might be time for an audience with the Norrian leaders. We haven't tried to make contact yet because Rem hasn't been able to tell us whether sorcery has gotten to them or not. There's a considerable divide between us, which I think you know."

"He doesn't know whether sorcery is in Norr yet? Didn't he come from there?"

Dax shook his head, drawing his mouth tight. "He didn't. I don't know where he came from. He hasn't told us. In fact, he didn't even knock on the door. One day, I entered this tower and found him here, waiting. He's been here ever since."

"That's so strange."

"He's made this turret his home. He also goes down and cleans the library, but he never leaves this wing."

"What about his identity? You seemed to know a fact about his mother," Kalea said.

"Yes, assuming he is who I think he is."

"Which is…?"

"Prince Remenaxice of Norr."

Kalea covered her mouth. "But…"

Dax spread his hands. "It's an assumption. He's mad as mad can be, girl. And he hasn't answered my questions about his identity. But I scoured some books and found his name in some old stories. A Norrian princess gave birth to a set of triplets, but the three princes were hated among their own kind. Their mother's power protected them from execution or whatever might've happened to them. Eventually, they were expelled from Norr, pushed out to wander the Darklands. Nothing else in our books hint at what happened next. Whoever Prince Remenaxice was, something happened to him, and here he is. He confirmed my belief earlier this evening too."

"How?"

"When he told you to look for his brother, Adrayeth. Right there in the books, it says that Prince Remenaxice had two brothers, one bearing that exact name. The other was named Hathrohjilh."

Kalea covered her mouth. She couldn't keep her eyes from darting to the door, as if Bowaen would enter bearing the sword with the same name. Maybe Rem's brother had owned it once upon a time. She withheld her questions about it from Dax. Bowaen might not have shown him the sword yet.

She looked back at Rem and couldn't stop staring at him. "I don't believe it. A Norrian prince."

Dax added, "This makes little sense to me, though, because it's like I said earlier: the mother of the triplets died fourteen hundred years ago. If that was when she *died*, it would make Remenaxice…older than that." He shook his head. "If this is indeed him, he hasn't been to his home in a long time."

"My lord," Thomas said, still sitting at the table, reviewing the phrases he'd recorded. "A word Rem used…"

"What?"

"Wikshen," Thomas said, grimacing at the last sheet of paper. "Did you hear it the same as I did?"

"What does it mean?" Kalea asked.

Dax shook his head. "So we all heard the same thing. But…a fairy tale is what it means. It's an ancient Darklandic legend about a monstrous man who murdered and raped."

Kalea bit her lip and looked at Rem. "Why would he mention that?"

Dax slicked a hand over his jaw-length hair, which was beginning to lose its neat shape in the late hour. "For any reason. It could be useful, or it could be a useless memory from his past. His mother might've told him those horror stories in his youth."

"It's eerie he'd mention it on a night like this."

"We'll have to try to decode it," Dax said. "This is what Rem does: he provides us with codes. Some have been useful already, like when he spoke of a black ravian and we realized a black ravian was the crest of House Carri."

"House Carri, as in *Carri*dax?"

"Yes. Not long ago, the Carri Manor welcomed a mage into their household for his counsel. The mage, we found out, is a sorcerer who poisoned the mind of the man who used to be my best friend."

"Oh dear Creator."

"Sorcery is eating our proud city."

Kalea turned her face away as Dax's expression darkened.

"Better go to bed, girl," he said. "Your friends are leaving tomorrow, and I suggest you get far away from here too."

In the morning, the trio and Lord Dax went to a store room where leather shoulder bags had been prepared, full of dried food, kindling tools, knives, and whatever else might be useful out in the wilds. Lord Dax even granted the men and Kalea fresh undergarments and cloaks with hooded mantles. Del was given a set of lethal knives, though he boasted about his heavy pipe even as he accepted them. A bedroll for each of them was secured to their packs.

"What's the matter, Kalea?" Del asked as hers was being tied to her bag by its leather fastenings. "Were you looking forward to nestling into the dirt and covering over with rotten leaves?" He followed up with a snicker.

She couldn't deny her face must've looked long as she thought back to her exchange with Dorhen about bedrolls. With a sly smile on his face, he'd offered to let her share his, and she had refused. The alluring and mischievous feeling that exchange had brought on… She would've looked forward to flirting with him more along their way. How sad it was to have that prospect stolen away in the night. But she'd find him.

"Listen now," Lord Dax said. "Lord Rem told you to go to Norr."

"Those elves'll skin us," Del grumbled.

"You're partially right. Things have been strained between Sharr and Norr for a long time, and the sorcerers work to aggravate the situation. But there are certain loopholes that haven't been closed up. More than likely, Damos will be flying over Norr on his ravian, though he'll have to take caution because of their hostility and their excellent ability with ranged weapons. He's not stupid; he knows all of this. What you should do is take the common trail. It's a prominent road that runs through Norr, built before the days of Hanhelin's Gate. Traders, elves, and human pilgrims all used to use it. Its primary function was to guide non-elven travelers through Norr without allowing them any sight of the elves' villages. Back in those days, you would've found station cabins to sleep in, made for that purpose, but I assume those cabins are no more."

Bowaen stepped forward. "This common trail is the loophole you were getting at?"

"Yes. Though non-elves aren't welcome in Norr, they've written nothing to Sharr barring us from using it. My people have reported that the road is overgrown because it doesn't get much use anymore, but it's still there."

"Well, how do we know we won't get skinned if we're caught on it in the heart of their forest?" Bowaen asked.

"I'm sending you with an official document bearing my seal. If you get waylaid by the *saehgahn* rangers, show it to them. They may take you into custody, but if you can show it to the right dignitaries, they may communicate with me and possibly ransom you back. Nonetheless, I'm not expecting them to harm you outright."

"Still sounds shaky," Bowaen said after clicking his tongue.

"It is, but it's the way things are. This is urgent, and your reward is waiting."

Del scoffed. "It's not worth getting skinned."

"They won't skin you, my good man!" Dax sucked air through his nose and relaxed his shoulders. "The elves conduct themselves carefully and with consideration. However, the sorcerers *will* skin you in good time. Go home and watch current events advance, and they eventually will—that's a promise."

Del shrank under Lord Dax's stare and twiddled the pipe hanging off his shoulder on its leather strap.

"If you see any elves along your way, they might appear…rough, but please don't judge their appearance. They all live under the same refined principles of honor."

Sighing, Bowaen said, "I'll give it a try."

"Remember to stay on the trail. Don't leave it," Dax warned.

The side of Bowaen's mouth quirked. "We can't leave it even to hunt a rabbit for dinner?"

"Best not to. Between the three of you, you carry more than enough food to get through Norr. I'm hoping you'll catch Damos before then."

Bowaen nodded sharply and hoisted his jewelry lockbox on his back. Del helped him with his cloak and took both of their new travel bags.

"Well." Lord Dax slapped and rubbed his hands together. "I suppose we're finished. Use your best judgment on whatever problems arise. I trust you. You've no idea how deeply I trust you."

Cocking his head, Bowaen snorted. "Why?"

"Lord Rem recommended you."

For hours, days, weeks, years, lifetimes, Dorhen fought to find his muscles and move them, still stuck in the thick, dark place. Every once in a while, he'd locate a finger or an ankle, and he kept looking.

He made a fist with his right hand. He still couldn't find his other hand because he had focused all his effort on the right one. The snakes slithered faster around him. He ignored them.

An enormous wave of hot tingles washed over his abdomen, as if the darkness itself were pleasuring him. It would seduce him again and put him back to sleep. To suppress his efforts and make him forget.

His head clouded over as some of the snakes coiled around in his skull to smother his thoughts. He would keep trying until it killed him. As heavy as the slime in his head grew, he'd keep fighting. He couldn't let it win. He couldn't lose the connection his brain had managed to reestablish with his appendages.

The snakes rushed around his form, many staying at his genitals—at least he'd found those. But if they made him feel too good, he'd fall asleep and they'd win. He ignored the pleasure and turned his thoughts back to moving his arms. The hot, slithering creatures squeezed. They were beating him at his game.

No!

There! He'd found his mind's voice.

Fool. What are you doing?

There was the other voice. The off-putting voice that had shared his thoughts since...since... How long had it even been? The caressing washed away his other senses and replaced them with a luxury he'd never wish to refuse. What little senses he'd reclaimed would disappear with the fast approaching climax.

Enjoy yourself, fool. You're not needed anymore. Lie back and enjoy yourself.

The snakes rubbed him a bit faster, like a hand, but as the pleasure mounted, he could no longer register it as anything beyond the warm enveloping bliss.

He moved his arm up. Hopefully, its movement wasn't his imagination. Tearing his mind away from the slithering around his lower body, he managed to wiggle his fingers. He searched for his face.

A flash of light.

There it was! He fought on, moving his hand, his arm, making a fist, stretching his fingers, and back again. Up. If he could keep pushing in that direction, he might find his face. His sleepy, lethargic existence in this darkness no longer made sense. He had a body! He should be able to move it. To wake up. A world existed somewhere outside of this dark place. Surely that flash of light proved his eyes were still there too, and soon they would open. And stay open.

The squeezing, pulsing sensation around his penis slackened; he had pushed it further from his mind, for now. Focus. Maybe he could open his eyes if he thought hard about it and tried.

His fingers met resistance. In the place where they touched, a feeling bloomed. His cheek! He'd found his face. He hadn't ceased to exist after all. He might not be dead either. The stroking sensation down below slowed but remained.

You're going to regret this, fool, the other voice said. *You are no longer needed. Lie back and have your orgasm.*

It took great effort to mold his thoughts into words of his own. *No. Go away.*

Make me.

Another flash of light seared his eyes. He *did* have eyes. It flickered and lingered a few seconds this time. Dark. Dorhen kept trying, though it drained his energy. A new wave of cloud crept over his thoughts. The snakes in his head thickened and slithered around in circles. He had finally grasped this level of consciousness after…years of trying—he couldn't give up.

The stroking snakes hastened their movement again, and more blood travelled down through his abdomen. A new awareness of his blood ignited. Each time he made note of any bodily function was a triumph. Piece by piece, memories of how it felt to be alive returned to him. He could try to find his left hand next.

The snakes gripped harder and continued the caress.

Shit, it feels good. Ha!

He had made another thought, and with minimal effort. Frustration mounted. Frustration was a thing. And "shit" was a rude word. He'd... he'd heard it...somewhere. He'd heard it from the mouths of men. He used to walk around. He used to drift through towns.

Light beamed into his vision again. It flickered and remained. He forgot about the snakes' seduction. They vanished. Numbness still plagued his body, yet his right hand was in attendance. He couldn't move it much, but it supplied a sense of feeling.

The light separated and seeped back together. All he could do was watch. Shapes. Lights. He could only feel the graze of air on his right hand, nowhere else. He still couldn't smell anything on the breeze. Shadows moved around, but the light didn't go away this time. The dark shapes organized into discernible structures.

You want control back, fool? Enjoy. Your efforts are rewarded with the return of your sight, the other voice said in a taunting manner.

Long, dark shapes materialized in the background: trees. And below him, smaller dark shapes hovered, some moving. He squinted. They were people. He loomed over their heads. One or two men nearly reached his height. His vision sharpened. A few turned around and he saw their faces, none of them recognizable. Rumbling vibrations rolled through his head until they settled into recognizable sounds. Voices. The voices weren't his or the other voice he'd shared his mind with; they were on the outside of his head. The snakes must've cleared from his ears.

"What's wrong with Wikshen? He just puked on himself." The volume of the voice rose and fell. Several more faces turned around.

"He's just weird. There's no excuse for 'im," another voice answered the first.

A wave of laughter.

"Nasty creature, isn't he?" That speaker's eyes drifted over him. "He doesn't seem to notice what he's done."

The extra voice in Dorhen's head asked, *Do you wonder how busy your body has been?*

Dorhen didn't respond. He tried to speak with his mouth. It didn't move. He hadn't won back control of it. His head moved, though not of his own will, and his vision shifted downward, where tied hands rested over a naked torso. All of it wore a splatter of pale-colored vomit. A length of rawhide had been bound around the wrists. They weren't his hands, though—they were too big with longer fingers. His vision panned back up and surveyed the area. About twenty men moved around freely.

A whole lot more were tied together in the back. The soft murmuring of women's voices registered behind him.

"We've still got a lot of dunces left," a different man said. "How long 'til we get to the breach?"

"Oh, about…two days, I'd say."

"Well, the dunces are dying fast. Should we put 'em to use?"

The other man looked at Dorhen. "You up for one more raid or two, Wikshen? Will you behave and contribute?"

Oh, yes! We will, won't we, fool? If the fool wants to be conscious, we'll have a good time. Let the sorcerers call the shots for a while. You'll see what we do, fool. Watch the world move around you. It's all you'll be able to do.

Dorhen's vision rose and fell as if he were nodding. The other voice in his head rasped a laugh.

Another man's head cocked, and he smiled. "What do you think Wikshen feels about attacking the land of his kin?"

"Bah!" another responded. "He may have pointy ears, but he's no elf anymore."

Someone to the left, standing in the hazier side of his vision, pointed. "Hey, look! He agrees."

Someone else snorted. "Yeah, we'll see about that."

A more prominent-looking figure shushed the lot. "Listen, gentlemen, keep your eyes peeled. Norr's coming to an end. While we're still here, let's find the kingsorcerer a gift."

Are you listening, fool? The greedy, lecherous kingsorcerer wants a gift. Let's be the one to find it. We'll use it to bargain for our freedom. Then I can show you the life of a god. What do you say?

What are you…? Dorhen struggled to say in his head. The words still flowed like slugs out of a mouth. *What are you planning? What are they talking about?*

The other voice's laugh rolled on until the darkness engulfed his vision again.

Nonetheless, Dorhen would never give up. He'd fight with all the strength of his mind to gain back control of his body.

Chapter 31
An Order for the Saehgahn

The air wheezed in and out of Gaije's lungs. He had run through the wilds of his homeland for two days, perhaps more, hardly stopping to sleep. His legs trembled and a shock of pain ran up his shins with each step. He chose southeast, based on a vague idea of where his home clan lived from where the attack had occurred. He realized he must be close when he broke into a meadow followed by another soon after. Clan Lockheirhen raised horses and used the largest of Norr's open fields for grazing and training. Lehomis loved horses…

"Gaije. Wake up, my son."

A bright red sunset flared in his vision when he opened his eyes. He was sprawled face-down in one of those meadows. Frightened horses whinnied faintly, and their hooves sent a tremor through the earth to his ear.

He groaned and tried to lift his head. "Father?" His muscles didn't want to move. "I'm sorry, Father. I didn't mean to run away. I lost my nerve, and I…"

"Hurry home."

The warm radiance of light shone down on him as a shadow passed away. Gaije worked up to his feet. "I'm coming. Wait for me." His numb arms hung and his legs trembled.

"Father?" Gaije stood alone in the tall grass. The clouds in the sky sopped up the red sunset like blood. "Father!"

He must've dreamt the voice. He stumbled on over the lumpy earth and through the tall, waving grass. The wind picked up. The horses didn't sound any calmer. He might have to spend all night helping to gather them up.

Through his dizzy and exhausted senses, some faint sounds echoed through the rushing wind. Screams. He ran forward into the tree line until a red glow, brighter than the red sunset, roared under the canopy. He shook his head. A village was being raided. First his company, and now a village.

He ducked his head and stepped onto the trail winding through the buildings, now reduced to earthen shells set alight from within. A *saehgahn* ran around the bend, dirt-smudged and without a weapon.

Gaije squinted and coughed and resorted to filtering the air through the side of his hood. He caught the other elf by the shoulder. It was a mere *saeghar* in his teen years, his terrified face gawking.

"What happened?" Gaije asked. When the lad didn't answer, he shook him. "What happened?"

"Humans!"

Humans.

The lad jerked away and ran, a cowardly thing which would earn him a beating if the *saehgahn* found out, something to worry about later. Gaije charged forward, holding his bow. He reached for an arrow. None remained in his quiver. He'd been so shaken since his own attack, he'd failed to keep stock of them.

Past the village center, fewer buildings burned and more people ran about. Screams. Some of them were female, but their location proved hard to pinpoint in the chaos. Many clansmen, young *saeghar* and old *shi-hehen,* ran wildly. A few bumped him as they ran past, knocking him off balance. Some *saehgahn* remained alive, fighting with the rest of their strength for however long it would last, and Gaije would join them. It might not be his clan, but that was what *saehgahn* did.

He combed the village, striking down the attacking humans with his knife and checking empty houses and sheds for survivors, all while harvesting arrows from the dead.

Like the ones who had attacked his company, the humans stank, even over the stench of the burning village, though these were dressed in maroon and olive livery—Sharr! What did the smelly humans want from them?

Leaning over to remove a dead one's helmet, he found bone with flesh barely clinging to it. He lurched backward, smothering his nose in his sleeve.

Before he could speculate, a spear with a curved blade whooshed toward his neck. Gaije threw up his arm to block the strike with the stone plate on his bracer. Sparks flew, and he fell all the same. He didn't have enough energy right now. The human, also stinking and wearing a Sharzian tabard, raised the spear. Gaije's head spun, but he rolled as far out of the way as he could.

Thunk-thunk-thunk! Three arrows stabbed into the man, and he stumbled to the side. The archer approached, and Gaije scrambled to his feet.

The archer ripped the arrows out of the man's neck, shoulder, and rib cage, and hauled him into the fire. Turning to Gaije, he yelled over the roaring flames, "Stay on your feet, *saehgahn!*"

"G-Grandfather?" Gaije pushed his hood back, and the other *saehgahn* paused. His long hair dangled in loops behind his head, the way Lehomis fashioned his ground-length hair when he needed to shorten it hastily.

This is my *clan!*

"Gaije, what in hell are you—?" The two stared at each other until Lehomis shook his head. "Forget it. Now that you're here, listen. Your father's dead!"

Gaije's mouth hung open. "What?"

"Shut up and listen! You'd better look sharp." He handed him the three bloody arrows. "Mhina's missing! You need to help me find her."

"Which way did she go?"

"I couldn't tell, but she's still out there. Find her!"

Gaije took off after Lehomis slapped his shoulder.

"Mhina!" For an hour Gaije had searched, killing and burning humans all the way. He made his way to the outskirts of the orange inferno which used to be his home, and paused to suck in the clean air. He bent over and coughed, persistently calling her name. Most of the stinking humans had thinned out, and Gaije welcomed the lull in their aggression.

Heavy footfalls preceding an equine snort caught his attention. One of the clan's horses, a smoky grey stallion, stood among the shadowy trees. Someone sat bareback upon it.

Gaije ducked behind a tangle of brush and squinted to make out the person's identity. He couldn't put a name to the form, but in this madness, he hadn't recognized that teenaged *saeghar* right away either.

"Who's there?" he called.

The horse snorted again and stamped the ground, but the rider didn't answer. It was a *saehgahn* with years of adult-length hair, whoever he was. Gaije didn't ask again. The stranger paid no attention, thank the Bright One. An ominous vibration radiated off this person, not counting the fact that he didn't pay a fellow *saehgahn* an answer.

Gaije lifted his bow and nocked one of the bloody arrows Lehomis had given him. The horse shifted to the side, and the distant firelight behind Gaije flared in the person's eyes like a cat's.

Gaije drew the arrow back and aimed at one of the greenish eyes. Even when the eye turned to him, Gaije held the bow and arrow taut. Whatever had befallen his village, this…creature must be involved. He'd even helped himself to one of their young horses.

The creature's head turned, alerting Gaije to Mhina, his little sister, who had wandered in from the forest. In alarm, he sent the hushed call,

"Mhina, run!"

She didn't listen. She went straight for a nearby injured *saeghar*, sprawled and wheezing shallowly on the ground beside a thick tangle of brush. Gaije would've dismissed the lad as dead. She put her hand on his wound and held the pose until he jolted up and ran away without looking back.

Gaije's mouth dropped open. Had she just...? Yes! She healed him—with her hands! Mhina could heal. She'd never told anyone.

The rider watched too, silent and calm. His sleek, shadowy form gave no indication of armor. The cocky bastard didn't wear a shirt either. His horse stepped into the light from the shadowed space under a tight cluster of trees. Hands clad in black fingerless gloves clutched the horse's mane. He also wore black bands around his biceps, and a long black sheet around his waist spilled down the horse's side. His hair shone blue! It clung to his pale, sweaty body in sticky streamers.

Gaije tried again. "Mhina, come!"

She stepped toward the rider, murmuring, "You need help."

Gaije's heart leaped into his throat. He cried out again, his lungs roaring like the fires eating his village. The blue-haired rider sat, watching. In a moment of anxiety, Gaije let an arrow fly. The rider's wrist snapped up and he caught the arrow, his eyes never leaving Mhina.

Gaije vaulted over the brush and dashed after her, taking his last chance to grab her and make a desperate run.

The rider kicked his steed to gallop forward. The horse's powerful legs beat Gaije to her. The rider leaned way over its side, hanging onto its mane with one hand, and scooped her up.

Mhina let out a squeal.

Gaije cried out again.

Cradling the little one against his side, the strange *saehgahn* rode back through the burning village with Gaije's frantic arrows flying past him.

The last two arrows sank into the rider's right shoulder blade and pierced the skin along the side of his neck. He didn't bother to flinch. The surviving marauders followed him into the cold, dark forest.

Chapter 32

Her Wound

Taking Lord Rem's advice, Kalea, Bowaen, and Del entered the Norrian forest border. It lay a day's walk from Carridax; the only town closer to the elves' sovereign state was Theddir. She'd been unable to think about anything besides Lord Remenaxice since they left the estate.

"So," Bowaen began awkwardly as they followed the grassy trail through the elven forest. "We're still walkin' together, aren't we?"

"I guess so," she said. "Thank you for letting me follow you. Again."

"Bah, I'm used to it by now." He waved a hand as he walked in front of her, not bothering to turn."

Del sniffed as he walked beside Bowaen. She hadn't managed to have a decent conversation with that one yet.

"I'm following you because I believe the sword will lead me to Dorhen," she blurted out.

Bowaen turned to glance at her this time. "Oh, I know. I wouldn't have questioned it."

She wrung her hands as she walked behind them, unable to get Rem's foreboding words about emptiness and dead ends out of her head. *Don't go looking for any saehgahn. They're nothing but trouble*, he'd said. How could words like those not bother her?

"Rem is sending me to meet someone he knows, not to find Dorhen."

"Yeah, we were there," Del snapped, turning around.

Pouting, Kalea watched the patchy trail pass under her moving feet. "I don't care what he said. I'm going to find Dorhen."

"Well, you're a free woman, Kalea," Bowaen said. "You're following me because the Creator sent you to find Dorhen. If you don't want to go to the Darklands to meet Rem's brother, who cares? Don't do it. I'm not going to the Darklands anyway. I'm gonna find that brat and drag him to Carridax by his ear. He'll never get that far."

She blew a breath out through puffed cheeks.

"Hey," Bowaen said. "I see what you're doin', and it's not good for your mood. Stop watchin' your feet. Lift that chin and take in some of this forest scenery. You might like it."

She took his advice and looked around. Butterflies flitted around over the flowery thorn bushes cluttering the land on either side of the path. Huge, twisted white trees with deep green leaves danced toward the sky in the welcome sunlight. Bowaen had offered good advice, for her heart lightened. In the distance, a flock of black deer bounded away as they were alerted to the travelers rustling along the grassy path. She'd never seen such animals before. A different breed of bird she'd never seen lived here too, singing a melodic *hah-woo hah-woo* into the air.

"Bowaen," she said after a long time of walking. "Rem said you have a daughter by the Lady of Logardvy…"

Bowaen interrupted her half-formed question with a sharp grunt. "He doesn't know what he's talking about."

"Crazy elves," Del mumbled to echo Bowaen's attitude.

Kalea stopped talking about Rem and decided to enjoy Norr while she could. An essence of peace permeated the atmosphere, its presence hanging all around, like the air of a sanctuary—before the sorcerers had arrived.

Bowaen took Lord Dax's words to heart, resisting his interest in catching a rabbit to cook, even though they had already seen three along the common trail. Wandering into the deeper wood could attract unwanted attention from the *saehgahn* rangers Dax had warned them about.

"Rabbit's my favorite," Bowaen mumbled as the third one bounded away. Weeds and grass threatened to overgrow the trail, but it remained discernible by the old stone borders and occasional pillars lining the path.

By nightfall, they found the path lit by magnificent glowing orbs hovering above the strange stone pillars along the road, and they argued whether it was a spell cast by the elves to light the way each night and why they would still cast the spell. The colors shifted to romantic new tones as they passed through the territories, some warm, some cool, but always soft and comfortable.

They ate their dried rations, courtesy of the Dax Manor, in a little clearing a few steps off the trail, and built a fire to combat the sharp wind whistling through the trees. Putting aside their wariness, they managed to relax and laugh and tell stories around their little fire.

All the while, Kalea's eyes kept wandering into the dark shadows beyond the fire's glow. After enough sad thoughts had drifted through her head, she switched her stare to Bowaen for a moment, regardless of Del's chatter about his favorite kinds of jerky.

"What'cha lookin' at?" Bowaen finally asked her.

She caught herself, unsure how many minutes had passed by, her cheek resting on her hand. "Oh, sorry." She straightened up. "I was thinking about how nice you are…to me. And I got to thinking again about your daughter."

Bowaen grunted and threw his hands in the air. "Oh, for cryin' out loud. Look, the Lady of Logardvy was kind to me. And it was her fault. Men have a way about them—they don't wanna pass up certain… opportunities."

"It's all right, you don't have to explain. I was thinking about the spiritual side of the situation."

Bowaen frowned and reared his head back. "Spiritual side?"

"Yes. I know you don't believe you have a daughter, and I don't doubt your belief. But isn't it interesting how patient you've been with me? I know you didn't want to hear me out at first, but you gave in pretty quick."

"I gave in because you paid me in rare seashells."

Del's musings trailed off, and he listened to Bowaen and Kalea's exchange.

"But ever since, you've been soft and kind toward me. You've been more than a flat-fact escort."

Staring at the fire, Bowaen shrugged. "What do you want from me?"

"Nothing. I just… I like you."

Keeping his eyes averted, Bowaen said, "Okay, look. I was never lucky enough to get married. But I always imagined… Well, I always imagined if I had a child, I'd like it to be a girl… But then Del showed up." Chuckling, he leaned over and punched the younger man's arm.

"Ow!"

Kalea smiled. "So if she's your daughter for real, how old would she be?"

He scratched his rugged jaw and gazed into the fire again. "Almost your age, if my counting is anywhere near right."

Planting her chin atop her hands, elbows braced on her knees, Kalea smiled again. "It makes sense now. I think she is your daughter. I believe it."

"If that's your choice." He bit into a slab of jerky Del had handed him earlier.

Kalea stretched out on her unrolled bedding. "Thanks again, Bowaen. For your patience and your escort. I'll pray for your well-being. Yours too, Del."

Del didn't respond. He didn't have to. Kalea threw the quilt from the convent over her bedroll blanket to supplement the warmth, and said her silent prayers.

By morning, the magic lights had dissipated. Kalea, Bowaen, and Del walked the trail in peaceful silence for a whole day and repeated the camping routine. The lights appeared again, but none could tell how they were lit. Did they light themselves or did the elves do it? For the whole two days, they didn't see anyone, to Kalea's disappointment.

She laid out the quilt she had taken from the convent over her bedroll as before, and snuggled into the arrangement. It was a hand-me-down quilt, gently used by the time she'd received it. Like previous nights during her travels, she debated with herself whether it made her uncomfortable in its reminder of the horridly unsafe convent or if it soothed her by being a relic of home. Joy might've made it. When that realization hit, she decided to let the blanket be a comfort.

From their campsite, one of the lavender trail lights could be seen. Tree trunk silhouettes stood in front of the glow, creating a lovely pattern like panels of stained glass. She wouldn't be in a hurry to leave Norr behind. She loved everything about this forest. The fantasy of living here with Dorhen touched her mind like sugar on the tongue.

Soft footsteps upon the leaves approached. Her eyelids cracked open as pale bare feet stopped inches before her face. A gentle hand landed on her shoulder. "Wake up, little lily."

Her eyes shot open, and a loud snarl greeted her renewed consciousness. The pale-footed stranger disappeared, only a dream.

Kalea screamed as she was ripped from her quilt by her foot. Bowaen and Del's voices shouted behind her. Dead leaves rustled against her bare body as her chemise dragged up to her armpits. Twigs and roots snagged her hair and scratched during the rough journey. Against the ambient trail lights, the shape of a tall, hunched creature solidified. Without those lights, she'd have seen nothing at all.

Bowaen and Del's running feet trod the leaves in pursuit. Suddenly, the creature's long, clawed fingers let go and she was left in the churned leaves. It fell to the side, growling. An arrow had burrowed into its thick neck.

As it paused to bother with the arrow, Kalea collected herself and tried to run. The creature lunged and tripped her with a swipe of its huge paw. A moment later, she noticed its claws had raked through the flesh on her thigh.

Bowaen burst onto the scene with the sword, Hathrohjilh, swinging. The blade's tip swiped across the creature's back, and it roared.

Kalea scrambled to her feet and ran, paying no mind to the direction, so long as she could gain some distance and find a hiding place. She'd have to check her wound later. It didn't hurt, but adrenaline rushed all through her.

Bowaen and Del worked together to distract the monster. Another arrow *twanged* from beside Kalea's hiding spot and embedded into the beast's thick skin. The shadowy shrubs hid the archer's identity. One of Norr's ranger *saehgahn*?

The beast sniffed the air, angling its face toward the moon. The face was an awful combination of human and dog. Not a tuft of fur grew on its face, and the surface looked more like bone than skin. Its eyeballs couldn't be seen, and the sockets which supposedly housed them were wide, almost circular. Long teeth lined the jaw, without any lips to hide them.

The creature dodged Bowaen's strike before galloping on all fours toward Kalea.

"Run!" a voice from the shadow warned her. The archer emerged from behind a dark group of trees and shoved her.

She obeyed, disregarding direction.

She ran until someone else's campfire glow appeared behind rows of black tree silhouettes.

She stopped and collapsed before getting too close. She'd have to try and guess whether these men—or elves—were friendly. If so, they might help Bowaen kill the monster. She crept closer, hugging herself and shivering, donned in her thin chemise—another reason to hesitate before approaching.

They weren't elves. A bunch of laughing, talking men were drinking and roasting a horse's leg over the fire. Live horses, tied together in a large group, danced in place nervously. Wagons full of goods stood around their circle, acting like a wall to close them in. Within the enclosure, they kept a collection of baskets bound shut with rope. Two men sat at each end of the basket cluster and one sat behind it.

She listened carefully.

"Speak up, you bloody freak!" one of the men grunted. A slap to flesh sounded.

"What does he want?"

"He said he has to take a piss."

The group laughed.

"Don't know if we should let him. Might be a trick."

The men were referring to a hooded figure with his hands tied. Kalea was tiptoeing around to the left to see more when a woman stood up from stooping over a stump used as a table. She held a pitcher. Kalea squinted.

I'm dreaming, she thought as she watched the young woman stumble through the camp, enduring slaps and gropes to her rear. The woman's face stayed solemn, as if she no longer noticed that sort of treatment upon her. She was a bit chubby, with stern eyes and dark hair. Kalea covered her mouth to stop the noise she wished she could make.

Vivene. She mouthed the name, resisting shouting it. A frantic quaking overtook her. She'd found Vivene! One of her sisters! Kalea's breaths came deep and noisy. Her eyes darted all over for more sisters. Or Dorhen.

A hand clapped over Kalea's mouth from behind. She screamed, but the hand held firm. Any noise she made was drowned under a swell of laughter from the camp.

"Shh."

"Bowaen?" Kalea said. Her eyes fixed on the sight of Vivene, of all people, pouring wine into the laughing men's cups.

"No," the person whispered, too clear and youthful to be Bowaen. "But stay calm. And get away from this place."

Kalea turned around to find an elf with red hair shining in the firelight. "Were you the one shooting the arrows when we were—?"

"Yes."

"What happened back there?"

"The beast is dead. You're safe now, and your friends are alive. They're looking for you. Go."

Kalea pointed at the camp. How could she explain to the elf about her situation?

He grabbed her hand and turned her away from the camp. He hissed, "They're bad people. Go now!"

The moment Kalea took a step, a sharp ache shot through her leg. Blood had soaked into the side of her chemise. That beast had scratched her badly, and she hadn't noticed due to shock. After her short rest, the pain set in. She moaned, and the elf shushed her.

"Be silent. Tread as lightly as you can." He turned his attention back to the camp and crept closer, traversing around the perimeter.

She'd be sure to tell Bowaen what she saw when she found him. Clamping her hands over her mouth, she picked her way through the leaves and stepped over fallen branches, praying to the One Creator to not let them see her white gown glowing in the moonlight.

She traced her steps back as best as she could. She had no recollection of the exact route she had taken along her wild sprint, but Bowaen and Del would be looking for her after killing the monster. She added a few prayers to her thoughts for Vivene.

Bowaen and Del worked together to distract the beast, using the faint moonlight to see. One of them could easily trip in the shadows and fall, rendering them vulnerable to being mauled. The beast tended to chase Del more often because he smelled strongly of tobacco. As it chased him, Bowaen followed behind, eager to stab it in the ribs if he could ever find the chance. Either its fur or its skin was too thick, or possibly both, because he couldn't find the best angle to drive the blade in. Those dense, silky hairs made the blade slide off.

After Bowaen's first attempt to stab between the ribs, the creature roared in annoyance and veered around to swipe at him. He leaped and rolled, dropping the sword. The beast charged at him, and he scrambled away.

"Hey!" Del yelled at the beast, waving his arms. "Come here! Hey!"

The creature ignored him, opening its humanoid jaw farther than any real human could. A thin membrane stretched between the bones. Strings of slobber dripped off the sharp teeth. Bowaen scrambled on hands and knees toward the shiny surface of the sword reflecting the moon.

"Hey!" Del yelled again.

Bowaen grabbed the sword by its hilt and raised it. The creature leaped and came down, crushing him under its hot, furry body. It roared and snapped its steaming fangs at his head.

He ducked and wiggled to sink down under it as far as he could, getting a mouthful of fur. He heard a few more arrows hit the creature's thick hide.

The roaring stopped and the snapping slowed. The beast sighed and went limp as a warm wetness spread over his hands and into his clothing. Heart pounding, Bowaen struggled under its weight.

"Oh, God," Del's voice moaned.

"Del!"

"Bow!" The creature half-lifted up as Del struggled in trying to get a grip and remove it. Bowaen pushed as he pulled until they turned it over. Bowaen rolled over on his hands and knees and panted.

The monster huffed shallow breaths with the sword sticking out of its chest. He'd managed to angle the blade to make the creature fall on it. Thankfully, the pommel hadn't jabbed into Bowaen's torso on impact; instead, it had braced against the ground under his arm.

"Good Creator, what was that thing?" Del asked. Bowaen wasn't ready to talk yet. "Bow, cut its head off to make sure it doesn't get up again."

Bowaen pulled the sword out with a serenade of squishing meaty sounds. His stomach churned. The creature lurched, and Bowaen fell back onto his ass and elbows. The full moon was enough to see its limbs…shrinking. The whole creature shrank and paled. Its hair receded, leaving the soft skin of a human instead. It shrank all the way down to an average man's size.

"Chandran?" Bowaen said, cocking his head in disgust. "What in hell…?"

"Go on, Bowaen, finish him off!"

"Hush!"

Chandran didn't writhe anymore. He lay naked on the ground with an open wound going all the way through his chest. The arrows were still pinned into his back, one of which had driven through his chest when he rolled over, while the others had broken off. His eyes stared into the dark tree canopy. Chandran didn't need Bowaen's help in dying.

Bowaen had killed only a few men before as the need arose, but tried not to be in the habit of such a thing. He would spare his conscience this one. He sheathed the sword and left Chandran to the elements.

After Bowaen left, Chandran managed to turn over, wheezing and grasping at the earth. He dug his index finger into the thick, reddened mud, chanting the phrase he wasn't supposed to have memorized yet— kingsorcerer's orders. What should he care now? Dying this way would be his last vengeance.

He begged and pleaded of Ingnet, the pixie known for mind manipulation, in the seductive language it favored. He completed the circle drawn deep into the earth with his finger. The ritual couldn't be completed until he shed someone's blood into the drawn circle.

He dragged himself over the circle so his wound could bleed into the spell. He chanted persistently, even as his vision darkened, fighting to stay alive long enough to finish the invocation. The last syllables emerged as puffs of breath.

A greater being crawled out of the portal drawn in the mud and loomed over the fresh corpse left as an offering. The hunger stirred in its being, and it wouldn't have been able to linger on the mortal plane any longer if the carcass hadn't been there.

The creature stooped to sink its long, dry teeth deep into the warm, moist meat. When it finished consuming every string of tender flesh, it crunched the bones until they were gone too. Thus it was properly fueled to walk the earth.

Tears leaked out of Kalea's eyes. *Poor Vivene!* She was making progress, however. She'd found at least one of her sisters, and that was a step closer to her goal. She would inform Bowaen, and they'd come up with a plan to rescue her. Maybe all her sisters were held captive at the camp. And Dorhen.

That red-haired elf had also seemed concerned with the bad people. The sorcerers. She hobbled along, dragging her pained leg and clenching her teeth. She'd never let a sorcerer touch her ever again!

A squeal creaked out of her throat when she stepped on a sharp twig. She stopped to let the pain pass. While she swallowed to loosen her throat and think of a prayer to recite to help her ignore the pain, the darkness thickened. A passing cloud covered the moon. The dense air grazed the prickling flesh of her arms.

Hands took her shoulders and squeezed. Kalea yelped. It wasn't the red-haired elf again.

She wriggled, and the hands tightened, digging large fingers into her muscles. A body pressed hard against her backside and bent her over like one of the illustrations in Vivene's book. A sour odor accompanied the tall presence. Little could be seen anymore with the moon covered up, but the long, heavy hair falling down around her face, which belonged to someone else, appeared blue in the strange lighting. Blue hair.

"No, fool," a deep whisper rumbled behind her. "Why would I harm this one?"

Kalea started to respond, but squeaked instead at the squeeze of his left hand around her belly. His pelvis pushed hard against her rear. The sultry aura of his body mingled with hers, raising her own temperature. He leaned in farther, until his nose grazed her jaw.

A long sniff drew in the air along her neck. The deep voice resonated again, this time beside her ear. "How would you like it?"

This was only the beginning. The story continues in the next book, *Unwilling Deity.*

Kalea shows kindness to a stranger.

Gaije becomes a saehgahn.

Dorhen confesses his feelings.

Wikshen is bound in a room full of light.

Glossary and Pronunciation

A Note on Elvish pronunciation: You'll find a lot of H's in Elvish words. Oftentimes a male elf's name contains the suffix "hen," it's the masculine suffix ("ah" or "het" being the female counterpart). Usually the H in "hen" is pronounced. Other H's found in elvish words tend to be "swallowed," such as the first H in "Daghahen" (Dag-uh-hen). How to pronounce the H's in Elvish words will largely be based on your own instincts. I, personally, tend to swallow the H in "Dorhen."

Also note: The section on Elvish words contains a few more words and phrases than you'll actually find in the story.

<u>Characters</u> (* main characters)

Alhannah: (Ahl-hawn-ah) the head Desteer maiden in the Lockheirhen village.

Anonhet: (Ah-non-het) A young elf woman who works in Lehomis's household.

Arius Medallus: (Air-ee-us Meh-dahl-us) A fairy who watches over Dorhen.

Chandran: (Shan-der-an) An ambitious sorcerer from the Ilbith faction.

Damos: (Day-mōs) a young Grey Mage.

Del: (Dell) Bowaen's apprentice.

Exaliss, Bowaen: (Ex-all-iss, Bō-ay-en) A rugged, middle-aged swordsman and runner for the Wistara White Guild.

Gaije: (Gāj) A young elf, talented archer, and debut *saehgahn* from clan Lockheirhen in Norr. Lehomis's grandson.

Gani, Sister: (Gah-nee) An old vestal who oversees the laundry duties in the Hallowill convent.

Hydenman, Kemp: (Hahyd-en-man, Kemp) A farmer who sells his produce in Tintilly.

Joy: (Joi) Kalea's best friend and fellow novice.

Kelenhanen: (Kel-en-hah-nen) the new queen of Norr and a member of the Tinharri clan.

Lamrhath: (Lam-wrath or Lam-er-hath) the current kingsorcerer.

Lehomis: (Lay-ah-miss) A legendary elf, master of archery, writer, and elder of the Lockheirhen clan.

Liam, Father: (Lee-ahm) A priest who works at the Hallowill convent.

McShivvy, Daghahen: (Mik-shy-vee, Dag-uh-hen) Dorhen's father.

McShivvy, Lambelhen: (Mik-shy-vee, Lam-bell-hen) Daghahen's twin brother.

Mhina: (Mee-nah) A young elven girl, Gaije's sister.

Orinleah: (Or-in-lee-ah) Dorhen's mother and member of the Linharri clan.

Rayna: (Ray-nah) Chandran's thrall.

Remenaxice, Lord: (Rem-en-ak-sis) A mysterious elf in Carridax. Also known as "Rem."

Rose: (Rohz) One of Kalea's friends and fellow novices at the Hallowill convent.

Scupley, Sister: (Scup-lee) The mistress of novices in the Hallowill convent.

Selka: (Sell-kah) The best chamber mistress in Ilbith's Lightland outpost.

*Sufferborn, Dorhen: (Suffer-born, Door-en or Door-hen) A young rogue elf who wanders the Lightlands.

Talekas: (Tal-ek-as) A sorcerer in the Ilbith Faction.

*Thridmill, Kalea: (Thrid-mill, Kah-lee-ah) A novice in the Hallowill convent and expert washerwoman.

Tirnah: (Teer-nah) Gaije's mother.

Togha: (Tōga) Gaije's distant cousin and the local letter carrier from clan Lockheirhen in Norr.

Trisdahen: (Triz-dah-hen) Gaije's father.

Vivene: (Viv-een) A spunky novice and friend of Kalea's at the Hallowill convent.

Wikshen: (Wik-shen) The flesh embodiment of the pixie, Wik.

Places and Things

Braies: (brā) Underwear usually made from linen. Also refers to a piece elves wear with their *sa-garhik*.

Bright One, The: See "Lin Yilbarhen" in the Elvish/Norrian language section.

Carridax: (Cair-i-daks) A city in the Lightlands established by two noble houses, the Carri's and the Dax's.

Chips: A motley assortment of valuable metal scraps used as currency in the Darklands. The Darklands have no official government and therefore no official mint. Chips can range anywhere from foreign coins or coins left over from old Darklandic civilization, to thin "chips" or nuggets, to broken jewelry.

Darklands, The: The northern side of the continent of Kaihals, consisting mostly of wild lands and territories, famous for being overrun with disreputable ruffians, warring tribal peoples, cults, and evil creatures.

Dendrea: (Den-dree-uh) the official Lightlandic currency.

Desteer, The: (Des-tīr) The largest spiritual order in the Norrian religion. The Desteer members are always female and referred to as "maidens."

Dunce: A slang term given by the Ilbith sorcerers to a person who is infected with a Darklandic brain parasite.

Gaulice: (Gôl-iss) A city in the heart of the Lightlands.

Hael: (Hāl) One of the five pixies favored by the Ilbith sorcery faction.

Hallowill: (Häl-oh-wil) A pine forest in the heart of the Lightlands where Kalea's convent is located.

Hathrohjilh: (Hath-row-schil or Hath-row-jill) A mysterious sword.

Ilbith: (Il-bith) A sorcery faction and also a tower located in the Darklands.

Ildahar: (Il-däh-här) A large town in Norr, founded by an ancient clan. A location for one of the army outposts.

Ingnet: (Ing-net) One of the five pixies favored by the Ilbith sorcery faction.

Kaihals: (Kāls) The name of the continent.

Kanarihen: (Can-är-ee-hen) An elven clan in Norr, around which the town of Ildahar was formed. They specialize in making silk and Norr's supply of paper.

Kingsorcerer: (king-sorcerer) The leader of the reigning sorcery faction in the Darklands within a network of many warring factions.

Lockheirhen: (Läk-air-en) An elven clan in Norr, established by the legendary Lehomis Lockheirhen, whose primary function is raising and trading horses. Gaije is a member of this clan.

Lightlands, The: The southern side of the continent of Kaihals, shared by the Kingdom of Sharr and the Sovereign State of Norr.

Linharri: (Lin-ah-ree) A large elven clan in Norr from which Dorhen's mother originated. They specialize in metal working and supply armor to the royal army. They are close cousins to the ruling clan, the Tinharri's.

Logardvy: (Läg-ard-vee) A gold mining city established among the southern mountains in the Lightlands.

Naerezek: (Nair-e-zek) One of the five pixies favored by the Ilbith sorcery faction. Lamrhath's patron pettygod.

Norr: (Nôr) The Sovereign State of Norr. A large forest in the northern Lightlands and also the country of the elves, consisting of a union of many clans.

Norr elves: (Nôr elvz) the most common term for the elves who originated from the region of Norr. Note: no other types of elves are known, but the Norr elves' own cultural worries point to there being others.

Pettygod: (petty-god) Any of various stray spirits (ghosts, fairies, demons, etc.) to have inspired cult followers whose appeasement of such spirits can often evolve into actual religions of various sizes and popularities. Pettygod cults are often hostile and their practices are frowned upon or condemned by normal society.

Pipa: (pēp-ä) A musical instrument with four strings.

Pixtagen: (piks-tah-gen) "Pixie-taken" A new being created as the result of a pixie taking possession of a human (or elf's) body. Wikshen is a pixtagen.

Ravian: (ray-vee-an) Giant mythological birds of brilliant colors, said to have once existed in greater numbers long ago. A few are still accessible through magical practices.

Sanctity of Creation, The: The belief in a single master architect, known as the One Creator, who made the entire universe. The official religion of the Lightlands. Belief centers around the sovereignty of the One Creator as he rules over all he created.

Sharr: (Shä-r) A large island south of the Lightlands and also the name of the ruling kingdom of the Lightlands (excluding Norr).

Taulmoil: (Tôl-moy-l) A small town in the heart of the Lightlands where Kalea is from.

Thaccilians, The: (Thak-shee-lee-ans) A race of people spawned by the power of the pixie, Thaxyl.

Thaxyl: (Thak-sill) A once-great pixie and pettygod.

Theddir: (Thed-deer) A town built on stilts to tolerate frequent flooding located immediately to the south-east of Norr. The last town in the Lightlands where elves are welcome.

Tinharri: (Tin-ah-ree) The ruling clan in Norr.

Tintilly: (Tin-til-lee) A town located on the edge of Hallowill forest. Kalea goes there often.

Wexwick: (Weks-wik) A rundown town on the west coast of the Lightlands, north of Ravian Cove, where bandits and thieves tend to hide out.

Wik: (Wick) A powerful pixie and pettygod. One of the five pixies favored by the Ilbith sorcery faction.

Wistara: (Wist-ahra) A peninsula between the greater Lightlands and Sharr, serving as common passage between the two land masses.

Elvish/Norrian Words

Aahmei: Informal "mama."

Ah: "Yes."

Ameiha: Formal "mother." Often used to address Desteer maidens and queens.

Amonimori: "Good morning."

Caunsaehgahn: "Coming into service." A coming-of-age journey male elves must complete before they can graduate to full adulthood.

Daghen-saehgahn: "Guardian-servant" a husband.

Desteer: "Whisperer." A religious order in Norrian culture.

Fa: "She"

Farhah: "Soon to be life carrier" young female.

Faerhain: "Life carrier" adult female.

Gaulaerhainha: "Choosing her fate" a female's coming-of-age ceremony in which she chooses the "hall" or the "home."

Guenhighar: A pet name for a young boy.

Guenhihah: A pet name for a young girl.

Hanbohik: The traditional Norrian dress, worn by females, consisting of a long skirt that fastens over the breasts with a collection of thin underdresses, long sleeves, tied lapels, and small jacket or hip-length tunic worn over top.

Laugaulentrei: "The lake of the dead tree," the final resting place for deceased elves.

Lin Yilbarhen: "The Bright One." God of the elves and the official religion of Norr. Seen as the "light" who leads his children through the wilderness.

Milhanrajea: "Mind Viewing." The practice in which a Desteer maiden uses her psychic ability to delve her sight into the mind of an elf to see their thoughts, intents, problems, and/or desires.

Pahkahen: Formal "father."

Pawbhen: Informal "papa."

Sa: "He"

Sa-garhik: Traditional leggings, worn by males, consisting of two separate pieces for the legs fastened to the braies, a garment that covers the pelvic area. *Sa-garhik* is similar to human culture's leggings, except for their open design, often exposing the hipbone and the sides of the buttocks.

Saehgahn: "Servant." An adult male. Also an official, sacred order to which all male elves must join and adhere.

Saeghar: "Too young to serve." A young male.

Sarakren: "He is forbidden." *Sarakren* is a status given to *saehgahn* who are forbidden to marry. This status comes with a brand on his left buttock (always visible between his braies and leg coverings) to warn *faerhain* away.

Shi: "Old" or "elderly."

Shi-hehen: A retired and elderly *saehgahn* who no longer has to answer the call of *saehgahn* duty, except in dire village or family emergencies.

Shi-helah: An elderly faerhain who's household workload has decreased and been taken over by younger females.

Tok: "No."

It means the world to me that you've chosen *Sufferborn*. If you enjoyed the experience, please consider leaving a review at your favorite retailer. Leaving a review is the best thing you can do for your favorite books and authors! It not only helps other people to make the decision to buy, it causes the retailer to show the book sooner in search results and in those "just for you" suggestions.

Let me tell you, writing books is NOT easy! It has been my dream ever since 1998 when I was a lonely, unpopular thirteen-year-old girl hiding away in my bedroom, surrounded by my hundreds of colored pencil drawings and stacks of rock and roll cd's. This story is something I've planned and developed ever since then. It was the steepest mountain of my life. I can honestly say that these characters, particularly Dorhen and his ladylove, Kalea, have been every bit a part of me as my shy personality, my odd fashion sense, and my love for metal music. When I finally reached the finish line of publishing the book of my dreams, I found life to be harder than ever before—not easier. That's why I'd like to ask you for your best, honest, kindest review. I love hearing feedback from readers and I do remember what they say and consider their advice while writing future books. You don't have to say a whole lot in the review, just that you liked it, or that the book was at least adequate—hahahah!

For more information, news of future installments, art, and merchandise, please visit www.jchartcarver.com.

Made in the USA
Middletown, DE
04 August 2022